The Yellowhammer's Cradle

by

Sally Spedding

PRAISE FOR SALLY SPEDDING

'Cut to the Bone is dark, intense and absolutely compelling.'
- *Sarah Rayne, author of The Silence, The Bell Tower and many more.*

'Cut to the Bone is chilling. Seriously chilling.'
- *Thorne Moore, author of A Time for Silence, Motherlove, and The Unravelling.*

'How To Write A Chiller Thriller' comes from the Mistress of the Macabre herself, Sally Spedding has the Chill Factor – let her help you develop your own. Highly recommended.'
- *Suzanne Ruthven, author and former editor of Compass Books.*

'Malediction is a horrifying tale of poisoned faith. No-one does the darker side of noir like Sally Spedding.'
- *Andrew Taylor, winner of the Crime Writers' Association Debut Dagger.*

'Malediction is an intense, visceral, intelligent thriller from the get-go. Dark, dark fiction, definitely not for the squeamish. If you thought Dan Brown was the last word in clerical depravity, think again.'
- *Peter Guttridge. Award winning crime/thriller author and reviewer.*

'Cold Remains will keep the reader on edge until the very end.'
- *Fran Lewis, New York talk show host and reviewer.*

'Cold Remains is the most complex, incredible, yet realistic Gordian knot I've read of in very long time – if ever.'
- *Mallory Forbes, Mallory Heart Reviews.*

'Her writing is so distinctly unique, it will truly chill you to the bone.'
- *Sally Meseg, Dreamcatcher*

PREVIOUS PUBLICATIONS

CUT TO THE BONE

HOW TO WRITE A CHILLER THRILLER

MALEDICTION

COLD REMAINS

STRANGERS WAITING

COME AND BE KILLED

PREY SILENCE

A NIGHT WITH NO STARS

CLOVEN

WRINGLAND

ISBN: 978-1533319272

Published by DEATH WATCH BOOKS

Cover images by Jeffrey Spedding

Author photograph by Jeffrey Spedding

To all those who have never been betrayers

The Yellowhammer's Cradle

In Scotland and northern England, children are urged
to destroy the yellowhammer's nest, eggs and nestlings
because according to ancient folklore, it is said to drink a
drop of the Devil's blood every May Day morning.

A guid new year to ane an' a'
An mony may ye see,
An' during a' the years to come,
O happy may ye be.
An' may ye ne'er hae cause to mourn,
To sigh or shed a tear,
To ane an'a baith great an' sma'
A hearty guid New year.

Anon.

Prologue

Although the gloaming has drawn a purple veil over forest, loch and sea, the local Fair is still in full swing with sounds of distant laughter, of men parading their prize beasts, and crabbit gulls from the Irish Sea fighting among feed sacks and left-over picnics. But the young stalker hears only the crush of twigs and old leaves underfoot as each sure step takes her deeper among those downy birches whose cool foliage and lichen-covered limbs touch her skin.

Sometimes she stops to hear if she in turn is being followed. Cleverly, she has wrapped a mourning veil over her hair and the lower part of her face. Now in this private spot close to the loch's shore, where birch gives way to whinberry bushes and the straight-boled alder, where the ground leaves her boot prints all too visible, she must draw breath and bide her time. She slaps at those persistent clegs and midges trapped under her veil, until the sinner arrives to lean against a tree to wait. A woman dressed like a Tail, yet nervous as if she knows being there is wrong.

Without warning, two Gordon setters, one black, one brown, appear from the undergrowth, sniffing the ground. No time to wonder where they came from or to whom they belong. These dogs spell trouble. The hunter snatches the nearest collar and, before the brown setter can bark a warning, severs his skull with a

1

rock. She pulls a length of mooring rope tight around his throat until those silky ribs stop heaving.

The Tail must be deaf or too busy waiting for her lover to notice anything amiss, but when the black dog lopes off alone along the shore, she calls him back. To no avail.

That mooring rope's taut again between the killer's hands, ready and waiting for her real target. Strong for her age and fit, she soon brings the adulterer down into the whinberries. Her already bloodied rock makes short work of this thicker skull and, while the Tail lies as still as the dog, her painted mouth agape and blue eyes fixed on the alders' crowns, those greedy, young fingers lift her torn dress, probe its petticoats and pull free the frail, peach-coloured undergarments.

Suddenly, a shout. Then a man she recognises hurtles towards the corpse. Shock and grief in his fox-coloured eyes. He's too late, but not late enough to avoid the leaking smell of death. The screech of Devilish curses aimed his way, rising from that secret place to scar the sky.

*

1.

10th January 1847

Where blood is thinner than water...

Although Christmas, the New Year and Feast of the Epiphany, had all passed in a blur of windless drizzle - or smirr, as the locals called it - even thirteen year-old Catriona Mairi McPhee knew Argyll was no longer a place for the sick or faint-hearted. For seven long days and nights, Atlantic gales had pounded its mountains, forests and lochs, severing trees and destroying all but the most sturdy of dwellings. So far, the McPhee's but and ben had survived, for Footer's Hill had shielded their two-roomed hovel from the westerly blast. Even so, water tumbled down the land's bracken-covered sides, flooding the nearby hill loch, turning her father Iain's once cultivated plot into a treacherous bog.

Her mother said the Devil was at work in a Godless land, and her daughter must therefore lay her innocent hand on the Bible and offer up a prayer for their continued deliverance. Her father, for his part, blamed Lord Melhuish whose brutal Clearance for sheep grazing, had ended his job as herdsman, leaving him to beg for the three of them to stay on in this pitiful shack until he found new employment at the next Feeing Fair.

With nowhere else to go, and a prisoner of growing tension between her parents, Catriona soon withdrew into her dreams. All the while, the mad wind whistled down the chimney, making the fire spit out wet wood, bringing a draught through every stone to torment the one candle and turn her blood to ice. Such storms made any outdoor life impossible. No walks to Cranranich to meet girls of her own age, or to peep at the huge, impenetrable Ardnasaig House on the shore of Loch Nonach. The one wonder of her own small world.

At least the bad weather had meant no visit to the kirk with her mother to endure yet another dreary sermon on the wicked ways of men; surely a blessing in itself.

Now, with each bleak hour that passed, she observed the cracks in her parents' marriage growing wider. Perhaps if she'd had a brother or sister, they could have invented different homes for themselves, complete with servants fetching freshly- baked dainties topped by coloured icing. Warming their sheets on beds hung with silk, and dressing them in the kind of clothes that only the very rich could afford from shops in Edinburgh and Glasgow.

But her mother's three late miscarriages meant these fairy tales remained unshared.

Mairi McPhee, a kirk minister's daughter from Tarbet, longed for a better life for them all. She'd married for love and the chance to flee the strictest of Presbyterian homes. But Iain McPhee's sudden, humiliating loss of work last June, changed her into a hermit, never mixing with her former women friends, or bothering with her appearance. Her pale hair had turned silver. Her frame thinned from slender to skin and bone. Her skin dry, pitted.

"Look at him." She angled her pinched face towards the once fit, handsome man lolling open-mouthed in his chair by the struggling fire. "Sleep, sleep, sleep. All he ever does," she wheezed. "And while he rests his lazy bones, what are we supposed to live on?"

Catriona had given up thinking of ideas for him to make money. Besides, who'd employ a man so wedded to the heavy, he was rarely out of bed before midday?

"Why not sell Bibles for the kirk?" She suggested to her mother. "Or all those other books you've kept for so long?"

"Never. Without them - the antidote for all his pagan blasphemies - my soul would break. Remember when I dared have you Christened last autumn? How he refused? Content to see you, his only child, spin in Hell when your time comes."

This protest made her poor mother clasp her chest, draw breath in rusty, agonising gasps, while a fresh blast of rain battered the one small window so hard, Catriona waited for the glass to break. And still her father slept. Still God wasn't listening.

She shivered, watching Mairi McPhee shuffle to the window and press both palms against the trembling pane as if to prevent it shattering. However, if she was honest with herself, her father's unbelief was far more interesting and believable than some kindly old god who looked after everyone yet had been happy to see his own son strung up with nails and pierced by a sword...

"You must raise yourself out of this mire," her mother was speaking, this time, barely whispering. "I've given you a good education here so you can leave and better yourself whichever way you can."

5

Again, Ardnasaig House and its lochside acres flickered into Catriona's mind. How many times had she stared at those dark granite walls, their many oblong windows and the daring young man riding his white pony around the estate with such abandon? James Baird, with a mostly absent father and a mother she'd never seen. This heir to Ardnasaig who didn't even know she, Catriona Mairi McPhee existed.

"When will that be?"

"Next May's soon enough."

Despite the stormy battle outside and the grim atmosphere inside, a surge of excitement brought a smile. The first in weeks.

"I'll be fourteen on May Day," Catriona announced.

"And a woman too, judging by the signs."

Mairi McPhee turned towards her, and once again Catriona saw how too suddenly she'd grown old and sick, with lungs unable to hold the air she needed. "You mustn't let him over there bring you down to my condition. You've a good heart, and with God's grace, could meet and marry a man with the means to make you happy. Give you children and make me the proudest Grannie this side of the Irish Sea." She planted a cold kiss on Catriona's forehead. A kiss already smelling of the grave.

Just then, her father woke up. More out of his chair than in, he righted himself to fix his bleary brown-flecked eyes on her. Not with any benevolence, but what appeared to be genuine fear. "I heard ye two gabbing on when you thought I were asleep. No bairn o' mine's putting hersel aboot till I say so. O'er me dead body."

Catriona eyed him, then her mother, knowing who'd be leaving this earth first. This made her fists clench against her much-mended skirt and burning blood to fill her head with a rage neither must see.

"Besides, the Dame of Nonach has her ane ideas for weans," Iain McPhee went on. "Born and unborn. Mark me words…"

"Who's she?" frowned Catriona. Her father's frightening stories about old hags and assorted trolls had surrounded her for as long as she could remember. But this was a new name.

"You don't need to know," rasped her mother. "Besides, it's just another myth he likes to peddle."

"Then ask yersel, wife, why nae fertile woman living near the loch has e'er birthed a live wean? E'en ye?"

His wife's hands covered her face.

"Why's that?" ventured Catriona, feeling her heartbeat quicken.

"The Dame waits 'til they give up trying, and die without issue. Ye began life and was born miles from here. There's the difference."

Catriona felt more than cold. This was the worst story of all. "So how did James Baird survive?"

Her father swiftly turned away.

"Perhaps this wicked Dame was too busy," rasped her mother with a sneer. "Let him slip through her net..."

Rainwater had begun to creep under the only door and spread like a dark omen over the stone flags. Catriona took a rag from near the fire and, closing her mouth against her father's fiery breath, his unwashed body, kept herself busy by cleaning. That way, her feelings of disgust and resentment would mean a tidy floor, scrubbed clothes and plates fit to eat off the next time. That way might lead to praise. What she'd longed for from him all her life.

Her mother was speaking again, with difficulty.

"Husband, if you had a care for this poor wee girl here, you'd not be filling her head with such nonsense. Nor keep her here until *you* see fit. The sooner she finds a placement after her next birthday, where her brains and beauty will give her a good life, the better."

This plea left her panting even more painfully for breath. She stumbled to another less comfortable chair than his, and Catriona quickly fetched her a cup of water from a rusty pot in what could hardly be called a kitchen. Mairi McPhee drank the light brown liquid as if it was nectar. Then, clasping Catriona's arm, asked if she'd help her into bed.

Her breathing had become more uneven and, with each breath, the grimace on her thin, worn face intensified. In an instant, Catriona imagined the unimaginable. Life without her, and the prospect of sharing this miserable shelter with her father after next May, made her eyes sting and burn in turn.

"I'll fetch Doctor Angus from Cranranich," she said.

"Ne'er in this weather ye don't."

Iain McPhee must have raised himself from the fire and crept up behind her. His footsteps lost to the thundering rain. "Come morning, she'll be back on her feet, giving me the usual trouble."

The flickering candle he carried, illuminated his bitter mouth even more clearly; the angry spittle gathered in its corners, while her mother's grip on Catriona's hand tightened as if pleading for help.

"You *want* her to die!" Catriona shouted at him. "And me!"

Without warning, a slap stung her ear, knocking her off balance. She let go of her mother's hand and fell against the low bed, pulling off its cover as she went.

"Nae wee lass e'er speaks to me like that! And unless I hear a sorry, ye'll get nothing more as long as yer under this roof."

"Nothing more?" she challenged. "What have I had already?"

A mistake the moment she'd said it. But before he could retaliate, Mairi McPhee suddenly let out the strangest sound, like Catriona filling up an empty ale bottle with the hill loch's water. One of her simple pleasures, when to be out of that shack was better than being in it. She stroked her mother's icy forehead, pushing back the meagre strands of hair, letting her fingers stray over her papery eyelids, bringing them down to shut out the man who wouldn't save her.

"Just remember," her father added, prodding her between her shoulders. "Ye'll be needing me a long while yet. I can tell by the way this candle's light leaves yer face untouched."

"Don't speak so," came a weak voice from the bed. "That's the Devil's tongue talking, just when I need to make peace with my Lord..."

She beckoned Catriona to come closer, but her father placed himself between them.

"Nae whispering, wife. If ye've summat to say, let's share it."

But the dying woman ignored him. "Catriona Mairi McPhee, never forget my advice. Never."

"I won't. I promise."

Mairi McPhee seemed to smile at this, and Catriona dodged out of her father's way, to place another shawl over her.

"I must take Communion. Please..." Her mother gasped, but before anyone could respond, a savage gust of wind rattled the old tin roof, driving a crow against the window glass. Its beak opening in a silent cry before it slid ragged and lifeless from sight. Catriona turned to see her mother's blind head tilting to one side, while from between those open lips protruded a thick, bluish tongue.

Her father's breath reached the back of her neck.

"Just ye and me, now, dochter," he smiled tobacco-stained teeth. "And ne'er forget it."

***

2.

July 16th 1848

Where a friend in need is a friend indeed...

With her normally faithful monthlies already eight weeks late, fifteen year- old Janet Margaret Lennox had thought of little else for the past week. But whom to tell? Certainly not her dear mother, set to join her as Cook-Housekeeper at The Manse on the Isle of Lismore. Nor her handsome older brother, Calum, waiting to join the Royal Highland Regiment's 42nd Foot. So who else could give advice and comfort in her hour of need? Why, her one true friend, who'd once been a nun, a half-trained apothecary and now Wise Woman. Linnet Garvie, gifted with what she herself had termed 'special powers.'

On Janet's twelfth birthday, she'd taken a pinprick of her blood, mixed it with her own and lain it on a small white feather which she'd flung into the air from the top window of her house at the better end of Fife Street.

"Blood sisters now," she'd smiled. "And whenever ye hear me voice, ye'll ken what to do…"

*

So began yet another pilgrimage up Fife Street under a burning blue sky, made hotter it seemed by the flares and heat from the Scott Lithgow shipyard that separated the long row of houses from the Clyde's oily waters. Up until now, this street of contrasts had been the beginning and end of her world, from earliest memories of her father's slam of the front door to yesterday when that cream vellum letter from The Manse had arrived, confirming employment.

Its envelope seemed almost glued to Janet's hands as she broke into a run over the mess of cinders and horse dung, past the half-finished *Jura Queen* heaving on the incoming tide. Here the shipyard workers' mean dwellings became taller, wider, cleaner. Where the 'up' folk lived. Those in professions whose few bairns attended paying schools to learn Latin and Greek, lifting them away from grime and poverty. Where a fresh oat loaf was a luxury.

She passed her brother standing stock-still, facing the open water. Never had he seemed so forlorn, so far away already. News of the move to Lismore had shaken him badly enough for their mother to remind him of the need to earn a living or starve.

"Whaur d'ye think yer goin'?" His voice pierced Janet like a dart.

"Harbour Hill. To Linnet's. Why?"

"Agin?"

"Ye shud find yerself a frein too."

"*Yer* me frein..."

So she was. And more. Why she quickened her pace uphill away from his anxious gaze. By next week he'd know if the renowned regiment had accepted him or not. By next week too, God willing, her own future would be made clear.

Her friend's window boxes were in full bloom and Janet caught the smell of phlox as she panted her way up the short path to the side door. Everything Linnet seemed to touch turned to success. No wonder Janet had always looked up to her and listened to that calming voice in her head whenever there seemed no way out of a problem.

The skinny, older woman whose yellow hair was hidden under a large straw bonnet, was busy cutting roses and laying them in her long basket.

Snip, snip, snip, while bony shoulder blades poked in and out of her black dress in time to the rhythm. Janet found herself wondering if her 'special powers' were simply due to starvation. She coughed and Linnet's knife fell to the ground.

"I ken why yer here," the gardener's shrewd eyes immediately settled on Janet's belly. Her skin still badly pockmarked from a childhood illness. "Tell me I'm mistaken."

Janet shook her head. She then picked up her friend's knife and handed it over. Once seated alongside Linnet on an iron garden seat, she began her tale of woe.

*

Later, in the cool indoors, where a delicate carriage clock over the grate was chiming midday, Linnet made a welcome pot of tea and reminded Janet of her rescue plan.

"Remember playing tea parties with our wee Morag?" she said finally, passing her a gold-rimmed porcelain cup. "How readily she joined in?"

"O' course. Could I e'er forget?" Janet's gaze fell on a small framed painting of the pretty, wee bairn, whose smile was sweeter than any of Linnet's blooms in the garden; whose short brown hair glistened like polished walnut. "How is she now?"

A pause in which Janet felt the temperature drop.

"Dead."

"Dead?"

"Aye. The 7th of June. Just one month afterwards."

"How?"

"I cannae talk about it." She handed Janet a matching plate bearing an iced dainty, but it suddenly seemed repellent. "Can ye imagine how stricken me poor brother and his wife are." She stared at her in a way Janet had never seen before.

"I can. O' course I can."

Suddenly, a tortoiseshell kitten bounded into the room and leapt onto Janet's lap. That too seemed all wrong, but she stroked it nevertheless, sensing that something in her friend had changed.

Once they'd exchanged farewells with Linnet giving her a lucky sign for Lismore, Janet found herself in the street with Calum waiting, arms crossed.

"Long enough," he complained.

"Yer right," she said, and as they walked back downhill, Janet took his hand and squeezed it. Meanwhile, back in that cool parlour on Harbour Hill, another's determined hand had found a pen and ink and was beginning to script an important letter to a Lord and Lady Bruce of The Manse, Lismore.

*

It hadn't simply been the island's remoteness, nor the lack of any other company in that wild, sheep-strewn place, but the bad atmosphere both Janet and her mother had encountered the moment they'd arrived. As July became August, and both employers succumbed to various accidents and illnesses which affected their dog breeding enterprise, she'd realised time was running out. After a strange, one-sided meeting ending in dismissal by Lady Bruce's bedside, Janet and her mother walked all of eleven miles in slapping rain to the quayside where there was no boat until the next day.

During that cold, wet night out of doors, she'd not only imagined the wean growing inside her, but also why Linnet Garvie had made her swear to allow it come full term? Without her mother knowing, she would have to buy a corset to keep prying eyes at bay. But worse was the prospect of no employment, no rented home in Fife Street to return to, and a future as bleak as that grey, churning sea.

***

3.

In which the truth must also be buried...

The inside of Catriona's mouth was even hotter and drier than the air outside it, so she moved her tongue around from side to side and top to bottom behind her pretty teeth, to make a supply of spit. But even her tongue was as parched as a willow twig ready for the charcoal furnace.

She picked up one of her father's empties - its original contents long passed through his body - and now full of hill loch water. Should she or shouldn't she drink from it? Difficult to tell the colour or its contents behind the brown glass, but she knew that during winter storms like the one last year, cattle and other animal dung leaked into that very loch. Several crofters and folk come up from the cities for fresh air, had died of the smallpox only last June, so no. At just fourteen years old, she couldn't risk going the same way as those wretched souls. Not while her cherished dream of escape to a better and paid life still flickered like that stubborn candle in draughty Footer's Cottage.

For a brief moment, she considered returning there, but Iain McPhee had woken from last night's sleep with a roar so terrifying she'd not stopped for her usual porridge or drink of spring water,

16

instead had run like a girl possessed up to her hidden treasures hidden near the top of Footer's Hill.

And here they all were, saved from various expeditions and adventures, ranged round her like so many loyal subjects. Also in remarkably good condition given that their specially knitted bag was damp and stained by the Hill's dark soil that had kept everything from prying eyes for two years to this very day...

She glanced up from twisting the sapphire-studded wedding ring around the fourth finger of her own left hand, to see three thin lines of black smoke rising from the forest above Baw Heid further down Loch Nonach. Idiots, she thought, kissing each of the ring's precious gems in turn. Landowners such as Lord Melhuish had banned charcoal burning during the summer months. But then Baw Heid and its few inhabitants always had been a law unto themselves.

The ring seemed reluctant to leave her finger, but just to feel it so snug in her hot palm, brought back memories of friends in Cranranich; many of whom had already gone into service throughout the length and breadth of Scotland. Some even to England. How she and they had passed a home-made version amongst themselves while chanting "He loves me, he loves me not," as the speed increased until a careless pair of hands - never hers - let it fall. Soon she, the motherless Catriona Mairi McPhee had a reputation for not letting go. For never giving up. Now no-one came to see her and not simply because she lived too far out, but that she was too ashamed of the hovel she called home.

The morning sun had cleared the top of Ardnasaig Forest and seemed to be punishing her even more, heating up her bare head, her cheeks and exposed ears until she changed position, packing away her special mementoes; choosing a new burial place for them.

But when she'd finished digging, she glimpsed her father standing in his ruined plot, staring up at her; making her catch her breath and cover the grave more thoroughly, hoping his beady eyes hadn't spotted its whereabouts. From so far away, he resembled one of those midges who during the summer, swarm near Loch Nonach's still water. Harmless enough from a distance, but not when sucking your blood, leaving a scar never to heal...

He was waving now, flailing the air. But she wasn't done. Her necessary ritual on Footer's Hill always brought her visits to their proper end. Why she wiped her hands clean on grass before pulling two small rag dolls - a boy and a lassie - from her old skirt pocket. Both shabby, well-used, but no matter. Who they represented and what she made them do to each other was much more important. Which was why, when she noticed Iain McPhee struggling towards her through the tumbled rocks and dense bracken, she quickly dug a fresh hole and consigned her coupling playthings to a safer darkness.

✱✱✱

4.

March 3rd 1849

In which love has a price to pay...

Not until early the following March had both Janet and her mother Margaret settled into their respective posts of housemaid and cook-housekeeper at Ardnasaig House, that gaunt mansion owned by renowned architect Donald Baird which dominated its own thirty-eight acres by Loch Nonach's forested shores, between the hamlet of Kilforgan to the west and Cranranich village to the east. However, it would take considerably longer to forget their five months in Cranranich's overcrowded Poor House, even though they now occupied an attic bedroom apiece with white cotton sheets and ate regular meals using proper knives and forks.

But how could Janet ever forget last year's damp August day, when they'd waved at the ferry to stop and deliver them to Oban from Lismore's little harbour? It was only because neither had admitted why they had been dismissed so swiftly from the Bruce's Manse, that the often absent Donald Baird had employed them. Within weeks, that Poor House in Oban had turned both women into people they no longer recognised. Cheating their way to second helpings, stealing whatever they could lay their hands on, and all the while Janet's growing belly had strained beneath her stifling corset.

Now, the downstairs clock struck midnight between Friday and Saturday with twelve desolate chimes and on the final stroke, Janet looked in on Margaret Lennox snoring gently on her back with a small bolster in place to prevent her double chin from growing bigger in the night, then stood on the small, chilly landing outside the three attic rooms. She listened as might a deer on the hill in that motherless, fatherless house, wondering if James Baird was still awake, or if his day's hunting boar in Draighnish Forest had worn him out. Wondering too, if the unfriendly handyman was on his usual prowl before trotting away to his own dwelling near Kilforgan.

She couldn't spare the time to find out, nor risk any kind of commotion elsewhere in the house, so she closed her own door and pushed her chair and the clothes chest against it. Her belly had told her the time had come. Time to commit a mother's worst crime before that clock's next hourly chime. And now by strange coincidence, her severe, low-down pain built up like those waves she'd seen on the loch when rough weather came in. She stuffed a handkerchief in her mouth, lest she cried out too loud. It smelt of onions, but her tears were already falling.

With trembling fingers she opened her blouse, loosened her skirt and unhooked the tight corset she'd endured for too long to disguise her condition. Immediately her pale, waxen belly swelled out, and the kicking she'd felt under the stiff, boned fabric came harder, for longer, making visible bumps in her flesh.

Next, she put a hand between her legs and withdrew it, wet. Linnet Garvie had never mentioned water when she'd gone to her for help. But here it was, running out of her like one of those wee burnies leading from the grounds into that big, bottomless loch. The chamber pot was already in place, together with a threadbare towel and a newly sharpened gutting knife complete with sturdy bone handle.

When her water stopped and a deep, searing ache began, Janet thought of Calum, her soldier brother in the Royal Highland Regiment, sometimes too far away. At others, not far enough. How fear for his future and loneliness had brought him into her arms for a sin she would live with for the end of her days. A secret that no other must ever know. Not even him, or their mother.

How she longed to be a simple bairn again, on Greenock's streets. A bairn with no coins for sweetmeats and trinkets, but love by the welcome hearth where her mother took in washing. Where Calum and his friends swam, boxed and leap-frogged the capstans lining the quayside. Dreaming of uniforms and grown-up lives far away. She'd known of girls gone into service miles from their homes - some as far as Lancashire - but the bond between her and her mother was too deep for that. Especially since her no-good father had left them while she was still a wean.

Her fist stopped her scream, and biting through its skin brought the taste of blood into her mouth. Her small room and its one faltering candle seemed to move around her, faster and faster until she was weightless, lifeless, losing everything. Mind, body and soul. Even the wee bairn pushing its way into the world.

Then, with its first cry, came darkness.

*

More tiny cries like the mewl of Linnet Garvie's new kitten was enough to wake her. The candle was dying, but in its last, wavering throes, Janet saw the bloodied, crumpled towel beneath her thighs, and how what had passed from her body was still breathing, connected to hers by a shining pink cord.

A boy.

No name. How could there be? And once the gutting knife she'd borrowed from the kitchen had cut her free, her hands twisted that little neck so tight, until the crack of small bones brought a terrible silence.

Having crossed herself, and wrapped the lifeless body in the towel, she dressed herself for the cold outdoors, still dizzy. Still hurting. Her breathing too loud, rasping like the forestry saws on the felled spruce, as she carried her dead burden to the linen room situated at the end of the narrowest of passageways. Here, carpet gave way to tiles and the temperature dropped so low, her breath came out like sprays of mist.

Don't stop...

But she did. Both large ventilation holes set at eye level into the linen room's wooden door, had always unnerved her. Now more than ever. She murmured the Lord's Prayer over and over, stumbling when "forgive us our trespasses" came along. But what would He have done in her situation? Or anyone else?

*

She used the oldest of the sad irons to weight the bottom of her linen bag. Next her son cocooned in her corset and his bloodied towel, followed by a swift knot and another murmured prayer as she left the house's relative warmth. Her boots found each slippery step down to the courtyard where the old well was waiting, its mouth white as the very milk that had swelled her breasts for too long.

Its thin ice soon split under her fist. Then came a dog's bark from somewhere, momentarily distracting her before she dropped the burden into the jagged hole where the rainwater's gloating suck drew her sin away. Deep and deeper into the stew of years, while unseen above and behind her, the watcher whose coat sleeve had cleared a patch of condensation from the window glass, moved away.

*

Janet had to wait until dawn's creeping light to enable her to properly clean up and rinse out her chamber pot and knife. Rather than use a tap from the linen room's water tank and risk her mother waking up, she chose one of the two 'necessaries' that Donald Baird had insisted be installed next to the Store in the courtyard. Grateful that the normally reliable flow of spring water hadn't frozen, she left the chamber pot's white china looking like new. As for the stains on her wooden floor, she soon rubbed those away, but not so her memories of that dead weight in her arms, and how those new, black eyes - identical to hers, but twice the size - had stared up at her. Into her guilty soul.

*

Having checked her working clothes bore no bloodstains, Janet sat fully dressed in front of the small mirror she'd placed in the middle of the one window sill overlooking the loch. She must behave as if nothing had happened. Perform her usual duties and rituals to keep memories and any suspicion at bay. And the day's new light would tell which parts of her face and neck needed the special seaweed cream she'd concocted for her dry skin.

The green mixture smelt of the sea loch as she worked it in around her nose, especially on that conspicuous blue vein across its bridge which had mysteriously appeared on the day she'd started work at Ardnasaig. Next, her eyes and mouth while she stretched both lips as she did so, then closed them when too many bad teeth came into view. This was the face James Baird saw first thing in the morning and last at night. It had to be worth looking at. The same for her hair. Too black, almost blue-black, when her mother's was grey-brown and Calum's almost fair.

"Yer grandmother on yer father's side were a gypsy," her mother had said. "Ye've had that blood come down to ye, and there's nothin' ye can do."

But there was.

Janet re-lit her candle and heated up her curling tongs over its meagre flame. She'd stolen them from The Manse on the Isle of Lismore, before the Bruce family had suddenly asked her and her mother to leave. The dog-breeding couple had said they'd neither liked the way she'd looked at them, nor her mother's cooking. The list had gone on, but beneath all this, Janet suspected something far less straightforward. Deep in her heart she knew that one day, that odd couple who'd rarely spoken to each other, would come back to haunt her.

*

With new curls on show under the edge of her white cap and her skin glowing from the seaweed cream's good work, Janet helped her mother prepare James Baird's breakfast. Still dwelling on her crime, she bore his cooked kipper into the dining room where he sat poring over a pile of letters, some accompanied by small brownish pictures of women's faces. The plate shook in her hand, and it took all her concentration to set it down in one steady motion.

"What are those, sir?" She ventured almost too brightly, placing a mother-of-pearl fish knife and fork to hand. At her first interview with his father, he'd warned her never to ask questions of her betters, interrupt or speak without being spoken to. But nerves were to blame and she kept her hands hidden behind her back.

Normally, with the architect away for so long, and never any friend come to visit his son, she and her mother would converse with him as if *they* were his family. Now, she hoped he wouldn't notice her unease.

"Daguerreotypes," he said, answering her question. "Papa wants me to commission a portrait of Mama to be finished in time for his next visit home."

"Oh."

Words such as 'daguerreotypes,' 'commission' and 'portrait' had never crossed Janet's lips, yet she could guess their meaning, and recalled something Linnet had said. "To paint a dead person's picture is to bring them back. Maybe agin their wishes..."

Best not tell him that, thought Janet, refilling his teacup. The young man, dressed for shooting deer, ignored this comment and turned instead to his kipper.

"'Tis a pity she won't see it."

25

He glanced up at her. Grief tightening his features the way a rope pulls a sail to ride the wind. "She's not dead. I know it. She just never came back."

Defying the rules she placed a comforting hand on his shoulder.

"I'll try and find her for you, sir."

James Baird's one blue eye reflected her in its iris. "Miss Lennox, I appreciate your offer, but you have your tasks and I have mine. However, if you see or hear anything while performing them that might lead to my mother being found, then it's your duty to let me know."

Janet blushed. "O' course, sir."

"And speaking of tasks, father wants me to take on more help in the house early next year. Some time from now I know, but the right kind of employee hardly grows on trees..."

Another blush. Janet re-filled his teacup from the pot, and was about to leave, when he held her arm. "What do you think of this portrait? It's by an Oban artist, Rory Baldwin." He held up the top sheet of paper, attached to which were two small samples. Certainly his letter-heading was impressive, as was his image of a young woman with Spanish looks and a knowing smile.

"Was yer mother dark or fair?" asked Janet.

"Is," he corrected her again.

"I'm sorry, sir."

A pause, in which she spotted a fishing boat churning its way east down the loch. Meanwhile, James Baird was studying the second image. This time, of an older woman with lighter skin and hair. Janet thought the subject's gaze possessed a magnetic quality.

"By William Rankin from Inverary. He's exhibited at the Royal Academy in London for the past five years."

"I'd go for him, sir. He really can do eyes."

*

When Janet returned to the kitchen with James Baird's used dishes and the kipper skeleton picked clean, her mother looked her up and down.

"Well, well. Ye look pleased with yerself." Margaret Lennox who'd been trimming fat off a piece of beef, pushed a crinkly strand of white hair back under her cap, and re-tied her apron. "Will ye tell me why?"

Because she'd already kept too many secrets from her, Janet relayed her the news about the Inverary artist, but saved the most contentious morsel until last.

"And Mr Baird's wanting more help in the house next year."

Her mother frowned.

"I don't like the sound o' that. When exactly?"

"I'm nae sure."

"Then say nothing. He'll soon forget. He's probably just had a letter from the Balkans, and knowing Mr Baird, there'll not be another for a while."

Janet gave her a hug and if it had lasted any longer, would have confessed what she'd done last night.

"We stick together," she said instead. "Safety in numbers."

"Indeed. Now go and butter up that miserable Mr Bogle. We may soon be needing him on our side."

*

Janet found the handyman out the front, cutting back a group of rhododendrons in readiness for their next show of blooms. Last summer's sad remains flopped to the frosty ground around his feet and occasionally, he'd pick up a brown stem and examine it for signs of disease. His tartan tam o' shanter had faded in last summer's sun, and his breeches, coat and boots all showed the same wear and tear. Why not offer him a haircut? She thought. The chance to have his clothes washed?

"Ye cud do with a full-time gardener here," she said instead, losing courage, holding out a tin bowl full to the brim with the kind of sweet tea he liked. "Ye've enough tasks, what with the logs and everything."

"He didn't turn round. Neither did he show any interest in the tea.

"Best keep busy. The way things are."

"I dinnae understand."

"What I've seen here; the gossip I've heard. 'Tis a wonder I'm nae gone in the head."

Despite the bowl warming her hands, Janet felt the raw March morning invade her outer clothes to touch her skin. Her shiver tipped some of the tea overboard.

"I've brought ye a drink. 'Tis still hot."

He appeared not to listen, instead increased his cutting rate so the only sound was the snip, snip, snip of impatient steel jaws and the odd sigh when the woody stems proved too thick for them.

"What did Mrs Baird look like?" She ventured, seeing a couple of forestry workers clattering past Ardnasaig's walled boundary in their cart. "Were she beautiful?"

He took his time to answer, probably searching for the right word. She was right.

"Eye-catchin's the word. Soft-spoken and kind. Nae like some I ken. Too guid for these parts, tha's for sure. P'rhaps why she took hersel away..."

Janet looked up at the big house behind her, unconvinced by his theory. How could anyone leave such a place for whatever reason. *She* never would. Unless she was bound and shackled, unable to fight.

"Ye don't like me and me mother here, do ye?" She said suddenly.

Finally, he turned round. Took the tin bowl from her hand, tipped its content out and handed it back to her.

"Wud anyone?"

Janet bit her lip, and for one terrible moment, wondered if he'd noticed anything last night. Her mother's advice evaporated like those misty, faraway fir trees on the opposite side of the loch.

"I'll tell Master Baird what you've just said."

"He won't care. I were ne'er consulted about ye and Mrs Lennox comin' 'ere. And since Mrs Baird went missing, I've always bin the invisible man with nae a livin' soul to ken what I really think. What I feel..."

Janet barely listened. The poisoned dart he'd thrown her way, was still stinging too much so that another wouldn't hurt.

"Why wudnae anyone like us?"

His deep-set eyes met hers. He pulled his cap further down his bumpy forehead, placing them both in shadow.

"Ask yersel, Miss Lennox. Ask yersel..."

As she turned away, clutching the cold, empty tin bowl to her chest, Janet cast her mind back to early February when she and her mother had first viewed Ardnasaig House in all its winter grandeur. They made a pact together, that after their earlier tribulations, nothing must jeopardise their new-found good fortune. Nothing.

Then she thought of the black, leather-bound notebook she'd first brought with her, now half full. How important it was for the future to keep up her daily entries of hopes, fears and secrets, because the simple act of writing, which had taken longer than most others of her age to master, could make problems seem less and dreams more possible.

***

5.

December 3rd 1851

Where rules are broken...

Three weeks before Christmas Eve in the year of London's Great Exhibition at Hyde Park, Catriona McPhee was making what might possibly be the last journey to her mother's grave in Cranranich. With each eager step she prepared her goodbyes, trying not to dwell upon what Mairi McPhee might be looking like now, with over three years' soil filling her ears, eyes and mouth. But at least the single plot and its stone angel clasping a Bible, was pretty enough. Prominent too, near the kirk gate so there wasn't too much long, wet grass to negotiate in her mother's old boots.

"God bless you," she murmured, placing three birch cones where she imagined her mother's head to be. "I've done what you wanted. I've found a good placement, even though it may not be permanent and, with your help, will make it so." She touched the guardian angel's cold lips and was about to kneel down to kiss the now weedy grass which had conquered the grave's marble frame, when a stout old man wearing a faded tartan cap, pushed his way through the gate and proceeded wide-legged away from her towards a more weathered slab where he stopped to make the sign of the cross.

Not wanting to engage in conversation with this seemingly devout stranger, Catriona gathered up her coat's hem and ran back the way she'd come, aware of his eyes on her until she rounded the stone wall and took the sloping path down to the village.

An hour later, she was hastily adding the last of her clothes to a selection of her mother's holy books already lying in her battered little case, when her father's cattle-calling voice reached her at the far end of their but and ben. Her fingers momentarily hovered over the rusted clasps, then, with added determination, pressed them down. She also held her breath, knowing what was coming next. The creak of that fireside chair. A bottle tumbling over. Iron-soled boots on stone and that body always in black, bent from life on the hills, propped up close by against the rough stone wall. The reek of heavy filling her space.

Ever since she'd boldly accosted James Baird on his way to Kilforgan a fortnight ago, and he'd agreed to give her at least a temporary post over Christmas at Ardnasaig House, Iain McPhee had raised vocal, and to her, unreasonable objections. But now, as the time for her to leave drew ever closer, they'd become louder. More angry. She hid what had been her mother's old case under her bed, bracing herself for what was to come.

"Ye dinnae ken those people," he shouted as he advanced, his face flickering red in the one candle's glow. "There's nae man about that hoose, tha's for sure. Only the young Jock who's ne'er done a day's turn in his life, and two women servants who folks swear ain't right in the head."

But Catriona thought of the worn, brown case that had once belonged to her mother when she'd been her age. The future it represented. A future with money to pay for proper food and medicines her father needed, especially if she was kept on after the festivities.

"When did you last taste a nice cut of beef and a proper pudding?" She tested him. "When did you last have no pain?"

The once big man seemed surprised. He tried to stand tall but his knees let him down. Catriona was soon by his side, leading him back to the fire and setting the fallen ale bottle upright.

Suddenly, without warning, he seized her arm and turned to face her. Eyes as deep as the hill loch behind the cottage, met hers.

"O'er my dead body would I let me ane lassie go to Ardnasaig. And there's the end to it."

"Why? You promised I could leave here once I reached sixteen. What else is there for me?"

His reply was a tighter grip. And was it more than a fleeting fear tensing his features?

She broke free to reclaim her belongings, call out her goodbye and pull the one solid door open to the chill gloaming outside. As she slithered down the wet hillside towards the track to the hamlet and beyond, with her mother's case still firm in her grasp, she glanced back at the man who'd kept her at Footer's Cottage too long against her and her mother's wishes. He wasn't following - how could he? - but stood in the doorway like a dark dolmen, both hands covering his face.

*

So *this* was the carriageway she'd peeped at so many times from behind its wall, and this the black, shiny front door to Ardnasaig

House that would soon, very soon, be opening on to the rest of her life. Oh yes, Catriona thought, eyeing its brass lion's head knocker. Temporary was a word already driven clean from her mind, together with that vision of her father weeping.

She primped her pale ringlets into place under her new bonnet and smoothed each finger of her gloves before bringing the knocker down hard three times. The sound alone brought a rush of pleasure and anticipation. Who would answer it? she tried to guess, but too late. Bolts were being drawn back and warmer air eked out as the gap between door and frame widened.

"Yes?"

Two black eyes fixed on her as if she were a pedlar or worse.

'...and two women servants who folks swear ain't right in the head...'

"Miss Catriona McPhee," she said, keeping her nerve, trying to forget her father's comment. "Come to see Master Baird about my job."

"My job?" That startlingly white, bony face turned away to call for help, and soon a short, equally stern-faced older woman took her place. Someone whose top-to-toe black suggested she was in charge.

"Master Baird's ne'er mentioned this," she growled at her. "Ye nae telling us some fable?"

"I never lie. Please ask him."

"Wait there." The door closed in her face and when Catriona placed her ear to its freezing wood, heard an argument that could, if unresolved, spell the end of her dream.

34

Suddenly, upon hearing footsteps to her right, she turned to see an unshaven young man of no more than twenty, dressed in hunting clothes and smelling of the outdoors, appraising her with the oddest eyes she'd ever seen, and not noticed before. One blue, one brown. But at least he'd recognised her and, without any greeting or welcome, escorted her round the mansion's far corner to a courtyard bordering a large well, from where double doors led into the biggest space she'd ever seen. Not only that, but filled with quantities of meat, fish and vegetables enough to feed a whole village.

"The Store," he announced, forgetting to scrape mud and black leaves from his boots. "Mrs Lennox's domain. She and her daughter have worked here almost two years now." This statement was delivered as if he'd referred to dogs or horses, not people. Nevertheless if Catriona's first encounter *had* been with the daughter, it hadn't promised much of a welcome.

James Baird led the way through into a Drawing Room three times the size of her father's humble but and ben, lit not by the six oil lamps but the nearby Loch Nonach reflecting the morning's strange brightness. His courtesy, however, didn't extend to offering her a seat, and when Margaret Lennox the Cook-Housekeeper, and her daughter Janet were summoned, they stood as far away from her as possible.

*

As Catriona later sorted out her few belongings in the attic room next to Janet Lennox and separated by the thinnest of walls, she relived how the tension of that interview with James Baird and the women had almost made her change her mind; forget her promise to her mother and to herself.

While he'd tried to trip her up at every turn, they'd behaved like two crows waiting to pluck out her eyes. Obviously not wanting her there either. Perhaps the hunting, shooting bachelor simply didn't like women. Perhaps having yet another one in the house was one too many, There'd been no evidence or mention of any female friend or sweetheart, and it was only having learnt that his father had insisted upon more help for his Christmas homecoming, which kept her from re-packing that little brown case.

*

Now, on the day before Christmas Eve with sun the colour of pale egg yolk staining the eastern sky over Loch Nonach, Catriona set down her bucket of seaweed on the loch's stony shore and straightened her young back. Just then, from where she stood, something unexpected caught her eye. A misty column rising from beyond the army of dark-leaved rhododendrons that seemed to guard Ardnasaig House from even those who rightfully lived there.

The more she stared at this almost human form, the more it seemed to grow; to devour the granite walls and their black oblong windows. Even reaching as far as the two chimney smokes trickling into the sky. Not only that, but a luminous stain seemed to bleed from the top end of it, making her catch her breath. Could this strange mist be the spectre of the Brocken that the kindly old handyman had mentioned to her not so long ago? Or something even more terrible? Supposing it lasted all day and night and was the Devil himself?

Her father's warning lodged in her ears as they had all night in her cold attic room while Janet Lennox had snored and muttered in her sleep. She forgot all about the seaweed she'd been collecting for this housekeeper's daughter. Instead, gathered up her rough woollen coat and began to run, slipping this way and that on the round, wet stones until having waded through the tide's leavings, reached higher ground.

That spectral creature still hung by the house as she joined the water-logged path leading through the alder grove - a place she hurried through even on the brightest of days - where, according to her father, the Dame of Nonach had lain in wait for a young villager delivering bread to the nunnery and, with a tongue as long as an adder, had sucked the growing child from her womb. Iain McPhee had once told her how despite living away at Tarbet and ignoring his wife's protests, he'd insisted upon covering her swollen belly with his coat and, for extra protection, sticking a knife into the new cradle's woodwork. Old and tarnished, that knife had become another of her playthings up by the hill loch. Only last summer had she finally thrown it away.

Catriona paused on the rickety footbridge to watch the torrent flowing beneath her feet, wondering if this wicked creature had ever been punished for such a terrible act. If any of the nuns once living here had gone astray with a man and been made to suffer. Also, who in more recent times might have felt that greedy tongue between their legs?

A dead salmon swept by in the foam, belly up, its waxy mouth agape as if in stricken surprise. Then broken branches prettified by the kind of sphagnum moss that tickled her cheeks whenever she helped the handyman gather in firewood. This wreckage jostled together as it sped towards the outfall into that bottomless loch. A place of such mysteries that both fascinated and repelled her. More than anything, she was curious to find out more about her employers; how they'd come to occupy this house built fifty years ago, centuries after a small Cistercian nunnery had stood here, and whose abandoned graveyard could still be seen amongst the unscythed grass.

*

Although this was the first day without rain since she'd arrived three weeks ago, the past year's bad weather still lay underfoot and, as the water's roar diminished behind her and her mother's boots sunk into deepening mud where her earlier prints were barely visible, Catriona sensed that nothing but trouble awaited her. And as for Ardnasaig's owner, Donald Baird, whose idea it had been to hire extra help for the Christmas season, he was far away in the Crimea, designing homes for wealthy Russian princes. Like his missing wife, she had no idea what he looked like. Was he responsible for his son's heavy jaw? Those same oddly coloured eyes? What she *did* know was that Ardnasaig resembled a miniature kingdom, but instead of a king ruling, two poorly educated women shared the coveted throne. The throne that one day would be hers.

"Them's twisted sisters, make no mistake." Mr Bogle the handyman had observed after James had signed her in until the end of January. "And on me deathbed, I'll tell ye things ye shudnae' ken. If I fall to Death's messenger, get yersel to me side."

She'd felt her pulse judder in her neck, while her father's doubts about her being here had grown like the spectre now obliterating the front of the house and its darkly recessed doorway that resembled an upturned coffin.

Despite not grasping what the old retainer had meant, Catriona kept a careful watch on his appearance and the way he went about his tasks. But to hear him whistle 'Can ye sew cushions?' with gusto each time he trundled logs from the outhouse through to Ardansaig's huge Store room, put her mind at ease. That he seemed hale and hearty enough was a relief to her, as in just a short space of time, he'd grown to be the kind of father she'd have much preferred.

According to Fergus Bogle - but always *Mr* Bogle to her - he was born on a fishing boat in the Sound of Mull. His mother, unaware she was expecting him, had just helped her husband reel in the last catch of the day when she'd felt pains never felt before.

"I were barely bigger than a terrier pup, but I entered the world with her lucky caul wrapped round me," he'd confided as he'd piled logs into Catriona's basket for the lower rooms' fires. "She always swore because of it, I'd never drown."

Catriona had never heard of that particular superstition, but with the rippling loch always in sight, it must be a comfort to know one wouldn't ever struggle in those deadening depths, and vanish, undiscovered for ever.

*

Next, past the alder grove, where the path became lost amongst the biggest ferns she'd ever seen and to her left, the house had disappeared from view. It was here, in this secret, ancient world that she suddenly craved her own mother's company. Her hand in hers. That continual encouragement to make the most of herself, until the very day she died.

Just then, Catriona noticed three figures huddled together at the top of the tree-lined carriageway that sloped up to the house. Margaret Lennox and her daughter together with Mr Bogle, all facing this growing, misty phenomenon. Because that's what it was. A phenomenon, when there was no vapour anywhere else. On most days, the sea water loch, its inlets and rocky crannogs containing bones of the ancient dead, would be veiled in thick moisture. But this wasn't most days. This was the day before Christmas Eve with everything to prepare for the architect's return home tomorrow.

"'Tis a bad omen," the handyman muttered, as she picked her way through the small, walled graveyard where, according to him, the long-gone nuns still lay, overseen by their five prioresses and the Dame of Nonach's disturbed soul.

"What d'ye mean, ye blathering auld man?" came Janet's accusing tongue sharper than an awl. Just to hear it, made Catriona slow her pace, realising she'd left the seaweed bucket behind. That the Glaswegian's sunken cheeks so at odds with the rest of her sturdy body, would have to wait for the creamy green lotion she'd make up every Tuesday evening once the house was tidy. Iain McPhee had warned against reading a book by its cover, but truly, Catriona had never seen such a daunting face, and had wondered more than once why the eighteen year-old was so convinced she could improve it.

She began to run again, up the slope between the rows of bare lime trees, towards the little gathering now themselves cocooned inside this slow-moving apparition whose 'head' was sheathed in a coloured halo. Mr Bogle's cheeks reflected the colour, looking like two ripe damsons. He stuck out his grizzled chin in defiance as if a mere housemaid like Janet Lennox held no terrors for him.

"Mind how ye speak to me," he said to her, "or I'll spread the word aboot the things ye've done. How ye've brought a fresh curse upon this place..."

What on earth did he mean?

"Nae-one threatens me ane bairn," snarled the housekeeper, slipping an arm around her daughter's thick waist. "Nae-one. 'Sides, what'll Master Baird that idle whipster do? He's ne'er here. Too busy with tha' gun o' his. Anyways," she poked Mr Bogle in the chest with her free hand. "Explain, sir, what ye mean by a *fresh* curse?" Her voice rose to an even higher level while the weak sun had given up trying, and in its place, snow clouds began to ink the sky.

He shrugged.

"What folks 'ave said."

Suddenly, as if snuffed out, the haloed apparition faded as swiftly as it had appeared, leaving the threesome drawing closer to each other against Ardnasaig's front wall. Janet Lennox with the advantage of a stick she'd hidden behind her skirt, had spotted Catriona empty-handed. Immediately she changed her focus.

"Where's me seaweed?"

"You'll have it tomorrow. I promise."

"There's a liar!"

Catriona tried to wrench the weapon from Janet's grasp, but the eighteen year-old, fattened up from extra helpings in the kitchen, overpowered her and, before Mr Bogle could intervene, had struck her left shoulder hard.

The pain stormed through Catriona's cold body as the wet cobbles came closer and closer to meet her, until she felt the dark, sweet bliss of nothing.

*

"I'm sorry I were nae' quick enough on my feet to help ye." Mr Bogle helped her up and took her arm as the worst of her pain and dizziness ebbed away. "But I swear to God I'll speak with those two Bairds once they're home. Yer a braw, wee lassie and by far the best worker since Mrs Baird went away..."

"Don't think I'm not grateful," Catriona turned to him, surprised by the suddenness of that last remark. Also, what it meant. "And if I didn't have my father so dependent on me, things would be different. I'd stand up to them both. Make them fearful to open their mouths. But I've too much to lose. Thank you all the same..."

"Mrs Baird wud have thought the world of ye," he said, his gaze misting over. "Just as I did her." He then squeezed Catriona's arm and lowered his voice. "I spent a whole week searching the loch and round aboot. Night and day, day and night. And on that first evening without her or the dogs, all the lamps in the hoose went out at the same time. And if I'm to speak the truth, a light died in me too. Why her son won't easily trust another woman. In his eyes, she'd abandoned him."

Catriona was lost for words as he let go of her to open the double doors leading into the Store, where Margaret Lennox herself had labelled every sack of tatties and tumsties, to deter pilfering. Where in the far corner, four pink hams together with other less unidentifiable slabs of flesh, hung from great hooks, turning in the sudden draught of air. Trout and salmon too, lay ready for the knife; their lifeless eyes staring in her direction, while several unskinned eels coiled together in a cold, slimy embrace.

"That Brocken spectre's not the first sign of wha's wrong with Ardnasaig," he closed the door behind him. "And I'd say this to ye, Miss McPhee, in case yer ever tempted to drink from the well out there..."

"Say what?"

"Ne'er bend o'er the side and breathe in its air. Ne'er e'en touch the water..."

"Why?"

"'Tis poisonous. And aboot yer room, ye still have its key?"

Catriona saw nothing but worry in his eyes, and wondered where this was all leading.

"Of course."

"See ye use it. And don't be openin' yer door to anyone once ye've retired for the night."

She felt more than the Store's deep chill sneak under her clothes as he removed his gloves, then his tartan beret and smoothed down what remained of his wiry, grey hair.

"And as for that linen room on the top floor..."

"What's wrong with it?" She eyed him. "Is that why you don't sleep here?"

He was about to answer when other voices took over. Immediately he laid a bruised and battered finger over his lips. *"Wheesht!* Master Baird's come hame. We'd best busy oursels."

*

With that strange, one-sided conversation filling her head, Catriona made her way along the marginally warmer corridor until she reached the kitchen where yet more toil awaited her. James Baird was laughing as usual from the back of his throat. Laughing with Janet Lennox if you please. A raw fish smell hung in the air making her secure her cap tight over her hair.

It wasn't simply jealousy, but reliving the housemaid's stick hitting her shoulder, seeing again that curling mouth and those hard black eyes, was almost too much to bear. The headless trout lay in a pool of pale blood next to the gutting knife. Its blade dulled by a ridge of scraped, scaly skin. Catriona's fingers closed around the bone handle, as for a moment she imagined the unimaginable.

What are you thinking of? Certainly not your father…

She set the knife down in case Mrs Lennox should return to her task of preparing lunch, and rolled up her sleeves to more easily lift the pot of boiled spring water from the stove and pour half its contents into the sink. She'd just begun to scrub at a stained old skillet when she sensed a draught on her back; smelt the reek of a man's sweat as two cold hands covered her eyes and a body firmed itself against hers.

James Baird had been drinking. The smell was the same as Iain McPhee's days and nights. He breathed it into her ear.

"Catriona Mairi McPhee, d'ye have a festive wish for me?" he chuckled.

The shock kept her mute as she attempted to prise those hands away. But the man who supposedly mistrusted women, pushed himself closer until the meaning of his crude rhyme became all too clear.

"I wish that you land the biggest pike in the whole of Argyll," she managed to say. "And the biggest salmon and the biggest carp..."

He laughed while his palms slipped from her eyes to cover her small breasts. A shot of pleasure allowed them to linger, before she pushed him way, giving herself the chance to duck round him towards the open doorway. However, she'd spotted Janet Lennox's shadow darkening the flagstoned floor.

"Not good enough for ye, eh? Ye cringing vermin," the older girl sneered, before her thick, booted leg jutted out to connect with Catriona's shin.

Sprawled out against the rough stone, she spotted a black rat scuttling away in front of her. How *dare* she be likened to something like that? She thought of the gutting knife. How close she'd come to using it. How close...

Suddenly, a different boot prodded her ankle. Not once, but three times. And he was shouting. Covering up for himself, no doubt.

"Get those dishes done, McPhee. I'll give you five minutes, and if you're tardy, we'll be taking a little boat trip to see Blae Crannog."

Rejection had edged his voice with iron, but there'd be another time, when it suited her better. When that black-haired witch wasn't around. Yet just to think of that grim rock cluster jutting from the loch beyond Fearn House's old jetty, was enough to see her upright, albeit limping to the kitchen. When he came to check on her again, this time wearing a black oilskin slung over his shoulders, she was putting the last dish away.

"Within the hour, my father's room must be ready for tomorrow. When that's done, there's foliage to be cut for the hall, oil lamps to refill, and wood to be laid in the grates. All of them."

Catriona knew anything was better than that threatened boat trip and at least, gathering fuel would take her outdoors to where Mr Bogle was sure to be busy chopping logs. But could she tell him what James Baird had wanted of her? Not quite. Not yet.

Now, she must exchange her white apron for the grey, and find some dry footwear. Her bootless feet climbed the shallow, oak stairs to the next floor where the temperature seemed to plummet. She paused to look out over the pristine sheet of loch water; its crescent-shaped beach and her abandoned bucket glinting in the weak but persevering sun. Could this be where Isobel Baird had vanished? A place so deep that according to her father, a weighted measuring line a mile long, had never reached the bottom?

Just then, a small noise from behind her made her start. Was Margaret Lennox making up the Master's bed nearby? Was this a cry of exhaustion, because that's what it sounded like. A cry... Catriona listened again, then spotted the housekeeper hurrying by outside while the grandfather clock on the floor below, struck eleven doleful notes. If that noise hadn't been hers, then whose? She willed her pulse to stop, to make sure her imagination wasn't playing tricks. But no. She swore on her mother's dead heart this was a real bairn mewling and, as she took the next flight of stairs to her attic room lying between those of Margaret Lennox and her daughter, the pitiful sound grew louder, more persistent.

She forgot to breathe, having realised at last where the source of the crying might lie. Running now, knocking her sore shoulder against the ever-narrowing corridor's wall, she arrived where her ears and anxious mind were filled as if to bursting. And then she saw them, as if for the first time.

The linen room door's two 'eyes' met hers, trapping her like that fly in amber used as a paperweight in the architect's windowless study. Her scream lay too far down her throat to be heard, and once the ghostly crying had stopped, in its place came the kitchen bell, dancing madly behind its glass cover, demanding she put in an appearance. As she hastened downstairs, she couldn't help but wonder if that pitiful noise was connected to the cook-housekeeper and her daughter. After all, in unguarded moments, they both seemed to harbour secrets. Secrets that might some day allow her to prosper at their expense.

***

6.

Where more difficulties prevail...

Janet ended her day's entry in her notebook with a short prayer for herself and her mother, knowing her writing was full of spelling mistakes she'd no time to correct. Of words that came nowhere near to her real feelings. Nevertheless, she set down her pen and secreted this precious book deep in her skirt pocket. Although this was her own wee room under the eaves, she couldn't trust anyone in that house, least of all her closest neighbour, and not even Master Baird. The notebook contained other things too. Ditties and sayings from her associates in Greenock, especially Linnet Garvie and her niece - a braw wee bairn called Morag whom she'd met at her house just the once, before becoming an angel in the sky. Jewels to keep hope alive in her heart.

Her short break was almost over. Her mother was standing outside the house shouting as she usually did when things weren't going her way. This time, it was for the handyman. But why so much din, straining her poor lungs? The old eejit wasn't that deaf...

Janet picked up her hand mirror, tilting it to examine her face more closely in the morning's milky light. Although her eyebrows were still too thick and dark, her lips altogether too thin, the seaweed cream seemed to have made her skin even softer to the touch, while lines that had previously aged her eyes, had become almost invisible. However, that stubborn blue vein across her nose still remained. Then she remembered her supplies of the special, green cream had run low. With Christmas nearly there, she was convinced the new maid had deliberately let her down. Already showing signs of rebellion.

Knowing that her mother with her breathing problems and loss of appetite, wasn't long for this life, and that she, Janet Margaret Lennox would soon be an orphan in a hostile world, it was more important than ever to pay such attention to herself

She often wondered if she should have agreed to come to Ardnasaig House at all, but Linnet had forecast she'd find the love of her life here, and end up with a fortune in land and property. So how could she have refused the Bairds' offer of work? Even though the Dame of Nonach still seemed to exert a malign influence over the loch's inhabitants, and Master Baird with his differently coloured eyes and strange laughter, spent his time up the woods with his rifle, he was worth the chase. Anything could befall his father. Anything at all. Why, when he, the keen huntsman had lifted her skirt in the still-room on that late November day, she'd let him take her, silently, urgently, filling her with the kind of heat only a fire could deliver.

*

According to her secret notebook, her next 'wee frein' was due on Ne'erday, but what if it didn't appear? What then?

Margaret Lennox's cooking smells hung in the stairwell, but before going down to help herself from the pot as usual, Janet placed her right eye over the spy- hole she'd made in her panelled wall adjoining her rival's room. She saw how the single bed was neatly made, and at its side, on the floor, lay a pile of plain-looking books. Novels, maybe. And what had Linnet Garvie said about novels? That more often than not, they came from the Devil's soul, and to open them would only take the reader back there.

Just then, came the sound of voices and footsteps coming up the first flight of stairs. Janet closed her door, pressing her ear tight against it to listen to James Baird and another man who sounded older and not from Inverary at all.

"It's as if my mother's actually here looking out over the loch," James said. "Incredible."

"I'm delighted, sir. I do try to capture the subject's spirit. I only regret it's taken so long bringing it to you, but my wife's been ill..."

"That loch's where she always walked the dogs and where..." James Baird added as if he'd not listened. Then paused. "Their footprints ended."

"You did say. But you must never give up hope of finding her, Mr Baird. Never. And just here, outside their rooms where natural light will catch her unique eyes, seems an ideal spot to hang the work, Would your esteemed father approve, do you think?"

"I'm sure. But there *is* someone else I could ask."

Janet was ready and came down from the attic. The moment she saw what the bearded artist had delivered and now held aloft for her to see, she knew the beautiful, mysterious Isobel Baird had indeed come home.

"The perfect place for her, sir," she agreed, unable to stop staring at how the painter's brush had re-created skin and hair to be so real; the silk fabric of her dress so vivid. Her sapphire wedding ring, too, that the missing woman seemed almost alive. Janet followed the direction of those blue eyes over towards the loch, and could have sworn that both eyelids had flickered and the lips almost invisibly moved. "She'll be weel happy here."

*

"We'll be in the drawing room," James Baird announced to Janet once the painting had been hung. "I'm sure Mr Rankin would appreciate a wee dram before he leaves."

Feeling almost like a trespasser, she quickened away from the painting, unable to shake a gnawing insecurity from her mind. Despite being included in the choice of artist and the hanging decision, her own and her ailing mother's situation there had changed with Catriona McPhee's arrival. Not long ago, after an evening's solitary drinking, the huntsman had shouted he wanted Ardnasaig for himself. And the expression on his face when the lass from Footer's Hill had arrived a night early, had hardly been one of pleasure.

Since then, more than once, she'd caught him looking her up and down. And hadn't that recent incident in the scullery, borne this out? As for the old handyman, who did he think he was? Favouring that glaikit over herself and her mother who'd worked there far longer. She'd have to tread carefully, given that the maid was clouding her sky and possible future in a grand house with burnies running through the land. The kind of life Isobel Baird had enjoyed until her late evening stroll five and a half ago, when neither she nor her two pet setters had returned.

*

Pigs' liver. Normally Janet's favourite, where she only had to imagine the offal slivers floating in a thick gravy sea, for her hunger to make its demands. And normally too, she'd have dipped her index finger into the pot for her tongue to savour the tasty sample. But not today. She'd already been sick in 'the stanks and still felt queer…

Her mother glanced up from wiping down the kitchen's wooden table. Brown gravy rimmed her mouth, while deep lines almost buried her eyes. Whatever illness she had, wasn't improving.

"Why all that commotion upstairs?" She asked.

"Mrs Baird's portrait arrived."

But Margaret Lennox's interest didn't last long. "Where's McPhee? I rang for her ten minutes ago."

"She's nae in her room. Anyway, why bother with that piece o' gristle?"

"She's paid to help us."

Janet used her elbow to clear a space on the misted window pane.

"She deliberately forgot me seaweed. I ken what she's up to."

Her mother returned to the stove and stirred the stew. "By the way, how well did ye sleep last night?" She asked.

"Like a rock. Why ye askin'?"

"So nobody touched yer blanket? Peeled it back to stare at ye then lay like an incubus atop *yer* body?"

Incubus?

The cook's spoon trembled and she dropped it into the stew before hauling herself into the nearest chair as if that imagined

52

weight was still upon her. Janet placed a hand on her hot forehead. "Your'e not goin' mad are ye? Tell me the alphabet letters and no hesitation."

"A b c d e..." Having reached z, Margaret Lennox tried untying her apron. "Lunch will be later today, for the first time since I walked through Ardnasaig's front door." She eased herself from the chair and, gripping Janet's arm, managed to rid herself of the apron and stand unaided. "Come upstairs quickly. I've something to show ye."

Two pairs of boots clattered up the oak stairs towards the attic. With her mother's wide but skinny hips in front and James Baird calling for his meal behind her, panic flushed Janet's cheeks. It was while pausing for breath, on the first landing, that Margaret Lennox noticed the new picture. Whether her own unsteadiness or the surprise of seeing such a haunting face, caused her wobble and reach for the banister, Janet couldn't say.

"She were the one staring at me! I'd swear on my Holy Book..."

"Come on, mother. Let's get upstairs."

She herself tried not to meet Isobel Baird's accusing gaze, but there was no denying the aura of blame leaking from the canvas behind the glass. If she touched it, would the woman spring into being? Start speaking?

"In here." Margaret Lennox pushed open her attic room door and closed it tight behind them.

A stale smell hung in the air, while beyond the small window, a sly drizzle obscured the sea loch's view. Her mother took her hand and guided it to the top edge of the brown, woven blanket

53

that lay in disorder on her bed. "That's how it was left after the visit. I swear on me Saviour's heart. See there, that bunching? Touch it, go on. Touch it..."

"What visit?"

"Her on that landing below. Isobel Baird."

"That's impossible, mother. Please dinnae think that way..."

Yet Janet knew those same, unflinching eyes would be there by the stairs each day, boring like a diviner's rod into her soul, almost as if pleading for help.

"But tha's not all. When I were alone again, I got up to re-light my candle and heard this wee bairn wailing on and on it went... On and on..."

"Bairn?"

Janet's heartbeat quickened.

"No mistaking it, and when I stepped into the passageway, it grew louder and louder 'til I had to stop up me ears like this..."

Suddenly it was as if a match had been struck behind Janet's own eyes. She slapped those red, cooking hands away from that stupid, stupid head. Once, twice, three times until she fell silent.

"I'm sorry to hit ye, but Mother, ye'll be dragging me to the land o' the demon faeries with ye. Can't ye see?" she cried. "And there's Christmas comin' and Mr Baird will be here at noon tomorrow and..." She drew breath. "We'll find ourselves at the gate like the last time and then what'll we do while McPhee takes our place?"

Like the last time. With a growing belly beneath her coat...

"Hit me agin, daughter, and I'll be speaking to the master, make nae mistake. Since ye took up with that Linnet Garvie, it's as if our lives are on the Devil's platter and his appetite's returned."

"Who's Linnet Garvie?" Janet prayed she could fool her.

"The Devil's picking up his irons, ready to eat. I can tell."

"Have a care, mother." Janet edged away. "The wrong ears could be lissening."

"They already have."

"Meaning?"

"That witch woman in Fife Street will be the death of ye. Mark my words."

How had she known?

Then remembered Calum.

"She was ne'er a witch, mother. Just a wise woman I could speak with."

"Ye father was a stubborn auld pudding too. Ye've his looks and his ways. Be canny, daughter. All I'm saying."

*

Janet let herself out of the room to run down to the kitchen, only to find James Baird waiting by the stove. His eyebrows met in a frown above his nose. A sheet of paper and a pencil lay in his hands.

"I've listed kitchen tasks for Christmas," he scowled. "Miss McPhee's doing her best, but it's your mother we pay to do food. Besides, I've a shoot over at Browburn in half an hour."

Damn the maid...

"I'll see ye get your lunch, sir," Janet nevertheless reassured him. "Me mother's nae feelin' her usual self, but it'll pass." And

55

with that, she stirred the pot and checked the tatties weren't overcooked.

*

She'd not said one word to her younger rival during the final preparation and serving of the meal, but once James Baird had wiped his dinner plate clean with a heel of bread, and snatched his rifle from near the Store, Janet cornered Catriona McPhee by the plate cupboard.

"Ye'll fetch me seaweed before dark." She ordered. "'Tis still out there in the bucket."

The girl's mouth set into a pout. "But I've floors to sweep. Holly and baubles to get in place..."

Janet resisted placing her fingers around that fluttering throat. She was in enough bother already. "We'll go together," she said. "And on the way I can show ye things about Ardnasaig ye didnae' know."

"What things?" Those grey eyes narrowed. "You're just trying to make trouble. I knew it the first hour I was here."

"Did nae one e'er tell ye that one day, yer mouth will bring disaster unless ye curb it? Who was it brought ye up?"

Silence save for the soft rain falling outside, darkening the carriageway; everything it touched.

"My mother, then my father."

"That oxter." James Baird's description, serving her well.

The maid faced her, lips quivering. Janet saw her then, as an old, empty woman, full of nothing but hatred.

"He's the finest, braw man this side of Argyll. You insult him, so you insult me."

"Ye skin's thinner than a flea's. And isnae it odd ye've always a man to run to? To fight yer battles?" Her hand crept under the girl's cotton cap. The pale hair felt soft as whey. Too soft, compared to her own. Reason to pull it hard until several strands curled between her fingers.

"Get off!"

"Come wi' me, then."

But why had her expression changed to something which made Janet's pulse slow down? Surely a warning, deep as the loch's gullet into the very earth, yet she couldn't heed it. Instead, reminded herself she was in charge. Had to be. There was still work to do.

*

Despite her protective cloak, this was the kind of rain Janet hated most of all, sneaking into her eyes and down her neck to chill her skin. She turned to see Margaret Lennox's face at her window staring after her. Heard James bring his cob from the stable, but shut her ears to the maid nagging on about where Mr Bogle had got to, because now they were entering the small graveyard and its hidden population of long-dead nuns.

Just six weathered, granite stumps remained as their memorials, half-hidden by weeds and separate from another more prominent marker.

Her follower hung back and Janet, fearful she might run off, pulled her alongside, feeling her cold, small hand in hers. She then lowered her voice so as not to be overheard. Poachers weren't uncommon, so too other wandering vagrants hidden by the evergreens.

"See that smooth stone blacker than the rest?" She pointed at it. "Who d'ye think lies there, set apart from the others?"

An indolent shrug.

Janet had known from the first day that the bonnie, fairy-like girl from near Cranranich would be trouble. So, reel her in, like a gasping carp, she told herself. Show her who's in charge…

"Yer dyin' to ken, aren't ye? I can tell," she said.

The maid cast an anxious glance towards the house.

"Lissen to me guid. I ne'er give away nothin' for free. First, ye must pass the test."

"Test? What do you mean?"

Janet let go of her hand. Forced her voice to a whisper as raindrops from the moss-encrusted overhead branches fell on their heads. And when she'd finished, saw her listener's face crumple like those fat fungi her mother added to the pot for flavour and substance. But that act didn't last long. Soon those grey eyes had hardened again; that sweet little mouth turned sour, emitting a curse so foul as to send even the lurking Dame of Nonach back to her grave.

✱✱✱

7.

She should have controlled herself. Mistake number one.

Now she had to eat a stone.

Catriona observed her tormentor bent low along the crescent beach, searching for the best instrument of torture and possible death, probing the ramshackle ground strewn with peeled branches and root clumps whose tendrils occasionally trapped her feet.

She weighed up her limited options. To flee, attack the bully, or put into practice her dead mother's trick of pretending to eat. But supposing that went wrong and the stone lodged too deep in her gullet? Would the cook's cold-hearted daughter clear the obstruction? Save her life? She doubted it. Of course she wanted to learn more of Ardnasaig House and its mysterious surroundings, but not enough to kill herself.

The housemaid chuckled as she compared one stone with another, while Catriona waited with the seaweed bucket she'd reclaimed, weighing extra heavily in her hand. Its cold handle searing into her palm as the bully approached. That wicked smile still in place.

"This one'll do," she said, holding out an oval specimen, spliced by a white vein. "Just pop it in, shut yer eyes and swallow."

Catriona's throat immediately closed up. Just to think of her dead Grannie's overcooked bannocks had been enough. Now the thing was by her lips smelling like both stanks in Ardnasaig's inner courtyard. Hers to clean every week.

"I'll make up your cream instead," she pleaded.

"That's for me to do in me ane way. I've decided. Now open yer mouth and ye'll soon ken a secret to scald yer heart. And what kind o' place it is your father's let ye come to."

Enough.

Catriona hefted the almost full bucket of seaweed to shoulder height and aimed its slimy contents at that mocking face. The din soon stopped, giving her the advantage.

She ran past the skeletal posts of an old jetty swaying in the shallows along the shoreline where that same rejected stone hit the ground behind her. Through the six burnies emptying into the bigger water and a ruined bothy whose broken walls were green with ivy. The only short cut back to the house. Her one goal.

At least she was fit, unlike some girls her age. At least she could run when she had to. Helping Mr Bogle with his tasks had built up her stamina, and although she often had to employ devious means of adding to her mealtime portions, the weight she'd recently lost was now an asset.

"Miss McPhee? Is that you?"

She glanced round, peering through the drizzle. James Baird with his rifle strapped to his back, was drawing closer with every stride. His chestnut mount, breathing heavily, was piled up with a red deer's corpse; the tips of its antlers scraping the ground. Dead meat beginning to taint the air.

"You don't have to run away," he said. "No-one'll harm you."

"*You* won't, but someone else will."

"Who's that, then?"

Catriona stalled. Bad enough she'd humiliated Janet Lennox, but worse would be to give her name. She was normally a quick thinker, but his bristled face was bearing down on hers. Brown and blue eyes widening in anticipation. Blood showed inside the cob's nostrils.

"A shadow, that's all," she panted. "Just a shadow."

"Don't lissen to her, sir," came Lennox's voice from behind the beast. "Look what she's just done to me." Her eyes like black as a shrimp's. Her mouth an angry hole. Seaweed strands lay trapped in her hair, and she stank. Catriona had witnessed moments like this in Cranranich's one ale house when her father had drowned his grief for his dead wife in drink. More than once she'd been able to calm him, lead him away from whoever he'd offended. More than once stopped a fight developing.

Now however, she felt a certain menace. These two people were still strangers to her. To run was cowardly, but to stay? And then she remembered her promise to her dying mother.

*

The rifle shot's echo hung in the damp air, and when Catriona reached the sloping carriageway up to the house, saw Mrs Lennox with arms folded standing by the front door. Her thin, old hair sealed to her skull by the rain.

"Did ye hear that?" she rasped, then coughed. A deep rattling sound from a hollow chest.

"No."

"Then why run as if the Devil was after ye?"

Devil?

That word had made Catriona start.

"Have ye seen me Janet or Mr Bogle?" The crone persisted.

"Mrs Lennox, my stomach's bad. I need to visit the…"

"Not so fast, Missy. I can sniff a liar a mile off." Both arms reached for her, but Catriona took the steps two at a time and entered the tiled hallway where smells of wax polish and stew met her nose. The safest place was the Store. Besides, Mr Bogle was sure to be there at this early time of day, but once she'd pushed open its wide, heavy door to where wood lay stacked like mountains, and apples from the last harvest rested in rows of newspaper, realised she was alone.

What now?

She shivered long and loud enough to grip onto the nearest shelf where tatties and tumsties bought in from Cranranich market, lay ready for peeling.

Where else could she look for him?

But only the rain replied.

Perhaps he'd returned to his bothy to fetch a new axe. Perhaps wearied of the day already, taking a rest. Whatever the reason, she had to find him. She had no other friend in this hostile place. Had that rifle shot out there been meant for her? If so, surely the handyman who'd filled her head with such disturbing thoughts would have investigated it immediately.

The adjoining stable where he kept his skewbald mare during each day, was also empty, and just then, his mysterious words filled her mind.

"If I fall to Death's Messenger, get yoursel to me side…"

She had no choice but to make her way to Kilforgan where he lived, and the quickest route was north, through the glade of elm trees, away from the house and that alarming encounter.

*

Nothing but elms, green moss and a suffocating silence. Bog water had soon entered her mother's black, smooth-soled boots, weighing her down as she crept beneath bare boughs whose bark was so skin-like, so twisted, they seemed to belong to living giants, pausing to let her pass. Some of the ancient trees felled by winter storms, still lay strewn on the ground, and rather than risk losing her sense of direction by walking round them, she clambered over their recumbent bodies, tearing her stockings and scarring her boots with their neat, little heels. All the while, that recent encounter with Janet Lennox and James Baird thrummed in her brain. But she mustn't be driven away. She must cling to her dream and do right by Mairi McPhee, who was owed nothing less.

No breeze either. Just the slightest sniff of woodsmoke and the small disturbances of birds gathering food. The lucky ones, she thought. With no prospect of anything to eat until she found the missing handyman, hunger began biting her own stomach. Lennox had helped herself to the last of the oats and milk, leaving her with just half a cold tattie and a cup of water. And now the black-eyed besom would be indoors filling herself up yet again.

*

This was taking too long. Soon, there'd be a search party out for her and already the day was growing old. If dusk fell too soon, she might lose her way and instead find herself heading down towards the loch.

Catriona clambered onwards up a steep bank where the biggest boulders she'd ever seen stood embedded in its side, like warts delivered by some long-ago curse. Mr Bogle had once remarked upon how they seemed to grow year on year until one day, he'd wake up to find they'd imprisoned him in their midst. So, she reasoned, his bothy must be near and, sure enough, beyond a layered bank of velvety-green stones, she saw a small roof and its one bare chimney.

Why no smoke? If he was home, a fire would be his priority. So, where was he? She was distracted by a group of small, red deer who'd invaded his garden beyond the barn, turned on their heels and fled as soon as they saw her. Terror in their gentle eyes.

*

Mr Bogle's front door was ajar, its keyhole empty. Catriona called out his name and sensed its echo haunting the air around her. Just then, more than anything, she wished she could see his familiar form. Feel his steadying hand on her shoulder. She crept into the one main room whose already low ceiling bore a thick black beam that must have caused him to stoop to avoid it. Squinted into that mean light from a single window curtained either side by a wall of empty trees.

To her, this was no bothy, but a gaol. Yet he'd spoken of it fondly as a haven. Somewhere to forget the needs of Ardnasaig, especially after Mrs Baird had gone missing. So, why leave his door unlocked? There were still Irish troublemakers around after the famine, and the recent Glennish clearances further up the loch had caused hundreds of the dispossessed to take to the road. She'd heard whispers that Kilforgan was next. That a Colonel Ritchie had already called his tenant farmers to a meeting and threatened to fine them if they didn't attend. In the old days, her father would be the first to get there and support the underdogs. So why had James Baird said nothing? Done nothing?

Wedging the door open behind her, she moved towards the dead fire and touched the one remaining piece of charred pinewood with her cold fingertip. No warmth here. It hadn't been lit for hours, possibly the night before. So what had happened? Mr Bogle only travelled into Kilforgan for his few necessities on Friday mornings. And then she remembered his pony. If she was neither here nor at Ardnasiag then he must be out and about on her. But where?

She trembled in that bleak afternoon and retreated outside to check the muddy ground for signs of recent foot or hoof prints. But there was nothing to suggest the handyman had returned. And the empty barn proved it.

Hurry...

But she wasn't quite finished and, before closing the bothy door, curiosity impelled her to take another look inside. She'd been too quick and might have missed something. This very door was a start, for behind it hung a lined, tweed cloak stiff with age and neglect. A garment she'd not so far, seen him wear. Beneath this, were two gnarled sticks and a long, black crop. His bed - a horsehair mattress - lay directly on the stone floor while a curled-up print showing the birth of Christ had been nailed to the wall above it.

Odd that, she thought. According to him, he'd neither attended the little kirk in Cranranich nor Kilforgan, and had expressed no interest in Christmas or the faith. As for her, that grainy image of a bearded almost naked man pierced by nails, suffering for the world's sins, brought back the memory of her mother's preaching mouth. The cut of that angry hand on her head whenever a bad word slipped out...

And then she remembered that day she'd visited her grave to say farewell. He'd been there too...

Having examined the handyman's bed, she found nothing under the lumpy, hessian-covered pillow, nor beneath the three brown blankets he'd left smoothed over. The same for an oak cupboard, home to a hand-knitted shirt which she held against her face, smelling him deep in its fibres. Tears stung behind her eyes. He'd never spoken of a wife or bairns, or indeed any other relations. It seemed the Bairds at Ardnasaig House were the only family he had.

She moved on to the area to the right of the dead hearth where a cracked stone sink and a pitcher stood upon two pieces of granite. Between these ran an iron pipe from the sink into a 'stank' below the floor. Its smell reminded her of Cranranich churchyard after rain.

Next to this sink stood a small metal cupboard with a mesh front. She knelt down to open it and let her hand explore first the upper then lower shelves. A block of cheese with a small knife embedded in its side. A jar of skinned onions, a bread crust and two apples with crinkled skins softened by age - the way he liked them because of his teeth.

The knife was, however, irresistible. And then came something unexpected. Nothing to do with food or any supper remains, but a folded up sheet of *The Scotsman*, yellowed and brittle to the touch, wrapped around something that felt hard between her fingers.

Without reading the enfolding newsprint, she bore the package to the window for its extra light. Had the handyman saved himself a few crusts then forgotten them? Or discovered a special stone by the loch on those days he cleared the leavings from the shore? Her fingers unpeeled the paper with the same care she'd once explored herself when her first bleed had finished. With no mother to explain what had happened to her body so suddenly, so frighteningly, it had been her father who'd done so. Not until weeks later did she discover he'd taken a portion of that dark, sticky blood from the pot she'd used and kept it in an apothecary's phial by the but and ben door.

"For guid luck," he'd said, without a blush. "And to keep trouble from the hearth."

At the time, she'd wondered what Mairi McPhee would have made of such a primitive act. The woman who believed witches should hang and be fed to the wolves. That burning in Hell was too kind for folks conniving with the Devil and his familiars…

A comb.

But clearly not just any comb. This was fashioned from cream-coloured ivory with engraved images of a sun, moon and stars along its short handle. Catriona stared at the delicate handiwork, imagining the elephant it must have come from. Which other fingers might have used it. And her next thought was, had the canny old bachelor once had a wife? A lover, even? And if so, this item certainly wasn't from anywhere near Kilforgan. Nor were Isobel Baird's clothes. Once, while Margaret Lennox was in the 'necessaries,' she'd peeked inide the missing woman's elegantly furnished bedroom and there, in the huge mirrored wardrobe, still hung garments from another world. They'd transported her from that grey-drenched lochside to those faraway eastern palaces where Donald Baird was paid not only in roubles, but also in bolts of rich fabrics inlaid with gems and small mirrors. She'd also found fine woollen cloaks and shawls with collars and cuffs of white fur, smooth as skin. Dresses and skirts in red and russet brocade and devoré, tailored for the slender figure that Mrs Baird must have possessed. Trousers too, gathered in around the ankles, summer boots, and indoor slippers embroidered with every kind of beading.

Having always had a weakness for other people's possessions, Catriona resolved to return to search some more, and sample the exotic potions trapped inside their beautifully coloured bottles.

'You're a light-fingered little minx,' her mother had said more than once. Light-fingered, possibly, but a minx? Catriona dismissed it as another puritanical exaggeration.

In the losing light, she studied the comb again and gasped inwardly as she suddenly spotted a single hair, neither fair nor dark, long nor short, trapped between two of its middle teeth. But, when freed, curled itself around her index finger. Was this some accidental remnant or a deliberate keepsake, the way her father also retained her moon-blood and nail clippings whenever he'd cut them? Or her own 'souvenirs' still buried on Footer's Hill?'

For safe-keeping, she returned the hair to its host, interweaving it between those same two ivory teeth. Once her discovery was safe inside her coat pocket, she placed the folded newspaper back in the mesh cupboard and closed the bothy door behind her, wondering if Mr Bogle had bought that comb at London's Great Exhibition.

While quickening away from the deserted dwelling, she glanced upwards at those same black clouds now conjoined together, chilling the air, bringing the first flakes of snow to melt on her forehead. She wished she'd glimpsed at what the newspaper had contained. Perhaps something or nothing, but the desire to check grew overpowering.

After just two minutes, she had the answer. Grateful yet again to her dead mother for teaching her to read and, safe under a sheltering tree, she scanned the report dated 20th August 1846.

ARCHITECT'S BELOVED WIFE AND DOGS NEVER RETURNED HOME

Catriona stared at the three images shown below. One, a sketch of the loch near Ardnasaig House, and two depicting the rocky crannogs beyond the old mooring posts, still occasionally explored by local divers. Donald Baird was then quoted as saying that 'if she'd been in peril, both Tam and Rabbie, her Gordon setters, would have guarded her with their lives…'

Enough.

She screwed the paper into a tight ball and stamped it to a pulp underfoot. Her curses burning her throat. A sudden noise from behind made her spin round, almost losing her balance. Nevertheless, she was just in time to see a dark-clad figure stumble away into the forest.

***

8

In which corners are turned...

By the time the whole of Ardnasaig's grounds lay softened and smoothed by a whiteness that made Janet shield her eyes from its glare, her mother had taken to her bed, leaving McPhee to clear away the remains of the late luncheon and finish gutting the brown trout for supper. Janet had reluctantly agreed to feed the cocks and gather their eggs before darkness fell, and now, she slipped and slid past the mound where, if rumour was to be believed, bones from various warring clans had long infected the soil. That strange fern-covered lump of land always made her hurry by and with each step, her resentment at having to do this task rose inside her like a winter sea.

She noticed two sets of identical human tracks in the snow. One leading from the house to beyond where she stood, and the other, from there to the shoreline. Most of the prints were spoilt as if their owner had been stumbling along, or perhaps had deliberately obscured them.

If her hands around the basket and grain bag hadn't been so stiff with cold, she might have investigated further but, having reached the fenced-off chicken plot, she flung the seeds at the snowy ground where they sank, leaving pock marks akin to Linnet Garvie's skin. And that reminded her...

Seaweed.

Her own fresh tracks around the plot conjoined with those others she'd seen, and it wasn't until she'd reached the shore's path that she realised none of the hens had come from their coop to feed. In the early days, when they'd heard her mother coming from as far away as the alder grove, they'd fair bit her hand off as she'd thrown in the food. Now was quite different with just the murmur of snow settling and icy wavelets lapping against the shore. Janet turned round to check the coop once again, but soon wished she hadn't.

*

She ran without stopping from Satan's handiwork, and returned to the house still stricken by what she'd seen in the coop. Her lungs were drained of air, her mouth dry with fear as she noticed James Baird with his rifle once more on his back, saddling up his chestnut cob in the stables to hunt for Mr Bogle. The animal, restless at this change in routine, took his rider hop-hopping round and round his loose box with one foot in the stirrup until she managed to stop him.

"Thank you."

"I'm nae frightened o' horses, sir. Only people."

James gathered up his reins, preparing to leave, but she still held the buckle where the nearside rein met the bit. Was this the best time to mention what she'd seen? She doubted it.

"Is it wise to be going out alone after dark, sir?" she said instead. For those that did, were said to return changed in some way.

"Who else can do it? The good man may have fallen ill, or worse."

Silence.

She let go of the rein. He was right. However, with the architect's arrival less than sixteen hours away, too much was going wrong. She couldn't hold back any longer.

"There's nae cocks left, sir," she began. "They've bin slit open. All of them. Not a one left alive. 'Tis a dreadful sight."

He stared at her. The last time he'd done that was in the Store's darkest, most private corner. His poker the colour of a ham bone. This was very different.

"You saw them with your own eyes?"

She nodded.

The estate owner's son brought the cob closer. Ale, not whisky on his breath. "So where's your gutting knife?"

He was serious.

Think...

"In the kitchen, of course. Do ye believe, sir, I could do such a thing to those poor, dumb creatures?" She clamped her bottom lip between her teeth until warm blood reached her tongue. Her mother had always said she was born with too much of a mouth, but now wasn't the time to check herself. Too much was at stake.

"You were working on the trout with it. That I do know," he said.

Janet felt dizzy. "There is other knives, sir. Ask McPhee. She likes trouble. And," she added, narrowing her eyes for the greatest effect, "she ne'er spares ye neither wi' her talk."

"*Miss* McPhee," he corrected her.

His bored chestnut mount tugged at his hay, while outside, snow had been driven in by a wind off the loch.

"I'm listening," he said.

Janet swallowed hard. Dabbed her lip with her sleeve. She might well have his bairn inside her. This time next year, be a woman of means...

"She says ye pester 'er, sir. She has to lock her room at night and wear an extra pair of undergarments to protect herself. And tha's not all. But I can see I've said too much. Please forgive me, sir. But remember how she didnae even look round when ye'd shot yer rifle after 'er."

That mouth had shrunk to a thin, angry line. Above his scarf, a vein leapt in his neck. Within three seconds, he was ducking beneath the lintel, kicking the gelding out into the wintry world where stars still lay hidden as deep as the trouble stirring within her heart.

*

The hallway clock struck half past four as Janet lit the lamps and checked on the fire still glowing well enough in the drawing room where James Baird liked to pore over his maps for the best hunting, and weapons' manuals for the latest products to match his prey. She'd seen the detailed drawings of rifles and traps enough times and been repelled by their functions. To her, animals possessed feelings and souls as much as human beings. Some were even nobler. All in fact, nobler than the new maid, and if she, Janet, were ever to become mistress of Ardnasaig, she'd wean him off his sport, like his mother had probably tried to do. Make being indoors more interesting than traipsing over bogs and burnies...

Suddenly, a thudding noise came from upstairs. Alarm numbed her heart. Supposing whoever had slaughtered those hens was still abroad in Ardnasaig, with that sharp gutting knife to hand? How she wished her soldier brother was by her side to steady her nerves. To wrap his strong, warm arms about her. Even the surly Mr Bogle would do. Wherever he was…

*

In the dusky light, Margaret Lennox didn't resemble her mother at all. It was as if her old blood had frozen and her body, curled up on the top of her bed facing the door, had shrunk to half its size...

Her eyes were tight shut, her mouth set in a fearful grimace and the breath coming from it little more than a faint crackle. Beyond the curtains that didn't quite meet in the middle, Janet saw snow still falling with far too much determination. She lit the one candle and brought it over to see her mother more clearly. The one who'd used her meagre savings to bring her to The Manse at Lismore from Greenock's back streets and finally via the Poor House to here.

"Has yer blanket bin touched agin?" she asked her. "Have ye felt another presence?"

A tiny nod. Nothing more.

"I'll not see in the Hogmanay," she croaked. "And when I'm still, just tow me out on the loch and let my boat drift..."

What a queer request...

Janet took her cold hand and placed it under the thin blanket. It was as if the window glass had gone and snow was actually in the room. "'Tis a terrible thing to ask o' me. I could nae more do tha' than kill me ane bairn."

Those rheumy eyes opened and fixed on her. Were they full of too much knowing? Or reflecting her own guilty conscience? Janet looked away.

"What was good enough for the lady of the house is good enough for me," her mother continued.

What?

"Say that again."

"Once is too often."

"Please..."

"She told me that herself. Just now. Afore ye'd set foot on the stairs. She won't be troubling Ardnasaig again. Not now she's spoken."

Janet took the candle over to the fireplace to prod the sullen logs into life. Their warmth mean and intermittent, and amongst the ash, she noticed scorched and ragged feathers; singed pieces of twig. Was her mother to be believed? If so, surely James Baird should be told...

"Tell Calum to come soon," her mother then murmured. "I must see him again. See the both of ye together as ye always were... A wee brother and sister sent from God."

Janet faced the grate, sensing fire beneath her skin. Her pulse on the run. "He's sailin' for Sebastopol any day now. There'll be nae address."

Margaret Lennox closed her eyes.

"But I'll see what I can do." Janet stood up and without looking back, left the room, aware of two black shadows leaking into her soul. One a secret she should share. The other never. Not even on her own last breath…

*

The snow was settling but not falling. Every tree branch drooped under their glistening burdens and if her mother wasn't so wabbit, this wintry scene would have surely have lifted her spirits. Just then Janet caught sight of a familiar figure struggling up the carriageway dragging a clump of blackthorn blossom in each hand. Snow on her shoulders, on her bare head. Two distinct tracks of footprints led down from the house. She was making another, going the wider way. Bigger, more patterned than those near the coop. Two sets of which had been quite smooth.

Janet blinked. McPhee must be living in fantasy land.

She pulled her own shawl tight around her shoulders and stepped out to meet her. "Can't ye see how short o' hands we are here in the house?" she challenged.

"That's why I've brought these from the forest. I want to make Ardnasaig look more like Christmas. 'Specially with Mr Baird coming home."

"Why blackthorn? There's plenty of spruce around."

"For luck."

But according to Linnet Garvie, that prickly shrub signified quite the opposite.

"'Tis unlucky to bring it indoors," Janet said. "There'll be a death in the family."

McPhee's laugh was high and bright as she plucked off a newly-opened white blossom and set it defiantly into her hair.

"What did ye use to cut them with?"

A startled pause.

"Why?"

Janet stopped herself. She had to be careful. On her guard. "Ye've taken long enough. Have ye seen Mr Bogle anywhere?"

"No. Should I have?"

"Or the hens?"

Another look of surprise. Real or false was hard to tell. "Aren't they laying?"

"Worse than that." Janet stared at the girl's feet. "And why change yer boots?"

McPhee gave a puzzled frown, but before she could reply, a black cloud of crows soared from the snowy trees as shouts from near the gate grew louder. James Baird astride his cob, was cantering up the carriageway holding on to a slightly-built young man by the hair. The stranger kept stumbling against the animal's front leg and once they'd reached the top, fell into the snow, moaning and muttering.

Where on earth had he come from, and why had the hunter picked him up in this manner? Before the rider dismounted, the dark-haired man struggled to his feet and began to run faster than a whippet back the way they'd come. But Janet, never losing sight of her plan to ensnare James Baird, blocked his way, gripping his sodden shirt with both hands. Feeling his shivering bones through the too-thin wool and McPhee's eyes on her every move.

"No, ye don't! Ye stop wi' me." She said to him.

"What's your name, fellow?" James Baird leapt from his cob and passed the reins to the maid. His fists ready to fight.

"Falcon Steer, sir."

"And from where have you crawled, Mr Steer?"

"Dunblane. No work there, but heard there was plenty up Argyll way."

"Nonsense. You heard wrong. You must be with those gypsies over at Tarra."

"No, sir. I don't like their ways. I'm a free man. A free thinker."

"So you try and steal my horse while I'm searching for our handyman. That it?"

"Not true. I was just admiring him. He's half Clydesdale, sir, in case you didn't know. A right fine specimen."

Janet couldn't help but admire his spirit. He had a good body too. Tight as a young tree. Hair grown long like a woman's tied back with green cord. For a second, she imagined him all dressed up. Then guiltily, all naked...

"Make an apology now, Mr Steer, or I'll be walking you to the loch and not stopping until you drown, full of water..."

"Tell your woman to leave me be, or you'll be the one drowning."

Your woman...

As Steer turned towards her, Janet felt as if that recent snowfall - that luminous whiteness in the gloaming - had melted. His deep brown eyes bore the same fire she'd seen in those of her brother. She let go only for the huntsman to take him and slice his crop against the other man's calves until he screamed.

"Let him speak, sir. Give him a chance," she pleaded, but James Baird ignored her.

"So you've been at our cocks too?" He said to Steer.

"What cocks?"

"They're all slaughtered. Every one."

The stranger turned to Janet not for help - he seemed too proud for that - but perhaps because he too sensed an inexplicable affinity.

"How could he be in two places at once, sir? And where's the blood on him?" She challenged the hunter.

"Washed it off in the loch, I wouldn't wonder," sneered McPhee. "Or on the snow. Easy enough to do."

The stranger turned to face her with enough anger in his expression for her to withdraw behind the chestnut's shoulder. "Check the snow for prints, Master Baird," she then added, undeterred. "A match will show up nice and clear. At least till the melting."

"There'll be no melt," Steer said ominously, then faced the huntsman. "And I'll wager the killer you seek belongs here at Ardnasaig House."

Silence, save for the cob's breath and the world freezing over. McPhee's pretty little mouth had fallen open in surprise; and the white blackthorn blossom floated down from her hair. Janet shivered as James Baird gripped the man's tangled scalp again. "Come with me, Mr Steer, unless you prefer Kilforgan's police constable."

"He'll be too tied up with the Clearance to bother with me. Haven't you heard? Writs of Removal are out already with Colonel Ritchie."

McPhee crept from her cowardly hiding place to drag both blackthorn branches around to the Store. Janet, still none the wiser as to how she'd cut them down, was tempted to follow, to search her pockets for a knife, when all of a sudden, James Baird shouted in her direction.

"You and your mother - get the pot and fires going. Then we need to talk. This time tomorrow, my father'll be here, expecting everything running to plan. And what'll he be finding? And who'll get the damned blame?" His voice rose. "Me!"

*

Woodsmoke drifted upwards from charcoal burning deep in Ardnasaig Forest and the slam of the Store's door and muffled talk diminished as Janet watched the two figures with the cob move away towards the stable. How could she have revealed what her poor mother had said about Isobel Baird? Things were surely going to get worse. She was no Linnet Garvie but could feel the future smothering her like that strange misty spectre that had devoured the house that very morning. Was Mr Bogle, to whom she'd never listened with any great respect, to be proved right? Was Ardnasaig, despite its lofty rooms and the space most folk from her part of Glasgow would envy above all else, cursed beyond any human understanding?

And who'd be next to succumb?

*

Janet decided the half-gutted trout would keep chilled until Boxing Day, but with the cooking pot empty, she must resist the temptation to use for James Baird's supper what was set aside for Christmas. And then she remembered the beef her mother had cooked two days ago. So, cold beef it would be, with its hard, purple rind soon scraped away. Hot tatties too, and the last half of her mother's custard cake to finish with.

As she worked, she thought about the stranger's fine brown eyes - how they'd fixed on her and then McPhee in quite different ways. He'd wanted another suspect for that recent slaughter, and had seemed disappointed when no name passed her lips. And, as Janet set the dining room table for one, decided it was time to keep track of her.

*

She called for the girl to revive the fires, and found her in the hallway, setting the first of those black, prickly branches and their fragile blossom into a bucket. McPhee sang softly to herself as she patted the soil around it with her bare hands, as if nothing else mattered, while the second fir lay against the stairs, giving off an odd smell. Light from the nearest lamp turned her hair the colour that Janet herself had longed for since she was a bairn. Pale, soft gold. But not her face.

"Them's nae important," Janet snapped. "Fires are."

McPhee ignored her, letting her fingers rest on the earth in a way Janet had never seen before. That voice seemed to belong to someone much older, delivering a ditty she didn't recognise.

"Bring us all eight days of cheer,

Till Hogmanay and the new year.

Bring good thoughts in, drive evil out

With God's fair grace, the Devil rout.

Trefoil, Vervain, John's Wort, Dill,

Hinder witches of their will."

Janet sensed a sudden slowing of her blood. So she'd learnt things from Linnet, but nothing like this. Besides, with the cocks all dead, how could she sing anything?

She backed away to stand by the door as if to keep herself clean.

"It's Master James who wants the fires kept up," she said.

The maid looked up as if she'd seen a ghost. Her trance over. "You're always eyeing me. You and that damned mother of yours."

Don't rise to the bait...

"When the fires are done, there's vegetables to scrape and stuffin' to make."

"And Mrs Lennox? What's she up to?"

Janet saw impudence personified. "It'll be just ye and me for the time being. So get used to doin' as yer told."

"Does she need Dr Angus? If so, I could fetch him."

"She wants peace. That's what she's said."

McPhee lifted her hands out of the bucket and brushed dirt from both her palms. "There'll be no peace now." She stood up to shake white petals from her skirt.

"Why's tha', then?"

"I saw how Falcon Steer looked at you."

"Yer jealous."

A little laugh, yet sharp as a dawn breeze.

"I prefer a man to have lighter coloured hair. Fair skin."

"Not fussy, then?"

A strange, small smile followed.

"*He* is. I can tell. Like a deer hunter ready to strike at only the biggest, most meaty carcass."

✳✳✳

9.

Where endings are not in sight...

Poor Lennox, lapping up flattery like a thirsty dog. So thought Catriona, obediently making a start with the cold carrots from the Store. With the gutting knife mysteriously gone and Mr Bogle's own one far too small for the purpose, she chose another whose worn, wooden handle chafed against her palm. Her rival's hinted accusations making her scrape all the harder, pretending she was scraping the skin off that ugly, bony face.

She should be pleased the pony-tailed stranger had eyed her rival that way, but there was another side to the coin - how quickly he'd changed when she herself had dared utter a word against him, making her shiver, wanting to be invisible. But who did he think he was? Impertinent creature, too ready to take Lennox's side. And as for James Baird, he was as fickle as a weathervane, turning whichever way the wind blew. In the greater scheme of things, that was immaterial. What did matter was that he must perceive her as whiter than that clinging, untrodden snow lying beneath the elms.

*

While she worked her knife blade up and down the sides of each carrot and cut them into four sections apiece, she wondered what if Falcon Steer were to meet her rival again. Perhaps she should encourage it. And what about those poor, helpless cocks? Lennox *must* have known, as she'd shown no horror or surprise at their cruel fate, and if James Baird had spoken the truth, they'd suffered a merciless attack. Those black-feathered females had been her favourites from day one. Following her to the edge of their domain whenever she'd passed by. Although they'd been the housekeeper's responsibility, she'd have gladly stepped in if need be. Dumb creatures had often calmed her nerves while demanding nothing in return, and at first light tomorrow, she'd go to the coop and witness the grim aftermath for herself.

Catriona tipped the peeled carrots into a pan and began preparing three onions for the Christmas stuffing. She hated onions for making her cry, and her chopping soon became more haphazard. According to the doctor who'd helped deliver her, she'd not only left her mother's womb in a hurry, but 'dry-eyed and smiling. An oddity if e'er there was,' so he'd said, and here she was, wiping away all wetness off her cheeks as if her life depended on it.

*

She realised she was starving, and pushed some of the stuffing mix into her mouth, gobbling it down before anyone should find out, feeling more alone than at any other time since arriving at that unwelcome, black front door. Perhaps if she closed her eyes and willed the old handyman to appear, he would, bringing everything back to normal.

But it was neither Mr Bogle who appeared, nor Falcon Steer. Catriona, having sensed a sudden draught on her back, whipped round and immediately sniffed stagnant loch water. And why was the cook-housekeeper's gaunt body draped in a thin sheet, standing behind the one wooden chair? And stranger still, why had those dry old lips turned a fulsome, trembling red? The watery, hazel-coloured eyes become such a startling blue? Hard as steel, skewering her with hatred?

A shot of terror touched her soul, for this was no solid, living housekeeper, but an oddly-altered spectre whose bony forefinger pointed her way, as she moved away from the chair, coming closer, step by step.

"What's the matter?" Catriona backed away. "What are you doing?" She felt the cold kitchen wall reach her skin. "Do you need a doctor? Do you want to sit down?"

But by then, that finger with its jagged nail was resolutely pressed on her breastbone. Pinning her against the exposed granite stones as old as the earth itself, so that any earlier concern for this sorry, silent figure slipped away like rainwater off Footer's Hill.

"Get away! Leave me alone!" Her push met only air accompanied by the distinct crack and crumble of old bones. Meanwhile, the creature's breathing had quickened, releasing more of that unmistakeable fishy smell. In a moment of panic, Catriona realised that whoever Margaret Lennox had become, wanted her, Iain McPhee's daughter, gone.

*

Catriona stifled a scream as that trailing sheet moved away, leaving the same fishy stink in her wake. Then, with her pulse still throbbing in her ears, she followed the smell up the first flight of stairs and paused on the landing to catch her breath and let the last of the window's light show the way up to the attic..

But what's this?

It hadn't been there that morning.

A black-framed portrait of a woman wearing a dark blue dress, executed so delicately, so realistically that Catriona couldn't resist reaching up to touch those barely tinted cheeks, then the exquisitely red-painted lips. But it wasn't until her fingertip reached the nearest sharp, blue eye, that she realised who had accosted her in the kitchen. And reading the first two words below, was all the bad news she needed.

Isobel Baird, July 1846 Oil on canvas. William Rankin R.A. 1851

She steadied herself against the banister's mean rail, wondering how in the Devil's name this painting had got there, and had the artist worked directly in front of her, or from some other image? But these questions were immaterial because the more she stared at this woman whose prominent, sapphire wedding ring glinted from behind the protective glass, the more she knew that from now on, unless her guardian angel was on full alert, any future in Ardnasaig House would be doomed.

*

Loch Nonach's smell lingered by Margaret Lennox's attic door, but evaporated the moment Catriona opened the bedroom door to a numbing chill. On the bed, lay the housekeeper herself, bone and muscle as still as a length of wood washed up on the loch's shore. Her beak-like nose upturned. Her mouth half-open and it seemed, silent for ever. Catriona prised open those veiny eyelids in turn just to make sure she'd not been hallucinating.

No...

Gone were the two lifeless, hazel-coloured orbs she'd been expecting. These were blue. The very same vivid colour that had so startled her in the kitchen. Identical to those eyes in the painting on the landing below.

*

Minutes later, on trembling legs, she ran back downstairs, while Donald Bairds' contribution to *The Scotsman*' that she'd seen in Mr Bogle's bothy, accompanied each step.

'...*if she'd been in peril, both Tam and Rabbie, her Gordon setters, would have guarded her with their lives...*'

She collected her candle, then paused in fresh fear, because Lennox was bellowing out her name like a fishwife.

The carrots hit her first. Then an uncut onion connected with her cheek. Black Eyes was in full flow until James Baird placed himself in front of her, with a damp-haired Falcon Steer looking on as if he'd entered Bedlam. The loch's saltiness clung to his clothes. Lamplight yellowed the whites of his eyes.

"Sir," blushed Lennox when her rant had finished. "I told McPhee to get these ready for tomorrow. And what does she do? Pleases hersel. I'm sick of it."

"Your mother interrupted me." Catriona protested. "At least, I *think* it was her."

Lennox glanced past both men towards the corridor. "Where is she, then?"

Catriona felt the force of the stranger's dark stare. Now more than ever, she sensed an enemy, the way a stag knows its stalker is closing in...

"Took herself off. How am I supposed to know?"

Falcon Steer looked at her. He'd stuffed half a carrot into his mouth and was chewing on it like a horse. "There's a death in this house, I can tell," he announced before swallowing. "Be mindful..."

Lennox reached for his arm as if she was suddenly drowning. What was left of his woollen shirt hung in shreds from his arms, his body. "Ye mean me mother?"

"And others to consider."

Catriona saw James Baird turn pale.

After that, it was as if she was invisible, trailing the little party to the top of the house. Lennox led the way, and her scream when it came curling down the stairwell, seemed to bruise the very walls and cause the absent architect's framed watercolours of Loch Nonach and one of his son on that white pony, to tilt on their pins. Nobody mentioned the new painting. There were more important things afoot.

*

Half an hour later, James Baird's orders, Catriona had placed Falcon Steer's chair on its own further down the dining table to be nearest the fire. The traveller who to her mind had been made too welcome, devoured his beef and drunk his spring water before the huntsman had even picked up his knife.

Nobody spoke, and she certainly wasn't going to mention that revolting apparition in the kitchen. Lennox's back was to the door, her head lowered, not even stealing the odd glance at the new man at the table, while Catriona thought only of what was happening overhead and two floors up. The housekeeper beginning to decompose.

She drew the long, velvet curtains tight against the night which the mysterious interloper had predicted would freeze all the fish in the loch by morning. And if Donald Baird was arriving tomorrow as expected by pony and trap from Inverary, there'd be certain danger from black ice.

"Father promised me he'd pay for telegraph equipment here when he's next home," said James Baird. "Just think of it, no more relying on the post to take messages."

Lennox looked up, wet-eyed. Another opinion on her lips. "Mother told me there'd bin at least thirteen designs for them instruments at the Great Exhibition," she said, causing a small stir. "'Tis a pity Mr Baird didn't act sooner. And put a window in that dark study of his, now there's nae tax."

"If you loan me your cob," Steer said to the huntsman as if to fill the awkward silence, "I'll fetch a priest for Mrs Lennox, and on the way see there's peat put down where the track slopes too near the loch."

Ingratiating himself rather too quickly, thought Catriona, still stung by the other employee's sudden display of knowledge.

"Loan you my cob?" James Baird laughed. All his big teeth on show before he finished his wine in one long gulp. "I don't think so."

In that moment, Catriona imagined the future; herself at his side, ordering their butler to refill his glass. As his wife, she would sacrifice her own ambitions to ease his path and keep him content. Let his father see that despite her having lived in a but and ben, she'd be good for him. This inner vision appeared so strongly to her, was it possible he'd felt it too? Was this why he turned to her. Red lips glistening?

"Miss McPhee, I've never found myself in such a situation as this before, and I hope never to again. We have our housekeeper Mrs Lennox dead as a stone upstairs, Mr Bogle and his pony have gone and all our cocks lie slain by a cruel hand." He eyed Falcon Steer. "And here sits a stranger I've yet to trust."

Catriona felt the weight of the world upon her slight shoulders. Also, the weight of the tramp's recent pronouncement. "What did Mr Steer mean by other deaths to consider?" she said.

"Can we please keep to the point?"

"Sir," aware of Lennox turned her way, "I also have to ask. Was the mirror taken down from opposite the deathbed?"

"Why?"

"For the soul to leave this house, sir. Otherwise..."

But Lennox was already running from the room.

"It's too late," said Steer. "Spirits will linger until ready to depart."

James Baird wiped his mouth with his napkin and set it down.

"Enough of this fanciful talk." He turned to her. "Miss McPhee, I want your mind on this, or my father will say I'm not responsible enough to have charge of Ardnasaig. He'll employ someone else to take my place. Imagine it..."

"I can, sir. We must remove Mrs Lennox from the house at once. I've seen dead cattle and how quickly they rot, even in December."

"In this weather?" He rolled up a slice of cold beef, before cutting it into three equal portions and eating the first.

"In this weather."

"So what now?"

"I have a different solution to Mr Steer's. At least until travelling conditions improve."

James Baird seemed very interested. "What's that, then? Put her among the nuns in the old graveyard?"

"No," interrupted Steer with surprising feeling. "That's a cursed spot. I knew the moment my feet passed through it. The Dame of Nonach also lies there under that black stone and if you linger, she'll draw you down to Hell. You need a holy man to cleanse it first. We must spare the deceased that."

Catriona frowned. Was *that* what Lennox had wanted her to know? And a stone was the price of it. James Baird's mismatched eyes were on her again. "Back to you, Miss McPhee. What are *your* thoughts?"

Even thought the fire was still lively, Catriona's skin began to cool. When she'd finished her theory, both men were already standing.

"But we must let Janet think there's another way," she added, careful to use her Christian name, hoping her sly adversary was eavesdropping. "We can't have her falling sick. She's in enough shock already."

Just then, as she'd guessed, Lennox returned to the dining room. Her face streaked by tears, her black hair in disarray. Under her arm she carried the offending mirror and leant it against the wall below a watercolour of the former nunnery set against a vivid sunset.

"I told mother she'd have the best," she announced. "And that means a proper Christian burial in sanctified ground. I've kept most of me wages to pay for it." She turned to James Baird. "Are burials costly round here?"

The huntsman nodded.

"But, as she's been a loyal worker, I shall ask my father to help out."

"Thank you, sir."

Catriona watched her crude half-curtsy while Falcon Steer parted the curtains then closed them again.

"I've noticed your neighbour at Fearn House down the loch keeps a number of barks," he said. "To avoid the snowed-up tracks, I can fetch one and row Mrs Lennox up to Kilforgan before the loch freezes over."

"Dauvit Hendry never takes risks."

"We can but try, sir." Black Eyes was colouring up. Her bony cheeks pink with excitement. "It's nae far, and when he finds out why we want one…"

"Miss Lennox," said the over-helpful stranger. "First, your poor mother must be moved from this house. Then we can decide."

Catriona refilled James Baird's glass and, as they both waited for the din of two pairs of boots to diminish up the stairs, he tipped the blood red wine down his throat.

"Let them be for a moment," he said. "Then I'll follow." He threw her a crooked smile. "I'd never have thought of that ice house in a million years."

Catriona returned his smile. Then asked what he and the stranger had deduced from their visit to the cocks' coop.

"Nothing to worry your pretty little head about," was all he said.

She began to clear the table, keeping busy, alert for every sound coming from above. Despite James Baird's reassurance, her pulse was leaping so fast in her wrists that she almost dropped the plates on her way to the scullery. On her return, to her surprise, the narrow stairway was blocked by four people. Mrs Lennox's corpse at their centre, swathed in that same, thin bed sheet, emerged head first. What little hair her cap had covered, now hung free like that floaty, pale moss on every winter branch. The unmistakeable whiff of human dung ever stronger as she approached.

"Steady," urged James, himself less so. "Use the rear door."

"Why, sir?" complained Lennox.

"In my father's absence, this is my property and in it, you'll do as I say. Your mother's to stop in the ice house until the morning."

That bony face dropped in amazement. Looked even more ugly. "Mr Steer, tell him nae. *Please...*"

Lennox almost lost her grip on those gnarled bare feet, and the corpse tilted against the banister; white eyes scrolled upwards, blank to the world. Her few teeth askew in her gaping mouth. Hard to imagine how she'd once ruled this kingdom and kept food short on her plate, thought Catriona. At least Mairi McPhee had spared her own daughter such a sight. Even her father had refused to keep her coffin open for folks to pay their respects.

"Tell him nae!" Roared Lennox again, but before the man from Dunblane could utter a word, further chaos had begun from higher up the stairs, causing the procession to halt. The reason soon clear.

Fluttering and scratching sounds preceded a black veil of bats whose velvet bodies brushed both the dead and the living as they swept by. Of all God's creatures, Catriona feared these the most. And now it was as if every single one in the whole of Arygll had descended upon Ardnasaig House.

*

James Baird squeezed past the housekeeper's body on his way through to the hallway, and re-appeared with his rifle cocked, ready to fire at the rabid intruders.

"No, sir!" Catriona cried. "If they die, trouble will shadow the rest of your days. Is that what you want? Is it?"

"Speak for yersel," said Lennox before James Baird began firing here, there and everywhere.

Catriona stopped up her ears as one shot after another brought blood and the glistening fall of innards. A black, wet autumn wherever she looked. One squealing bat lay warm on her head, flapping its wings. She screamed, disentangling it from her hair as Falcon Steer added to the din.

"Sir!" He shouted, picking two writhing victims from the dead woman's breasts and letting them fall to the floor. "I can't be a part of things here any more." He glanced back at Lennox. Softened his voice. "If you come with me, we could have a good life. I've a trade, I can work. We could go to America. To California. Far, far away..."

Catriona watched the orphan's plain mouth open.

"'Tis guid of ye to think of me," she said at last, "but me mother needs proper attention." Meanwhile, more tears fall to mingle with the bats' blood. "And sir," she addressed James Baird. "I'll take her to the loch meself. There'll be nae wicked freezin' for her."

Let her go, thought Catriona. The rifle was still in the huntsman's hands. If she insisted on disobeying him, she must face the consequences. And why should she care? The architect's son was showing no real interest in that rocky face, those hard, black olive eyes.

And then, what happened next, made her heart tremble beneath her clothes. Margaret Lennox dipped perilously towards the floor as Falcon Steer, having gripped her arm in a farewell gesture, suddenly walked away, shoulders hunched.

"Come back!" Lennox cried after him. "I need ye here."

"I meant what I said."

With that, Catriona and James Baird took his place and began pulling the old body this way and that until the sheet that had protected her modesty, slipped free, exposing her yellowed flesh, skin wrinkled as the sand on Benronan beach after high tide. Catriona sneaked a glance at those flattened breasts and worse, down below, between her thighs, bald as a plucked chicken from where both a daughter and son had entered the world.

Lennox caught James Baird looking too, before she snatched at the sheet to make swift amends. Catriona thought of her own father - how age and cruel events had left him a mere shadow of his earlier self. How corruption of the flesh wasn't as her mother said, a way to life eternal, but a frightening end in itself, with no more mystery than that. If immortality was the next stage, why hadn't she appeared to her in any dream? Where was she hiding? Where?

She held her nose, forced to leave the struggle, then pushed her way into the dining room and peered through its one window overlooking the gloomy carriageway. Falcon Steer was striding along it through the snow without any backward glance. Was he crying too? Hard to say, but, as the commotion behind her increased, instead of continuing on his way through the open gates, he turned right along the now buried track to the loch side. A track she knew led eventually to the cocks' coop. If she wasn't so behind in her tasks, she'd have followed him to see what was he up to. Be witness to what might he find second time around.

*

Having cleared up bat blood from the hall tiles and flung their stubborn remains out amongst the rhododendrons, Catriona filled up the bullet holes in the wall by the stairs and rubbed beeswax into the dining room table. She was imagining tomorrow's scene with Donald Baird in place at the head and his son the only company. Imagining too, the housekeeper waking up in the ice house, not dead at all. Eyes wide awake. Blue, not hazel.

Unlike the daughter, she'd first of all been taught to read and write at Cranranich's small kirk school, and since mistakes meant a beating, her spelling and the way she formed her letters with a pen, were as near perfect as they could be. Then, after the move to Footer's Cottage, her mother had taken over her education, making her copy out the Scriptures, learn the history and geography of Scotland and other more faraway countries. Perhaps why Master Baird had offered her work.

She'd also learnt of Sikhs and Zoroastrians who leave their dead on towers of silence; the Aboriginal notions of death and rebirth, but strangest of all were the inhabitants of Baw Heid at the furthermost, inland edge of the loch. Amongst other odd rituals were their woven wicker caskets designed to fit both a corpse and a chosen animal. Only last month, the bodies of Colonel Neville from Braewhelan Lodge, killed by angry tenants, had been burnt alongside his favourite horse.

As a useful exercise for her future status, Catriona created a Yuletide list divided into two parts. *Tasks to be Done* and *Menus Without Chicken* for the next four days and, as she sat on an old wooden chair in the kitchen, felt Mr Bogle's loss more than ever. The dependable father-figure still hadn't turned up, and she found herself wondering what he'd have advised for the dead housekeeper. With his often skewed view of life, he might have caused quite a stir.

She finished her lists and pinned them up in a prominent place on the window frame, at the same time looking out for Falcon Steer's return. But it seemed the night had claimed him. Instead, came the distant slamming of doors and Lennox's weeping and wailing. Not for the first time since starting work, did Catriona ask herself how long could her main plan sustain her.

Iain McPhee had never made plans. Especially during the years since her mother had died. But what if word reached him about the unexplained goings-on here? She dreaded to think. Would he forcibly try and remove her? But what else could she do with herself? However stormy the weather, this was *her* place, *her* future. Not his.

Catriona reached for the little ivory comb safe in her pocket. Something to remember Mr Bogle by, should she never set eyes on him again. And then James Baird appeared, in need of a wash and change of clothes. And was that Margaret Lennox's dung still clinging to his breeches?

"Are you well, sir?" she asked.

"I will be if you can heat a bath for me, and leave a dram alongside."

"Of course, sir."

That would mean at least half an hour of boiling up enough water. But if it led to the chance of her catching him undressed or even half undressed, then every second would be worthwhile. As he left the kitchen, she called out after him.

"By the way, sir. That's a fine new painting upstairs. Who is it of?"

"My mother. Who else?

That word 'mother' came as a shock.

"Why so surprised?" he said.

"I'm not, sir. It's just that... "

"What?"

"Forgive me saying, sir, but you don't resemble her at all."

✱✱✱

10.

Where certain hearts turn to ice...

It was still Christmas Eve, and Janet had fallen asleep dreaming of Falcon Steer and his distinctive, long hair sailing away from Glasgow like so many of the Clearance workers, to a foreign shore. He'd waved once, only to be obscured by others. Now she opened her eyes to a hard, white world beyond the window and the same biting cold in her mother's room. It was like being back in the ice house again, laying that stiff body on the straw between those glistening Arctic blocks, while James Baird looked on, tapping his rifle impatiently against his boots as she'd tucked in those few strands of grey hair that had escaped the half-frozen sheet.

But how to inform her brother? His regiment had moved on, but whether to Sebastopol, she didn't know. Nevertheless, her yearning to tell him was tempered by reality. He'd ask too many questions, adopt a stance. Taint the rest of her life with more guilt. He'd torment her like McPhee. Give her no peace, and yet she would always have a place for him somewhere in her heart.

She felt a sudden, spreading hollowness, but not from hunger. As if her own skin contained nothing. However, she'd met Falcon. The man with the beautiful eyes and teeth whiter than anything beyond the window. Whiter too, than James Baird's. And the more she thought of him, the more her nipples tingled and less was her resolve to stay in that bleak, friendless house. But what if her *'wee frein'* wouldn't come on time? What then?

She watched a group of hungry gulls fly southwards against the streaked dawn sky and promised herself if a wean *were* on the way, she wouldn't commit the same sin as before. Nor would she let the Dame of Nonach help herself. She'd give it some sort of life, but not here. Not with James Baird for a father...

*

The grandfather clock brought from Paisley by wealthy Malcolm Baird, the first incumbent of Ardnasaig House, chimed six o'clock. In eight hours' time there'd be his grandson at the table. A man of considerable reputation who paid all the wages. Who'd find his home so changed there was no knowing what he might do.

Janet and her mother had met him just the once and not for long, because of his business appointment in Glasgow. He'd seemed as cold as a Loch Nonach carp, with no smile even for his son. No wonder his spirited, glamorous wife had left him. She'd have surely done the same...

Suddenly, came sounds that were nothing to do with starlings or crows foraging among the roof tiles overhead. Janet sat up, pressing her right ear against the wall behind her bed. McPhee was moving back and fore along that very wall, with just half an inch of pine wood separating them. And what else was she doing? Murmuring, that was for sure, like she'd done while potting up the blackthorn. Shaking things too, by the sound of it. Perhaps she was sleep-walking. Linnet had once said that the Devil lures slumberers from their rest at the point of death, to wander forever without peace...

Janet flung the blanket free of her legs, driven by the realisation she barely knew her attic neighbour. To her and her mother, she'd been the 'one from Cranranich' with a drinker for a father who'd married above himself to a kirk minister's God-fearing daughter. Nothing more, nothing less.

She collected a bowl of water from the tank room next to the linen room's most hateful door she'd ever known, which, now that her mother was dead, would be her task to regularly open and delve inside for bed linen. Maybe she should beg James Baird to give that work to McPhee instead.

It was almost too quiet, and her wash didn't last long. The freezing water stung her skin - down below as well - rekindling the image of her mother on that straw floor, where the few prayers had changed nothing for the better. Forcing Janet to wonder again where Falcon might be. And how after everything, that special seaweed didn't matter a jot, for her handsome iron worker was out there somewhere, waiting.

So too, was Ne'erday…

Her ears pricked up again, hearing the drag and drop of other water. Was the maid rinsing out her undergarments? She certainly never put them in the boiler along with everything else, where often her own mother's bloomers would emerge entangled with table napkins and James Baird's shirts. At least two pairs of her own drawers had gone missing just after the girl had arrived. Never to be found.

She discovered an extra bodice and pulled her thicker stockings up her calves before lacing up her trusty boots with their stoat skin lining - a gift from Calum while Greenock still sweated under a summer sky. Reminding her, like that linen room door, of things she'd rather forget.

Without making a sound, she crept downstairs from the attic landing, glancing behind her every so often to ensure no-one was following. Down that same dark oak stairwell where her mother's corpse had recently passed, giving Janet the chance to touch her hair, shoulders and feet, so there'd be no haunting. At least, that's what Linnet had always advised after a death.

What in God's name…?

She paused on the next landing. Stepped back in case she'd been seeing things, and froze in terror at the sudden creak of old wood beneath her feet.

Not even the dim light could disguise the fact that the fine portrait had gone, leaving only the two empty hooks. However, Janet could still feel the woman's penetrating gaze upon her, as if searching her soul. Trying to reach her to tell her something she ought to know.

*

"Miss Lennox? Is that you?" James Baird's voice reached her from somewhere, but because he never normally rose until eight o'clock, she didn't bother to answer. Instead she gathered her cloak tight around her and was soon outside in the rear courtyard, skirting the frozen well on her way over to the ice house. If the snow thawed by Boxing Day, the local hunt would be invading Ardnasaig's acres, trampling everything in its path.

A sky of torn grey shreds - some light, some dark - with a hint of brightness battling through. And over the elm glade,

104

twinkled the sad remains of stars. Cobblestones lay treacherous under their icy skin, just as they had been almost two years ago for another of her grim journeys. Her boots skidded this way and that, but still she was resolved to walk to Kilforgan if necessary for the kirk minister to arrange a burial. Margaret Lennox was, like her, baptised, confirmed and on most Sundays in Spring and summer, had attended the kirk's outdoor services above the loch. She could recite most of the psalms by heart, and believed every word. She deserved a proper ending…

Time was shortening before the master's expected return, and Janet had two missions to accomplish. The first began with her bare, cold hand closing round the ice house's frosted door handle to check her mother hadn't miraculously begun to breathe again. She hadn't. Just lay rigid in her straw bed. Gone it seemed, to another world. Next, however, upon closer inspection, came the scene of slaughter.

*

Janet didn't stop slithering down the carriageway out of sight of the house, until she'd reached the old graveyard. The taste of sick still in her throat.. Here, in this secret place, she refilled her lungs and rubbed the snow from her knees where she'd fallen. The silence that enfolded her was more profound than ever before as if, like a too-soft blanket, it was there to smother that barbaric sight in the ice house. A sight no God-fearing person should ever see. She half expected the wicked Dame of Nonach to rise from her grave in protest at the intrusion, but instead, came the faintest of whispers, lighter than a summer evening's breeze blowing off the loch. Whether from a man or woman she couldn't tell.

"Guard yer tongue, Janet. Ye'll need it to save yourself..."

What kind of warning was that? And why? Perhaps someone already dead was trying to frighten her into keeping silent.

Her mother?

It was possible. With Donald Baird due back within hours, another terrible crime had been committed, and Janet herself could fall under suspicion. This possibility, however unjust, gnawed at her resolve to trek to Kilforgan to fetch the police. Instead, there was still something else she had to see for herself before any melt.

Still in shock, she moved on past oaks whose giant-sized boles jutted like wean-filled bellies from their trunks. Just as hers had been that fearsome cold spring almost two years' ago, but not from gluttony, from love.

Through other trees whose sprawling roots almost floored her again – and on by Druids' Mound, mysteriously bare of snow - towards the rougher pasture spiked by various reed-filled bogs and the hens' fenced-off portion. Janet focussed on the snowy track, ruptured by various footprints which she tried to identify, and soon matched up two sets of what were probably Falcon and James Baird's boot prints skirting smaller ones she'd seen yesterday. Unpatterned, showing a dainty heel, yet not as deep. Unlike hers and the others, and in dawn's untainted light, discovered these continued to the small gate and then on to the coop itself.

Her heartbeat quickened as she memorised the scene and the precise shape and depth of just one of these distinctive prints which had included a small heel. Was it possible a man or youth could possess such delicate feet? Or was the real answer too alarming to consider?

And then, again, for the second time, while thinking of her mother's hideously violated face, viewed what lay within the pen.

*

"Oh, ye poor wee things!" Janet cried out loud, unable to look at the clods of black leavings mingled with blood. The neat slittings, the frozen uravellings. The open beaks and staring eyes.

Just as she was about to hurry away, a twig snapped behind her. She twisted round and there she was. Wee McPhee looking like a precious little doll, trembling, rubbing away her tears. Gloves, mind, Janet noticed. Taking care of herself, obviously.

How had she known she'd be here? Was she tracking her night and day? If so, why?

"It's the Devil's work, that's for sure," sniffed the girl not at all convincingly. "But can a wild animal be possessed by Him?"

"Nae animal's done this. Nor the butchery on me dead mother."

Guard yer tongue…

"Butchery? What are you talking about?" asked McPhee, still sniffing, but Janet sensed her surprise was fake.

"Just ye wait."

That not-so pretty face tightened, puckering her spiteful mouth.

"No-one threatens me. Ever."

Yet all the same, Janet could tell that the cunning maid was thinking hard, trying to divert things. Lay blame elsewhere.

"I know nothing more about Mrs Lennox," said McPhee. "But that gipsy with a woman's hair could have done all this. I saw blood under his nails. The way he wouldn't look me in the eyes. Only you..."

Only ye...

"He hardly stayed, though, did he?" she taunted. "How does that make you feel? When you needed him most?"

Never mind the slippery grass, the treacherous hidden ice. This was much more dangerous ground.

'Guard yer tongue...'

Easier said than done, thought Janet, eyeing McPhee's brown, buttoned boots probably bought at some local fair or other. She knew they didn't have a heel, but she had to test the girl's reaction.

"Let's see beneath yer boot."

"Why's that?"

Instead of replying, Janet reached for the nearest leather-clad ankle, but the younger girl was too quick, swerving away, calling her a witch because that's what she'd learnt before arriving at Ardnasaig. A witch who'd be wanting to steal her piss next, and her monthly blood. And who'd named her so? Why, none other than James Baird, following in Mr Bogle's footsteps.

Janet stood under that slow-moving sky feeling dizziness and despair. Even the brave sun cracking open the clouds over Nonach Forest didn't help. And then, having turned her gaze downwards, saw how all the previously visible boot prints and those fresh ones leading back to the house, had been destroyed.

*

"Sir," she panted, standing by the Store's open door. "What have ye and Mr Bogle been tellin' folks round here about me?"

James Baird sat on an old stool facing away from her, cleaning his rifle with short, measured strokes that reminded her of things they shouldn't. He neither stopped nor looked round. So she wasn't worth even that any more. It hadn't occurred to her that since her mother's passing, her days here might be numbered. That Donald Baird might hire a new cook and keep McPhee on as housekeeper. Especially if he knew about Margaret Lennox's stolen eyes as well as the dead cocks.

"Telling what?"

"That I'm a witch. That Falcon Steer disembowelled yer cocks."

"Who said?"

"Miss McPhee."

Without a word, he stopped polishing the wooden barrel and set the rifle on the floor. The stool's iron feet grated against the stone flags as he turned to face her, eyes shaded by the rim of his hat.

"Miss Lennox, I may not have had the education my father enjoyed, nor known the kind of company he and my mother kept during their years together, but," he stood up to stand at the doorway as if on guard. His face reflecting the snow. "I've no truck with that kind of talk. We're in 1851, not the Dark Ages. I'd have been happy to keep Mr Steer on as an extra pair of hands. When he saw the cocks, he cried like a bairn. Real tears…"

Janet could imagine it. Also a noose, swinging against a black, stormy sky.

"They still hang in England," she said, without thinking.

"So I've heard. But then Sassenachs are savages. Every one."

"What about half-bloods?" Because his accent suggested it.

"All I know is Miss McPhee seems very interested in the slaughter. Every time she sees me, she speaks of it."

"To say what, sir?"

"How sad she is. That some savage beast must have come from the forest."

Janet saw that noose again.

"She's sayin' one thing to ye and another to me, sir. Playin' tricks."

This wasn't getting anywhere. James Baird's interest fading like that Brocken spectre. Until a surprise.

"Tell me, was it you up and about so early this morning?"

Be careful.

"I couldnae sleep from thinkin' about me mother. How she needs proper rest in the Lord, and also, sir, how come Miss McPhee's so knowin' about witchcraft? Have ye heard her chantin' and singin' round the house? Because I have. 'Tis very strange. Remember how she foretold trouble before ye shot those bats?"

By way of a reply, he pulled out his grandfather's watch from his waistcoat, and frowned.

"We have five and a half hours until my father arrives. I can keep Miss McPhee busy until the moment he sets foot in the hall.

As for you, Miss Lennox, the kitchen, scullery and Store are your domains."

"And the laundry?"

She held her breath.

"Why d'you ask?"

"I cannae sew nor iron to save me life, sir."

Was that a smile creeping along his lips? Some small warmth in that bleak place? That same smile as when he'd lifted her skirt and pressed himself close?

"I'm sure Miss McPhee can oblige until we find her replacement."

Replacement?

Janet blinked. He really was full of surprises. Pleasant ones at that. He retrieved his rifle and patted her on the shoulder.

"Keep your own counsel, Janet Lennox. That's one lesson I've learnt."

"Thankye again, sir." And, emboldened by his show of support, added, "could I have the loan of yer cob to find the Reverend over at Kilforgan? "

"Why?"

She had to think quickly. Guard her tongue.

"Me mother needs a proper grave."

"I'll go. The track's sure to be bad, and he'll have to bring his special trap with him. Our dog cart's too small for a hearse."

"O' course, sir."

That smile again, like a glow in the gloom. "Perhaps, Miss Lennox, there'll be something hot for when I return?"

She blushed.

"I'll see to it personally."

"Good. And instruct Miss McPhee to get rid of those dead cocks. A fire's best. Whatever's the cause, my father mustn't suspect anything. Once he's gone again, we can discover more. But there *is* another matter we must resolve this morning."

"Sir?"

"William Rankin's missing painting. Where on God's earth can it be?"

*

Janet hurried through to the kitchen with those last words thrumming in her ears. Glad the dour Mr Bogle wasn't around to add to her mounting problems. From the moment he'd set eyes on her, she'd been aware of his resentment. Perhaps he himself had given McPhee that wicked notion about her. Perhaps he wasn't the uncomplicated hewer of wood and ice he'd appeared to be, but a mischief-maker in disguise.

She tipped a pile of tumsties into the stone sink and had just begun to peel off their purply skins, when she heard the door behind her scrape against the floor as it opened.

"I heard every word." Came a voice soft as a summer breeze. "And I won't ever forget."

Janet smelt the outdoors, the bone-numbing cold that McPhee brought with her. Her peeler slipped from her fingers into the brown water. "Yer to burn the hens," she said, fishing around for it. "Master Baird's orders. And put a hot stone in his father's bed once the linen's bin checked for repair. When that's all done, report to me for yer next tasks…"

112

"Is that it?"

"And those boots ye wore when Mr Steer first arrived. I'd like to see them."

"They were ruined. I got rid."

"Where?"

The girl shrugged.

"Down the well. What's wrong with that?"

Janet stopped. Felt faint again, her normally sturdy legs about to give way. The same sensation as she felt in the days before her monthlies came. She clutched her belly with wet hands, aware that behind the fleshy womb wall that Linnet had termed the safest place in the world, lay not safety, but danger.

***

11

In which secrets are known...

Catriona knew her lie about throwing Mairi McPhee's black boots into the well was a mistake, but she must neither panic nor run. Rather, do everything she could to stay on at Ardnasaig House and enhance her position. The painted woman on the first floor landing was exactly that. Just oil paint and canvas and, despite what Margaret Lennox had said, and others working against her, she must strive to be the best domestic servant in Argyll, winning over James Baird by her attention to detail and to him. She could almost hear her dead mother's voice telling her so. But what about her troublesome father?

I'm not listening... I can't...

And before wrapping a woollen scarf around her head and searching for her thickest gloves, Catriona glanced at herself in her small unframed mirror. Her well-proportioned face, large, grey eyes, a slender nose and full, pretty lips were timeless assets. Worthy successors, surely, to those of Isobel Baird?

Thankful not to have that same blue vein blemish that made Lennox's nose look even worse, she practised her biggest smile of welcome, inwardly renewing that promise she'd made to her mother so no-one either quick or dead, could take it away. And then there was the question of boots. It was no-one's business what she'd planned for them. As for her new, brown, buttoned ones, they were also soaked through, and to have worn them any more would have soon seen her back broken.

A hasty search in the Store led to a cupboard. Donald and Isobel Baird's footwear for the winter. No matter Iain McPhee had often warned against wearing dead men's shoes, Isobel Baird wasn't dead. Was she?

Yes, Catriona told herself as she chose a fine pair of grey, moleskin winter boots with dainty, brass fasteners, she must swallow her pride and burn the hens as instructed. Nevertheless, burning the dead cocks wasn't a task she was relishing, and as she ventured forth, admitted to herself it felt odd to be wearing the lady of the house's footwear. However, not only did their patterned soles without a heel offer the best grip on the icy ground, they were also a perfect fit. Falcon Steer had been right. There'd be no thawing today or for the foreseeable future.

*

As she shook each fallen branch free of snow and laid them in a pyramid formation the way Mr Bogle had shown her, Catriona thought of the tyrannical, lying Janet Lennox with a hatred as pure as that first acid light heralding the dawn. The low-life from Greenock had enjoyed ordering her to do this. Yes, *enjoyed.* And to make matters worse, had turned James Baird against her so that the word 'replacement' had readily fallen from his lips. She'd seen the way he'd smiled - twice - and touched Black Eyes' bony shoulder…

Catriona sealed her lips and snorted the freezing air through her nose as she lit the taper and held it against the bonfire's innermost branch until it bore a tiny flame. While adding more wood and strengthening the weave, she had the strongest feeling of being watched.

She scanned the high rhododendrons whose normally dark, glossy leaves were now crystalline white. The pine plantation on the burial mound and the sliver of loch water mirroring the yellow dawn. Had Falcon Steer returned? If so, he'd know how to noiselessly conceal himself - unlike her with Lennox. How she cursed that twig which had earlier given her away. And just to think of that stranger and other disconcerting morsels of news, made her work faster, lifting up the first dead weight of the cocks' frozen guts on to the shovel.

Woodsmoke, flesh smoke cracking, spitting, sending burnt remnants into her hair, the corners of her eyes, while a pair of buzzards hovered overhead. They'd feasted already, leaving the pen's snow carpeted in black, broken feathers.

Four to go…

Soon with the last corpse added to the flames, the pyre collapsed in on itself with a sigh, and when the ashes had cooled, she extracted a small souvenir for later. A charred claw. For luck.

She scraped most of the strewn feathers into a heap and added them to the embers. Their blue smoke thickened, smelling of old clothes. Of Mairi McPhee's wardrobe.

The worst was over.

*

On the way back to the house, Catriona thanked the lucky claw she'd not been approached to help with the storage or eventual removal of the housekeeper's body. That Lennox with her devious ways, was too full of bright ideas to see anything through. So why then did she feel a quickening inside her chest? Was it because she'd watched those cocks spit and burn on the fire, or because she'd just been made responsible for the laundry - a task she'd never been trained for? No, it was the prospect of a Christmas without her father and Mr Bogle, where one malicious person's word would weigh double her own. Where her dream of being mistress of Ardnasaig House was in imminent danger of slipping away.

*

As she grappled her way up the icy stone steps leading to the back of the house, Catriona knew what she must do to restore her hard-won status with James Baird. Hadn't she heard him say loud and clear, 'have something hot for my return?'

And by the time she'd reached the stable and found his cob gone from its stall, she promised herself to do just that. At midday, there'd be two men, possibly three, to feed. The Reverend MacKinnon, the architect and the huntsman himself.

When she opened the Store door, her magic helper was staring her in the face. A round of pork belly, not too fat and, despite the poor light, still a good colour. The letters D F McT scored into its orange rind. To reach the meat, she had to pass the newly-killed stag hanging over a large tin bucket filling up with blood from its open mouth. Its eyes still and black as those of the housekeeper's daughter.

She'd seen enough gore for one day and, cradling the heavy ham in her arms, hurried along until she reached the big, square kitchen.

No knife.

To find one would mean venturing further afield and risking a possible encounter with her adversary who'd humiliated and even tried to kill her. Who surely would again. She listened hard for the slightest clue that Lennox was nearby. Even a whiff of that unwashed body.

Where was she?

With her own clothes still reeking of woodsmoke, Catriona slipped into the scullery where she knew Margaret Lennox had kept spare of everything. Sure enough, in a lower cupboard lay a set of four carvers set in size order, into a block of elm. The name BOGLE as its maker, gouged into its side. She chose the middling one.

Back in the kitchen, she locked the door behind her and slid the bolt across, knowing that before long, the Glaswegian would come looking...

Damnation.

The pork rind was thicker, more slippery than she'd imagined. Her fingers almost numb with cold against the knife handle, her mind elsewhere on the never-ending mysteries of Ardnasaig House. Especially that wean's pitiful cries from the linen room, enough to break your heart. She hoped the ivory comb lying next to the handyman's cheese knife and her room key, deep in her skirt pocket, would be some protection. If the comb *had* belonged to someone he'd cared for, it might care for her too.

118

With the pork belly safely in the oven and the coals beneath burning brightly, Catriona prepared a mash using the tumsties Lennox had already peeled, all this with bated breath. Surely the cooking smells would have attracted the enemy by now? Surely she'd on her vengeful way? But no. It seemed as if, in that warren of a house with that white, silent world outside, she, Catriona Mairi McPhee was the last person left on this earth.

*

With mounting curiosity as to where Lennox might be, she noticed how dust had gathered in the join between each stair even since she'd cleaned up those bats' scattered entrails. Once she'd checked Lennox was safely in her own quarters, she'd fetch a duster, then add some holly with berries to the mirrors and pictures in the lounge and dining rooms. Survival depended upon making a good impression on the architect and his son. To tip the see-saw her way, and show the real difference between herself and the thick-waist from Greenock. How she, not the daughter could replace the frozen housekeeper.

*

On the first landing, Catriona passed various engravings of bleak, mist-swathed Scottish castles she'd never seen in real life, to that gap where the portrait had been. Whoever had removed it, must have had a reason. But what could that be, and why now? And then she found herself thinking about William Rankin's commission. Had it been meant for some special occasion or even a votive offering to bring the subject home? If so, the wait could be a long one.

*

Unlike her own door, Margaret Lennox's was unlocked, and through the narrow cranny between its wood and the frame, Catriona saw the bed in disarray and on top lay her rival, face down. She was muttering lines Catriona recognised as belonging to the Bible, mixed up with less intelligible words - referring to her brother, begging him to pray for her and for God to forgive their unholy sin. She was also begging for her mother's soul to find peace, and from her place among angels, help her daughter find who'd been responsible for taking her eyes. Endow her with deserved rewards.

Unholy sin? Taking her eyes? Deserved rewards?

Catriona forgot herself and all her recent troubles. To listen was far more intriguing, and might just shine a small but useful light into the Glaswegian's troubled soul.

She moved closer to the bed where death's aftermath still lingered, forming a sour-sweet taste on her tongue. Nevertheless, it was time to help.

"Janet? It's me, Catriona," she whispered. "Can't we be friends and stop fighting each other? Ardnasaig's a terrible mess, and Mr Baird will be here soon…"

Lennox didn't move.

"Keep away from me. D'ye hear?" she muttered. "Keep away."

"How can I when there's been such suffering? For you especially?" Her voice sounded convincingly sincere. Good.

Those black eyes then turned on her. Crease marks patterned Lennox's cheeks, and Catriona observed that most of the undersheet was stained by yellow and brown patches.

"I ken nowt about ye," she snarled. "So why trust ye?"

"You must, and I'm sorry about your mother still unburied. I lost mine too long ago. At least she was prayed for and taken away quickly. But taking her eyes? What's happened?"

"I cannae talk about it."

"At least Master Baird's gone over to see the Reverend so she'll have a proper burial."

At this, Lennox pushed her face deep into her mother's pillow. Spread out like that, with her cap askew and her boots still on her feet, she resembled a body washed in with the tide. But curiosity, outweighing any pity, trickled into Catriona's mind.
"Do you need to talk about your brother at all?" She ventured.

At this, the other girl reared up, reached for her cap and swung her strong, thick legs off the bed. Catriona caught the smell of her sex. She wrinkled her nose.

"Why's tha', then?"

"You tell me."

"Mention him agin and ye'll regret it. An' where's Mrs Baird's picture? Ye bin playin' tricks? I wudnae put it past ye…"

Catriona sighed. However upset Lennox was, she could still spit out poison.

"All I'm saying is, with Mr Baird arriving soon we should make an effort. Why I started a meal. I couldn't find you."

Lennox pushed past her and out on to the landing. Catriona knew it would be easy to follow her, make more excuses, but that's what the other was expecting. Let her take all the credit, she told herself. For she now had other more important matters on her mind. The housekeeper had gone. What more was she waiting for?

*

Half past eight. The old clock again, tolling away the bleak morning. Catriona knew she'd always possessed a curious nature. Both her parents had said so, but it had been Mairi McPhee who'd warned that too many questions can lead up the Devil's path. That some secrets were best kept that way, untouched. However, Calum Lennox was clearly no ordinary brother. It was only right and proper she find out more.

*

As befitting her status, Margaret Lennox's room possessed more than a simple bed, chair and small locker, for here stood a walnut tallboy, a rustic desk with four drawers and an oval mirror set above it where times without number, the woman must have viewed her stern, big-boned face.

Compared to Mr Bogle's bothy, this was a palace, yet Catriona had never once heard him express any envy for those in Ardnasaig. Instead, "death is nae respecter of the wallet," was his favourite expression. As she opened one drawer after another, she found herself wondering if he really knew what had happened to Isobel Baird during her fateful evening stroll. And could the comb she'd found be part of the mystery? That single hair from the woman's actual head? If so, she might have to make some decisions. And fast.

It was clear that Margaret Lennox hadn't been taught to write properly and each word of her weekly lists and goods to be bought or ordered, contained missing letters and crossings out. What was legible, bore red ink blobs like blood from a bullet wound. Her labels in the Store the same. Catriona rummaged beyond these, past a small, brown print of Christ on the cross and a quotation from the New Testament marked by a dried, pressed celandine, until a letter from her soldier son from the Royal Highland Regiment's barracks near Glasgow, made her pause. The badly-smudged date had been countersigned by his 42nd Foot's Commander. Nothing remarkable in that, thought Catriona, beginning to read. Until her pulse seemed to stop.

I'm opening mae heart tae ye, dearest mither, but ye must take what ye ken o mae grievous sin to the grave. It was all ma fault all mae doin and there's nae a day passes I dinna dwel on what I did with mae Janet, but if deth shud take me in battle, tha will be mae penance...

She smiled to herself. What a gift. He must have written this after his Commander had checked the contents and signed. Pain seemed to coat every misshapen word. She forced the note into her skirt pocket, already taken up with other objects. So she was a hoarder. No shame in that. All part of her curiosity. Her need to get to the root of things, which was why she continued her swift search, aware of an idea prodding at her mind.

The fire had almost given up and when she realised there was nothing else of any further interest in the housekeeper's room, began to strip the bed, making sure her bare hands didn't accidentally touch those still-damp stains.

Ignoring that same sensation of being watched by those staring, blue eyes which had dominated not only that painting, but Margaret Lennox's ghostly face, Catriona finished her task without drawing breath and silently closed the door behind her.

***

12

In which friendship is tested...

'*Guard yer tongue...* '

There was no time for Janet to search her mother's room for any personal items and unlikely objects of value to take care of, because already the noise of men's voices and whinnying horses was drawing closer to Ardnasaig House's front door.

Having checked the maid's ham hadn't blackened to charcoal, she closed the oven, snatched her cloak from the peg and hurried outside where two riders - James Baird together with a top-hatted man whom she didn't recognise, swathed in a black cape and mounted on a matching horse - drew up alongside the Reverend McKinnon's pony and trap. On it perched a light brown casket with rope handles. As plain and simple as could be. Her mother all over.

Janet glanced away, blinking back tears. Thinking when and how to mention the mutilation to her body.

Despite a weak sun lightening the far end of the loch, three silhouetted fishing boats were already heading towards the sea to beat the freeze, leaving rippling trails in their wake. She knew more snow would fall before nightfall. But now help was at hand, and the grey-bearded Reverend MacKinnon soon caught her eye, giving her a sympathetic smile. He'd always seemed a benign enough man and especially so when she and her mother had attended his harvest service in October. No doubt he'd been grateful for two extra people in the pew.

As for the unknown rider, James, still astride his cob, introduced him as Constable Seumas Coyle, transferred from Inverary to help quell Kilforgan's displaced tenants now in revolt. His tight red curls set above a small, pointed face, made him look like a weasel. Bad skin too, like Linnet's, perhaps from childhood smallpox.

"But why's he here, sir?" she asked James Baird, only for him to turn away and greet the Reverend with a warm handshake.

"Falcon Steer and the serious matter of our dead cocks," he called back to her. "Besides, the constable's never been to Ardnasaig before, and was curious."

So it seemed, the way he scanned the house and grounds from his vantage point. Also, James Baird had listened to McPhee.

Janet hadn't heard the word 'constable' for a good few years and hoped she'd not seemed too surprised. She also wished she'd had time to wash herself and set her hair into a more demure style, for Coyle had appraised her with his strange green eyes as if she'd committed a crime and he'd already judged her guilty.

'Guard yer tongue…'

*

"I would have arrived sooner," said the Reverend MacKinnon, blowing into his gloved hands. "But apart from the black ice, my exorcism over at Glenvallich Farm took longer than usual. Mrs Farquar's poor troubled soul just wouldn't depart. As stubborn in death as she was in life…"

James Baird dismounted his cob and, with exaggerated movements, tied it up. He clearly didn't like this kind of talk.

"There's a disturbance on Colonel Ritchie's land," he snapped. "We must progress."

Coyle nodded. "Once yer late housekeeper's gone from here, I suggest ye bar the big gate or his tenants'll be in like a ravenous pack o' hounds."

"The Clearance is a real sin." The Reverend stepped down from his trap and laid his crop across its seat. "Those poor women and their weans. We'll have to open up the kirk for them. At least over Christmas."

Janet thought of all Ardnasaig's empty rooms. The amount of food stored up since the autumn. "Why nae let some come here, sir?" She looked at James Baird. "I'd take care o' them."

"Absolutely not. My father's due in three hours. He'll be weary. More than weary. I've seen it before."

The Reverend laid a gloved hand on her shoulder. "Kind thoughts aren't enough, Janet. Master Baird's right. There are practicalities to consider. Now then," he glanced towards the ice house. "'Tis time for us see to your dear mother."

'Guard yer tongue...'

But Janet could wait no longer and was just about to blurt out what she'd witnessed in the ice house, when inside her head began to spin. Her legs to give way and morning suddenly become night.

*

She eventually woke in the dark of her attic room still believing it was night.

Nae, it cannae be...

Her head, instead of lightness, felt as though a rock lodged there. Heavy. Unmoving. Her whole body was stiff with cold. Even stiffer than her mother's which had frozen and softened enough in the watery ice to have allowed an unknown attacker to strike. The ice house door, facing away from the house, had somehow been left open, so no wonder the melt hadn't been noticed. The water, pink with blood, had run off inside, down the drain.

But that wasn't all.

She tore the now frozen strips of cloth from her own forehead. Someone must have dampened them, placed them there after she'd fainted at the thought of her mother being found.

Her right hand slipped into her apron pocket.

No, please God...

Yet the notebook had gone.

Suddenly, a tap on her door.

"D'you fancy a tot of whisky, Janet?"

McPhee trying too hard again, and the thought of her impersonating a nurse, made her insides clench. She also noticed smart, grey boots each bearing a line of wee brass fasteners showing below the hem of her skirt.

"Leave it by the door."

"Are you feeling better? You've had such a shock. The worst shock of all…"

"Wouldn't ye be, with yer mother's eyes taken out like that? And where's me notebook gone?"

Silence in which McPhee pointed towards the window.

"Falcon Steer's down by the loch. I'd swear it was him."

Why were the little vixen trying to divert her?

128

"Shall I tell him you're recovered?"

Beneath this light, sing-song voice lay steel, reminding Janet of the bright new man-traps James Baird set down every spring to keep muntjacs off the land.

Could this be a trap too?

"Just tell me where me notebook is."

McPhee shook those fair curls which Janet wanted to pull from her head.

"I didn't know you kept one. What does it look like?"

"Ye tell me."

"I'm not staying any longer just to hear your ridiculous lie." McPhee backed out, but when Janet raised herself to follow her on to the landing, the girl had gone. In her place, those same men's voices rising up the stairwell, and the noticeable smell of burnt ham. Time to set her cap upon her head, smooth down her apron, organise the whisky. Make an appearance. But before doing so, Janet peered from the small attic window to see the Reverend McKinnon's pony and trap with the unadorned coffin heavily secured, as if ready to go.

*

McPhee had beaten her to it.

As if already mistress of Ardnasaig House, the fair-haired maid was busy passing round a tumbler of Glengoyne apiece. All three men seemed in need of it. They stood in a semicircle in the hallway under the trophy stags' heads, surrounded by glass boxes containing all manner of stuffed, forest creatures. The badger, with its doleful expression and plump pink paws poised as if ready to break through its glass box and make an escape, always moved her the most. Apparently, Isobel Baird had paid good money to have these sad victims of her son's gun preserved and Janet often wondered if James hadn't resumed his hunting and killing in earnest once she was out of the way.

"How are you feeling now, Miss Lennox?" The Reverend MacKinnon stepped forward. Kept a fatherly hand on her arm.

"I'm sorry to have left all the work to Miss McPhee."

The other girl glanced at her. A half smile in place.

"It's no trouble."

The Reverend let go of Janet's arm. His cracked lips on the move.

"And I promise to leave no stone unturned in finding your mother's savage attacker. To stand firm with James Baird here, and Constable Coyle."

"Thankye, Reverend," she said, thinking also of her missing notebook. "I hope whoever's responsible, is made to pay. But there is one thing…"

She looked from one to the other. "I dinnae want Mr Baird burdened with all this on his return." She then fixed on his son. "And I ken ye feel the same the same way about the cocks…"

"Justice takes precedence at all times, Miss Lennox," said Constable Coyle before James could respond. "And in that context, I have a warrant out for the arrest of a Mr Falcon Steer."

While McPhee didn't hide her little smile, Janet's instant dislike of this particular officer was growing, and not just because there were more Coyles than anyone in Inverary's graveyard. A dynasty of lawyers, administrators, and of course, police.

"We've already searched the grounds and weather permitting, it'll be dogs this afternoon," Coyle added.

"Dogs?"

"Trying to help, that's all," James Baird reminded her. "We should be grateful."

McPhee refilled his glass without catching his eye nor mentioning she'd seen Falcon Steer by the loch. Janet also noticed how her white cap set off the neatly braided hair beneath. Her apron ironed crisp and flat. Unlike hers, and when she told her to clear the table and check the main rooms' fires, the girl stuck out her tongue so no-one else could see.

Coyle fingered his moustache. Squeezed the ends between his fingers so they stayed turned upwards. "I've heard this Mr Steer took a shine to ye, Miss Lennox. What d'ye say to that?"

Suddenly that enormous granite dwelling with all its gloomy rooms, its maze of stairs and corridors, seemed to be closing in. Shrinking bit by bit, stone by stone until Janet felt their chill next to her skin. Less a house, she thought. More a grave.

"No more than to Miss McPhee, sir."

The girl ignored her, cool as an eel.

"We've waited a good while for ye to recover upstairs," said Weasel Face. "To answer some questions. Please do not move on to other matters. The fact is, someone, and it could well be him, had the opportunity, cunning and skill to wreak havoc here. Meanwhile we still have Fergus Bogle's unusual absence…"

"Mr Bogle's a good man," the maid stepped in. Please don't tar him with the same brush as evil folk."

"Yer nae supposed to offer an opinion," hissed Janet. Remember yer place."

"You as well, remember?"

Janet let it go. Lowering herself to the maid's level would achieve nothing. Instead, she looked from one man to the other.

"But why take me mother's eyes?"

The Reverend lowered his gaze while James Baird picked up a table mat and studied it. Only Coyle faced her fair and square.

"Steer's not one of us and we don't trust strangers, wanderers, persons with grievances who enter our lands to take the part of the undeserving poor. The filthy Paddies are bad enough, and now as well as the mob coming off Colonel Ritchie's land, we have a no-good. But a no-good skilled enough with a knife, as your coop and the ice house can attest." He placed his empty tumbler on an occasional table near one of the potted blackthorn branches and moved closer.

"What's puzzling me is why not take a piece of your mother's hair or a toenail instead?" said the Reverend, while Coyle maintained eye contact with her like the vermin he was.

"Did he wear any strange emblems or speak o' the Devil by name?" he asked.

"Ne'er a word, sir."

"Incantations, then? Odd sayings ye might have understood?"

"None that I heard."

"And his abode?"

"You wouldn't think he had one, given the state of him," said McPhee still basking in the glory of having put a meal on the table. "He sleeps where he can. Takes what he can. That's clear as day."

Janet felt her already wounded heart begin to fold up and die.

"So would I if both Mr Bairds had nae been good enough to take mother and me in."

The maid pursed her lips, excused herself and went out, leaving the kind of silence that hangs in the air before a storm. Janet wondered again why she'd not mentioned Falcon Steer being by the loch? Had that been a lie as she'd thought, or could she be protecting him? If so, why?

*

The nearby fire suddenly burst into life, sending pink and green tongues of flame upwards, licking the chimney's blackened bricks. The red-haired constable was starting to speak again.

"The Bruce family on Lismore didn't hold on to ye for long," came out like a bullet. "Just a few months."

Janet started.

"Forgive me, but that's nae yer business, sir."

However, James Baird was clearly interested.

"It might be," he said, and Janet felt like a hooked sewin floundering on a slippery rock. The hook stinging her mouth... She pointed to the Reverend MacKinnon's pony and trap beyond the front door. The full coffin still strapped to its sides. The bay pawing the ground, impatient to be off.

"Me mother's still unburied. I cannae say till she's at rest."

"I've a note from Lady Bruce herself," said Coyle. His hand poised to slip inside his cape. "Shall I read it out now?"

A tremor passed from Janet's neck to her feet. That same dizziness hovering. Now more than ever, she wished her mother was alive and by her side. And then without warning, Linnet – she was sure of it - whispering in her ear.

"Remember yer first bairn... Who thinks ill of a guid mother?"

"I were expecting a wean," Janet began, to save her life... "Three months gone and sick every day and night. We left Lismore to give him a chance. The Cranranich workhouse were at least a roof. That's God's truth."

"Where's this bairn now?"

Janet had often imagined a place, far better than she could have ever provided.

"On a farm near the Borders. He's doin' well..."

"Where exactly?"

"Duns." The only place there she'd heard of there...

"Did ye take him yerselves?"

Janet nodded. Her neck and head weighted it seemed, by lead.

"So, he'll be on this year's Census?"

She hoped her hesitation went unnoticed.

"Aye, sir."

Was Coyle writing down her answer in his own small notepad? Her already bad belly began to heave. Not for the first time that day...

"And who did ye lie with to conceive this bairn, Miss Lennox? Who would have been the father?"

McPhee re-appeared, coal scuttle in hand. "What she isn't saying, Constable, is that her brother was the father. And he's that ashamed of what he did."

*

Linnet had been wrong. Badly wrong. The disarray following this announcement lasted for what seemed beyond eternity. Janet saw McPhee's piously kneeling figure now laying pieces of coal on the fire's struggling flames, and wanted to kill her.

"We should be lookin' for weapons!" she shouted to deter any more talk of an unborn wean. "The guttin' knife, for a start, with a bone handle, whose blade is sharper than glass, sharper than…"

"Why listen to her?" Came that voice designed to win over foolish men. "She tried to make me eat a stone the size of a duck egg. Just imagine it. I could have died a dreadful death."

"Eat a stone?" Coyle clearly warming to his task. "Tell us more, Miss McPhee."

"In a moment, sir."

The maid got to her feet, wiped her filthy hands down her clean apron and ran from the hallway up the stairs. In the time it took for Janet to recount what she described as a 'brief misunderstanding' in the old graveyard, the maid re-joined the small gathering holding Isobel Baird's distinctive portrait in front of her body. A gloating gleam showed off her little teeth, like those of the bats that had defiled Margaret Lennox's corpse.

"I found this in Miss Lennox's bed, if you please. Hidden deep."

James Baird stepped forwards and checked the painting over.

"In her *bed*?" Constable Coyle turned his gaze on Janet. "Are ye sure ye've not an overactive imagination?"

"They both have," the huntsman took it from her and set it down near the door. "And now we urgently need to get Mrs Margaret Lennox away from here, while you, Miss McPhee, kindly return my mother's picture to its place."

The girl held her ground. Was there no end to her stubbornness? Janet saw her pointing her way.

"Miss Lennox also knows things about the Dame of Nonach… Bad things. And that's not all…"

"And *I* heard ye chanting about trefoil and vervain hindering witches of their will. And where's me notebook, me undergarments? Two pairs o' them?"

Coyle's cheeks reddened. His weren't the only ones.
"Sir," Janet continued, her conscience quite clear about the lie to follow. "She's made a spy-hole in her wall so she can follow me every move, and put hexes on me and Master Baird. See that blackthorn? Only witches would bring that into a house, ne'er mind for Christmas…"

"Please, please…" The Reverend clapped his big hands then reached towards the coat stand for his cloak. "Compared to what's happened to Mrs Lennox, this is bairns' talk. I suggest Constable Coyle completes his investigation of the ice house and its environs, then the cocks' coop."

"They've been burnt to a cinder, sir." McPhee eyed Janet. "*She* made me do it."

Before Coyle could respond or Janet defend herself, James Baird stepped towards the trouble-maker and thrust the framed painting into her hands.

"That was *my* order. Here's another. Go! And no more tricks or God help me." Then he added, "Miss Lennox, you come with us."

"First, sir, I need to use the 'necessaries.'"

No gentleman would query that request, and he didn't.

*

While McPhee was on the first landing, about to lift the portrait on to its hooks. Janet squeezed past her without speaking and once inside her mother's room on the next floor, slammed the door shut behind her, causing a trinket from Lismore to topple from the top of the desk.

She picked it up, but soon realised that one of the three glass bottles with their strange little corks from the Crystal Palace was missing from the same place.

Am I going mad?

Then the reason she was here seared into her mind. Apart from her notebook entries which were damning enough, Calum must have written to their mother and McPhee then found it. Why else had the dead woman more than once implied her daughter's deep sin? And now, more importantly, who else had stripped the bed and folded the blanket? Taken the opportunity for a good look round? And not just in this room...

"...her brother was the father. And he's ashamed of what he did..."

Janet soon realised each ramshackle drawer told the same story. A cruel hand must have explored here since the corpse had been removed. Yes, a small, well-shaped hand now just a door's width away, waiting to strike.

"Me notebook, if ye please." Janet gripped it tight. "That would be a start."

*

On her way to the ice-house for the last time, and to find something suitable to lay on her mother's coffin, Janet knew she should have felt some relief that Falcon Steer, not her, was the main suspect for both crimes, but didn't. Constable Coyle was taking the easy way – perhaps because of Christmas - when all the while, she knew deep in her bones that McPhee was nowhere near the young innocent she pretended to be.

And then, she noticed the unmoving sky overhead. Darker, like a bad omen inland; paler towards the Irish sea. Loch Nonach matched it exactly, while on the far side, contrasting with the dense and gloomy forests, strands of white woodsmoke rose up from Baw Heid's few settlements that clung to the water's edge.

Still light-headed from her tussle with McPhee, Janet wondered where Falcon was, and had the maid poisoned Coyle towards him to cover up her own sins? McPhee, within an inch of her life, on that top landing floor, hadn't broken on any score. Nor had her skirt pockets yielded the notebook or any other clues...

*

Relieved that no-one downstairs seemed to have heard the short but deadly fight two floors up, Janet slipped her cloak over her sore shoulders while the constable finished making his notes. He then addressed James Baird whose cob was neighing and banging its hooves from inside the stable.

"I'm very interested in what yer remaining employees have to say for themselves, and to that end, I suggest ye bring Miss McPhee over to the Police House at Kilforgan at midday on the 27th. And as for ye, Miss Lennox," his green eyes seemed to narrow as they turned on her. His mouth behind the ginger fur to grow more stern. "I'll see ye separately at eleven o'clock prompt the day after."

But James Baird clearly had other ideas.

"I can't commit to that, sir. My father's not here for long and…"

"Leave things to me, if ye please, Master Baird. And let's hope by then, our absent friend Fergus Bogle has made an appearance. I'd like to speak with him too."

It wasn't winter's unyielding grip that touched Janet's very marrow, but the prospect of leaving Falcon Steer in grave danger, and her own precarious employment for even a few hours to face more questions from this hostile official.

"May I ask, sir, why yer seein' Miss McPhee first?"

"In our alphabet, Miss Lennox, C comes before J."

"And Lennox surely before McPhee?"

Silence, in which Coyle turned away to stare down the drive at the few curious locals gathered by the gate, while the Reverend made the sign of the cross on his chest. Just to see it, made Janet's sickness rise up inside her. She clamped a hand over her mouth until the bile subsided.

"I'm offerin' fifteen pounds reward, sir," she then said. "To help catch whoever violated me mother. I dinnae want it forgotten…"

But the constable still ignored her. She could tell he was already leaning towards the younger, more bonny girl who, while opening the front door, had appeared as gentle as falling snow. All the more reason to make time to find just one piece of proof that she was working against her. The gutting knife and those missing smooth-soled boots would be a start.

*

Having added a few stems of laurel to the top of the cold, makeshift coffin and kissed it farewell, Janet watched her mother's wobbly departure as the Reverend coaxed his horse up the hill away from Ardnasaig House. The crunching of snow beneath the wheels diminished, and those few hamlet dwellers who'd gathered to pay their respects, began to disperse. One in particular seemed familiar. In fact, more than familiar. Especially the way he stood in that big brown coat, hands clasped behind his back.

Falcon? Could it be him? She hardly dared think so. Besides, with his description already circulating in the area, would he be brazen enough to show his face again here? Should she warn him he was a wanted man in case he didn't know? That might make matters worse, so she turned away, wondering too, whether Constable Coyle would eventually take up her reward offer. Fifteen pounds - all she had. But should she risk it? Supposing McPhee's accusation of her bairn being her brother's was proved? It could cost him his post in the regiment. Could reduce him and herself to paupers. And what if her wee boy was never found in Duns? What then?

*

Janet began the lonely trek up the snow-pitted carriageway and saw McPhee standing arms crossed in the dining room window. With chin stuck out, the whole pose was one of self-righteous defiance. However, this was grist to her mill, and she resolved before the week was out that Christmas or no Christmas, to have solid proof that whoever had committed two such evil acts, was being fed and sheltered under Ardnasaig's roof.

"Another question."

Janet spun round in surprise to see James Baird clasping a full tumbler of the single malt in his leather-gloved hand.

"Aye, sir?"

"Your blood's due on Ne'erday, so you said. Is there any sign yet?"

Janet stared into his mismatched eyes. He'd thrown her a lifebelt and she must grab it. Or else…

"Nae, sir."

"You must tell me when it comes."

"O' course, sir. Why would I not?"

Then, before he could ask any more, she took herself indoors back to find a quiet spot in which to memorise her plan not only for her own survival, but the peaceful passing of her mother's soul from this sore and troubled place. And that meant searching in earnest for two very different kinds of knives and a pair of smooth-soled boots.. Beginning with the maid's locked room.

Time to get her own back...

***

13

Where spirits are further disturbed...

She had survived that fight. Just. And, having blocked Lennox' spy-hole yet again and re-locked her room against the prowling monster, Catriona left the house via the courtyard door, with her bruised throat hidden by a scarf, and Lennox's threats still ringing in her ears. Bodily harm was nothing compared to the risk of her secret hoard of mementoes coming to light. She must be brave and resolute. Nothing less would do.

With just one hour to go before Donald Baird's arrival, and the snow clouds over Ardnasaig Forest conquering the last of the sky, she, on his son's orders, cleaned out the two 'necessaries' whilst holding her breath, then busied herself in the ice house. The first task was to brush all soiled straw towards the door, and push it with all her might up the slope to outside.

So, there'd be no syllabubs, chilled drinks or ice creams this Christmas, but these were the least of her concerns. The most serious being that James Baird, the Reverend McKinnon and PC Coyle might have heard some of Lennox's vile accusations against her. Secondly, that iron grip around her throat had almost snuffed out her life. Only her resolve to make Ardnasaig House the most welcoming, well-run home in Argyll had saved her.

Her one regret ought to have been that Iain McPhee wouldn't be sharing the festivities. But on balance, better he stayed at home with his bottle and an unreliable fire for company. At least until her future became more clear.

Having made a tidy heap of the sodden straw and returned inside that dank, domed space, the possibility occurred to her that if she plied both Bairds with enough drink, they might let her deliver some of the left-over food to his but and ben. He'd be grateful for sure. And perhaps less anxious about her staying on here.

She stopped her labours to bite into a plain scone lifted from a tin in the kitchen. This was men's work and she was starving, so why not take care of herself? By mistake, she bit down into her frozen lower lip and yelped. Tasted her own blood on her tongue.

Next came the drain where melt-water lay in a sluggish pool blocked by what, she couldn't quite tell. She bent over to see what the problem was, only to recoil in disgust. Of course. Margaret Lennox had thawed. Including her bowels.

A moment's panic. Should she probe and prod about and risk splashing herself with the foul waste, or leave well alone? Constable Coyle would be questioning her in four days' time, so she must claw back her original status - the trusted, reliable girl from Cranranich.

Finish the job…

She could almost hear Mr Bogle telling her so, as she crept outside for a suitable stick, but more unsettling was the sense that the missing mistress of Ardnasaig's burning blue eyes, seemed fixed on her every move.

*

With midday only thirty minutes away, helped by the handyman's little cheese knife, Catriona cut an armful of holly branches and, taking care not to pierce her tongue, licked snow from their hard, red fruit. Warmer than her numb lips and her thinning blood, it tasted almost sweet like those blueberries she'd picked as a child with sun on her back and a breeze in her hair...

She heard the cob kick against his stall as she carried her prickly burden towards the Store, aware again of being watched. Then James Baird emerged from the stable, red-faced and pre-occupied. No doubt anticipating his father's critical ways. Normally, Mr Bogle would have seen to his sweating mount, but since he'd gone, neither she nor Lennox were allowed near. More than once she'd offered and been turned down.

He glanced at her, unmoved by the holly.

"Ice is what we need. See what you can get."

"Where will I keep it, sir?"

"In one of the Store's buckets."

"And fresh straw?"

He indicated the stable.

"For Christ's sake, girl, be quick!"

But before she could ask where this new, clean ice might be found, he'd marched towards the ice house, arms swinging as he went.

*

Ice...

Catriona slid round to the front door and, rather than use her holly to adorn the many pictures, plunged it into the first available containers. A tall green vase decorated with embossed gilt leaves which Donald Baird had brought back from his travels while he still had a wife. Next, a more plain affair whose single, painted lily spread itself around the generous opening. A souvenir from Hyde Park's Great Exhibition delivered by the housekeeper no less, who'd also brought back three curious little glass jars, each with a cork stopper in the shape of a baby's head. Catriona hoped she'd be forgiven for taking just one of them for herself and hiding it inside a boot under her bed, but now the woman's corpse had been taken away, perhaps the other pair could belong to her too.

Seeing those strangely cherubic heads had also made her wonder if the ghostly wails she'd heard near the linen room door, might be connected to Lennox's lewd activities with her own brother.

*

More snow on the way and still no sign of the dead housekeeper's daughter. Ardnasaig's inner courtyard, sheltered from what little light there was, seemed as forbidding as a prison, with those dank granite walls enclosing the central well.

No gloves, but at least she'd had the foresight to bring that reserve carving knife and a straw-lined bucket, all the while resisting Mr Bogle's warning.

"Ne'er bend oe'r its side and breathe its air. Ne'er even touch the water..."

Leaning over the well's stony rim sent a stab of nerves to her heart. It was all very well him giving her the benefit of his wisdom, but he wasn't her, desperate to win her way back into favour. To counter Lennox's cruelty with her own good intentions.

She prodded the icy crust with her sturdy knife, but unlike on its previous outing, the tip buckled against a far greater strength. This wouldn't do at all, but she knew the answer. With Kilforgan's kirk bell ringing out midday, she fetched a sledge-hammer from the outhouse, and struck at her obstinate enemy until it split into several jagged islands, jostling together in the deep, black water. She sniffed, then dangled an already numb forefinger below the surface thinking that perhaps Mr Bogle had simply tried to scare her. Some men were like that. But wouldn't it look good if James Baird spied her full bucket?

The first and biggest piece of ice slipped from her grasp before she leaned in a little further and reclaimed it, pleased that her story about her mother's jettisoned boots seemed to have been believed. The second and third slab proved easy and her bucket was gaining weight. Just then, from the upper corner of her eye, a shadow appeared. Perhaps a raven hovering, or soot falling from a blocked chimney?

She turned to see neither but a blurred figure standing motionless at the second floor's middle window. Real or a phantom, man or woman was hard to tell. And if real, then why spy on her? She shielded her eyes for a more focused view but, as she did so, the watcher moved away behind the curtain.

Glancing down at her bucket, she wondered if there room for one more piece of ice. A pity to leave the last remaining slab, she thought, placing both hands beneath it, aware that something other than the smooth, hard underside had torn her glove wide open and scraped her skin.

The sudden shriek of a hunting horn almost made her drop her harvest by the Store's door. It came again and, because no hunts went out on Christmas Eve, she knew something was wrong. Perhaps, as that green-eyed constable had predicted, the Colonel's tenants were already marching towards Ardnasaig. If so, where was James Baird?

Cocking her uncovered head to listen, she also picked out the faintest echo of the grandfather clock's twelve sorrowful chimes.

Midday.

Having dropped the last section of ice on to the others and when it landed upside down, Catriona realised what had snagged her skin. A piece of bone, frozen to its host. She'd seen enough animal carcasses in forests and fields to realise that this particular specimen belonged to a vertebra, cleaned of all flesh, with that same translucency as her mystery comb's ivory handle.

On her way across the snow to the small door leading to the rear corridor, she kicked away her tracks as she went, wondering whether a whole creature lay concealed in the well or if some bird had accidentally dropped part of its prey. Whatever the bone's origins, she would add it to her small collection of mementoes. Maybe even present it to Constable Coyle when her turn came. But it was Mr Bogle's grim caution that had re-attached itself to her mind, like those giant barnacles crusting the loch's rocks where the Irish Sea rolls in.

Once inside the marginally warmer corridor, Catriona paused for breath, gathering hot spit in her mouth to heat her hands. Her eye then alighted on the little bone that seemed to be telling her to make haste and loosen it. She did, and soon her puzzling treasure lay safe in her deepest pocket.

"Miss McPhee?"

Hearing her name returned her to that white, brittle world where nothing was as it seemed. Where sly Lennox lurked in every shadow, hoping - she was sure of it - to catch her out. The call had come from the lounge at the front of the house and she took longer than usual to reach it, leaving her bucket in the doorway. Although the fire she'd lit earlier still glowed with vigour and the beribboned blackthorn in the far corner added colour, the atmosphere was far from festive. Lennox, who'd set her hair into clumsy ringlets, kept her back to her, polishing the walnut lowboy and then both bookcases standing side by side.

"You called me, sir?" Catriona addressed the young man pacing back and fore by the window. The sky almost black beyond the sudden snow flurry hitting the glass. He turned, saw the full bucket and moved into the middle of the room.

"Yes. Miss Lennox will put your ice in the Store next to the cold east wall, while you are to fetch the lantern and stand on the shore."

Catriona started.

"The shore, sir? Why? I thought Mr Baird would be arriving by road."

Lennox's black hate touched her heart as she passed her by. The bully put her duster in her apron pocket and snatched at the bucket.

"There's been a change of plan," James Baird went on while Lennox stood stock still. "Old Hendry's just called in on foot. The trap bringing my father turned over by Cranranich. He's safe, but the pony's been shot. At least there's a boat coming up and the water's calm. All should be well…"

"What a worry for you, sir." Catriona saw her adversary lower her plain head to sniff at the bucket. "I'm so sorry."

"Where did this ice come from?" Lennox demanded.

"A pool in the ash grove. Why do you ask?"

"Sir," Lennox ignored her. "If this came from the well, we could all die."

"How would you know that?"

Black Eyes blushed and left the room. Catriona then realised *she'd* been the silent watcher at the window, also that the nervy huntsman was deaf to anything but news of his father's journey home.

"I have the strongest feeling today will be marked by yet more misfortune," he added, making Catriona delay her important question for longer than usual.

"Sir, regarding your request," she ventured. "As I've never met your father, how will I know he's really Donald Baird?"

His son's odd eyes fixed on her.

"You've a suspicious mind, Miss McPhee, I'll give you that."

"Only because I don't want *my* eyes gouged out. I come from Cranranich, remember, sir? Seen too many tragedies there. Heard too many lies…"

The young man moved towards a dark oak bureau set against the wall opposite the fire, reached for a small key inside his waistcoat and with it, unlocked the top drawer. Moments later, he held out a small, embossed leather case and, having undone the clasp, passed it to her. Catriona stared at the oval-shaped image which at first, seemed to bear no more than a collection of brown stains, reminding her of Margaret Lennox's undersheet. Then, having banished her nerves, she picked out two people clad in outdoor clothes, standing close together…

"A daguerreotype," he explained. "My parents."

Underneath were the words *August 10th 1846*.

"Four days before… before she never came back."

To Catriona, his mother's bright smile seemed almost shocking, while her eyes stayed mysteriously blank, matching the bleached background of the loch's shore. She picked out the darker shapes of two dogs running behind them into the water. Although both the Bairds' heads leaned in towards each other, she nevertheless recognised the pale, lean man who was no more a stranger than her own father. Who hadn't changed a jot.

Her pulse changed tempo. Her lips dry and numb as cuttlefish bones. What if Donald Baird found out she was at Ardnasaig? Could that spell the sudden end of her plans for betterment?

*

Despite no birthday until 1st May, Catriona felt as old and worn as a crofter's wife, weighed down by her imminent meeting with two men she didn't particularly want to see again. Donald Baird and Constable Coyle. Even recalling her mother urging her to stay strong didn't really help. *She* hadn't been humiliated into re-hanging a picture she'd not moved in the first place, and do other horrible tasks in the ice house and that unlit, bone-chilling laundry room.

Suddenly a pair of hands settled on her shoulders. A familiar whisky smell reached her nose. James Baird with fear in his fingers, she could tell. They dug into her skin.

"Does your father know I'm here?" she asked first.

"Of course. Why?"

Was that too quick? Besides, she didn't believe him. Nor dared repeat her question.

"You said you knew Cranranich and its folk, Miss McPhee. Is there any reason for my father's boat to be delayed?"

"Whose is it?"

"George Sorrow's. Glencardle. He took some persuading."

Her own father had used the man many times for evening fishing expeditions and the occasional treat. Despite his name, he was a jolly old sea-dog.

"He's reputable, sir. But as you know, the southernmost water there is always the first to freeze. Things can change quickly..."

He freed her shoulders. Picked up the lamp he'd brought and passed it to her.

"Take the track through the rowans. That'll give you the best view of the water. But if you see trouble, have a care. Hide its light. Keep out of the way. For your own safety. I know those tenants from Kilforgan. Constable Coyle was right. For two pins they'd be at the gate and up to the door. This is the worst time of year for evictions. The worst time... And I hope for all our sakes, that the minister and the late Mrs Lennox reach their destination..."

His voice faded as Catriona gathered up her skirt and ran from the dining room with further questions especially about Falcon Steer unasked, and a growing sense that the planned Christmas would, like the day's embers, lie in a cold, dead grate.

*

Lennox stood half in, half out of shadow uttering not one word as Catriona proceeded through the hall towards the front door before hefting her cloak over her back and forcing her woollen mittens over her already bloodless fingers. The silence between them hung like a thick fog, and not until she'd slithered down the slope away from the house and reached the most westerly access to the loch, did it lift.

*

The rowan grove apparently planted by Isobel Baird shortly after her marriage, formed a snow-weighted holloway over Catriona's head, haphazardly releasing its wintry burden. One clump of snow fell into her left eye. Another on her nose. Half-expecting the cowardly Steer to show himself, she bent down to pick up a stout, fallen branch encrusted with the blue-green moss she'd once found so pretty. Sure enough, before long came the crackle of trodden twigs. His unmistakeable smell…

"Busy, busy, I see…" came the taunting voice she dreaded. "But don't you know, the Dame of Nonach's still waiting?"

Catriona gripped her stick, its icy wetness seeping through her gloves. She turned her lamp upon Falcon Steer, even more dishevelled than before in a brown, loose-fitting coat. His tied length of hair gone. And then she spotted the rifle in his hands.

"Waiting for what?"

A laugh, cold and crisp as the very ground she walked on.

"You know what they say about her in these parts? How she rules her kingdom of barren women. I'm here to protect you and your unborn, Miss McPhee. For who else will?"

"Protect *me*?" she laughed. "Protect yourself, Falcon Steer. You're wanted for violating a dead body, and butchering those cocks. And as for *my* unborn, it's not me who's late with the monthlies, but Janet Lennox. And not for the first time. I can tell by her eyes, and I've heard her being sick. It's James Baird's bairn, I'm sure of it, why she wants me gone."

But the unkempt man didn't appear to be listening.

"I said I'm here to protect you. To save you from the fire."

Fire?

That word which would normally conjure up warmth and colour, hit her heart like a frosted spear.

"The fate of witches, where I come from near Dunblane. They're strapped to a ladder and tilted towards the flames…"

"I'm no more a witch than you're Queen Victoria. How can you say that?"

"Your father's a loose-mouth. If he really cared for you, he'd be more circumspect. Don't say you've not been forewarned."

At mention of her father, that icy spear dug deeper.

"You've been to my home?"

Now it was his turn to laugh as he loped away through the snow towards the rowans.

"Home, she calls it. I wouldn't keep pigs there. Looks like money's in short supply and might be welcome."

She couldn't argue with that, but still had question to ask.

"And if the Dame of Nonach rules like you say, how did Mrs Baird manage to carry her son full term?" She called after him.

Another laugh that answered nothing.

Catriona felt the lamp suddenly too heavy as she stumbled away and positioned herself dutifully by the westernmost burnie's exit to the loch. Where ice crystals already made the pebbled beach look almost pretty. Where the incoming tide was now a lifeless, stone-grey sea.

She turned to make sure Steer wasn't following and, satisfied she was alone again, positioned herself in front of the silent water from which nightmares seemed to lift and hover. What if Donald Baird were to step ashore and recognise her? What kind of things had her drunken father been saying? And why had the devious Falcon Steer bothered to follow her?

***

155

14.

Where claws are sharpened...

Janet knew she must examine McPhee's ice bucket as soon as possible. But firstly and most important, was the liar's locked room.

She waited until her adversary had picked her way down to the shore. A figure as small and spindly as the bare trees through which she passed; the only moving thing in that desolate scene, soon lost to sight. Then, having checked that James Baird was still in place by the lounge window, she crept upstairs. Each step an effort she'd never felt before. Her laboured breath threatening to extinguish the small candle she held at chest height. The hastily-set ringlets brushing the back of her neck.

Past that wretched portrait and on to the rough-boarded uppermost floor with its three rooms set in a row under the eaves. Inhabited by a succession of Ardnasaig's domestic staff since great-grandfather Baird had spent much of his building fortune on the construction of the biggest house for miles around. Originally, or so James Baird had said, all three rooms had boasted locking doors while the housekeeper guarded the keys at night to deter thieving. Now, only McPhee's door to the smallest of those three rooms resisted her weight.

No more bats. Something at least to be thankful for. Just a bare, cold fear as the fingers of her free hand closed around the small length of wire she'd found earlier in the Store, and eased it into the empty key-hole. She moved it from side to side - a trick

Calum had taught her when they were bairns - thinking all the while how Constable Coyle would be speaking to McPhee first on the 27th, letting her fill his head with fables.

Silence, save for the scrape of steel on iron and the sudden slide of snow from the roof above. The overbearing stillness made her forget all about her mother's eyeless face, her own imminent 'wee frein,' and the whiff of almonds in that Greenock bedroom lit by bursts of brightness from the welders' flames…

Then came the click she'd waited for.

*

She closed McPhee's door behind her, drawn first to those books she'd first spied through her peep-hole in the wall, now filled with a blob of raw pastry. There were Bibles and texts on the Scriptures old and new. The words Jesus, God and Lord prominent on each one. Yet not once had she ever heard McPhee recite anything from the Christian faith. In fact, quite the reverse. Nor was her own missing notebook anywhere to be seen.

Janet blew a thin warmth on to her hands, returned the books to their exact place, in the right order, making sure none of the pages were bent over. Saw the snowfall beyond the window and prayed in her own fashion that Donald Baird was making good progress home. She also willed her cold fingers to move faster, searching through those few spare clothes that hung from iron hooks by the bed. But apron and skirt pockets were empty. Her own missing underwear and that strange glass bottle with a cork baby's head for a stopper had been spirited away.

Next, the plain white china bowl and jug she'd seen McPhee use at dawn and last thing at night. Never much washing round the back of her except for her neck and ears. And the way she rubbed at that pale pelt below her belly with her skinny legs wide open, it was a wonder it was still there. Janet scrutinised the bowl's cracked glaze for any trace of blood, but if McPhee *had* washed herself clean up here, she'd been more than thorough.

The bed.

She dropped to her knees, stretched an arm into the dusty, neglected world beneath the mattress and pulled out a pair of wet, brown boots that she immediately recognised. Their patterned soles matched up with those left by McPhee's surprise visit to the coop but, unlike her black, smooth-soled ones, were far from new.

Just as her fingers were set to probe inside each one, Janet heard footsteps approaching up the stairs. Slower, heavier than McPhee's. She sprang to her feet and was just about to place the one chair by the door to give herself a moment's grace, when a familiar voice uttered her name.

"Miss Lennox?" It said. "Don't be afraid and please don't hide from me. I can't stop long..."

Falcon?

Her heart was galloping inside her chest. What to do? "Please, Miss Lennox, I beg you..."

How had he got so far into the house without being seen? And what if he was caught? With her?

She let him in, frightened not just for his welfare, but her own. His appearance made her catch her breath. That once long hair had been hacked off short and lay in ragged spikes around his blue, frostbitten ears. A fresh bruise framed his left eye and his bottom lip bore a wine-red cut. His shivering reached her own chilled bones.

"Who's bin at ye?" She said, seeing his eyes rest upon the brown boot still in her hand. "Is it the Colonel's mob?"

But before he could explain further, a strange sonorous noise eked into the room from the direction of the loch. And again, for longer this time, slowing up her busy heart.

"Danger," he whispered. Then put out freezing fingers to touch her bare wrist. "Mr Baird's boat is taking too long. Something's amiss…"

"And McPhee? Is she still out there?"

"Yes."

"The she-cow."

"Take care, Miss Lennox, that the blame for all ills here don't fall on your shoulders. That you have justice on your side…" He took the boot from her.

"Justice?" Janet almost choked on the word. "Why? I've done nothin' wrong." She stared at the ruined man to glean what she could from that ravaged face.

"Listen to me. The Devil's army is at work here. This house stands cursed beyond redemption. I felt it in every stone, every unlit corner the moment I walked in. The disappeared are all around us. I hear their breaths, their restless sighs…"

Janet also heard that low, warning sound for the third time, adding menace to a tale she knew all too well from a travelling pedlar the first summer she was at Ardnasaig. How the Dame of Nonach's terrible deeds had caused her sleepless nights and distracted days.

Falcon lowered his voice, all the while, studying the boot inside and out. "And I know why you're here in this room. Your instincts are right, so please, Miss Lennox, I urge you now to come away with me. The *Heilan Maid's* sailing from Portnonach in an hour's time."

A hot blush hit Janet's neck. He was asking her of all people. Her, when there were plenty of others with neater waists and finer faces. His offer very, very tempting.

She'd been to Portnonach once with her mother on a rare Summer's afternoon off. The pretty village beyond Kilforgan boasted a ruined castle and a shop selling the most delicious shortbread... She could see it all so clearly. Feel its temptation touch her miserable soul.

"But me mother's nae been laid to rest. How can I?" She argued, hating herself. "Besides, I want proof that McPhee's bin stealin' from me for her ane ends. Constable Coyle is seeing me on Sunday. After her."

Falcon frowned.

"*After* her?"

Janet nodded. The falling snowflakes white on white were now as big as dandelions' heads she'd blow from their stalks to make wishes. She pulled her shawl tighter around her shoulders. Torn between this appealing man and the unburied, eyeless woman who'd been her one true companion for so long.

"I want the chance to speak me mind," she said.

"Look, I've heard talk..."

"What talk? Where?"

"In the Poacher's Arms, Cranranich. About McPhee's father and his carrying on before his wife died."

Janet felt as if an icy snake had uncoiled itself in her stomach and was making its way north.

"He was questioned twice after the woman here went missing, but," his gaze shifted to the window and its whiteness seemed to bleach even his dark eyes. "No connection was proved."

"Did she know?"

"Who?"

"McPhee?"

"Never ask that of her. Do you understand?"

His tension seemed to bind them together. He handed her back the boot which she replaced under the bed. "The tracks I saw by the hen coop weren't made by that sole. The best ones were smooth as Welsh butter."

"Until they all got scuffed over. I'm convinced they'd bin her mother's. She said she threw them in the well, but I dinnae believe her."

"Nor would I. And why do such a thing when boots cost so much?" He touched her hair and his hand then stroked her cheek. The feel of it brought another burning sensation that ended high between her thighs. "Did she say why?"

"No."

"Nor will she. One last time, Janet, are you coming with me?"

Janet...

"The mob are like animals. They're already at the bridge. You won't be safe here. Look at me..."

"I said, I cannae leave me dead mother."

He pointed to the thick, black Bible. His eyes hardening. "Don't be fooled by that Holy book over there. Oh yes, Miss Catriona will place her pretty little hand on it and swear to God what she'll say about you is true. And about me. Do you want her to be the death of you? Is that it? She thinks you're expecting a child by James Baird, when it should be her. She told me so. She's heard you being sick, so she says. Do you want The Dame of Nonach to suck it from you?"

The word *suck* brought a shiver.

"Nae, but..."

"Then come with me," he breathed in her ear. "I've had a child of my own. I can help you care for it."

"Thank ye. That's very kind." But instead of enquiring further about his remark about a child, her other unasked question remained.

"Tell me, how did James Baird survive full term? And others around these parts?"

Falcon frowned, as if gathering his thoughts.

"Who can say? He must be as rare as a square moon. As for your so-called 'others,' none of them was born within ten miles of the loch."

Bile again. On the rise.

"I cannae believe you."

"You'd better."

He moved away. Turned the one pillow over, sniffing both sides. "McPhee says it's not your firstborn. Is that true? You must trust me."

"I'm not pregnant."

"I can tell that you are."

Janet saw tenderness in his eyes. The first she'd seen for too long, making it easy to unplug her woes. To take herself back to that summer night in Greenock when she'd lain in her brother's arms. When the resourceful, persuasive Linnet Garvie had given her advice. Advice she'd regret until the end of her days...

*

Once she'd finished her sad story, she walked over to the window, only to stiffen at the sight of a diminutive, dark figure wending its way towards the house from the lochside, a lamp swaying with each stride. Its eerie light illuminating the girl's crumpled, red face. From sorrow or hatred, Janet couldn't tell. And then she turned to find the room's door wide open and her kindly Confessor vanished from sight.

***

15.

With Falcon Steer's words ringing like a death bell inside Catriona's head, she reached the end of the carriageway and climbed the unswept steps to Ardnasaig House. Utter weariness had kept her from persevering with the thankless job of waiting for a boat that might never arrive. Instead, she must save what little energy she had, to get to Footer's Cottage, even for just an hour. But if James Baird's anxious mood was anything to go by, that also might prove impossible.

She'd stood too long on that unforgiving shore feeling her bones turn to ice beneath her clothes, and still the architect hadn't come. Was it his boat's horn that had sounded three times? If so, she'd not heard a more mournful noise, and it surely meant trouble. But what could she or anyone do? He should have stayed over in Inverary until the weather had changed for the better. But perhaps he'd wanted to return home as quickly as possible. Perhaps Christmas not the only thing on his mind...

"Sir," she addressed his son's back as he sat at the writing bureau, putting pen to paper in a way that made her flinch. His gold nib grated against the paper, often penetrating through the blotting paper to the wood beneath. "I could get Mrs Masters to send out one of her fishing boats. We must *do* something."

The writer didn't look up as he signed off and found a matching envelope. Catriona strained to read his words without success.

"No. I can already hear her answer. She lost too many barks in last year's storm and won't risk another on the ice." He licked down the envelope's flap and the glimpse of his wet, red tongue made her insides quicken. For one thrilling moment, imagined it exploring her mouth, between her legs. Then came the stabbing thought that Lennox might have got there first, but he was speaking again. "This is a better cry for help. A matter of life and death, Miss McPhee. My father's life or death. I cannot leave Ardnasaig for fear the mob will break in. So, go as fast as you can to the Police House at Kilforgan and give this to Constable Coyle." He then glared at her. "Tamper with it and I'll see you never work again. Understood?"

She lowered her head. Where was any gratitude? Awareness of her efforts so far?

"Be swift, then," he urged. "You're young enough…"

Catriona left the room, relieved at least that he'd not noticed her wearing his mother's grey, moleskin boots again. How she'd feigned enough anxiety about his father. She took the stairs two at a time up towards her room.

Lennox's lingering smell was bad enough news, but worse how her own key normally a perfect fit, laboured in the lock. There was more. Mairi McPhee's *'Pathways to Our Lord'* lay not beneath her *'Stories from the Scriptures'* as before, but on top.

*

Sky the colour of old cream and the snow crisping to ice underfoot as Catriona skidded through the elm grove and up the bank to join the track leading north west from Ardnasaig. More than once she stopped, tempted to soften the envelope's glue with her hot, panting breath, but James Baird's threat had been serious. His letter and its unknown contents, must be delivered intact.

Each time, she glanced round to see if either the housemaid or the tramp from Dunblane, or both, were following. Not such an unlikely notion, for behind her back, they could have trespassed in her room. Found things they shouldn't, and that thought made her ignore her soaked stockings and feet beginning to freeze.

*

The journey to Kilforgan was two miles as the crow flies, and after wards, she'd continue to her father's cottage in the opposite direction. Three more miles; nine in all, during which she could lose her toes to frostbite. A frightening prospect forcing her cover the ground more quickly.

As the track narrowed around the bend to Kilforgan and the forest of Draighnish's older trees formed a domed ceiling blocking out the struggling sun, Catriona wondered if Mr Baird had landed by the shore after all, and how come Falcon Steer from Dunblane had gathered enough local folklore to preach against the Dame of Nonach's ways? Never mind the threats he'd made.. Who'd been spreading rumours, wanting to see the back of her? Lennox of course, who'd had no more intention of leaving Ardnasaig with him than walking to Africa…

Just then, she heard a distant voice. Noticed scuffed, blood-stained snow which brought a rush of terror. Colonel Ritchie's displaced mob could have been here already, planning to return. Hunger and desperation making them fight each other, perhaps. That might explain the spoilt whiteness rumpled like sheets on a birthing bed.

Catriona paused, her rapid breath sending plumes of steam into the crystalline air, reminding her of last autumn's birthday visit with her father to see the first steam locomotive set off from Dunrossie to Kilmore. A pity today's reunion with him wouldn't be so pleasurable, but this time the boot was on the other foot. Time she was treated like the concerned and caring adult she really had become. How she wished those iron railway tracks came closer to Ardnasaig House, then her feet would be dry, her mood quite different.

Suddenly James Baird's white envelope slipped from inside her coat on to the snow, but before she could rescue it, a black, collarless dog came careering through the snowy trees towards her - its glossy jaws spraying spittle as it ran. She gathered six pine cones and threw them in turn at its head, but the ribby cur, having pawed at the envelope, bore it away and squatted down to tear the paper apart.

This time, armed with a heavy, spiked branch, she sneaked up behind the thief and landed a severe blow on its skinny rear. Too hurt and surprised to attack, the creature yelped in agony and moved away, dragging both rear legs behind it. She retrieved the sodden, smudged remains of handwriting, and tried making sense of what its sender had been so keen for Constable Coyle to see.

*

fearful Coyle Steer and soon

information I beg you arrival here

for safety detain no sleep as possible Misses

How did these random words connect with what James Baird had uttered about the risk to his father's life? Whatever the reason, they continued to test her as she followed the wounded, wailing dog deeper into the wood, all the while muttering a protective verse Iain McPhee had used when out on the hills with his cattle..

"Nae curse me wi' yer unquiet life,

A wand'ring soul seeking only strife.

For the De'il will come and pull ye down

Where the dead lie fast and the dead lie drowned."

Catriona felt a spasm of fear hit her heart. Those piercing blue eyes last seen in the lifeless housekeeper's face, were emerging through the hazels' branches as if they didn't exist. Fixed on her. Willing her mission to fail, perhaps?

Just then, a man's growling voice brought more fear, accompanied by a hint of woodsmoke, reminding her of her father's hearth. Sly Falcon Steer immediately sprung to mind, because her days of trusting anyone were gone.

"Whaur ye gaen, Missy?" He spat out a bolus of phlegm. "An' wha's tha' yer bin sayin'?"

Damn him too.

"None of your business."

"Ye nae from these parts, tha's for sure."

"I certainly am, and I've a weapon to protect myself…"

"A weapon, eh? Let's see ye use it, then."

Catriona's right hand felt for the gutting knife in her coat's outside pocket and, gripped it in the attack position. She then turned full circle until spotting a short, bow-legged figure stumble towards her from the cover of a lime tree. A battered, wide-brimmed hat sat low on his head, while his bare left hand gripped an almost full sack of pine cones. In his right, lay a small axe. As he drew closer, she saw how both his cheeks had been sliced open, losing blood. Whether old or middle-aged, was hard to tell, and just then she willed Mr Bogle to appear to help defend her. For she could lose her head and die here, and not be found until spring, especially should more snow fall.

Two rheumy eyes scanned her body in a way she found unnerving. At least they weren't bright blue. His gaze then lingered on her hand deep in her coat pocket.

"Ye look weel enough fed," he observed. "Whaur ye from? Ardnasaig? The Bairds' palace?"

Think…

"No. I crossed from Baw Heid."

"One o' them damned pagans, then?"

"Never. I was taught the ways of Christ."

"How come ye crossed over the loch? 'Tis freezing by there. Are ye a faerie? A witch o' some kind?"

The sight of that axe and that purple blood leaking from his cheeks, turned her empty stomach. She must find something to divert his venom.

"I skated."

"Show us yer skates."

"I hid them by the shore back there. I've come to see my mother buried at the kirk in Kilforgan. Today's her birthday."

His gaze still rested on her coat pocket.

"Empty-handed, are ye then?"

"I'd give you some money if I had it. God's truth."

"That's wha' McKinnon told us. Then locked the kirk doors." He suddenly dropped his sack of fuel and, wrapping both hands around his axe shaft, slammed its iron head into the nearest tree trunk. "I pray the Hounds of Hell tear 'im limb from limb. An' as for Colonel Ritchie. Hell's too guid for 'im an' all. See what 'e did to me face." He placed a forefinger in his cheek's old blood and waggled it at her till a dark drop fell into the snow, spoiling its whiteness.

"I'm sorry, sir. Truly I am." She managed to say despite her fear; still keeping her fingers around the knife's comforting bone handle. "But with more bad weather coming, I'd best be on my way."

"If yer seein' tha' McKinnon, son o' the Dei'il he is, tell 'im what ye ken. Tha' ye'll be prayin' for the souls of me fellow workers."

"I will. I promise."

However, his tone changed to wheedling as he attempted to free the axe from the tree.

"Are ye sure ye've nae money for me, Missy? A few farthings mebbe?"

She sensed fresh danger. Her fingers closed tighter around the knife's handle.

"Your mob took what I had. I never stood a chance."

"Mob? 'Tis a bad word, Missy. Me freins are nae mob, an' they ne'er came this far. They've gone up Fort William for a better chance." He peered at her without mercy. "Summat in yer hard wee eyes tells me yer a leer."

Close enough now for her to smell his breath as the knife's bone handle warmed up in her hand. Her meagre earnings, wrapped in one of her father's old handkerchiefs, were for her alone. Why she never kept the money in her locked room or stitched it inside a pillowcase like Lennox. And that instinct had been proved right...
"I ken who ye are," the troll's gaze was on her again. A sneer on his lips. "Iain McPhee's sin. He cursed me herds so I slaved for Ritchie instead. And tha's nae all. Ask 'im aboot his fancy women. One in partic'lar..."

He grabbed her neck, but she was quicker, more supple, surprised by the strength of her first stab below his ear, which sent a spray of blood, far redder than what lay on his cheeks, up towards the snow-weighted branches. He lurched backwards, both hands clamped on the wound, and while he was down, causing the pink snow to deepen in colour, she knelt beside him, tore off his coat buttons and finally found his heart.

Then, for continued good fortune, she stuffed a pine cone in his gaping mouth, lifted her own garments and directed her hot, pale piss on to his face.

fearful Coyle Steer and soon

information I beg you arrival here

for safety detain no sleep as possible Misses

What use that nonsense now? Yet as Catriona moved on, dragging another branch behind her to destroy her footprints, those random words assumed a frightening significance, forcing her to turn on her heels away from the dying man's gasps. If she kept a straight path through the Browburn plantation, then up and over Footer's Hill, she'd be at her father's dwelling by dark.

All at once, something completely different made her stand stock still. A red shaft of light rising upwards from the suns' spread of colour behind Baw Heid's skull-shaped mountain. Was this lucky or unlucky, like yesterday's Brocken Spectre? Her father would know. So would Mr Bogle.

A distracted glance to the right where his cottage and stable lay, barely distinguishable from the snowy carpet around them. Where the one chimney was still quiet. Where, in the eerie silence, the peppery smell of wild boar met her nose, she prayed the axe man's wagging tongue had already frozen under the cone in his mouth. There'd been enough tittle-tattle from human tongues in the past few hours to last her a lifetime.

As Catriona stared at the hovel, she tried again to guess the real contents of James Baird's message…

Misses… Who else but her and Black Eyes? *Detain…* Was he asking Constable Coyle to put them both behind bars? Only the huntsman himself could say, and certainly she'd challenge him about the remaining words and watch his every reaction. In the meantime, to redeem herself, she must find a rescuer in Cranranich for his father. And if that meant showing a dainty ankle to whoever had a spare boat, so be it.

As that mysterious red pillar of light dispersed behind the mountain, Catriona picked her way between the white lines of oak and larch, on to the plantation of new spruce barely taller than herself, which her father had sworn would be a curse on Argyll for ever.

Not only was she dizzy from hunger and the sheer effort of placing one booted foot in front of the other, but also from churning James Baird's written words over and over in her mind. What else could he have meant? And then, as if she didn't have enough to think about, two other words intruded.

Falcon Steer.

Strange how that name had been mentioned after so long. As if dark forces were hell-bent on giving her more grief. She was glad she'd finished off that rabid trouble-maker back there. He'd been the liar. Not her.

*

At last, the brow of Footer's Hill. She'd recognise it anywhere, and even though the sun's orange glare made her shield her eyes, she could still make out her father's but and ben, lying like a black omen on the hillside below. Overhead, an eagle glided out of sight, it's claws frozen to its prey. A rabbit, squealing, like some old Gaelic song.

Downhill now, with a last look at Loch Nonach's southernmost end, where, instead of any boat, a ragged gash of broken ice scarred the white water.

***

16.

In which the past is a fraying veil...

With still no sign of her 'wee frein' and the growing possibility that the Dame of Nonach's deadly powers might be waning when she could be needing them most, Janet set down her candle by the Store's east wall and examined McPhee's ice - still intact - on its straw bed in the bucket. Having seen her poor mother's fingerprints peeled away by too many of the loch's frozen trout, she'd made sure to wear gloves. These were thin enough to detect what, if anything, her enemy had appeared to find at the well.

With her heartbeat pummelling her chest, she examined the topmost slab that tilted upwards near the bucket's rim. A small, almost wing-shaped depression in its surface, made her hold the candle closer, careful not to let its small warmth melt any of the ice.

She peered at the strange hollow, and the longer she did so, was reminded of a book on human anatomy Linnet had once hown her. Of bone and muscle, the journeys of food and blood - all in the name of the self-healing arts in which she was so expert. None of which resembled what might have lain in that ice, or indeed might have helped save her mother's life.

She turned the piece of ice over, wondering who else, having crossed into an earthly Hell, was seeking the Wise Woman's advice? It also occurred to her that should Coyle decide to pursue her own lie about the Border farm near Duns, and she needed Linnet as witness, would the Glaswegian simply save her own skin?

No use torturing herself. Whatever had cast its shape into the frozen slab of water was nothing to do with her.

*

Earlier, Janet had searched all she could in McPhee's room, and with the light fading, it was time to attend to the abandoned luncheon and prepare the evening's dinner, whatever those later hours might bring. James Baird hadn't eaten a thing since his breakfast kipper. Time to divert his attention to his stomach, especially as that little vixen was out of the way, running some errand or other

"Sir?" she called out once she'd re-heated the spiced wine her mother had taught her to make, and re-arranged the cold meats in a fresh design by his plate. "Ye'll be better able to greet yer father on a full belly."

"And I hope yours isn't filling." His voice preceded him from the hallway. "I've enough to be thinking about."

He obviously hadn't seen Falcon arrive or leave, but why this sudden, bitter tone? She fussed with his napkin, turning it into a lily flower. What she was good at.

"I can promise ye, sir, there's nae wean on the way. Do ye think I could raise it on me wages, me prospects? I've bin in the Poor House once, remember."

"Just fetch the wine and talk to me."

Janet swallowed in surprise.

"What about, sir?"

"Wine first."

She hurried out to the kitchen stove, ladled out the cinnamon-scented drink into a jug and delivered it to his elbow, wishing she'd paid her loosening ringlets more attention. But he wasn't interested in her hair. Instead, his mismatched eyes stayed on the one tall window overlooking the icy loch as he cracked each of his knuckles in turn. The harsh sound of it made her grip the back of the nearest chair.

"I should have bought another dog," he said, out of the blue.

"Why, sir? Because of the mob?" Janet let go of the chair to fill his glass from the jug.

"The mob's nothing to what reached my ears at midday. It's *you* I should have entrusted with my letter to Constable Coyle. I was asking him for help. For us and my father…"

Panic soon replaced any flattery as the clock struck a quarter past three.

"*Coyle?* Is that where she's gone? Sir, I hope ye don't take offence, but how *could* you? I'm older than she. Better able to defend meself if need be."

James Baird half-turned and she noticed his unshaven cheeks. How the bald patch on his crown, was gaining new territory. "Miss Lennox, please understand he might have detained you over Christmas and beyond. And I couldn't risk that. Not today of all days… You see he's convinced that you and your mother were… are…"

"What?"

"I can't."

"Ye must."

"The Dame of Nonach's heirs…"

Two pairs of ravens hovered over the frosted Rowan trees. Soon the deepening gloaming would make them invisible to the human eye. Just then, however, Janet imagined they'd grown and grown to form a black, malevolent cloak to smother her soul. As if she had just four days left to live.

"We're ne'er them!" She protested. "Tha's a terrible accusation. I read to myself from the Holy Book every night, and mother always heard me prayers..."

Mother...

Lying alone and unburied in the cold kirk.

His untouched wine was the colour of wean blood. Reminding her too vividly of what she must forget. "Has Mr Steer been making mischief?" she ventured, then wished she hadn't.

Her companion seemed genuinely surprised.

"No, no. Far from it. He seems to have the highest regard for you, Miss Lennox. According to the Constable, it's all to do with the Bruce's letter from Lismore."

"There ne'er were a letter! Did *ye* see it when the Constable were here? Nae. He were trying to frighten me. Besides, the Bruces was harder than granite. They wanted us gone the moment I began to show."

"Constable Coyle is our Procurator Fiscal's brother. A man of growing influence. When he speaks to you, I'd say as little as possible. If only for your brother's sake."

Janet blinked.

"What's me brother to do with anythin'?"

Her companion turned away. Best change the subject, she thought, and quick. "So why nae stop the Clearances? Make provision for them tha's fallen on hard times?"

James Baird finally put his glass to his lips and drank. The wine turned them red.

"Because there's nae money in it." She added before he could answer. "I'm nae glaekit, sir."

"My father said the same after your interview with him. He also noticed your hard-working hands."

Janet blushed. Glanced down at her bitten nails, the raw skin in which they lay. Would these be enough to save her?

"So, I'll be safe?"

He looked up at her. The one blue eye darker than usual.

"With me you will be."

"Thank ye, sir."

"It's Miss McPhee who's troubled me ever since Mr Hendry bought this letter over from Helen Fergusson down in Bar-Beithe earlier today. And why would she be spinning me such yarns? My family has known her for years. She was a special friend of my mother's. One of my Godparents, like Roberta Masters..."

From his breeches' pocket, he extracted a folded piece of blue paper and laid it next to his plate.

"What yarns, sir?" Janet challenged. "And may I ask why ye referred to Iain McPhee as an oxter the other day?"

James Baird absently used his fork to reduce a slice of ham to a mouth-sized portion before eating it. He then indicated the nearest chair. "Sit down, Miss Lennox, and I'll attempt to tell you."

"Shouldn't Mr Baird be informed too?" She asked afterwards; her mind spinning.

"How can I? I hired Miss McPhee without his knowledge. He'll blame me. Punish me again."

He wasn't the only one feeling troubled. Janet now felt too uneasy to be in the house or out of it. However, the Store's supply of wood was running low with no-one else to replenish it. Should the architect return before nightfall, he must have good fires and a warm house to welcome him.

Minutes later his son who'd not even bothered to saddle his pony, was cantering away in a wild spray of snow, heading east along the loch's frozen shore.

Before locking all three outer doors and hiding the keys in her drawers, Janet lifted one of his heavy coats from a hook by the scullery. Its weight and smell of man-sweat in the lining, providing the shield she needed more than ever, as she pushed the wheelbarrow out towards the elm grove where the shrouded, fallen trees lay ready for the taking.

She'd never used an axe before, but had seen Mr Bogle working one enough times to know that if the first cut was clean and true, the rest would follow. Every few yards, she kicked the barrow's iron wheel clear of snow, and with each kick making the keys judder next to her skin, wished instead that wheel was the fork-tongued maid.

According to Helen Fergusson, the twelve year-old herdsman's daughter had been at home by Footer's Hill on both occasions when the architect, accompanied by Constable Arthur Wildman - her brother and Constable Coyle's predecessor - had come calling, only to leave empty-handed. He'd felt sure the girl wasn't as innocent as she looked. That she was certainly privy to Iain McPhee's roving eye. And now, the maid with that same golden hair and black heart was out there somewhere.

'Twere the pretty bairn that unsettled me. The way she tried to protect her father. How, during the second visit, she spat out the vilest curse on me when she thought I wasnae lissening...'

The contents of Mrs Fergusson's letter that James Baird had shown her, repeated over and over in Janet's head as she set the barrow down and willed her ears to pick out the faintest sign of danger. The dutiful godmother didn't seem the sort to invent falsehoods. And given this damaging account, could herself be in danger...

*

Dark already, with a moon sliver and stars like pin tops dotting the sky, but bringing no added light, Janet wished she'd brought the oil lamp, despite the risk of attracting unwanted attention to herself. The awesome silence in the elm grove seemed to fill her throat, her whole body, so that when at last she stood, axe raised over the chosen branch, her arms lost their strength. Then without warning, something brushed against the back of her legs.

Her axe skewed into the snow. Her first thought was McPhee. But no.

This blood and piss stink wasn't human. She turned to see a miserable clutch of black, matted fur and, despite the purply darkness, two beseeching eyes.

The dog was barely able to stand. The deep wound on its rump showed bone and enough torn flesh to suggest that hungry crows might have added to its distress. But where was it from? Part of the Ritchie mob, maybe? And why here, with her? For food or something else?

"Och, ye poor thing," she stroked his head. "Who's harmed ye so bad, then?"

Suddenly, the dog - surely a Gordon setter - began to bury his nose into a nearby mound of snow and seconds later, held up what she assumed was a piece of wood. Even a filthy old bone. But a closer look showed a left-footed boot, in unlined black leather. The stray let her take it from his jaws, brush off the rest of the clinging snow, and run her hand along its smooth sole. Its small heel.

Where's the other one, then?" She asked, her pulse skipping as she slipped the boot into her borrowed coat's pocket. "Come on. It must be nearby…"

However, after several attempts, the dog whom she'd call 'Robbie,' gave up and let the snow take the weight of his weary body.

What else was lying buried in this elm grove? Janet wondered, trying to control her rising panic. What other secrets had her enemy gone to such great lengths to hide?

With her load of wood threatening to topple over at every opportunity, and the stray staying close by, Janet ever vigilant, cajoled the wheelbarrow back to the Store. The shock of seeing McPhee's boot had made her stack the last few logs any old way, just to finish the job and get back to the relative safety of Ardnasaig House's thick stone walls.

Each glance over her shoulder was more nervous then the one before; each breath shorter as she finally bolted the Store's door behind her and hunted for a candle. In its meagre light, she saw Robbie stagger towards the stag's hanging carcass and realise the beast's head that had stopped bleeding into the bucket which was thankfully too high for him to reach. She eased the boot from her coat's pocket and after a moment's deliberation, secreted it deep inside a heap of swedes she knew wouldn't be disturbed for weeks. Long after she'd had use of them.

Her mother's handwritten label fell to the floor, but before she could return it to its place, Robbie had gulped it down. He coughed then looked up, whining for more. If he was so starving, why hadn't he devoured that boot? Its leather wasn't so thick… Then she realised, he might have *wanted* her to see it.

*

She tore open a packet of oat cakes and while her new friend gobbled them up, cleaned his rump's open wound with pages from the *Oban Times* normally kept for the apple harvest. He growled as one by one she picked out those pine needles that lay embedded in his raw flesh, but when finished, licked her hand with a dry, hot tongue.

His smell was beginning to fill even that huge space, so to encourage him into the main part of the house was too big a risk. In a world of few friends, she'd found another. He must be safe and given a chance to heal. He'd probably saved her life out there. She must save his. The Store would be his home at least until the weather improved. Meanwhile, James Baird would have to be told.

Soon, a rough bed of old sacks lay ready in the darkest, furthest corner and, after another feed of ham rind used to make broth, Robbie slumped down into a snoring sleep.

Water…

Rather than travel to the scullery tap, she could melt a piece of ice. Yes, *that* particular piece of ice would be ideal…

*

Another haunting bellow rose from the loch, reaching her ears in that too-silent house, and for a second she was tempted to risk more numbing cold outside to see what was happening. But should McPhee arrive back, she'd most likely lock her out and watch her freeze to death, all the while with that pretty smile on her face. Until she realised her room had been broken into. Until she discovered Robbie…

Janet blew out her wavering candle and lit another, mumbling another prayer for her mother's soul as she bore it into the Drawing Room to light the six lamps around its walls. The maid's holly looked all wrong and not just because of the way it had been stuffed into various vases and trailed along the mantelpiece. And, still thinking of the owner of that smooth-soled boot, Janet went over to the writing bureau no-one was allowed to dust, and scoured its surface for clues as to what James Baird's letter had really contained.

The old oak bore the usual scratches and indentations from years of use. She moved her head's shadow to one side to see more clearly which of the marks seemed newer than the rest, but the candlelight wasn't strong enough so she replaced the cap on the bottle of dark blue ink and tidied the various pens into neat lines.

He'd been angry and alarmed with good reason. And then, a snatch of white caught her eye. Trapped between the desk's lid and the drawer beneath. It belonged to a sheet of blotting paper, hurriedly returned to its place.

With all the care she could muster, for fear of tearing its softness, Janet pulled the edge until bit by bit, the sheet used from new, scored with that day's date and a message clearly visible in reverse, lay in her trembling hand.

***

17

Where sleeping dogs are best left to lie...

No wind, no sound, save for those few crows moving leaden-winged from tree to tree.

Catriona always felt sorry for them at this harsh time of year, with food so scarce and the huntsman's bullet never far away. She'd once kept a thrush as a pet for two years until a sparrow hawk swooped on to its head and carried it off into the sky. Its pathetic little cries had torn at her heart. Even now, ten years' later, she'd not forgotten the way its tiny, fluttering form had filled her cupped hands, warming her fingers while that eager little heart pumped away at twice the speed of her own...

Having negotiated a colony of fallen boulders which Iain McPhee had sworn was a Neolithic site of ritual sacrifice, she soon left the plantation to slither down the eastern slope of Footer's hill, and onwards over hidden hollows and tufts of the Ghost Hills heather that more than once, tipped her forwards on to her knees.

Sometimes the gutting knife jabbed into her thigh, as if reminding her of its further potential. She'd already cleaned its blade to an unblemished shine, and now it lay in her coat's inner pocket, along with the cryptic, half-chewed remains of James Baird's letter.

Two forces now drove her onwards. Her father's careless mouth and that God-fearing Presbyterian, Roberta Masters of

Nonach Cottage, who might, with some persuasion, bring Donald Baird home for Christmas and repair her reputation.

Out of breath, with every limb chilled and aching from the kind of journey she'd not made since December 3rd, Catriona stopped at the bottom of the white, rutted track leading up to her former home, where several sets of footprints pointed towards it but none led away. Her father rarely had visitors now, and this apparent activity was a mystery. Normally, he'd already be at the door, but things were different now, and in the snowy dusk, that but and ben's small, dark oblong made up resembled less a dwelling than a coffin.

He'd seen her.

The mean door was opening inwards; a hand like a pale stain on its wood. But nothing else. Not yet. No smoke either, like at Mr Bogle's bothy, and this made her realise that in the twenty-one days she'd been away from there, something really had changed.

At least her feet hadn't frozen, so, avoiding the footprints, at the same time trying not to slip sideways from the path, she moved nearer that ever-widening slab of blackness. The hand had gone, but not the face and body it belonged to.

It's him…

Shock left cold breath in her mouth. Surely, this was an apparition, like Isobel Baird's accusing eyes in that stupid housekeeper's face…

Fergus Bogle's haggard demeanour and dirty clothes made him almost unrecognisable. But worse was the look of a stranger; the rifle propped against his leg as if ready for use. She then noticed the Apothecary's phial of her first-blood had gone from its usual place in the mean hallway.

"What are *you* doing here?" She blurted out at last. "I thought you'd come to some harm. I even went..." She stopped herself. She'd taken that comb and the cheese knife from his bothy. Perhaps that's why he was standing in front of her, staring at her expensive, grey boots.

"Come in, come in, Miss McPhee." He said without his usual welcoming smile. "Please. Ye, I and yer father shud talk afore it's too late..."

"Too late for what?"

"Afore ye see Constable Coyle..."

"Who told you about that?"

"So, 'tis true?"

She didn't answer.

"And talk about what?"

"Only a gowk would ask me that."

With that not-so-kindly voice hogging her cold ears, Catriona turned on her heels out of the front door and ploughed her way down the track. She'd been frightened by his tone, yet knowing that within ten minutes walk, lay Nonach Cottage mercifully hidden from above and beyond by lines of young spruce planted by Lord Melhuish in memory of his wife, dead from a miscarriage two years ago.

As she went, questions jabbed at her mind like summer's clega and midges. Had Mr Bogle known she'd be arriving there? And did she truly believe her father was in the next room? If so, why not come to the door? Was he that much of a coward?

Whatever the answers, that handyman might already be making his way back to Ardnasaig House to stir up even more

188

trouble. As if she wasn't in enough already. He wasn't nice Mr Bogle any more, but *nosy* Mr Bogle. Nosy and unpleasant. To be avoided at all costs. Just then, he represented one of those old mooring posts by Ardnasaig's shore. Weathered above the water line, rotten below.

"If I fall to Death's messenger, get yersel to me side..."

Not now she wouldn't...

Cranranich one mile.

*

This familiar scene seemed like a different country. In one of her mother's books, Catriona had pored over small copies of various paintings depicting Europe's finest mountains in winter. The Alps, Pyrenees and a Swiss town called Kitzbühl, enveloped in pristine snow. She could, without too much effort, imagine herself there, away from what now was beginning to feel like a steel trap closing around her. However, with Mrs Master's help, that trap might open a little, and her forthcoming interview with Constable Coyle be less an ordeal, more a victory.

She picked her way across the lochside track, parting the dank bracken and hearing the happy gurgle of a wee burnie, too sheltered to have iced over. Its widening over boggy ground to either side, told her the loch shore wasn't far.

Once through the bracken, and a wooden gate set into a shoulder-high wall, the cottage, its chimney's trail of black smoke and small, boatless harbour came into view. No time for second thoughts now. Catriona placed her numb feet carefully over the lumpy ground where horses' hooves had been and, avoiding a pile of steaming manure, headed for the cottage door.

*

She'd only seen the widow attend Cranranich's kirk on the rare occasions when her mother had coerced her there for the Sunday service. The childless woman built like a cromlech had sung and prayed the loudest, but no-one complained, because she represented money. Both her and her late husband's contributions to the collecting plate had made the difference between a new bell or no bell; a restored window or one that stayed boarded up. Now widowed and the sole owner of six fine fishing boats, with talk of starting excursions to add to her income, the zealot would soon be facing another call on her Christian values.

The brass knocker's coldness penetrated Catriona's torn glove and she swiftly rubbed away trapped blood from between her right thumb and forefinger. She wondered where these boats were. Why there was no sound coming from the icy loch. Whether all this would be too late...

"Round the back I am." A woman's voice rang out. "Who is it?"

"Catriona McPhee, the maid from Ardnasaig House. I need your help. Mr Baird's boat's not yet arrived with us."

"I cannae hear ye."

Catriona followed the path leading past the substantial cottage to a brick-built boat shed from where the reek of tar grew stronger as she approached. She peered inside to see Roberta Masters halfway up a ladder against the side of the *Nonach*

Princess. In her thick-gloved hand lay a tar brush, stroking the black treacly stuff along the fishing boat's water line.

"Well, well, well, if it's nae the herdsman's daughter from Footer's Cottage. After all this time…" Small, brown eyes appraised her visitor from head to toe, and to forestall any personal remarks, Catriona repeated her reason for being there.

"If no-one acts, he could be stranded there all night," she pleaded, alarmed at the woman's sudden laugh. At how she had to hold tight to the ladder's side for fear of falling off. "With all due respect, Mrs Masters, I don't see anything amusing in Mr Baird's predicament. He was due back home at one o'clock. Dauvit Hendry brought news that his trap had turned over and his pony shot. Why he'd taken a boat from George Sorrow."

Another laugh, making Catriona want to pull the fat creature off her perch and make her see sense.

"I think, child, someone's bin fanciful. There's bin nae boat on the loch since yesterday morning. And that was this one." She tapped its side with her brush. "I should ken."

"But…"

Catriona's empty stomach seemed to shrink. Her heart to turn still. And with no words coming, she heard the faintest sound of a horse neighing. Another puzzle. Surely a woman of this size and girth wouldn't keep a horse. Besides, with no grazing to be had, where was the stable?

The boat owner continued her chore with annoying regularity. It was time for some explanation.

"So, Mr Hendry's a liar?"

"He'd nae more lie than string his own mother up."

"And James Baird?"

She paused.

"Ah, that one."

"Please explain, Mrs Masters."

"I'm his Godmother, but that ne'er stops me worrying."

"He made me stand on the shore for an hour today, waiting for his father. I almost froze to death."

A glance her way. A smile lasting too long.

"Ye look well enough now."

"That's because I'm strong. I survive because I have to. For my own father's sake. I'm all he's got."

"And he should be proud of ye for being so concerned, but Mr Baird's nae fool. He'll be stopping over somewhere until Boxing Day, and by then, as God's me witness, all this snow will be water."

"But I saw the ice broken on the loch. As if his boat had gone down." Catriona pointed to beyond the scrubby shore. "Further down from here."

Instead of replying, the woman nodded in the direction of Ardnasaig House.

"If ye care for yer father and Mr Baird, ye'll be gone before ye freeze to death. Would ye fancy a piece of bread and cheese to take with ye?"

Catriona thanked her, but declined. In truth, her nerves would make eating anything impossible. At least until the ordeal of seeing the architect again was over.

*

More than two hours after her fruitless errand to Constable Coyle, with still no sign of the promised police dogs, Catriona left Nonach Cottage and made her way in the near-dark along the loch's shore line, through ghostly, wind-tangled alder groves, past a long-abandoned rowing boat half buried in snow, until the pebbles gave way to rising ground strewn with larger stones whose bright green mossy tufts poked through their white coverings. Any relief she might have felt that Roberta Masters had found her helpful, now submerged by imagining what the next day or two might bring.

More than once she paused to stare at the loch's dead, white surface for any sign of life, but there was none. Even the usual birds were absent, and that dark scar of broken ice she'd seen earlier, had gone. But worse, as she trudged upwards towards Ardnasaig House under the frozen lime trees, she sensed again those same powerful blue eyes following her every step.

*

As she neared the black front door, she saw woodsmoke billowing from both chimneys. Not only that, but each loch-facing room glimmered with their oil lamps' honeyed light. Lennox has been busy, she thought, turning the big brass handle in her torn, gloved hand. She repeated her efforts again and again, and used the matching knocker, but the door stayed shut.

With now no feeling in her toes, she hobbled round past the empty stable to the Store door, with the same result, except that this time, a low growl seemed to come from within. She listened more intently then, taking a gulp of bitingly cold air, called out. "It's me.

Miss McPhee. Is anybody home?" Instead of any human voice, came a bark she recognised.

She pummelled the wide, black-painted door causing that same bark to become a blood-curdling warning to keep away.

How in Hell's name had that creature got here? And who was giving it shelter?

Just as she prepared to knock again, there came a commotion from the end of the carriageway. The crunch of wheels and hooves on ice. Men's shouts, and James Baird swearing at the top of his voice.

Catriona crept round to the side of the house beneath the dining room windows, past the rhododendrons from where she could make out the blasphemer's cob, throwing his head up and down, clearly unused to pulling the kind of cart her father once used to deliver hay to his snow-bound cattle. James Baird crouched perilously on its front bench, but of far more interest was the passenger behind him, swaying to the cob's wild movements. The black hatted, whey-faced Donald Baird, looking her way.

She snatched at a fallen pine branch, heavy with frosted needles and, having dragged it to the front steps, began to sweep away the trampled ice as fiercely as if her life depended on it.

***

18.

Where worms seem to be turning...

Robbie was making that much din and Janet understood why. McPhee had been trying by hook or by crook to get back into the house. Despite James Baird's traitorous letter to Constable Coyle, this brief moment of power - the same as when she'd held that buried boot - made her even more determined to resist.

Minutes later, a light from the carriageway pierced the gap between the dining room curtains, casting a reed of brightness down a mournful oil painting of the house in autumn. Was this Falcon Steer? She wondered. Even Constable Coyle again?

Janet parted the red velvet curtains a little more and let out a gasp of surprise to see James Baird leap down from the front edge of a rough cart to help its other occupant, a tall, gaunt-looking older man dressed all in black, clamber down from behind him. She recognised the architect immediately from that haunting old daguerreotype. She rarely forgot a new word.

Donald Baird stared up at the house, his hooded eyes scanning each window, mouth half-open as he did so.

Immediately her pulse quickened. Her hair, face and clothes had been untouched since dawn. What sort of impression would *that* make?

Indecision…

Should she see to herself first, or be ready by the door with a forced smile of welcome on her lips?

Mother, what to do?

And because Margaret Lennox had often been quick to criticise her appearance, she ran upstairs to her room, cupping her candle with one hand and tearing off her white cap with the other. There were too many knots and tangles in her ringlets where normally her hairbrush would have glided through. And as for her face, several dark smudges, probably from the Store, marked her right cheek, while the blue vein on her nose seemed bluer than ever.

Spit and her mother's handkerchief soon cleared away the dirt, leaving instead a bright red blotch. If McPhee could see her now, she'd laugh so much, all those perfect little sheep's teeth of hers would be on show. Her bladder - another word learnt from Linnet Garvie - would be under some strain.

McPhee could stop outside for all she cared.

Janet peered out of her window expecting to see the little party busy collecting the architect's luggage. But no. The girl had reached the two Bairds first and, despite her recent journey to Kilforgan and back, still looked a hundred times better than she. The architect greeted her warmly and smiled. His son seemed relieved.

Moments later, she herself was hovering by the front door. The steps had mysteriously been swept. Not one stray leaf or speck of snow remained.

"Well, Miss Lennox, where were you?" James Baird shouted at her while freeing his cob from the cart's shafts. "What kind of welcome is this?"

"I've bin worried sick, sir. Where did ye go?"

McPhee answered first. "He reached Glencardle, but with no boats going out, not even for someone as important as Mr Baird, Mr Sorrow lent his cart instead. The ice has been bad all the way along. It's a miracle they're here at all."

Indeed it is... But little do ye ken...

Meanwhile, James's cadaverous father who now stood in front of her, pulled off his gloves and slapped them against his hat to dislodge the snow trapped above its brim.

"Janet Lennox, sir," she reminded him. "Please let me take those."

His welcome was a tired grunt before turning away from her to check on his son and a flushed McPhee who was pulling his heavy brown suitcase from the cart. He'd brought with him smells she couldn't place, while his hooded eyes seemed pale from grief and overwork; his white, bony wedding finger still bore a ring. She'd also noticed nails bitten to the quick. Just then, in the middle of her anxieties, it occurred to her that he seemed the least likely of men to have fathered a son. A son as stocky and solid as the huntsman.

"I thought, James," he said pointedly, "that our well-paid staff were trained to present themselves promptly to new arrivals. Particularly their employer."

"I've done my best, father," he retaliated, leading the cob away. "Perhaps, dare I say it, a few more trips home might help."

His father's mouth shrank. His fingers' tightened on his gloves and hat brim. Perhaps the two men had already quarrelled and it still simmered. What did she care? She'd be away from it all soon. Janet held the door wide for him, aware of her stupid red cheek. Her blue vein across her nose.

"Me mother's just passed away, sir," she explained. "I've had that on me mind. And the wicked takin' of 'er eyes."

The lizard in black hadn't even blinked when she'd added that bit.

"Miss McPhee did tell me," he said. "As did my son. You have not only my deepest sympathy, Miss Lennox, but also an assurance that Constable Coyle will leave no stone unturned to find the perpetrator of such wickedness."

Words were easy. Money was different, and she could tell straightaway there'd be no mention of him contributing to a proper funeral for the woman who'd worked so hard to keep his home running smoothly. He was as cold as he looked. As cold as her own hand closing round the door's icy handle.

"Where's Mr Bogle?" He asked, rather - it seemed - than pursue that particular conversation. .

"I think, sir, Master Baird 'ad better explain."

The architect brushed past her with the maid in tow, hefting his calfskin case up the last step to the front door. Its steel corners causing small sparks against the newly-swept granite slabs.

"Ye just wait," Janet hissed at her. "Did ye deliver that letter to the police house after all?"

The other girl's complexion turned whiter than the snow. Her grasp on the suitcase weakened, letting it bump to the step below. "May the Devil twist your rotten guts. What's it to you?"

'Guard yer tongue…'

"Have a care, McPhee. Yer famous for cursin'…"

198

And to see her so affronted, made Janet more reckless. "I ken what Master Baird had written in tha' letter."

Just then, Donald Baird turned round, finally holding out his coat, hat, cane and gloves for her to take. All lay stiff on her arm from exposure in that cart. She wanted to whisper to him what was plaguing her mind, but too late. He'd begun to speak. "My son and I need a brandy, then tea. Make haste. My bones have taken a battering for too long, and as for my equilibrium…"

Another new word to learn.

"Would ye fancy some cakes, sir?" Wondering if he yet knew about the portrait of his wife.

He nodded, before glancing around the hall where last year's silver baubles set amongst the blackthorn branches, sparkled in the lamplight.

"As you can tell from my sketches, I don't like fuss or over-embellishment. Whoever's made these festive decorations has extremely good taste."

"Me sir." McPhee's composure had returned. "Thank you, sir. And can I be unpacking your case while you warm yourself by the fire?"

"My, my," he smiled for the first time. "Such consideration." He then eyed Janet as she poured out two glasses of brandy from the decanter. "She'll need the keys, Miss Lennox."

Janet froze.

"But sir, they've been me ane responsibility since…"

"Please, do as you're asked. And given that you now have other tasks in the kitchen, I feel Miss McPhee could keep them from now on. I believe she also braved the cold to wait for me by the loch, and Mrs Masters told us of her efforts to find a boat there."

"Thank you sir." Those perfect, tiny teeth on show again.

"And dinner will be at eight," Janet added, pulling the heavy bunch of brass keys from her apron pocket and handing it over, all the while controlling her contempt. Only her mother had been allowed to clean in that particular bedroom. A symbol of her status. "I remember tha' as being yer preferred time."

She then hurried out to organise the best crockery ordered from Bell's of Glasgow for last Christmas and, despite her recent humiliation, set a pretty tray, all the while aware of McPhee's jealous gaze on her back. With that blotting paper's incriminating message still safe in her own drawers, this maid - keys or no keys - was the unarmed soldier in the battle to come. And James Baird another possible foe. But supposing he should find the blotting paper missing? That thought made her hesitate about keeping it. But not for long.

*

She returned with the tray to see McPhee plumping up the various cushions that Isobel Baird had embroidered during the endless Argyll winters. Her husband had settled himself by the fire in a generous leather armchair, twisting his ankles to and fro by the flames as he watched her. When Janet had placed his tray on a nearby table and enquired if everything was to his liking, the maid came over and, hands on slender hips, placed herself between them both. Janet saw the house keys form a bulge in her apron pocket, and hated her all the more.

"Sir," the enemy began. "Did you know we have a dog here?"

Donald Baird's thin grey eyebrows rose. His pale eyes registering more interest than for the dead Margaret Lennox.

"A dog?"

"Yes, sir. I'd swear to God I heard it barking in the Store before you and Master Baird arrived back. Hasn't he or Miss Lennox mentioned it?"

The architect still looked at her, but in a different way. He seemed so engrossed, Janet could almost taste her own bitterness.

"*He* certainly hasn't. What about you, Miss Lennox?"

She didn't reply, instead fussed over the tea leaves in the silver strainer. "So, tell me more, Miss McPhee," he added instead. "I'm all ears."

Janet poured his cup of tea then indicated the cakes her mother had baked from a French recipe on her last afternoon on this earth. Madeleines, bulging with raisins. She wanted to interrupt. Let him know what had really been happening. To say how wary she was. How scared...

"It sounds like a guard dog, sir," McPhee didn't waste any time. "And if you did want to keep it, I'd take care of it. I love dogs. Always have."

"So did my wife, but..." Here he hesitated, "after she and her two Gordon setters went missing, I've expressly forbidden any others to take their place. They let us down. Whatever befell her, neither animal returned here to sound the alarm."

Gordon setters?

"Unless one of them's come back to try and tell ye something, sir," said Janet unable to prevent his tea slopping over the teacup's gilded edge as she passed it to him. She used the hem of her skirt to wipe away the surplus from the saucer.

"After five and a half years? Rubbish…"

"I'm sorry sir, but I disagree. When I found Robbie in the elm grove, so wounded, 'is eyes filled with gratitude and 'e wanted to follow me. As if he ken where I were from. Anyone wud 'ave taken pity."

"Robbie?"

"Aye, sir."

"We Bairds aren't anyone, Miss Lennox."

"No, sir."

He took a sip. Licked his lips with a bloodless tongue. "Wounded? How?"

"As if someone had clubbed him 'ard above the tail."

McPhee gasped in horror. Turned her attention to the fire.

"Go and fetch this dog," said the architect. "If he recovers, and has a good nose, James can use him for hunting. That should keep him from any more mischief."

…any more mischief?

"*I'll* go, sir." The fair-haired maid laid down her poker.

"Best if I do," said Janet forcing a smile. "'E'll recognise me. After all, I rescued 'im."

"And while you do that," said the architect. "I'll go and see what this William Rankin of Inverary has made of my dear wife…"

*

A small triumph, but a triumph nevertheless, for which she'd doubtless pay the price. The corridor beyond the lit drawing room suddenly seemed as black as Hades and Janet felt her way along the expensively papered walls dotted with Donald Baird's framed sketches of fussy palaces adorned with pillars and carvings of lions and other wild beasts. So different from his own home she'd often wondered where these fanciful ideas had come from. But not now. She was too full of loathing to bother.

Past the kitchen and scullery into the truly cold nether regions where the Bairds' various capes, coats and cloaks hung together off single pegs, looking like so many dead men's garments. She guessed immediately something was wrong. The icy draught hitting her face for a start, and once she realised the Store's outer door must be open, and the dog gone, she let out a cry. For beyond this outer door, blurred paw marks, alongside human prints had been mostly obliterated, just like near the cocks' pen.

"Robbie!" She shouted with all her heart scolding herself for not finding out his proper name. Then whistled. A skill she'd excelled at in her Greenock days. But nothing replied. She listened to nightfall settling over this frozen world, wishing she'd grabbed Falcon's unexpected offer of escape. That her mother's soul might soon hear Christian blessings, and her body be placed safe and deep in holy ground.

Janet listened again, aware of her beating heart. Was that a laugh, or had she imagined it? There it was again. Some bird, maybe, calling from deep within the elm grove? She wasn't a country girl and couldn't tell one call from the next.

Another decision.

She'd made the wrong one half an hour ago, and must now make the right one. The tired traveller, having seen the portrait, would doubtless be dozing by the fire and his son, judging by faint noises coming from the stable, was still seeing to his cob.

One step at a time then, taking care not to give herself away, Janet negotiated the stray lumps of granite that Mr Bogle as handyman should have cleared, and up a treacherous small slope into the glade's mouth.

She'd fight if she had to. After all, hadn't she already beaten McPhee into submission, even though the girl had freely used her teeth? Calum had taught her how to box, to guard her breasts and do arm-locks and kicks where they hurt most. And it was him she thought of as she stopped to hear that same strange cackle, sensing a waiting trap into which she must not go.

Now came the faintest of barks. But her brief courage had slipped away, leaving a fearful void in its place.

*

Janet tripped up more than once on her flight back to the Store, and once inside, leant against the nearest cold wall, pressing her hands over her belly. Breathing faster than she'd ever done in her life.

Having recovered, she picked up her candle and trained it on the keyhole where there was no obvious sign of damage. However, outside was different. Here, the opening bore deep, recent scratches made with a sharp instrument. So, the injured dog had been let out deliberately, perhaps with a smile he'd trusted, and most likely the prospect of more food. But why?

And then she remembered that black boot.

Of course.

Was someone worried that clever creature might find more hidden things in other places? If so, what, and whose? As for the door, McPhee could have opened it - she'd been outside for long enough. So where was its big key now? There'd be trouble if, with all those food supplies ready for the taking, it was the only one.

Janet stared down at Robbie's makeshift bed knowing she'd miss not seeing him get better; hoping he was being cared for. She'd owed him a haven and had let him down by not bolting the door.

And then she spotted the ice bucket.

Having tipped its contents outside, she turned her attention to the pile of swedes, using both hands to grapple with the bulky vegetables, sending too many tumbling to the ground. She should have realised there'd been something different about the way they'd been arranged, or rather, re-arranged. Why? Because someone else had got there first.

***

19.

In which fortunes could be improving...

Although Donald Baird hadn't spent long with the new painting, he returned to the drawing room with relief relaxing his face.

"James chose well," he said to Catriona, settling himself back into that same armchair and opening his silver cigar box. "The eyes especially, capture her exactly. It's quite uncanny."

"I helped him choose the artist," she said.

"Really?" He looked at her, puzzled. "Mr Rankin was commissioned over two years ago."

She gulped on her mistake, then smiled to hide her embarrassment, "Well, sir," "I think he should do one of you."

"We'll see about that."

"Your wife must have been so beautiful," she added, placing his empty tea cup on the tray, as another diversion.

"Been?"

Another gulp.

"I mean, must *be*."

"Indeed. The kind of woman who'll never grow old." He eyed her feet. "Have you no indoor shoes?"

She nodded, glad he'd not noticed her wearing his wife's grey moleskin boots when arriving back home.

*

Catriona then hauled the architect's case upstairs just as Lennox was returning to the house from where, she couldn't imagine, with no dog. And what about her claim to know what had been in James Baird's letter? Was she lying to give herself the upper hand? Or had he trusted her enough to actually tell her?

As she dragged the steel-cornered burden up one stair at a time, changing her grip to spare her palms, cursing under her breath when her stockinged toes got in the way, she realised the next few hours would either keep the door open on her dream or shut it in her face.

The last step, with both arms aching as if pitted against the whole world. What a fool to have offered to take the thing, but given her situation, she'd had no choice. At least its owner hadn't flinched upon hearing her name, and she could hardly have made up another. His apparent short memory was to her advantage and she must keep it that way. That's what she told Isobel Baird's portrait, deliberately tilting it with her elbow as she passed by. Cursing those pervasive blue eyes and already planning in the not too distant future, to fling the wretched picture into the loch.

*

The keys to all the rooms in Ardnasaig House, felt like so many gold ingots in Catriona's hand and, having slipped her feet into a pair of black leather slippers kept in a handy little cupboard on that same landing, she unlocked the door to what had been the marital bedroom.

For a moment, she stood in awe at its size and the colours that made her head spin. She thought of her father's home; the dark, weeping walls and sense of gloomy entrapment. Here was another world altogether. The kind she'd imagined for too long. And the pale, thin man who'd apparently planned this adventure in blues, greens and yellows, climbed even higher in her estimation. Leaving his son a long way behind.

Two tall, curtained windows faced towards the still-frozen loch's eastern end. Its brightness adding to the vivid scene. Lennox had already made up the fire with its guard safely in place, while the four oil lamps' new wicks were likely to last for at least three days. Two tasks she'd been spared, leaving her time to really come into her own.

Forgetting the suitcase, Catriona sat on the edge of the four-poster bed, letting her sore fingers trace the raised, bejewelled patterns on its tasselled cover. She wondered which side of the bed had been whose, and during coupling - for that's what her father called it - did the architect lie on top of his wife? Had she been eager or coy? Wet or dry? She felt uncomfortable thinking about it, but whenever she'd met with her few friends before leaving Footer's Cottage, 'coupling' had been their main topic of conversation.

Apart from the portrait outside the door, she could find no other images of the woman who'd never returned. A surprise, given how long she and her architect husband been married, and seemingly devoted to each other. Her own father too, kept a few blurred images of Mairi McPhee taken at a stall in Cranranich Fair where a man from Paisley used a contraption using small sheets of glass to keep her uncertain smile alive. Even the cattle dogs had been immortalised at play.

Catriona's eyes travelled upwards to the silk hangings festooned from the top of each bed post. Strange how years ago, she'd dreamt of this very luxury. Of maybe sharing it all with that youthful rider who'd so transfixed her. She suppressed a little laugh at how things had turned out. Who'd have imagined her in this paradise of painted butterflies, pretty little monkeys and all manner of vegetation that her mother, for all her learning, had never shown her? Even the enamelled chamber pot near her feet looked too beautiful to be used.

Mr Baird's work must be making him exceedingly rich, she thought, recalling how Mairi McPhee had been left nothing by her own family. And as for Iain McPhee, his prospects were no better. The but and ben not even his. So, what would eventually fall to her? Just a pile of old bones at best…

She then took in the intricately carved bedroom furniture - all in walnut, judging by the wood's streaks and whorls. Also the room-sized rug bearing yet more shapes and patterns from far away. She mentally added up the cost, wondering what her father might say to see her so settled. So well thought of. Surely he'd change his stubborn mind about her being here? And the longer she sat drinking in the splendour, another idea came to her like a worm tunnelling into a ripe apple, while he memory of her recent visit home, for the moment, forgotten.

*

Her tasks seemed suddenly lighter, more purposeful, and once she'd returned the last velvet smoking jacket to its padded hangar in the wardrobe and collected all the items for the wash, fell to her knees and prayed. Not, however, to her dead mother's god, or his naïve son, but the Dame of Nonach, long since interred under her black stone. She begged for that invisible tongue to reach up inside Lennox's wild, black muff and suck out whatever hindrance might be hiding there.

It must have been true about the architect's Christmas presents being left at Inverary for delivery when the weather improved, because there'd been none in his suitcase. Nor any underwear she could sniff and examine. Just shirts, cravats and pyjamas giving her no clues as to whether or not he'd had a woman whilst away. Why did that bring another smile? Because, as her mother had often said, she wasn't stupid.

"All done, sir." She addressed the back of his balding head, just visible over the top of his armchair in the drawing room. A column of blue smoke rose from his cigar towards the ceiling then dispersed. "There's a change of clothes laid out ready if you wish."

"I can see you're quite the efficient young lady," he said. "And I'll be informing James of our new arrangements with the keys."

Our...

She was glad he couldn't see her blush.

"Thank you sir."

"Speaking of keys," he half-turned, gesturing her to come closer. "I wonder where Miss Lennox and that dog are. And my son."

"I'll find out right away, sir."

A long white finger beckoned.

"In a moment. When you've told me a bit more about yourself."

Just then, the fire's flames seemed too bright, too vigorous. Their hiss and spit too loud, like the noise from the crowd at Baw Heid when an old witch together with her six cats had been sealed alive inside a wicker casket and burned to ashes. Mairi McPhee had wanted Catriona to witness the fate of someone who couldn't keep her dangerous tongue still. Who'd railed against the kirk and made potions to cause illness and death. The terrible scene had stayed with her ever since. Why burning those dead cocks had proved such an ordeal. Why Falcon Steer's warning had cooled her blood.

She perched next to her employer on a plainer chair, willing a smile to her lips, as that imagined door between dream and doom hovered half-open in her mind. He was waiting. Those eyes the colour of dawn on the loch water, fixed on her in a way she couldn't fathom.

"In case Master Baird didn't mention it, sir, I reached sixteen years of age when the Great Exhibition opened in London's Hyde Park, and I'll be seventeen come the next May 1st. I'm from Footer's Hill Cottage, near Cranranich, but was born in the kirk house in Tarbet; the daughter of Mairi McPhee, although she passed away some years ago."

"*And* of Iain McPhee," he added, studying his now shorter cigar before returning it to his mouth.

Catriona swallowed hard.

"Of course, sir. After faithful service, my father had a bad time of things with Lord Melhuish. But he did his best for us, especially after mother passed on."

Those half-closed eyes flickered as if on a memory.

"I know. I called on him twice with Constable Wildman just after my own dear wife never returned home. I thought that with his knowledge of the area and his tracking skills, he might prove invaluable. And so he did. But sadly, the trail of both her and the dogs ran cold by Dauvit Hendry's boundary."

"I'm sorry, sir."

"Even in August, that bog around there will leave no trace of anyone or anything... Incidentally, when you next see your father, if he needs work, he can come here. Lord knows there's enough to do when I'm away."

Catriona's stomach tightened under her working clothes.

"But sir, Mr Bogle might come back."

Donald Baird shook his head.

"I need reliable folk, not those who desert their posts on a whim..."

Catriona kept her fixed smile in place to disguise her real fears. Her father being here would be a disaster of the worst order. She must mention his drinking, his inability to rise in the mornings. That would soon put an end to the notion. It was time to take a risk. She watched her employer as a hawk might its supper.

"I remember you from then, sir," she ventured." Did you remember me?"

"On the second occasion I called, I spotted a delightful young girl busy peeling potatoes. Despite my sorrow," he lowered his voice, "it occurred to me how idle my son was by comparison." He glanced at the door, then pulled his watch from his waistcoat.

"When you've removed the tea things, do please ask him to come and see me straight away. And then Miss Lennox."

"Certainly, sir, and as it's Christmas Eve, can I fetch you a liqueur or a whisky, whichever you prefer. With ice, of course."

He skewed the last of his cigar into a cut glass ashtray, leant towards her and touched her arm as she reached for the tray. Normally, she'd have recoiled at such familiarity, but not now. Not from him. She'd noticed a new liveliness in his eyes, and the hint of a smile creating two equal creases at each side of his mouth.

"It's almost as if you know what I want before I say it. A whisky with ice would be most welcome. And incidentally," his gaze stayed upon her. "You have a most delightful name, Miss McPhee. It sits very nicely on the tongue, unlike some I could mention."

On the tongue…

She lowered her head to hide another blush, yet still had something to say.

"Sir, I should warn you that there's a certain vagrant called Falcon Steer up from Dunblane, who's been to the house several times, making eyes at Miss Lennox and causing other mischief too. Constable Coyle has a warrant out for his arrest. He's a dangerous man, sir. It's only fair to warn you."

"Arrest for what?"

"I think Master Baird had best tell you, sir."

"And his appearance?"

She stopped short of mentioning both men having lunch together and of Coyle and the vicar standing where she was now. Then answered the question.

"His hair and eyes are dark as coals, and he speaks in an odd way. As for his clothes… Well," she gave a shy smile. "They're not a patch on yours, sir."

"Thank you, Miss McPhee. I shall confer with my son, and we shall all be on alert in case he pays us another call."

Catriona closed the solid oak door behind her and, despite the heavy tea tray and a quickening pulse, almost skipped along to the scullery where the sight of Lennox with her broad back to her, washing a red cabbage, made her pause to wonder if her latest request to the Dame of Nonach was taking effect. Her enemy seemed hunched over, as if in some discomfort. Twice the slippery cabbage fell into the bowl of water.

"Do I wash these tea things here or in the kitchen?" asked Catriona. The former housekeeper's keys in her apron pocket giving her the edge she needed.

"Where ye like, ye good for nothing."

"Mr Baird's asking to see the dog."

"Surely ye'll do? Dog or bitch, no matter."

Catriona focussed on that black block of a body and begged inwardly for the Dame's dark forces to make haste and do their work.

"And Master Baird? Where's he?" She said.

"Find him yerself. Mind, he won't want nothin' to do with ye. Not now. No wonder yer butterin' up an old grandfather instead…"

"Die, please, why don't you?"

"After ye, Miss McPhee."

Six chimes from the hall clock added to Catriona's sense of urgency. She set down the crowded tray on a table where a large mincer stood secured to its edge; the haggis's raw meat leftovers deep its open mouth. With the benefit of surprise, she was able to separate Lennox's right hand from the cabbage and, with a strength not fully used for five long years, pull her towards the contraption. She plunged that clenched, pale fist into the iron throat.

The scream didn't last long. Catriona had always been good at kicking.

"Remember that stone I had to eat? She snarled. "The lies you told me? My turn now, so tell me what you know about James Baird's letter, or I'll mince your hand for the haggis and you'll be back to the Poor House quicker than you can say Janet Margaret Lennox, witch..."

Those ugly, black eyes were wet from weeping, due most likely to the peeled onions, and for someone of her size and build, Lennox seemed weakened. To have lost the fight already. But not quite. "The dog's gone," she said. "So's the boot it dug up. Yer mother's."

Boot?

Catriona let go of her. Picked up the tray with suddenly numb fingers and backed towards the door. "And as for Master Baird," her enemy continued in a gloating tone. "He wants Constable Coyle to detain us, because, accordin' to him, since we've both been here, he's nae slept a wink at night."

No...

"But a little bird's just told me he's put his needle into you. And why write in your notebook that I have 'odd habits?'"

215

Funny to watch how Lennox changed colour.

"Where is it?"

"What's it worth?"

The cook frowned. "Nothin'. All fairy tales."

"Liar. And how about that coward Falcon Steer coward you fancy? Has he been at you, too?"

"Why wud that bother ye?"

"It doesn't."

"Now who's lyin'? Because ye know our friend is makin' hisself far more useful on the loose than behind bars. He's heard how yer father ogled other women before his ane wifie were even cold."

***

20.

In which important matters are addressed...

That had stung; given the minx something to think about. As for Janet, herself, it wasn't her imagination that James Baird was ignoring her, and it came as no surprise. He wasn't going to listen to anything she might say. Despite his recent confidences, his greater friendliness, that letter had claimed she was part of the problem. The hardest statement to swallow.

Since his father's arrival, tensions had grown, even though James had ridden for ten miles over ice to find a cart and shafts, and probably saved the architect's life. While James tried to defend himself, the older man attacked. Not in a noisome way, more like the drip-drip-drip of rainfall from the full gutter above her window.

While bringing more logs to the dining room, Janet had also heard snatches of arguments about replacing the handyman and re-filling the ice house. She'd strained every muscle to listen in case her name was mentioned. In case McPhee had betrayed her over the revealing notebook.

She hoped dinner would be enlivened by tales of the architect's travels in the Crimea, or the princes he'd worked with. Anything to lighten the atmosphere. As she checked the gravy for unwanted lumps, Janet felt the folded sheet of blotting paper rub against her skin inside her drawers. During her tussle with the maid, it had slipped between her legs, and when her hand had been thrust into the mincer, her bladder had leaked enough to blur some of the words. *Misses was* now *Miss...*

She slipped upstairs for a clean pair of drawers and return the paper to its former place, wondering when she should start packing and leave. She could see the way things were going, with McPhee ingratiating herself with the architect in readiness for the Constable Coyle's questioning. As for herself, 'The Weasel' could follow her to the ends of the earth and never find her.

She checked the spy-hole. Still blocked. Glad now that she'd thrown out the ice. Glad too, that if she needed him, Falcon Steer was out there somewhere in that white, silent world.

Before she went downstairs, Janet let her hand rest against her mother's room door and immediately felt its cold wood invade her skin. She made a promise to see her buried properly before she left Argyll for good, and hoped her soul and that of her dead grandson - even though he'd not been baptised - had already united in Heaven. She also promised herself never again to set eyes on that linen room door.

*

"Miss Lennox?" The new keeper of the keys called up, sounding as fresh as a spring morning. "I've set the table. Is it to be red wine or white, or both?"

Janet took her time. Nothing now to lose. Let McPhee have it all. At least if she left with her savings, she could pay the Reverend McKinnon for a headstone and find herself a bed on the way to Glasgow. 'Wee frein' or no 'wee frein,' she'd be on her way south.

"Both."

As she reached the last few steps towards the hall, that sickly-sweet voice tinkled away as she did all the right things in the right order. Tasks she - Janet - had done without fuss for almost three years. But she'd never forget that singer's face when the words 'boot' and 'dog' had come out. White as a sheet wasn't the half of it. But not enough fear to make her hand back the notebook. So how much fear could the girl from Cranranich take?

Boxing Day morning would come soon enough, and in the meantime, Janet urged herself to follow Linnet's advice more closely than ever. The friend who'd been strangely silent of late…

Guard yer tongue…

*

The maid had obviously found time to arrange her wheat-coloured curls so that they not only peeped sweetly beneath the edge of her cap, but also around both her shell-like ears. They bobbed up and down as she delivered the haggis on its silver platter to the table in the dining room,

Janet saw how Donald Baird's pale eyes followed her every move, and how his son at the opposite end, facing away from the drawn curtains, frowned at his plate, saying nothing. As far as she knew, his mother's portrait hadn't been spoken of again.

"I stepped outside a moment ago," said the architect to no-one in particular. "And I believe a thaw's on the way."

"About time too, sir." Catriona passed him a large silver-plated knife for him to slice the meaty mound himself. "I've never been so cold as when I was out on that shore waiting for your boat…"

At this, James Baird looked up.

"Why not tell my father how you searched for Mr Bogle too? Cleaned the 'necessaries' and had to burn the cocks?"

The girl turned white for the second time that evening.

"I thought, Master Baird, we weren't to mention that."

The architect stopped, mid-slice. A startled expression on his face.

"My cocks? My special black beauties? And what do you mean by 'burn,' son?"

"They'd met a most terrible end, sir." Janet stepped in, uncorking the bottle of red wine from somewhere in France called Bordeaux and setting it next to him. "Only yesterday it were. And I ken who's responsible 'cept I wudnae want to spoil yer Christmas…"

"No wonder I couldn't hear them just now."

Three pairs of eyes were on her as she focussed on the bottle's label depicting a vineyard stretching away towards a sunset horizon…

Donald Baird eased himself from his chair, passed behind his son and parted the curtains.

"If you know, Miss Lennox. You must say."

"In private, sir. If tha's alright with ye. I have me safety to consider…"

"That's a very curious remark to make. I hope you can substantiate it."

"I can sir."

"It's either that tramp or her who's to blame," McPhee said suddenly, tapping the side of her head with her forefinger, suggesting madness. "Trying to cause trouble here."

"That's enough!" The father turned to his son, who still pecked at his food without interest. "Once dinner's over, we'll go and take a look."

After that, the meal proceeded in silence, save for the click of cutlery against porcelain plates and strange pop-poppings from the hazel logs in the grate. Like icebergs in an Arctic sea, Janet and the other girl passed each other back and fore to the kitchen. Neither the red cabbage nor any wine, barely touched.

It was only during 'dessert,' as the architect called it, that any conversation resumed. "Describe this dog you found, Miss Lennox, and how do you think he was able to pick a lock and leave the house of his own accord?" A thin, greyish hand mapped by fine purple veins, gestured towards the other girl. "Miss McPhee told me all about it."

"Sir," began Janet, with difficulty "He were taken because he'd dug somethin' up, which again, I can't say. I hid it amongst the swedes in the Store for safe-keepin', now 'tis gone. And the lock, sir, had been picked from the *outside*."

McPhee bristled, like a cat spying its prey.

"She should know all about locks, sir. She picked mine too. And made a hole in her wall to watch me do private things." She glanced around for effect. "I won't mention them here, but I soon blocked it up."

Donald Baird attacked his meringue and it crumbled into the pool of cream turned purple by last July's blueberries. "I'd like a *description* of this dog, Miss Lennox."

"Black all over, with a big nose and amber eyes, sir, but with pain in them. A feathery kind of tail - what were left of it. Like I said, he'd bin badly injured. Beaten most likely…"

"Could he be Rabbie, I wonder?" Suggested James Baird, looking at her. "Tam was the brown one…"

"Too much of a coincidence. Surely, sir?" said McPhee.

Just then, a length of holly slipped from behind a small oil painting near the room's far corner, It showed two Gordon setters with ducks in their mouths. Their legs deep in loch water. Janet retrieved the holly, her mind going too fast. She pricked her thumb and drew blood.

"Sir, he were the one on the left. I'd swear it."

"Plenty of that breed in this part of the world, sir." McPhee prodded the fire that she'd not been bothered to lay. "My grandfather kept one for years…"

James Baird wasn't listening. He pushed back his chair, drained his wine glass and strode over to his father.

"We could go and look for him, Papa. He knows your special whistle. He'd come to you like a shot."

The architect stayed in his seat, as if even being called Papa wasn't enough to stir his weary body.

"Five years is a long time, especially in the wilds here. If traps didn't get the both of them, there'd have been wolves or bullets."

Janet shivered at the thought.

"Perhaps if I'd not returned to work so soon after the mystery, they might still be with us," mused the architect. "Dogs do seem to have a sixth sense."

His son's face grew even redder as if matching his impatience.

"If it *is* Rabbie, and what Miss Lennox says is true, he may have been trying to find my mother and Tam. After all, they were full brothers from the same litter."

"It *is* him, sir." Janet insisted. "Believe me."

"Then," said Donald Baird, "you must tell us what this dog dug up and where."

The maid straightened. Stayed motionless as his son began to shout.

"Later, Papa. Please! If the ice is thawing like you say, we may have a chance to discover something useful. I can show you the cocks' coop as well."

His father sighed as he left his chair. Eyes more sunken now. But why should she care? Janet asked herself. She only had to survive till Boxing Day morning, and that meant not being left alone with the golden-haired maid still holding the glowing poker. Robbie, however was a different matter. If still around, she'd be taking him with her...

*

Despite a rising panic, Janet led father and son the way down the unlit passage towards the coats and cloaks, aware of the persistent maid bringing up the rear.

"Sirs," she kept walking. "I must come with you both. Please."

"Miss McPhee may not appreciate being left on her own," said the older man, briefly turning round. "I've heard about the Clearance in Kilforgan. And what with the cocks and your mother, best you do as I say."

So, her mother came last...

"Please, sir."

"Men's work it us." His son collected a lamp from the Store. "You two get that table cleared and have a hot toddy ready for us when we get back."

"There's nae spare key to the Store's outer door, sir." Janet let them pass her, tempted to cling on to his cold cloak.

"I'll try and find one. Meanwhile, shoot the bolts and put something heavy by it till the morning."

And then, like a pair of ghosts they were gone. The door's slam like a stab to her pumping heart. She was alone in Ardnasaig House with her mortal enemy, whose shadow was growing like a thunder cloud on the passageway wall behind her.

***

21

Where troubles multiply and promises are forgotten...

"I must come with you, please!" Catriona mimicked that hated voice over and over as she obediently returned to the dining room making sure that for the next few moments at least, she stayed busy at the furthest end of the table.

While she stacked up James Baird's half-finished plates and laid them on a gold-plated trolley, she tried to imagine the conversation going on by the cocks' coop. Whether as a result, she'd have to undergo more awkward questions, with Lennox harping on about that damned boot. And damned it was, with its distinctive smooth sole and little heel. She wished now she'd buried it properly along with those other items, further away from the house. Out of harm's way...

With her index finger, she scooped up a little left-over cream and licked it too hard, catching her front teeth on skin. Would Black Eyes' weaken and describe in detail what she'd alleged that black dog had dug up? And while brushing stray crumbs into a sliver tray, Catriona frantically tried guessing where not only that boot was now, but its partner.

*

Nine o'clock, with the table cleared, but not her troubled mind. The clever mincer plan had failed. But something else might be more effective, and she resolved there and then to test her adversary into confessing everything she knew. Lennox had taken the trolley into the scullery and judging by the noise of her footsteps on stone, was on her way back.

"Be showing him yer drawers next." Came that same voice from the other side of the door. "And the rest of ye. I can't tell yer game. And dinnae think ye'll get away with it neither." Lennox moved towards the marble fireplace and picked up the huge, mesh guard to position it in front of the flames.

"*You* can talk while his son's wean feeds off you."

But Lennox surprised her. "What made ye think I meant Mr Baird?"

Catriona felt that familiar boiling rush of blood to her head. She ran at the target, arms outstretched until her outspread hands connected with that hideous body. She pushed her as if she was a logger pushing his prize downhill, so that a bony shoulder cracked against the hard, veined stone. Lennox then toppled backwards, her backside landing on the grate's black iron prongs. She let out a scream that could surely be heard for miles away.

"Shut your din! Save it to save yourself."

And every time Lennox tried to rise, Catriona kicked her down until her cap fell off her head and blue smoke bloomed from the hearth, consuming her skirt.

"I want answers from you before the men come back. Or else…"

"Yer wasting yer time." Discoloured teeth on full show. Hair a straggling mess.

"This boot you said the dog found. Describe it."

"Ye'll find out soon enough."

"You're going to say it's mine?"

"Why nae? Ye'd ne'er save me skin."

"Where is it?"

"Why shud a stupid boot matter so much?"

Catriona watched Lennox hit her skirt with both bare, sooty hands, spreading the smoke into the room. Making her own eyes water.

"What else did Steer say about my father?"

"I said, ye'll find out soon enough."

"Ha." Yet inside, that boiling rage threatened to spill over again. Catriona picked up the poker. Held it close to that black, unkempt head. Watched the plain mouth shaped by fear, start to move.

"I were told ye'd uttered the most vile curse at Mr Baird when he and Constable Wildman went to yer hovel."

"Who said?"

"The Constable hisself."

"He's long dead. And the dead can't speak."

"Well, I'm sure yer hoping our employer won't be reminded of it." Lennox's eyes fixed on the poker. "If yer so bent on killin' me, get it over with quick."

"*I* don't need to kill you. I've your notebook. Remember? And was that a lie or the truth about Master Baird's letter I had to deliver?"

Lennox rolled her ungainly body away from the logs, reached up inside her ruined skirt and into her drawers.

"Give me the notebook back, and ye'll have this."

Catriona was tempted. She smiled.

"After you."

"Much good may it do ye."

Lennox passed her the piss-stained blotting paper and, holding it away from her nose, Catriona angled it in front of the mirror over the mantelpiece where her hand seemed to turn numb. "And ye were happy to deliver that treachery?" added Lennox. "To cause the most harm? I wudnae have. I'd have taken a look, aye. But then, traitors always do as they're told. Why they ne'er leave the gutter. Why ye'll always be a dreg."

She tried to haul herself from the hearth and Catriona stared, as if the bullying, monstrous Lennox, no longer human, was some dangerous creature in a trap. Yet so very vulnerable. That James Baird had threatened her with her job, was her secret.
"Now, where's me notebook?" glowered the dead housekeeper's daughter, still struggling.

"Why the fuss? All lies and fairy tales, you said."

With a huge effort and clinging to the slippery marble, Lennox managed to stand upright, tear off her smouldering skirt and add it to the fire. "Ye shud know about them."

"I do, since I was a child. So, does 'unholy sin together' mean anything? I heard you say that in your sleep."

Without another word, Lennox then turned off all the lamps one by one and, trailing acrid smoke behind her like a living phantom, left the room.

Catriona set down the poker. It had felt good in her hand and she resolved to take it to bed with her, just in case.

*

She re-read the blotting paper message for the third time before consigning it to the reviving fire. Not for the housemaid's sake, but her own. If Constable Coyle were to see it, Black Eyes would be in the same sinking boat. However, those carefully chosen keepsakes of hers might just keep herself afloat, and of course, the architect who seemed to be showing her - a mere maid - considerable interest. If Lennox was foolish enough to open her mouth against her, she, Catriona Mairi McPhee would deny everything, and doubtless be believed.

With lamps re-lit, the dishes washed and dried, she thought ahead to the men's return. Time therefore, to bring the whisky glasses from the cabinet, then the whisky bottle itself, showing a noble white stag on its label. When she was ten years' old, her father had gone out at dead of night to the high hills beyond Lord Melhuish's boundary, and shot such a one. She'd glimpsed him from her bed separating that glowing skin from the red flesh beneath. Cutting what remained into pieces for the pot. But he of all people should have remembered that to cull such a revered beast brings a terrible curse on the one responsible, and their next of kin.

Next of kin...

Stupid man, and that was one of many reasons why he mustn't come to Ardnasaig House in any shape or form.

She turned the bottle round to avoid seeing that image again. And then remembered ice. Both the Baird men liked three blocks apiece, and to this end, Catriona trekked to the Store and shone her candle to where she knew the bucket lay.

It was empty.

No ice, no straw, no nothing. Lennox had again wrong-footed her. She hurled the empty bucket against the Store's stone wall and called again for the powerful yet elusive Dame of Nonach to do her worst to the housemaid. Why not a haemorrhage like the three her mother had endured at Footer's Cottage, where her blood turned the bothy into an abattoir? Why not pain so severe it would cause her heart to stop beating?

And just then, another of her father's warnings shattered her memories like a hunter's shot. "If ye curse too much on another, Catriona McPhee, it'll find its way back home."

*

Mr Baird was right. Christmas Day would see the ice that had encased Ardnasaig and its land like a suit of armour, melt as quickly as it had come. That would be too late. She must act now.

With a vengeful Lennox still around, it would be foolish to light a taper to take with her. Instead, she'd trust her memory to guide her to the chosen spot. As a bairn, she'd often taken things up Footer's Hill to bury along with all the other remains said to inhabit its rocky, heather-strewn slopes. Nothing of any real use, but significant in other ways. A short length of coarse twine, a bottle top and so on, until the best treasure had come her way. That lustrous ring she'd come across whilst playing 'house' in the bracken. Those six torn strips of peach-pink silk, some edged by cream lace, found on other travels.

Hurry...

The smell from the hanging venison was beginning to ripen and turn her already delicate stomach. She brushed past its dead weight, feeling her way like a blind mole towards the outer door. In her haste, she'd forgotten it was locked. Panicking, she ran back along the dark, labyrinthine corridors, through that windowless cave of a study that led into the marginally lighter hall at the front of the house, with its formidable parade of trophy stags' heads jutting from the walls. She'd never get used to their dominating presence, however many times she walked beneath them.

All at once, a dense chill curled around her body, slowing her progress. The thaw might be happening outside, but not here. She stopped to unbolt the front door and glanced back to check Lennox wasn't lurking with a knife.

Instead of Lennox, it was the last stag in the row who seemed to be gazing down at her in such a lifelike way that the more she stared back, the more that doleful expression began to change. Its brown glass eyes lost their dense colour, slowly changing to blue. Yes, the same persistent bright blue eyes she'd already encountered.

She let out a cry.

"Leave me alone, do you hear? Go back to Hell where you belong."

*

The front door's main bolt was too heavy and unyielding even though she tugged and tugged on it, desperate now to accomplish her mission before the Bairds' return. How she wished Mr Bogle was still there. The kindly old man she preferred to remember.

231

Then, suddenly, Catriona sniffed the remains of smoke, growing stronger. From where, she wasn't sure.

"Please let me help ye, Miss McPhee. I can see yer in a rush…" Said a hoarse but nevertheless sickly female voice as Lennox's arm reached past her for the bolt. With one movement accompanied by a sharp, grating sound, she pulled it aside to let in the night. Then a fist in the small of her back, sent her tumbling out on to the iron boot scraper screwed into the top step. She screamed as her knuckles took her weight. Smelt her own blood, not that of her enemy who was shouting at her.

"And if ye want more ice for the whiskies, Miss McPhee, ye'd better get some in afore the melt."

*

Ice for the evening's drams was the last thing on Catriona's mind. Shaken, disorientated and nursing her stinging, grazed knuckles, she crept round the front of Ardnasaig House, past the dining room and living room windows until she reached the rear courtyard. Her slippers, although leather, gave little protection against the wintry ground. From there, as if by one of those miracles Mairi McPhee had often preached about, she remembered where she should go.

A new smell made her pause and look down to where her feet stood on the softening ice. She bent lower and soon realised that not so long ago, someone had been sick. If this was Lennox's foul waste, then the bitch could still be pregnant…

Moving on, she soon found the familiar stone she'd used as the first marker. The second, a long-abandoned mounting block whose mossy growth showed darkly from its white disguise. Six more steps up the slope and into the elm grove where cushat doves perched high on the dripping branches, gave out their gentle songs. Where, in the silence once they had flown, she was sure other unquiet souls lingered, waiting to torment her.

*

The watery ice on the ground was kind to her damaged skin as Catriona cleared it away, tempted to retrieve a few pieces for the Bairds' drinks. But not now. Something or someone had been here first. The exposed soil was a mess of excavation, and of the three little refuges so carefully dug for her other treasures, none remained.

Mercy...

It was impossible to tell whether or not a human being or that damned, half-dead dog had been at work, but whoever the culprit was - and if Lennox's yarn about her dug-up boot was to be believed - then this had been just the start.

She stood up, and while shaking wet dirt from her skirt, detected men's voices coming closer through the elm grove. The Bairds were returning, and what they were saying, made her hold her breath. They'd come across an old man's body, stabbed twice over, lying in the forest just up from the track linking Cranranich with Kilforgan. He'd been part of the Clearance, collecting cones for fuel, but what was a real puzzle to them both was why his axe had still lain embedded in a the nearest tree trunk.

***

22.

In which the yellowhammer sweetly sings...

Janet had been too hurt in more ways than one to follow McPhee on her travels, but while on the stairs seeking her bed, she'd heard the maid and father and son in brief conversation upon their return. Judging by the hall clock's chimes, the girl had only been outside for fifteen minutes. Fifteen minutes for what? Janet wondered, before barricading herself into her unlockable room.

Not only the constant slide of ice off the roof above her room kept her awake all night and into Christmas Day, but also the pain of scorched skin on her backside and left thigh, where her thinner-than-usual skirt put together in the Poor House, had given precious little protection from the fire she herself had laid. Its smoke too, had thickened her breath, made her throat sore.

While she'd tossed and turned on her unforgiving mattress, that same nightmare had come to visit her as it had since she'd been a wee bairn. Of feeling a wind-fanned fire lick her bare feet, then her legs and body until her mouth filled with hot ash.

And now Christmas Day was dawning, with her bleed still not come despite falling into the hearth, and her mother still eyeless, unburied. A day when it mattered not a dead trout's tail what she did or did not do. With the architect's blessing, her younger, less experienced enemy in the next room held the house keys. Let her keep them. Play at being housekeeper. She, Janet, would soon have better things to do, like packing her belongings and planning her escape. There'd be no more worry about being followed, nor fear of attack. Never again would the scheming liar from Footer's Hill have the chance to laugh in her face. And there was still the possibility, thought Janet, rubbing the last of her seaweed cream on to her sore places and pulling down one of her mother's warmer old skirts over her legs, she might even meet Falcon again. The one person who'd offered her some small hope. Only to be turned down.

*

Margaret Lennox's unoccupied room still smelt of death, but this wasn't going to take long. Driven by the anxiety that at any moment, McPhee might barge her way in and realise what she was doing, Janet got busy. She crammed both remaining glass bottle souvenirs from Crystal Palace, clean underwear, two starched aprons and caps as well as one best skirt and a dark green cloak she'd knitted at the Poor House, into a clean sack from the Store. She dared not stop for anything else, apart from a few housekeeping notes which McPhee would never bother with. It almost broke her heart to leave the pillow that had borne her mother's head to the last. The thick, well-used Holy Bible and a collection of dried flowers picked from near her small, summer herb garden. Perhaps she might return for those later.

Back in her own quarters, she heard McPhee splashing water into her bowl. Even without the spy hole, she knew that after this would come the preening, especially now that the owner of Ardnasaig House was paying her so much attention.

Then she remembered her money. At the end of each week, she'd sewn it into the back of her pillowcase Almost twenty pounds in coins, with fifteen already earmarked as a reward for finding her mother's violator. Just before leaving, she'd unpick her handiwork and transfer the hoard to her drawers. Surely the safest place, should she meet the predicted mob from Kilforgan?

*

The favoured maid was now singing at the top of her voice. She sounded happy, without a care in the world, but anyone could put on an act. Janet would never forget the shock on her face when she'd spoken of that thin-skinned, smooth-soled black boot.

"Sing on, ye little Dei'l," she whispered, leaving her room. "Sing on…"

"'Tis nae for the land of my sires to give birth

Unto bosoms that shrink when their trial is nigh:

Away! We will bear over ocean and earth

A name and a spirit that will ne'er die.

My course to the winds, to the stars I resign…"

But why had that second line make Janet stand so still, then lodge in her mind as she made her way downstairs, leaving her packed bag behind?

*

Despite the new fire and a low sun licking the ice from those treetops around the loch and turning the water into a mess of black and white, breakfast was a chilly affair. The opposite to last year when, after the service at Kilforgan kirk, Dauvit Hendry together with Roberta Masters and Helen Fergusson had arrived at Ardnasaig House to mulled wine and a selection of home-baked cheese tartlets. Even Mr Bogle's face had worn a smile, if not for her.

Despite being only the fifth Christmas without Mrs Baird, the architect had let Mr Hendry play his pipes while the two women glided through their Strathspey steps and sung in voices that to Janet, sounded more like those of trapped hares. Only James Baird had seemed lost in his own gloomy thoughts.

Now, while Janet ladled porridge into both of the Bairds' bowls, neither seemed to notice how her movements weren't as quick as usual. And would they have cared anyway? James Baird, dishevelled and crumpled, in the same clothes he'd worn for a week, ate without speaking then, to her surprise, got up and followed her out when she went to fetch a portion of venison from the Store. So, the traitor still had nothing to say. But she did.

Again, guard yer tongue...

But why should she? What did plain speaking matter now?

The corridor grew colder, darker and he was catching up, his breath coming quickly, his sweaty smell meeting her nose.

"Sir," she ventured, seizing the opportunity. "Did ye find the black dog last night? Ye ne'er said."

His body pushed close to hers, in too much of a hurry to reply.

"And the cocks' coop, sir? Were Mr Baird upset?" She pressed herself against the wall to let him go by, observing how his stocky frame soon became part of the shadowy gloom ahead. She heard him snatch his coat from the hook and curse for having to pull at it twice.

"I understand why ye cannae speak to me," she called after him. "But I'm nae the fool ye think. I ken what ye wrote for Constable Coyle to see. That ye wanted me and McPhee detained. But," she lowered her voice. "E'en if I carry yer wean?"

Suddenly, the thunder of running boots. The smell of him again as he ran back towards her. His damp coat against her clean Christmas Day clothes. Although his cold hands were holding her arms tight, those odd-coloured eyes burned like the hazel log flames that had devoured her skirt.

"I'm sorry, Miss Lennox. Not my idea. Understand?"

"Then whose?" She persisted.

"Have you ever been bribed? I think not."

Bribed? Another new word...

He loosened his grip. Began to whisper.

"My father's still recovering from his long journey. How can I tell him? I've never been able to confide in the man. Surely you could see how things were when we both hired you and your mother?"

Janet nodded, puzzled, also embarrassed.

"What does bribed mean, sir?"

A pause, in which the huge house seemed to be closing in on her.

"That Dunblane fellow offered me five hundred pounds, but only if..."

"Falcon Steer?"

The corridor felt more like the coffin constraining her mother.

He nodded.

"On condition I made that request to Constable Coyle. He's convinced you and Miss McPhee are witches. What happened to the cocks and your mother confirmed it. He says he and his wife have suffered too much from – quote – 'these Devils' ways.' He plans to cleanse our lands of them because he believes their only child – a wee girl - died from a vicious hex."

Janet gulped. This couldn't be true. Her ears were deceiving her.

"So why come all this way?" she demanded. "To here? Besides, he's a beggar."

"He never said. That's the truth."

She thought of happy, little Morag and her daisy chain, but that sunlit scene brought fresh fear.

"Sir, 'tis nae me place to ask, but can't *ye* stop any questionin'? Clear me name? I've twenty pounds saved. Ye cud have that if that wud help."

James shook his uncombed head, bringing a shiver that made her teeth judder together. "I may seem to be wealthy, but look at this…"

He let go of her arms to turn both his breeches' pockets inside out. Empty, save for a few spent rifle cartridges, strands of dried grass and his set of house keys. Then, from a coat pocket, he withdrew a battered, leather purse and opened it. She straightaway recognised that same blue, folded letter from Helen Fergusson that he'd shown her, squashed up against just three pound notes. It was pitiful.

"I've more pennies than ye," she observed. "Nae wonder five hundred pounds were temptin.' And is that why ye ride to Inverary once a week? To yer bank?"

"Not *my* bank. His. And everything must be signed for by a Mr Andrew Stephenson there. Father's lawyer and executor, in case he has a fatal accident on his travels and doesn't come back. Can't you see, it's as if I don't exist? Before my mother left, things were quite different. She'd bought me my first pony and my cob. Made sure I had a regular allowance until I found my feet and decided what I wanted to do with my life. Now that allowance has stopped, I must account for every damned farthing. Why you and Mrs Lennox had to hand over all receipts from our deliveries, however small. Why your wages never went up and why my friends have stopped coming. Why my old rifle's on its last legs..."

Janet's sickness rose in her throat. She swallowed, but it made no difference until in her mind's eye came a pinprick of hope.

"What if yer message never arrived in Kilforgan?"

His blue and brown gaze fixed on her with an expression she couldn't read.

"Although Miss McPhee lied that it had, in the end that didn't matter."

"Why, sir?"

His voice came no more than a whisper. "Coyle and the minister..."

"Coyle and the minister what?"

A pause in which Janet could hear her heart. He was speaking again, sounding quite different in a way she couldn't describe.

"I'm sorry, Janet. I really am. Whatever I say or do, money or no money, you're looking at a dead man. Steer's mad and dangerous. Remember that if nothing else."

Janet?

He'd never called her that before.

*

Dramatics. That's what her mother would have said. What feeble men do when life doesn't go their way. That 'sorry' word wasn't for her or McPhee, but himself. And, if he was to be believed, she and the maid were in the greatest peril.

Janet listened to the diminishing clamour of his boots on stone as he left the Store. Feeling sick again, she pressed some old rag to her mouth, willing the bile to stay down. Yet, the longer the utter silence lingered in his wake, the more she believed his story to be a clever lie. The coward was passing the blame for his own deceits on to Falcon Steer, an innocent man. Someone he barely knew who, apart from that poor dog, had been the only one offering her another glimmer of hope. Also justice. Something her mother had believed in to her last breath. Despite their treatment at Lismore and Cranranich's Poor House.

If James Baird *had* asked the Constable to detain her and the maid about recent events, surely there was the process of law? People couldn't just be held for questioning on whims and rumours. Or could they? And why mention the Constable and minister in that way?

Janet began her walk back to the kitchen with a heavy heart, realising now that McPhee's attentions to the architect were so obviously to keep herself in his good books and out of trouble. But the big question was, how much, if anything, did *he* know?

"Feeling better, are we?" Came the last voice she wanted to hear. "Well, you certainly don't look it. Telling him you'd a wean on the way, eh? No, you wouldn't do a thing like that with him and risk losing your precious little job."

"'Tis bigger than yours."

"Not for long."

"Wash yer mouth out with vinegar and keep it away from me."

At this, the maid's gloved hand dug in her apron pocket, pulled out Margaret Lennox's bunch of keys together with a piece of paper bearing the architect's fancy writing, and dangled them close to Janet's head.

"You can't bear me to have these, can you?" She gloated. "Well, here's something else for your big, red ears. My wages are going up as from tomorrow and I'm being kept on here for as long as I like. According to this letter, every Saturday morning I'll be given two whole guineas."

Janet choked back her indignation. Then remembered her plan. "What about Saturday with Constable Coyle?"

Lennox cocked her head. Smiled.

"Mr Baird's agreed I don't have to go. That he'll vouch for my - and these are his words - 'impeccable behaviour and steadfast devotion to duty.' Oh, and he asked why I was wearing these gloves, so I showed him my grazed knuckles and said you'd pushed me on to the top step outside. He'll be speaking with you later."

Janet elbowed her way past the girl and into the kitchen where, with her mind out of control, she shovelled more coal beneath the already hot oven. With water in place under her mother's Christmas pudding, the venison to go in at ten o'clock, and the vegetables all peeled, she would take the initiative.

*

She found Donald Baird in the strange, tomb-like study. A room lined with mysterious, leather-bound books she'd never felt tempted to open. Lamplight and the fire - smaller than those in the main rooms - lent his face such an alarming colour that she almost changed her mind.

"You wanted to see me, sir," she began. "As lunch is under control."

"It seems, Miss Lennox, you are not."

He looked up from the papers on his lap and set them aside on a nearby occasional table. "Miss McPhee's hands are in a dreadful state and she tells me her nerves are more frayed than an old mooring rope. Which is why, when she mentioned Constable Coyle's plan to question her next Saturday, I felt duty bound to step in."

If two horns had sprouted either side of his head, Janet wouldn't have been surprised. Now was the time was right to divide and rule. Another of her dead mother's sayings.

"Sir, yer son had arranged that," she retorted, without mentioning the manipulative liar from Dunblane. "I've seen written proof. He's bin fearful o' her from the first day she stepped through yer front door on those pretty little feet in those smooth-soled boots. One of which that dog dug up. And," she took as deep a breath as her smoke-filled lungs would allow. "She put a Hellish curse on ye that second time ye called at Footer's Cottage after Mrs Baird had vanished. Do ye nae remember it, sir?"

"Who says all this?"

"Constable Wildman. The one before Constable Coyle. He told his sister. Said he'd ne'er forget it as long as he lived. Which weren't for long…"

Those pale, hooded eyes looked at her, unblinking. "Helen Fergusson is not only James's godmother, but also a special friend to my wife. I can only imagine how deeply distressed she'd be by your pernicious gossip."

"But 'tis the truth, sir. She had Mr Hendry deliver a letter about it yesterday afternoon when he brought news of yer trap turnin' over."

"So, where is it?"

"I have nae idea. Sir," she lied. Then took another risk. "Sir, 'tis nae me place, but yer son complains he's short o' money. If he only had some of his ane, say five hundred…"

To save my life…

The architect blinked. Twice.

"Five hundred? Have you any idea how much that is?"

"Yes sir. And it might just stop him getting into trouble."

Without replying, the architect whose accomplishments included at least four famous and sumptuous palaces near the Black Sea, left his armchair and went over to one of the many shelves. As he pulled out three thick tomes and placed them by his feet, the oil lamp's unsteady light played on his balding head, his green, quilted smoking jacket that reminded her of the moss that smothers every stone. Every fallen tree.

Janet watched him, open-mouthed, forgetting her other intended words as his right hand reached into the dark recess the books had left, to extract a cloth-covered bundle. "Ah. Now we have it." He unravelled this covering as he might a priceless relic, and she immediately recognised it as being her used drawers hiding a small, black leather-bound book. Her missing notebook which had contained a confession from Calum to their mother.

She made a move to go.

"I'd rather you didn't, Miss Lennox. Because there's this as well."

The one candle lit the last of her mother's miniature glass bottles, and although its baby's head cork was in place, what the added light revealed was so unexpectedly shocking that blood deserted her own head too quickly. And when he clicked his fingers for the shadow waiting beyond the door to enter, she barely heard him.

✳✳✳

23.

In which rotten apples are thrown from the basket...

It soon became clear that the Bairds' discovery of the elderly murder victim in Draighnish Forest and their trek to the Police House in Kilforgan to report it, wasn't the only factor bringing this special visitor back to Ardnasaig House on such a festive day.

While Catriona had hurried to relieve father and son of their soaking caps and capes just before midnight, she'd overheard enough of the one-sided exchange to wipe her smile of greeting from her face. How for the future well being of Ardnasaig House, drastic measures were necessary by January 5th if not before. These included the appointment of a new handyman, possibly Iain McPhee. The swift burial of the dead housekeeper to avoid a local scandal, and the questioning of her daughter in advance of the originally planned date.

James Baird however, had seemed unhappy. Why should Miss Lennox be the only one to be grilled by Constable Coyle and his Superintendent? he'd argued. Both had been at Ardnasaig House during Margaret Lennox's mutilation and that of the cocks. Both should go forward.

"You'll regret it, father." He'd said finally, before walking off.

"And you, son, had better respect my decisions."

"Forgive me interfering, sir," Catriona had interposed, brushing rain water from the architect's shoulders. "But you're

246

right. It's Miss Lennox who's made life unbearable here. Not me. I was brought up to believe in the Bible and our Lord's message of peace and love. I'm just sorry you've had to travel so far, back to all this..."

*

Despite the lack of any Christmas presents and melting roof ice blurring her dining room view of Constable Coyle's black horse and a brown carriage waiting at the top of the carriageway, Catriona couldn't help but feel a warm glow at how things had turned out.

With gloves still in place on her hands, as the architect had instructed her, she now hid behind the study door, while an irritable Constable Seumas Coyle ordered Lennox to gather up a few essential items for herself.

"After I've questioned ye," he added, "ye'll be delivered back here by the time darkness falls."

"On what grounds are ye taking me? And where's Master Baird?"

"Always too many questions, Miss Lennox." Coyle replied, unmoved. "Yer forgetting yer place."

"Why nae the 28th?"

"There've been further developments."

Catriona glanced behind herself in case the son was on his way. With hindsight, she'd never been sure about him since her first day there. Odd he wasn't present now. Odd too how her long-ago dream had shifted from him to another, who barely an hour since, had reached out to touch her arm as she'd passed by to collect her other treasures from their linen room hiding place. As for those so painstakingly buried, there'd be no relaxing until she knew where they'd gone.

Lennox was shouting. A hard, grating sound. She still smelt of smoke and of her 'down below' no matter how much soap she'd used. "Ye've no right, sir," she spat. "It's Christmas Day, and there's the dinner to get. And," she glanced in the direction of the door. "What about McPhee?"

"*Miss* McPhee," corrected the architect. There are ways to address people in my house. And as for dinner, thank you for your concern, but I assure you, we won't starve."

Catriona smiled again as that crow-call voice answered back. "Where did me mother's eyes in that bottle come from? And me notebook and drawers? That letter...?"

"Yer *brother's* letter," Coyle said as if he'd just scored a point. "Let's be straight about that."

"The eyes?" She persisted.

Coyle looked at Donald Baird for support, and wasn't disappointed.

"That's for Constable Coyle to investigate. And may I remind you, *I'm* in charge here. When I took you and your unfortunate mother in from the Poor House, despite a worrying reference from Lord and Lady Bruce in Lismore, you both assured me there'd be no animosity between you and my other employees. And no secrets."

"What secrets, sir?" Those white cheeks burned a dull red.

The architect paused as if to choose his words with care. "Improper relations between you and my son, for a start."

The explosion never came. Instead, a tense silence in which Donald Baird gestured for Catriona to show her face.

Lennox glared at her without speaking. She didn't need to. Catriona averted her eyes and saw the once healthy fire had died. How the loch beyond the window reflected cold, bright light on to everything and everyone. Black Eyes especially, who'd never looked so dangerous.

"Miss McPhee will accompany you upstairs to collect your essentials," the architect snapped. "Five minutes should suffice." He snatched at a small bell she'd never heard his son use, and shook it so fiercely, she jumped at the unfamiliar din. Then she spotted the carriage horse outside striking his front hoof on the ground, as if keen to be off. But now wasn't the time to offer to restrain him. She had a job to do. One she was dreading.

*

Constable Coyle picked up his briefcase and his black top hat. "There's also the matter of the murdered man that Mr Baird and his son stumbled upon above Kilforgan last night..." He glanced around the room. "Incidentally, where *is* Master Baird, sir?"

"Just gone out," said Lennox. "He seemed quite upset about something."

"Typical. Did he say why?" Donald Baird eyed her.

"No sir."

"And his rifle?"

"In the Store, sir. Usual place."

"Back to what I was saying." Coyle slid his thumb and finger along his moustache. Thinning it, twisting up the ends. "The poor fellow ye both came across had been dead at least a day, given how little of him remained in this land of ravenous predators. And as ye," his green eyes settled on Lennox, "have been absent several times from this house…"

"Who says?" She interrupted, quick as a flash.

"Miss McPhee."

Catriona swallowed too quickly and coughed.

"All lies, I'm telling ye," said Lennox. "All lies."

"Absences long enough to be of interest to us…"

"I don't know anyone from by there. Who was he?"

"There was nae name on him. Just a cone blocking up his mouth."

Catriona let out a gasp of sympathy. Donald Baird's eyes met hers.

"And certain other objects have come to light which I'd like ye if possible, to identify." Coyle enjoying himself.

"Objects? You mean McPhee's boot which the dog dug up and I'd kept safe as proof she'd bin to the coop before me?"

Catriona shivered. Caught the architect's eye again. He seemed to guess her thoughts. "Five minutes," he reminded Lennox sternly. "Go."

However, Black Eyes turned to Constable Coyle. Angry defiance disfiguring her features even more. She wasn't finished yet. "Master Baird's forced ye into this, hasn't he, sir? Ask him why. I dare ye."

And when she'd stomped from the room, Catriona saw how the constable had turned quite pink, while the architect handed him the bundle of treasure she'd given to him only hours before.

250

*

There they were again. Those ghostly blue eyes growing in intensity from out of the gloom above the stairs, just as Mairi McPhee's dream for her was so near to coming true. Catriona blinked three times in an attempt to rid herself of the menace as she followed Lennox in silence, clinging to the banisters on either side, as if letting go would bring her tumbling down.

When the Glaswegian reached the top landing, she spun round to face her, those heavy, unfashionable boots level with her nose. "What little bird lied to ye about me and Master Baird?"

"I'm not saying."

"Ye'd better. Or else…"

"No witch threatens me."

And before Catriona realised just how vulnerable she was, a sudden kick to her forehead tipped her over backwards, to bump down each hard stair until her skull impacted against the cold, stone floor below.

Those same blue eyes from the portrait were looking down on her. Becoming part of an all-too familiar face, screaming, choking, gasping for breath. Then later, her father, standing at Footer's Cottage door, shaking in fear.

Next, came nothing…

*

She awoke to a room she vaguely recognised, yet bearing unfamiliar smells. A strange yellow light eked in from between the brocade curtains, making her throbbing headache worse. When she tried

251

lifting herself from the pillows and exploring the bed on either side of her, she soon realised she wasn't alone. That the whiffs of soap and sleep belonged to a man.

Donald Baird.

Catriona turned to see the white-skinned architect lying next to her, wearing what seemed to be nothing more than a red velvet smoking jacket.

"I hope your bandage isn't too tight, Miss McPhee," he said. "I managed to get Doctor Angus out to see you, and mercifully, he concluded nothing was broken. He'll be calling again in a week's time to check on your bruise. And as for Miss Lennox, he said the hangman's rope will be too good for her."

That brought a genuine smile.

"Thank you, sir. You must have saved my life."

He faced her, cheek skin drooping towards his mouth. His wedding ring she noticed, had gone. "And I think, Miss McPhee, you're about to save mine."

*

Afterwards, she was still dry between her legs. Still a virgin, with a week to go before the architect was due to leave Argyll again. While he slept on his back, emitting small grunts from his half-open mouth, she resolved to pay the Dame of Nonach's stone another visit to help her better achieve her aims.

As his snores grew louder, she travelled back in time to that cold, damp cottage where her mother had also lain that way, making a similar noise. The difference now was, this was happening in one of the biggest private houses in the west of Scotland. If she kept making herself available, to sympathise at his failure to stiffen, by January 5th - his leaving date - Ardnasaig House would surely be her domain. James Baird or no James Baird.

*

That yellow light between the curtains had become a dull grey, and darkening every minute. Even through her head bandage, Catriona heard the clock downstairs chime half past three, and wondered how on earth she was to prepare his tea tray in time. She tried to wriggle towards the edge of the bed and in doing so must have woken him enough to ask the question she dreaded.

"Tell me, Miss McPhee, is it true what Janet Lennox said about you putting a Hellish curse on me when I visited your father for the second time?"

Remember, you have the upper hand...

She laughed. Discreetly, of course.

"Sir, as you know, I was born and baptised a Christian. I wouldn't know a curse, let alone use one."

"Is that God's truth?"

"Would you believe her over me, sir?"

His reply was to stretch out his left arm and stroke the curls that her bandage couldn't contain.

"And what was she implying about my son and Constable Coyle? Is there something I should know?"

Catriona looked up at the brown, billowing silk above the bed that matched the curtains and the walnut wood furniture. She imagined this extravagance descending to cover her, smother her.

She wriggled again to reach the bed's edge, with no luck. That headache was killing all her inventions. His questions, her dreams.

"She spits lies like a serpent, sir," she added. "Don't believe a word of them. But what she writes, is different. Why I thought you should have her notebook, and her brother's letter. What does *that* tell you?"

Donald Baird sighed, long and deep.

"I confess, Miss McPhee, my son has been the biggest, utter fool to walk this ancient land. He must have lost his mind to go near her."

"But she led him on, sir. Many times. You can't blame him not resisting."

She couldn't stop now. Didn't want to.

"He even made a play for *me*, if you please. Until I said in no uncertain terms, I wasn't interested. I just hope the wise Dame of Nonach will put an end to things." She twisted her head round to look at him. "For your sake, sir."

With another sigh, the architect sat up and left the bed to open the curtains on to the changed world outside. Damp and forlorn. Catriona saw the backs of his sunless calves. How his crumpled smoking jacket still hung from his bony shoulders. He was a walking skeleton. An angry, walking skeleton…

"I've asked Constable Coyle to have Doctor Angus do whatever's necessary to save Ardnasaig House for the right kind of heir."

She hid her smile. "And will Miss Lennox ever be coming back, sir?"

"I doubt that very much. The constable and the Superintendent have plenty with which to keep her in custody until the wheels of justice start turning. But what troubles me is how I was taken in by her and her mother's sincerity after their time in the Poor House. Their willingness to work…"

"Indeed they worked, sir. Against me."

"That I can see."

"Should you inform her brother, sir, in case he comes looking for her?"

"What's the use? I have it on good authority his regiment's preparing to sail."

"But sir, Miss Lennox wrote he was being sent to somewhere called Weedon in Northamptonshire."

"In the army, Miss McPhee, changes happen overnight. Lord Palmerston's unhappy about Russia's plan for the Balkans. And so, I might add, am I."

Catriona's head began to throb again. She wasn't interested in politics or wars, only that Lennox and the brother who'd been more than a brother, kept away. That soon, she might be gloriously on her own.

"And when you next go, sir. What then?"

But the architect's head was pressed against the window pane. He was peering down at the carriageway. "Someone's coming," he said. "Stay there." He walked over to the door, while a trickle of terror crept from her aching head to her feet.

"Who is it, sir?" She didn't dare look.

"I think it's your father, carrying some kind of parcel."

***

24.

Where wheels continue turning...

The sight of Margaret Lennox's wrinkled eyes cradled in their own thin blood inside her own little glass bottle, had left Janet in a state of terror, unable to fight her corner or think of anyone able to help. Whoever had carried out such a sickening act, must surely have the Devil's blood in their veins. And how had Donald Baird come to possess the item, and all her other personal things?

During the slow, often bumpy journey to Kilforgan's Police House, just one name had come to mind, spinning around to the sound of the covered carriage's wheels.

Catriona Mairi McPhee... Catriona Mairi McPhee...

*

"Our Father who shud be in Heaven, hallowed be Thy name..." She struggled to remember what she normally knew by heart, as Constable Coyle and the Reverend McKinnon pushed her down one of the Police House's short, damp passageways towards a wooden door reinforced by four rusted, iron bands. She hoped her prayer might soften the minister's heart, but he neither spoke, nor looked her in the eye.

Both men bore evidence of a recent Christmas dinner and from one of them came a pop of meaty wind.

"...as we forgive them that do wrong against us..." she continued.

"Shut yer mouth," snapped Coyle. "This isn't the kirk. Save yer breath for Baw Heid."

Baw Heid...

"Sir," she heard the minister whisper. "We weren't to mention it."

"'Well, 'tis a braw spot, there's no denying."

Janet's body slapped against the door, and her sickness, never far away, welled up to burn the back of her throat. Everything she'd clung to in her own defence was slipping away like snow off the hills. Baw Heid was a Hell on earth, so her mother had said. Tales of its ancient caves and strange goings inside them on had even reached Greenock, where Linnet Garvie told of live sacrifices and how a father was forced to eat his daughter while she still breathed because they'd been lovers. How its inhabitants seemed above the law.

What had she and Calum been, if not lovers? And the reason he'd joined the 42nd Foot was all down in black and white in her accursed notebook. She wondered what comforting words of wisdom and ideas for escape Falcon Steer, her special, crooked friend, might have now.

"Does Saturday still stand?" McKinnon asked Coyle, making her jump.

"Aye."

"Then I'll see she has a bucket till then. The usual things..." He lowered his voice. "We don't want trouble."

"Where's me poor mother?" Janet cried, keeping her head pressed against the door's damp, old wood.. "Is she still safe in the kirk?"

"Later, please."

"And Superintendent Lampard?" A friendly officer who'd come to their aid during trouble in the Poor House. "Why's he nae here to listen to me?"

"Holidaying in the Alps. Lucky man."

"I've nae bag. Nae things." What she'd packed for her escape still lay in her attic room.

But Coyle edged past her and, having selected a large key from a bunch of similar ones, unlocked the door, using his boot to kick it open.

The small, square windowless room smelt like an uncleaned 'stank,' and in the meagre daylight Janet saw how the walls glistened with moisture. But it was the extra chill breathed out by these ugly, grey stones that made her coat seem to be no more than cotton, freezing her fear. Was this really where the previously caring Falcon Steer wanted her to be? Her tempter with those deep, soft eyes? And James Baird, weak as a wren's feather? Or was his story about that mysterious stranger offering a huge bribe just another lie to cover himself and his devious ways?

And then the maid and the architect came to mind, bringing a fresh rise of bile. She couldn't stop herself from shouting.

"Ye men are all the same! Catriona McPhee's got the braw looks, the neat waist. Why I'm here and she's nae. And why, once me Calum hears about this, he'll be here with his soldier friends and see justice done. How ye've taken the wrong one."

Both her captors only chuckled at her outburst and the minister duly placed a bucket in the far corner, then threw in the same brown paper parcel she'd seen him collect earlier from an adjoining building. It landed on the low, iron-framed bed.

"If he'd kept his tumstie in his trousers in the first place, ye wudnae be here now," said Coyle. "It's all in yer notebook."

"Every last, sinful detail." Added the minister with relish, removing his black hat.

"Which Miss McPhee helpfully handed over," sneered the constable. "Unlike some, that wee lass has a strong sense of duty."

"She's bin out to break me since the day she arrived at Ardnasaig. As for me notebook, I like making things up. Fanciful tales, that's all they are, from being in the house all day."

"Do the godly Lord and Lady Bruce make up fanciful tales, then?"

"Show me their letter. Let me defend meself."

The Weasel turned his face to hers. A face dominated by hateful, narrowing eyes. "I'll choose the time for that."

It being Christmas Day, he probably had a family waiting. She had no-one. He glanced at the minister while she tried guessing what would come next.

"We have a wee bone, Miss Lennox. A wean's bone which Miss McPhee found in the well at Ardnasaig House. It had floated to the surface, embedding itself in the ice."

Janet shivered so long and so deep she almost lost her balance.

"And why would Fergus Bogle advise her ne'er to drink from that well?" added Coyle, keeping up his accusing gaze. "For fear of more death to follow?"

"I wonder what he might have witnessed to say such an odd thing?" said the minister, blowing warmth on to his bare hands. "Your notebook's no help."

"Good. McPhee's a liar. I've found all sorts of bones in that well - from birds, frogs, bats…"

"While yer in our charge, you refer to her as *Miss* McPhee. And Doctor Angus has examined the specimen already and confirmed our suspicions that it's a human bone."

"I will nae admit to something I didnae do."

"If you have something to confess, Miss Lennox," said the minister, "I'd be pleased to hear it. And so too, would God."

Janet pressed her cold lips together as Coyle opened his. "We're searching for Mr Bogle at this very moment, because Miss McPhee also claims she's heard a wean crying."

"Where?"

"By yer room."

Damn her.

"When is *she* being questioned?"

"When it's necessary."

Janet curled up her cold fists. Why not box her way out of trouble? It was possible…

The minister took a step back, before both men turned away and locked her door behind them. She was alone in that miserable cell.

"So I'm here on the strength of a wee bone, a notebook of make-believe and… and…" she faltered. Saying the next words was far harder than thinking them. "Me dead mother's eyes in one of her own little glass bottles?"

261

Coyle's voice carried through the stout wood from the other side. "I wish the list ended there, but that gutting knife we were given…"

"Given?"

"I mean, found. Slip of the tongue, It happens. As I was saying, it leads us to ye, Miss Lennox who used it most. Ye and ye alone."

"I was asking him for help. For us and my father…"

With James Baird's other falsehood churning around in her head, Janet's already ragged fingernails clawed at the rough wooden door. Pregnant or not, if she ever saw him again, she'd slowly kill him and watch him beg for her forgiveness with those mismatched eyes wide as those lids on the potted meat jars at Ardnasaig House. The same for the heartless maid…

Splinters tore the tender skin inside her nails, but this agony only drove her faster and faster to defeat this obstacle to freedom. Such pain was better than a trip to Baw Heid. In fact, anything was. As she sucked at her own warm blood, she worked out in her frightened mind how best to alert her brother. What to say, and lastly, how on this unholy earth, could she reach him.

*

More by touch than sight, with stinging fingers she unwrapped the brown paper parcel thrown on to her bed. Every rip, every tear she made represented a part of herself destroyed with no means of repair; her small defences scattered to a lost place.

Inside, lay half a stale loaf. An odd-smelling pie with a sunken crust. Two apples soft and puckered with age. Nothing to drink, when just a mouthful of clean water was all she craved. She set aside her rations and peered into the bucket, before dipping a sore finger into the opaque liquid at the bottom.

Was this water? Possibly. What came from the spring at Ardnasaig House was also often discoloured, especially after heavy rains. She lifted the bucket and poured its contents down her throat. At first, it felt good. An ordinary pleasure, until something more solid brushed against her tongue, releasing a foul, dung-like taste when she probed it. She was sick twice and crammed the brown paper into her mouth to stop any more from coming up.

Why not leave the obstruction there? She thought bleakly. And hold her nose at the same time until a swift death take her? No. She pulled he paper free, knelt down to smooth it out against the damp stone floor and, using that that same finger that had so rashly tested the 'water,' pierced the pie. With barely any light to guide her, her brown-coated finger began to write.

***

25.

In which further journeys are undertaken...

Free at last of her cumbersome bandage, and with a dose of Doctor Angus's laudanum soothing the severe ache behind her left ear, Catriona climbed into Donald Baird's little-used dog cart that she'd hurriedly brushed free of cobwebs.

Having helped pull her cape over her already damp curls, the architect passed her his highly-prized Fox umbrella. However, a sudden sneeze made her lose her grip, and it landed on the floor.

"Bless me!" she called out, reclaiming it and settling herself on the wet leather bench. "Even if no-one else will." For one glance had told her the man up front, whip at the ready, was still tense and pre-occupied, with a raindrop hanging from the end of his nose. His wedding ring finger still bare beneath the glove.

James Baird still hadn't returned home, but now at least they were going to Kilforgan to ask Constable Coyle and his Superintendent for help in their search.

"We couldn't have done this with the ice still down." He slapped the reins against the cob's broad back. "And with so few daylight hours, we can't waste time. Next April when I'm home again, I'll have a telegraph system installed. Relying on neighbours and the Penny Post is mediaeval. One's private and personal correspondence can all too easily be pryed upon or stolen."

"Has yours been, sir?"

"I've no proof." He snapped, then apologised.

Since she'd started work at Ardnasaig House, yes, she'd sneaked a look inside those more intriguing envelopes addressed to him, before handing them re-sealed to James Baird for safe-keeping. One in particular, from Lord Aberdeen congratulating his father on his fine work overseas, had needed all her skill to steam open then repair the wax thistle afterwards. But bills for coal, items for the Store, and requests for funds from Glasgow charities hadn't merited such effort.

Now was another chance to keep her enemy from Ardnasaig's door.

"I once saw Miss Lennox trying to open one of your envelopes, sir. She soon stopped when she realised I was there."

He paused. The droplet fell from his nose. "I'm not obliged to take her back, you know. And as for any reference..." He slapped the reins again, this time with more annoyance. "It'll have to tell the truth."

"Of course, sir. She can't be inflicted on someone else as generous and trusting as you and your son."

"I do so like your directness, Miss McPhee. Very refreshing in a muddled world."

"Thank you, sir, and if I may be impertinent, has your wedding ring been mislaid?

"No. I was born a gentleman and I'll die a gentleman. That's my answer."

*

As the chestnut cob picked his way out of the rear courtyard towards the parade of elms, Catriona looked back at Ardnasaig

House, empty now of that witch and her influence for ever. Or so she hoped. Its charcoal-coloured stones shone with an extra gleam while the rhododendron army still guarded its western wall. To the east, the parade of limes drip-dripped their surplus water to the ground in a muffled beat, and she tried to imagine the summer to come, with their green crowns in full glory.

Yes, she should have been feeling elated at her growing prospects here, but three more shadows had recently cast themselves across her path. For a start, her father's puzzling Christmas gift of a pair of expensive-looking peach-pink drawers edged in beige lace. He'd not appeared drunk as he'd walked off down the carriageway, ignoring her calls to stop. So why leave such an item for her? He didn't know her size, for a start. And as for the small cryptic card attached to the parcel.

To me canny wee lassie for auld lang syne

It was a complete mystery. Why for old time's sake? Was this some stupid joke?

"Was that your Christmas gift?" Donald Baird had asked while dressing for breakfast. She'd nodded then lied again.

"Just some new stockings and a necklace of my mother's. It's a pity he didn't stop longer, but I know your rules on followers."

"Any father of yours is no follower." And, as he'd stretched his braces over his mean shoulders and searched for his waistcoat, she'd hurried downstairs to poke the strange offering into the kitchen boiler's greedy flames.

However, two other crucial matters still remained. The idea of her father working alongside her for six days a week, month in, month out, had blighted her mind since the architect first mentioned it. Surely Donald Baird would change his rash decision? But so far, there'd been nothing as reassuring as that. And thirdly, the creeping realisation that this man of means now whipping the cob once again into action, might never provide her with an heir. If so, questions had to be asked.

*

With the large, open gates behind them, her driver half-turned to her. Another raindrop already on the end of his nose. "You claimed last night that before my son left the house, Miss Lennox had shouted at him? What exactly?"

Keep calm. Think...

She was ready.

"He must rid himself of the Devil eating at his heart, sir. A terrible thing to say. She also said if he didn't get himself cleansed, he'd be damned for ever."

"Damned?" he repeated in an incredulous tone, guiding the cob too loosely around the sharp turn, and having to rein back a few paces to avoid the opposite wall. He wasn't used to this kind of physical work, thought Catriona, holding on to her seat with her spare hand. Her mind on full alert.

"Yes, sir," she said. "Clear as a night-jar's call. But surely no son of yours would listen to that nonsense?"

"I most sincerely hope not."

"When I warned her how such words might affect someone with more good in their heart than her, she pushed me downstairs. Could have killed me, as you saw, sir."

267

The dog cart rattled and splashed its way past a couple of beggars whose calloused hands were outstretched towards them. The cob quickened his trot, spraying them with mud. She wondered if that old fool she'd met in the wood was one of their number. Whether they were on their way to an unguarded Ardnasaig House.

"She has much to answer for, does Miss Lennox," said her driver.

"Did you know, sir, she'd been planning to leave us?"

"No. When?"

"She never said. But I found her things all packed up."

"And her wages?"

"Gone from inside her pillow case."

"Ah."

Catriona shivered, lowering the umbrella closer to her head. The muffled hoof beats adding to her unease. He might ask how she'd known the money had been hidden there. Might waver in his opinion of her. Her prize catch must now be steered away to safer ground and, seeing the nearby loch so bright and still between the black trees, lining the track, made her tap the back of his coat. "Sir, I know the water out there's as cold as Miss Lennox's heart, but your son may have decided to explore it."

"No. No. Never." He interrupted, glancing round with a tortured look on his face. "He hates that loch. Won't even fish there. Did you know that? Either he goes up to those in the hills or over to Loch Fyne."

"I didn't know, sir. Keeping an eye on Miss Lennox and running the house, especially since her mother died, has taken all my time."

"Of course… And," half a glance in her direction. "Now you've got *me*."

"*That's* a pleasure, sir."

Another pony and trap suddenly appeared round the next bend and squeezed by.

"Speaking of the loch, although James seems to avoid it, he's convinced his beloved mother's somehow connected with it. He begged me to pay for two navy divers to explore it last year. But nothing was found."

"I'm truly sorry, sir. But as for her portrait, he's certainly proud of it. And I like how the artist has made the flesh colours are so real and her hair so perfect."

"As I remarked when I first arrived, Miss McPhee, you have extremely good taste."

Taste…

A deep blush scorched her cheeks as she remembered last night. How, unlike the previous occasion, his pointed tongue had become bolder, making her dizzy; bringing cries she'd never made before. How his curious yet persistent finger had brought blood from below. But then, in the aftermath, those horrible blue eyes had hovered over her, and her body had soon felt like cold, dead marble.

*

They passed more foul, unkempt beggars, this time accompanied by three mangy dogs who yapped relentlessly at the cob. The animal swerved, nearly unseating the architect for whom composure surely came next to cleanliness. Then without warning, two bedraggled rams with the biggest horns she'd ever seen, lunged out from a gap in the trackside wall and crashed through the briar bushes on the other side leading steeply down to the loch. Before they disappeared, Catriona noticed the letter M on their matted flanks. Something in the forest must have badly frightened them.

"Lord Melhuish." Her lover announced, pulling on the reins and steadying the alarmed cob into a walk. "'Tis easy to preach about his predicament. You take on too many workers from the goodness of your heart and there's invariably bad feeling when plans change. I'm not saying your father or his friends gave him any trouble. Far from it."

"My father's a good man, sir. And he'd have had that beast roped with one throw and moved from harm's way."

"He also had you, Miss McPhee."

Another blush. But pleasure didn't last long. To the right, up on the brow of the rough, wet hill from where streams of water were tumbling down to the loch, something caught her eye. The figure of a man with a large, black dog limping alongside him. She recognised both.

Falcon Steer, and the greedy creature who'd eaten that letter.

"Look to the left, sir," she gestured at the loch to divert her driver's attention. "The fishermen are out."

"Indeed they are," he glanced at the sloping shore where several men stood with their rods, thigh deep in water. Another two perched in a blue and white rowing boat, the same size as that snow-covered one she'd seen near Nonach Cottage. "And no," he added. "We won't be stopping to ask them about James."

Nor Falcon Steer, she thought, lowering her umbrella again in case he glimpsed her. Even though he'd not met Donald Baird in person, he might well recognise the cob. What was he doing up there with that dog? And where was he going?

"Faster, sir, if you can," she said, seeing the sign, KILFORGAN 1 MILE. "I've never travelled very well…"

"And I wish to God we were here for some other purpose."

*

Moments later, with Steer and the cur safely out of sight, the chestnut shook his wet mane and began to canter. Having passed Mr Bogle's still smokeless bothy nestling amongst the bare woodland, that last mile seemed to fly by, and soon they reached the quiet village with its kirk on the right, and a small General Stores to the left. As she'd never been so far this way before, Catriona wondered where the Police House was, hoping that Lennox hadn't got free and was watching her with those frightening black eyes.

Donald Baird reined in the cob outside the narrow dwelling that housed the Stores and its faded sign, for her to take his place up front. Despite the bad headache, she was eager to please. To do anything to help find his son.

After just a minute, she watched him emerge from the shop long-faced, followed by a wrinkled crone dressed from head to toe in tombstone grey whose deep-socketed eyes looked her up and down. Too late the protective umbrella blocked her view, but not that that mischievous hole of a mouth.

"She's nae Mrs Baird," the store owner growled after him, pointing a bony finger in Catriona's direction. "And mark me

271

words, sir, whatever yer plannin wi' the bairn,' the Dame of Nonach'll soon be smackin' her lips."

Bairn? The crone was mad.

"Keep your nonsense to yourself, Mrs Kellaway," muttered Donald Baird as Catriona wished her dead. The cob's sweaty steam in her nose.

The architect's expression also reinforced what a thin line she still trod. If her dream was to be realised, she must be more cunning than a wolf by night. More careful than her father in the birthing shed bringing those big-boned Highland calves into the world. More willing than in that summer gloaming by the lochside where he'd been the piper, but she'd called the sweetest tune.

*

Alongside the kirk, Constable Coyle's black horse stood ready harnessed to that same brown carriage. Catriona also noticed how around that plain, stone building with its even plainer windows, stood a screen of wide-girthed yews bent sideways from the winds. At their feet, lay the gravestones of those who'd lived too long or not long enough. Of those fallen in wars on Scottish soil or abroad. And further back, between these trees whose roots were said to wander into the mouths of the dead, lay an area of neglect which, according to her mother, resting in Cranranich with a winged angel at her head, hid unmarked plots saved for unsaveable sinners. Catriona couldn't help but imagine the old housemaid lying there with a tree root working its way between her teeth while the Devil had snatched her soul for Himself.

The temperature seemed to drop even further when she and the architect entered the unlit, undecorated kirk. The Reverend McKinnon wearing a more expensive looking black hat and coat than for his recent visit to Ardnasaig House, was busy arranging copies of his last sermon together with information on next years' services for those few of the parish who could read. He looked up, more surprised it seemed, to see her than Donald Baird. Then he shook his distinguished parishioner's hand.

"'Tis by God's deliverance, sir, that you're with us at all," he smiled; their hands still locked together. "Is that why you've come? To offer thanks?"

Catriona couldn't help herself "His son James is missing, sir," she said. "Since Christmas Day morning."

"Is this so?"

"Yes!" snapped the architect. "And according to Miss McPhee here, Miss Lennox had told him in no uncertain terms to cleanse himself of the Devil. So I judged he might have made his way here to do just that."

"She's a fine one to talk, excuse my saying so."

"Indeed."

"Did he leave on foot?"

A nod.

"He's a strong lad. He knows these surroundings."

"You're right, but he's never just disappeared before. And why leave his rifle behind?"

Catriona, noticing his father's eyes begin to glisten, felt a twinge of disappointment. Men should be fearless, tearless.

Especially this one. Otherwise, he might waver like a reed in the wind when she needed him most. And what use would that be?

"I'm loathe to contradict you, Mr Baird," said the minister. "But my feeling is he'll be back to you soon enough. I've seen James enjoying his creature comforts too much to be away from them for long." He removed a large watch from inside his coat and frowned. "Excuse me, but I'm now needed at the Police House. Miss Lennox is with Constable Coyle. I have to ensure there's a witness before the kirk session."

"She's been very unfair to my son," countered Donald Baird. "Or he wouldn't have gone off the way he did. And, as someone who pays substantial taxes here in Argyll, I've a right to see the constable do his duty. A right to see *her*."

"I'm afraid that's not possible. Perhaps Monday, when the questioning will be over."

In the extra chill that hung between the two men, Catriona, thinking again of that ragged figure above the nearby woods, took a gamble.

"Has Falcon Steer been seen hereabouts, Reverend? Is he still a wanted man?" Donald Baird's eyes were on her, while beneath the clergyman's thick, black eyebrows, she detected a change of expression. As a child, she'd observed her warring parents for too long not to recognise trepidation.

"Mr Baird," he predictably ignored her. "Miss Lennox is being questioned now, and I need to hasten along."

"Monday then?"

"That's best, sir."

Just then, the architect reached inside his great coat and extracted a pale, pigskin wallet swollen by banknotes, both Scottish and foreign. Never in her whole life had Catriona seen so many. He was a walking bank while her wages had so far consisted of coins. The same as she'd found in Lennox's pillowcase.

"Take these," he said to the minister, peeling off two ten pound notes bearing Walter Scott's head. "For my former housekeeper's burial. I don't want talk, do you understand me?"

"Of course, Mr Baird. I'll see to it this very afternoon."

Catriona noticed how hat pink, plump hand closed over the generous donation. The flicker of deceit in his eyes. Margaret Lennox had already been disposed of, probably in that overgrown area of the graveyard, and this money would have been far better spent on something else. Her.

***

26.

Where wounds are opened and salt rubbed in...

After two days and nights spent planning her escape, despite numb bones, the ever-present sickness and a bed so full of broken, prodding springs, Janet had chosen the floor. But what was the difference? Damp was everywhere, as if Kilforgan's wet earth had not only seeped in under the uneven flagstones, but also between the gaps around each crude, granite lump that formed the walls to her cell. At least her makeshift note to Calum was finished, and she'd not died. While she still breathed, there was hope. As for her expected 'wee frein,' she wished it not to come, and once she was away from here, the greedy Dame of Nonach would be powerless.

Now, Constable Coyle with clanging keys and impatient grunts was unlocking her cell door. Was it time for more pie and warm, flecked water? Or time for Baw Heid? As he held no food bag, she watched his every move.

He sniffed then grimaced before handing her a new pair of black woollen gloves meant for smaller hands.

"Wear them now, and keep them on. Something smart about ye, at least. Might make a difference."

"To what?"

"Yer situation."

Was he trying to hide her broken, bloodied nails so he wouldn't be blamed for harming her? She also wondered if it had been his shit she'd eaten…

Time for a small disobedience.

"Is this how ye treat yer wife, in private?

A hit she saw coming, but was too stiff, too cold to avoid. Her left shoulder, already badly bruised from her fall into the grate, took the impact and stung so deep. He smiled a row of yellow teeth, while the tips of his moustache twitched up each cheek.

"Move yer carcass!"

With her brown paper message safe in her coat pocket, she stumbled behind him past another door similar to hers, with sounds of another woman, whimpering.

"God be with ye," Janet hissed to her. "He's nae wi' me."

At this, Coyle turned, snatched at the neck of her coat and tried to drag her towards the mean light of a wet day. But a vision of Margaret Lennox abandoned, still unburied, made her dig in her heels. "Afore I go anywhere, sir, I want to see me mother given proper Christian rites and laid to rest in holy ground. I've money set aside. When I can reach it."

"A burial's been done. God rest her soul."

Janet's spittle suddenly tasted foul.

"Where?"

"The kirk, o' course. The Reverend McKinnon saw to it yesterday."

Coyle, the weasel, was now a cat that had the cream. She wished for strength from somewhere to box him senseless...

"Why wasnae I there too? She's me mother..."

He pulled at her coat again, catching her off-guard. She fell against him and, having pushed her upright, brushed his gloved hands together, as if ridding them of a leper's touch. "And none too pretty a sight, I might add."

Keep yer tears to yersel... Dinnae give him that pleasure.

"Whoever took out her eyes should be put on trial."

"Exactly, Miss Lennox. Why yer here, and shortly to be travelling to where ye'll see the Bruces letter from Lismore and more besides..."

"A trial? At Baw Heid?"

"Ye've a good memory. I'll grant ye that."

The loch's solid chill seemed to invade her body, filling her lungs with its salty harvest. She could barely speak.

"But ye promised I'd be back at Ardnasaig House by dark on Christmas Day, and now look. So what am I charged with? Who else is blackenin' me name?"

"A friend in Greenock seems to hold more than a few keys."

Linnet?

Janet gripped The Weasel's arm. Took in his ale breath. His laughing, cruel eyes. That imagined weight of salt inside her.

"Ye've bin *there?*"

"How could I not?"

Guarding her tongue was no longer possible. "Yer deceiving me, sir. Her name and address in me notebook means nothing."

"There was far more than that, as weel ye know."

"What if I said that Falcon Steer who's supposed to be poor, may have offered James Baird who certainly *is* poor, five hundred pounds to make sure ye question me and Miss McPhee?"

A pause in which anything could happen. His eyes narrowed.

"Slander won't help ye. Justice will."

"James Baird told me hissel."

Coyle immediately blew his whistle and she flinched. Was that thunder growing louder from without or within? And why all of a sudden, was her mouth a hot, bloody cave and her head a night full of spinning stars?

*

Janet probed each of her teeth in turn with her tongue. Half were loose. Two front ones had gone, leaving pulpy holes tasting of raw liver. And then there was the rain, hitting the carriage roof and both its blind windows as the wheels dipped and rose along what must be a badly rutted track. She gripped her stomach with both hands, praying that these ups and downs wouldn't bring her blood down below. That having a wean beginning inside her would give her courage to face Baw Heid, for that name cut so deep into her brain was surely the plan. And once the questions were over she'd be free to see where her mother lay before fleeing from this terrible, wicked place. Unless Calum should find her first.

And then the thought occurred to her - what if he found out she'd strangled and drowned his wean and had another in her belly? What then?

The coach's wheels were now rattling along a hard surface. She opened her eyes and saw how instead of cords, both window blinds had been nailed to their wooden frames. In panic, she tore at the stiff black fabric with her gloved fingers, but found no purchase. Next, she tried what remained of her teeth.

More blood, but at least a grip. A nick in the weave big enough to give her a start. She blinked at the bright grey sky and matching water beyond the muddied glass. Saw a fishing boat pass underneath...

She was on a bridge. But which one? She'd heard of Eagle Bridge further south, where Loch Nonach meets the sea. Could this be it?

Somehow she found the strength to haul the window down halfway, letting cold, salty air hit her skin.

Quick...

She pulled the smelly brown ball of paper from her coat pocket, reached up and let it drop into the rain. Paper and gravy and a stranger's leavings. Dear God. But in her heart knew she hadn't got a prayer...

*

Every inch of her was hurting as the carriage lurched down a steep incline and curved a long way to the left into what seemed to be the beginnings of a forest. Despite a biting draught, she kept the window open in the hope of seeing someone, anyone, and calling for help but, as the sky and its rain vanished, leaving only patches of unmelted snow to relieve the gloom, she heard above the throb of hooves on earth, two voices she'd come to dread.

Constable Coyle and the saintly Reverend McKinnon.

"Steady, sir, or we'll miss our turning. Remember the last time?"

"I do."

"Weather won't be helping."

"What about this God o' yours then?"

"I'm praying to Him now."

***

27

Where to give is not always better than to receive...

The melt had lasted all day and the mournful silence around Ardnasaig House was enlivened only by the gurgling spates from every nook, every cranny. Dusk lowered its gloom over Catriona's future home, its towering trees and the loch where nothing moved save for two fat, glistening seals draped on a rock cluster near the shore. As if they knew she was looking, both slithered in to the water, casting ripple rings as far as the eye could see.

The so far fruitless search for James Baird had taken up the wet afternoon and left his father irked and pre-occupied. He was sitting in the Drawing Room, facing the loch when Catriona left him a tea tray complete with the last of Margaret Lennox's Christmas cake, before going back outside.

She unhooked the bedraggled cob from his shafts and led him round to the stable. Inside its pungent darkness, she refilled the empty iron manger and drew water from the tap in the 'necessaries' for his bucket, wondering why she wasn't more cheerful that Lennox was out of the way. Perhaps because her tongue might still be too busy.

Could the former employee somehow be connected to the huntsman's absence and be trying to pin it on her? And why hadn't his name - unlike her brother's - appeared in the notebook that the architect had passed over to the Constable? Was her shame at opening her thick legs for him, so deep that all she'd written was a daily prayer for her blood to come?

Catriona hit the cob's head when he leaned into her for his hay, rightly judging him too greedy to confront her. "Be thankful someone's feeding you at all!" She shouted. When *she* was mistress of Ardnasaig, she'd have a prettier beast that matched herself. A Palomino, perhaps, with a fine profile and delicate mane she could groom with her special ivory comb. She'd make the architect buy a new brougham. Dark blue with leather seats and gilt door handles...

But just as she was imagining driving it through Cranranich to Inverary under the admiring scrutiny of her former friends, the dream darkened and disappeared altogether when the prospect of her father sharing it, intervened.

While leaving Kilforgan after their fruitless visit, Donald Baird had again mentioned him being his new handyman, and the longer James remained missing, this bad idea could grow into reality. Unless she nipped it in the bud.

"He's far too old, sir," she'd said. And you must have seen for yourself how he's not that well. And he does enjoy a dram."

But clearly Donald Baird wasn't convinced by her arguments. Nor could he have heard of the herdsman's other weakness.

"I saw his hands," he'd replied. "Good strong specimens. And he'd a sharp look about him that I like."

She gathered a clutch of clean straw and rubbed it over the animal's back and shoulders, lifting off the day's muddy sweat. She'd once seen James Baird do the same and, as part of her plan to impress the architect, to make herself indispensable, this cob would be clean. As for ice for her lover's whisky, she must choose between the yellowish spring water from the tap or the clearer rain water in the well. Either way, there'd be none until a good frost returned, and in the meantime. She was sure to think up other compensations.

Having thrown down the muddied, used straw, Catrion picked her way to the half-door, aware of the stable imperceptibly turning colder and the cob himself stepping back from feeding as if in fear. Her skin seemed to freeze, her lips grow numb and her exposed ears so quickly frosted, she screamed. And then came the sound of creeping water. Not running over rocks or from some tap, but softly lap-lapping, while outside, hovering amid the remains of daylight, those same blue eyes she'd first seen transposed on to the housekeeper's face and later in that disturbing, all-seeing portrait.

Too ensnared by those frightening sensations to notice where she placed her feet on her way to the Store, she neither saw nor heard the small burnie formed by the melt, coursing down from higher ground.

"Leave me alone and go to Hell's darkest place!" she hissed at the staring spectre. "Or I'll plant an eternal curse on all you Bairds..."

With water-filled boots she let herself into the Store, using the architect's newly-found spare key now already on her overcrowded ring. Whether because she could still hear that creeping water and sense every step being watched, she suddenly saw those dark heaps of carrots, potatoes and especially swedes – where Lennox had hidden her black boot - as unbeatable foes, waiting to fill every waking moment with grinding toil. Added to this, the rank stink of half-gutted trout, the small mountain of venison pieces lying where Lennox had left them. The pork that should have been served on Boxing Day, smelling like the absent enemy herself.

Then his voice, calling for her. A man so lost without his son, yet who'd rarely written home or shown him much companionship when he was here. Whose almost colourless eyes had certainly not been passed on. And what if that son never came back? What then? With all things considered, it might be for the best...

"Miss McPhee?"

Donald Baird drawing closer.

"Yes, sir?"

By the open door into the passageway, lamp in hand, he eyed her sodden feet. It was a miracle he'd still not recognised her grey boots with their distinctive fastenings. Perhaps his wife had bought and worn them while he'd been absent. This certainly seemed to be the case.

"You may choose a pair of my wife's boots," he said, proving her right. "They're taller than yours and more practical, because we're taking a walk."

The last thing she felt like after her recent fright.

He indicated that same wooden cupboard behind the door that she'd already made use of. "Most are hardly worn, so I have little attachment to them." With that, he strode off towards the front of the house, leaving her flattered at this suggestion, but also wary.

"A walk where, sir?" She called after him.

"To look for James. What else? And when we've found him, I can fetch his Christmas gift from Inverary."

*

These fawn-coloured boots, so different from the earlier pair she'd taken, fitted like another skin, while the silver eyelets and their laces almost reaching her knees, were so much easier than those other brass contraptions. A label stitched on the inside of the right boot confirmed their worth. M D. Burnett. Edinburgh. By appointment to Her Majesty the Queen.

An honour indeed.

Catriona followed the smell of Donald Baird's wet, woollen coat, and when they met again, having glanced at her feet with an approving look, he helped fit her black cape over her shoulders. However, he missed her strained smile, unaware her headache had returned and her rear that had bumped up and down for too long in that dog cart, was sore. Yet she must get used to being obedient at least while he was around. Another hidden aspect of life in this most desired of houses that she'd never considered while watching his once carefree son on his white pony. Even while the Lennox pair had been fully occupied in their posts.

"Sir," she began as they dodged the dripping lime trees with him walking on ahead. "I've been thinking, with everything to do now I'm the only maid…"

"You're more than a maid, Miss McPhee."

She drew level with him. Tried to catch his eye.

"I'm grateful you've improved my wages, sir, but on Monday couldn't we try for a new housekeeper as well? Mrs Masters might know of someone who might suit."

"At the moment, my son has priority. Until he's found, I can't attend to anything else. I wish to God I'd ignored the Reverend McKinnon and just pushed my way into that Police House to speak to Miss Lennox."

"We can still go on Monday. He said so, sir." Yet she prayed he'd decline.

Her prayer was answered. He shook his head.

"There's others we can see for now. Closer to home."

"Sir, can't you use your position to summon the police from Inverary? Even Glasgow? I mean, you've had letters from several very important people. Lord Aberdeen, for example. You're well known."

He glanced at her, puzzled.

"I've seen them waiting for you on your desk, sir," she was quick to explain. "Like I said, it was Miss Lennox who used to read them."

She wondered if he was deaf as well as 'soft.'

"This search must be kept local at the moment. Just in case."

"Of what, sir?"

Another pause. Him slowing down.

"In case James has done something foolish."

Dwelling on that odd reply, and wondering what he could have meant, Catriona stepped into one unseen puddle after another. However, Isobel Baird's boots with their higher heel, kept her feet dry.

"You get what you pay for, Mairi," she remembered her grandmother's words to her only daughter while furnishing the Tarbet house before Lord Melhuish tempted her husband away to the hills.

And these boots must have cost a lot.

While the architect's lamp casting a wavering glow on the waterlogged track ahead and wet stones slippery underfoot, Catriona's gloved hand reached into her skirt pocket where Lennox's money lay snug in one of her handkerchiefs, to stop the twenty coins rattling together. With her own missed donations to her father and her new pay and prospects, she'd never again have to put up with second best.

*

Oak and birch, restrained on either side of the track by old moss-covered walls, loomed into the wintry sky. That horrible experience in the stable had chipped a hole in her fragile defences. And everything, even these trees standing where they had since the days of the Jacobite rebellion, were no longer familiar and protective, but ominous strangers bearing a warning.

The architect paused, lowered his umbrella and shouted out his son's name in a voice she didn't recognise. And again, with such ferocity she held her breath, while startled muntjacs skittered away into the black beyond.

"This way," he said afterwards, slightly hoarse, indicating with his lamp a smaller track leading over a footbridge to the base of Footer's Hill. "If neither the Reverend or the constable can help me, I know someone who can."

Without thinking, Catriona gripped his damp coat's left sleeve. "But sir, it's far too treacherous to go there on a night like this. Besides," contradicting what that filthy vagrant had said, "Colonel Ritchie's mob is sure to be around, bent on revenge. I couldn't bear to see you come to harm, sir. Especially after all you've endured. All you've done for me."

"You're a kindly soul, Miss McPhee," he said, holding his lamp high to check his bearings. "And your father was kind to me when I needed it. So, just follow me. He's the best hope I have."

★★★

28.

Janet must have dozed off after coming down that hill, and while asleep, her dream of Calum passing over that same bridge and finding her message for help had been so real, she'd expected to see him running alongside the carriage when its sudden lurch to the left had jolted her from sleep.

Now in the gloaming, there was nothing but loch water to her right, spread like a sheet of metal, almost level with the carriage's wheels. Opposite, a forbidding bank of briar, hawthorn and half-grown trees so spindly they'd never been worth a man's sweat to fell, almost shut out the sky. It was through an archway cut into this mass that her two captors urged the slowing horse. Could this be Baw Heid? The place of torments with no return? Or was it somewhere further from Ardnasaig, by a different water?

Forcing her tired eyes to find even the smallest clue on the opposite shore, Janet picked out the silhouette of what could only be Footer's Hill. McPhee country.

And there, by the shoreline lay three pinpricks of light. Nonach Cottage then Bar-Beithe, both belonging to James Baird's godmothers, and further down, Dauvit Hendry's bothy; lowly in appearance but certainly not in significance.

Which of these decent folk knew of her ordeal? Would they even care, or had they too been poisoned against her?

Seven chimes from somewhere, echoing through the cave's glistening, creviced walls.

No 'necessaries.' Not even a pot to piss in, but two shiny iron rings set into the rocky floor. Well-used, obviously. Making her wonder who else had been here before her, and were they still alive?

Seven oil lamps attached to the cave's ceiling, hung overhead, while seven playing cards, bearing strange, named pictures she'd never seen before, were being set out in a horseshoe on the rough wooden table by a masked dwarf, dressed from head to toe in green felt. The colours of The High Priestess, The Hierophant, Page of Cups, and others, spun before her eyes. She then noticed that the little creature had also delivered a pale purple drink in a tall, clear glass, and so sweet and cool did it feel on her tongue, her loose teeth, she drank it down in two gulps.

That strange visit had been brief enough, but then came another, with the dwarf bearing a lump of pale cheese, half a peeled beetroot and a dry biscuit shedding flaky crumbs. Despite a deep, hurting hunger, she couldn't eat for fear her remaining teeth might fall out, and then where'd she be?

"What is this place?" she asked the little servant brushing the biscuit crumbs into his or her tiny palm. "And where are those two criminals?"

"Criminals?" The voice as light as one of her mother's sponges.

"Yes. Constable Coyle and the Minister. I was supposed to be released by Christmas Day evening." Her tongue dislodged one of her wobbling side teeth. It dropped into her hand, bringing with it a small skein of blood.

"Released to where?"

For a moment, that dark, grey house and its two tall chimneys loomed into mind. The windowless study where the cowardly McPhee had hidden herself. The linen room with its watching door… Yet still she could give it no name. As the green-clad figure licked those crumbs from its palm and rearranged the food, she tested herself on other things. Her mother - but what was she called? Her brother? The street she'd been born in?

And then she remembered that purple drink.

"Get me out of here!" She shrieked at the fussing creature. "I beg you, with everything I have. Everything…"

"Turn the cards to know your fate, Miss Lennox. If the Hanged Man's first, you're too late."

"You know my name?"

"Of course."

The minion backed away towards the cave wall on the opposite side, while Janet caught the illustrated victim's dead eye, the gaping mouth. Then, when she looked up, saw that same portion of cave wall beginning to open.

Having forced the imp through the widening gap in front of her, she fell forwards on to her knees, dragging her booted feet behind, just missing the dull thud of both sides of rock jamming tight together. She realised her gloves had been left on the table.

*

Janet and her attendant were encased within a black tunnel, rank with the winter's dead, and as his splashing footsteps receded behind her, she noticed a grey light grow brighter with every frightened step she took. Was this from a moon? A roaming ghost? And then, almost like a benediction, came the smell of sea.

No matter her belly's sickness had crept to her throat, that promise of freedom drove her forwards, past the tunnel's barnacled walls, where small, white crabs and dried, splayed starfish rotted amongst the shells. Salt air stung her loose and broken teeth, her eyes and the bruise she knew still lay on her left cheek. A strand of her own hair blew across her face, blinding her to what lay immediately ahead, blocking her path, nudged by foamy, incoming water. The sorrowful sight of a black lump of fur ending in a distinctive feathered tail.

Her loyal friend whose name also escaped her. But what had he been doing there? Searching for his missing owner? Or killed then dumped where he might never be found?

Suddenly, voices she remembered.

"Down here!"

"Ye should have tied the witch fast, sir."

"Your job, not mine."

With that argument echoing at the far end of the tunnel, Janet picked herself up, gave the lifeless dog one last glance and willed her heavy boots to carry her quicker than ever before into the lapping tide.

*

Moonlight. She'd guessed right. But not the salt water's cleaving cold, drawing her and the bulky clothes on her back down and down until only by freeing her numb arms from her killing coat, could she begin to rise again. She watched it float away without her. Empty arms outstretched, filling with water. A pair of seagulls hovered above as a vicious cramp bit into her legs. She tried to stay afloat long enough to get her bearings. One creature landed on her head and pecked at her skull. Another her ear.

"Away wi' ye!" She gargled, fearing her eyes would be next. "Away!"

A shoreline to the left, dotted with the flickering lights of small, green dwellings, gave no clue as to whether she was on a loch or the sea itself. But just to imagine a warm hearth with food on the stove and a clean bed to sleep in was too much to bear, driving her arms and leaden legs to greater effort.

To her right, she glimpsed a rocky outcrop, bearing a solitary tree. If only she could reach it she might find somewhere to hide. To get warm again... And then piece by piece, her broken memory mended.

She must be in a sea loch. Was this Loch Nonach again?

Just then, a sudden splash some way behind her. Something slapping the water in a regular beat. What could that be? Was she perhaps in Loch Lomond with its mysterious monster or was this some huge, man-eating bird bearing down on her?

Sweet Jesus...

To her left, from the corner of her stinging eye, Janet picked out the moonlit prow of a shiny, blue and white bark, carrying at least three people. From it came a piercing beam of light. Shouts and curses, meant for her.

She prayed to that blue vein on her nose. "Dinnae let me drown here. Nae now... please, nae now..."

With every last ounce of life, her arms and hands clawed at the mounting waves and her leaden feet kicked out until her bleached fingers finally connected with rock. Part of a substantial crannog she didn't recognise.

She dragged herself closer through swathes of kelp that cradled a dead eel's slimy corpse and other leavings from the deep. From here she scrambled upwards wherever she could gain a hold. Slipping backwards more than moving forwards. Keeping her cries to herself, she managed to haul her shivering, drenched body into the first hollow and crouched down in a welcome nest of broken bracken and wet, cushioning moss.

The blue vein had heard her plea.

The vegetation surrounding her gave off an odd, sour-sweet smell, but it was the sea gulls and a spread-winged buzzard circling the one alder tree which worried her. Also her pursuers drawing closer while she gathered smaller rocks for ammunition, should they try to land.

"Give yersel up, while ye can, ye witch." Came a man's voice Janet thought she'd heard before.

"We can shoot you with less mercy than we would a deer," said another.

Try then...

Janet placed a few ferns on her head to disguise herself and peeped out in the direction of these threats, before that same, blinding beam hit her eyes. The generous moon showed three figures and a rifle barrel pointing in her direction.

Her first rock hit a man with rough hair wrapped up against the cold. The next took another's hat from his head and, while leaning over to retrieve it from the water, a third rock caught his arm.

The Reverend McKinnon?

"You foolish, Devilish sinner!" He hollered in pain. "You've just sealed your fate."

"Speak for yersel." And as her ravaged, gloveless hands groped for a bigger rock, they met with something just as hard, but smooth. And that odd smell wasn't from any sheltered moss, but stale, dark blood.

Human blood.

✳✳✳

29

Where wolves lurk in sheep's clothing...

Despite the unexpected moonlight and array of winking stars, Footer's Hill had never seemed so forbidding. Every jutting rock, every pocket of darkness were faces belonging to the long-dead guarding their sacred home.

Catriona let Donald Baird guide her alongside the narrow burnie in full spate that led from the hill loch behind her father's but and ben. Somewhere she did not want to go, and yet, for appearances must seem a willing partner. The architect had even suggested a novel Christmas gift to replace the one she'd not had time to deliver to him. To offer a permanent, full-time post at Ardnasaig House, with all creature comforts included. Starting in three days' time.

"And with you as my housekeeper, and another two maids in place - with this time, *two* letters of reference apiece - my son will be better able to manage the estate in my absence. So far, I'm afraid to say, he's had a woeful disregard for its possibilities."

"He does seem to prefer deer drives elsewhere," she ventured.

"Precisely. Anything not involving his own. And as for inviting that tramp from Dunblane in for luncheon…"

His own?

Catriona stared at him. The full moon above the hill seemed too oppressive. Too unwelcoming. Waiting for her dream to dismantle. For her to fail. "Is the estate not yours, sir?"

A pause.

"Of course."

She sighed with relief. But not for long.

"And my wife was - is still - my chief beneficiary, but every day without her is..." His voice was soon lost to the sounds of tumbling water, and Catriona touched his arm in a sympathetic gesture. "However, as a responsible father, I do have James to think of."

"Of course, sir. And he showed great loyalty when you were late coming home on Christmas Eve. I've never seen anyone so distracted."

"Is that so?"

"Indeed, sir."

The architect stared up at the moon. "When he was a lad, I was tempted to rename him Janus."

"Why's that, sir?"

"You're not familiar with the legend?"

"No, sir. And before this track gets too boggy, we could turn off here to the right. It's longer, but safer."

Not the first time she'd lied to the man who held her future in his hands. But to her mind, lies were often the only way out. Despite what those stupid Ten Commandments said.

"As I was saying," Donald Baird's feet stayed put. "The Janus legend concerns a Roman deity who kept the gate of Heaven. He had one face in front, the other behind. I won't bore you with details about his eponymous temple, but to many, he represents two-facedness. And James's apparent loyalty is the opposite to his wayward, lackadaisical side."

Just then, she didn't care if his son had the head of an elephant and the body of a mouse. She had to divert this man from going near Footer's Hill and her father.

"Sir," she reminded him. "I *do* know these tracks. We're sure to meet trouble after the melt, and I wouldn't want your wife's beautiful boots ruined."

His leather-gloved hand took hers and tightened its grip.

"Miss McPhee, you are in my employ, therefore my responsibility. If harm befalls us, I carry the blame."

This man was more than stubborn. If only that other part of him was as rigid, she thought, forcing a smile and thanking him for his consideration. Adding her steps to his on a route that would bring them to her father's door. No time to ask if he'd actually signed everything over to his son, or how that weak, devious individual had survived nine months in the womb without the Dame of Nonach's attentions. She'd spotted Footer's Cottage. Sniffed woodsmoke in the air.

Damn it for ever...

*

The one front window seemed little more than a pinprick glow between the bare oaks and alders lining the burn. And the nearer they came to it, the more Catriona discerned a blemish moving against its brightness. Then another, also in motion. Two figures, she was sure of that. But what they were doing, she couldn't tell. Was Fergus Bogle still there? And if so, why?

The front door opened before she and the architect reached the end of the weedy path, and although the night was turning towards a frost, she felt sweat prickle her skin.

"You go first," he said, letting go of her hand. "He's your father, after all."

Your father after all…

Four words that made her want to run as far as London. Failing that, she must sink the architect's little boat of plans.

"Please don't judge him, sir," she began. "Like I've said, he doesn't take his drink too well. Nor his personal appearance. And as for the state of the place, just shut your eyes."

"No-one's perfect, Miss McPhee. 'Tis the spirit that counts."

Inwardly, Catriona tried to calm her leaping pulse, but when her father came into full view, holding a half-done candle, this same pulse seemed to stop.

*

Iain Hamish McPhee was a different man altogether. Gone the mane of grey, greasy hair, the crumpled clothes and smell of heavy. Instead, here stood someone who'd spent some time on his appearance. Even the stone flags beneath his shiny black boots had been swept clean. Not what she'd hoped for at all.

Those same flecked, brown eyes looked her and her companion up and down, but this time, they were keen as a hawk's, no longer bleary. He let her peck his newly-shaven cheek.

"Thank you for my Christmas present," she said with forced cheerfulness. "It was very thoughtful of you. I'm sorry I didn't have time to bring you anything over. I've been that busy…"

"I'm sure ye have. And remember, 'tis far better to give than to receive," he said, holding a hand out to the architect. "Another unexpected visit, sir. My pleasure, I'm sure. Now what can I help ye with, this time?"

"Mr McPhee, your daughter's been abroad in the cold for long enough. At my behest, I might add. I'll explain why we're here, if you'd kindly let us share your hearth for a few moments."

Her father's eyes rested on hers, and was it an unspoken fear that passed between them?

"Mr Baird's not been long back from his travels," she put in. "And a terrible journey home."

"Very well. Cam ben the hoose. But I'm a man on me own, remember. Nae woman tae help me, ye understand. While ye," he looked at the architect, "without forgetting yer wife, are more fortunate."

"Your daughter is certainly an asset."

"She always was. Now sir, please step inside. As ye can see, 'tis nae palace."

"But it's so tidy," she protested. "You've really worked hard. Mother would be so pleased."

"Pride, it is, dochter. Lose it and yer nothing."

"Quite." said Donald Baird, as Catriona followed her father into those four walls that had shaped so much of her and her mother's lives. Despite the cleanliness and the well-made fire, she felt a deepening shame that the man who'd raised her wages and even shared his bed with her, promising her a future, should see again such a lowly dwelling.

She noticed the dark blue phial containing her moon-blood stood in the shadows behind the door. With the toe of her boot, she pushed it further out of sight. His old rifle stood polished and gleaming propped up in its usual place by his mud-free coat. A reserve pair of outdoor boots as buffed as those he was wearing. And then, amongst his various caps, something that made her stop. A Black Watch tartan one. Something he'd never worn. But she knew someone who had...

"What ye starin' at?" He challenged her.

"Nothing."

"Weel, come on now. Let me open a bottle. We've drinkin' tae do."

*

Too tense to eat or drink, Catriona sat next to her employer on two unmatched chairs in front of the fire, while the story - with her additions - of James Baird's absence unfolded. How his cob was still in its stable, all his clothes still in his room and his rifle where he'd left it by the coats near the Store. Without prompting, she poked the embers and added more wood - spitting larch, alive with wood lice.

"And keys to the house?" Her father asked, bending by a small cupboard next to the grate.

"He must have taken them. I've been looking all over."

"So where did this son o' yourn like to go?" Iain McPhee found three glasses and set them on a rough, wooden table. She noticed they looked washed and polished. "Up or down?"

"He means hills or the loch, sir," Catriona explained. "And, given what you said earlier, I'd say the hills."

The architect frowned. Had she spoken out of turn? Or was he lost for words?

No, he wasn't.

"I'd say the loch, Mr McPhee. That's where you'd found where my wife's and her dogs' tracks ended. Yes," he nodded. "Definitely the loch. But then you see, I'm quite out of touch. My work keeps me away for too long. Why I'm here with your daughter, asking for your help again. And although tomorrow's a Sunday, I'll pay you well to start a search for James. Use anyone you can, and whatever means."

"And the law, sir? I cannae work wi' them."

"They're too busy anyway," said Catriona, before the architect could reply, now ignoring all Margaret Lennox's advice about offering unwanted opinions. That bossy bitch was dead, buried in a pauper's grave, whereas *she* was alive, wearing another pair of Isobel Baird's boots, and not for the first time. And was that relief she saw flickering in her father's eyes?

"Fair seem to be," he said. "Only this morning, that throw-back Coyle and the minister from Kilforgan was driving past the loch towards Cranranich, beating the life out o' the hoss, too. Odd thing, but it weren't pulling no police carriage, and the blind on my side, were down. I did wonder where they was going, and who might have bin inside..."

303

Catriona imagined Lennox being carted off to her fate, and that thought brought a tiny smile. The architect however, still frowned.

"And there's this man from Dunblane, Falcon Steer. Your daughter tells me he's up to no good round here. A vagrant who's been welcomed into my house, courtesy of my son. Flattering my housemaid, if you please."

Her father set down his glass. Licked his lips. Looked to her for a description.

"Tall, black hair, roughly cut, around twenty-six years old?" she volunteered, before standing up. The longer she stayed here, the greater the risk of too much being said. Iain McPhee was shaking his head.

"Nae. Cannae say I have."

"Or a black Gordon setter. He'd be fourteen by now..." Donald Baird, looking wan despite the firelight, drained the last of his whisky. "One of the best."

"Sir, I'd have told ye if so."

The architect placed his empty glass on the stone window ledge and as a reminder, patted her father's arm.

"Tomorrow, Mr McPhee?

"At your service, sir. And if yer agreeable, I'll report back to ye Monday morning."

Catriona shivered at that earth-coloured smile. Even as a bairn she'd never trusted it.

Both men shook hands. But worse was to come.

"And another matter. Just as urgent. I'm seeking a replacement handyman by January 4th," the architect added. "The day before I leave. The post involves six days a week. Three kirk holidays a year. Full board..."

"E'en without yer son there, sir?"

Pause.

"James will be found. Now, would you consider it?"

"I'd be honoured, sir."

*

Another handshake, which Catriona couldn't bear to watch. Which also made her walk over to where she'd seen that tartan cap. With her back towards the two men, she slipped it inside her cape.

"Father," she then began as if the missing handyman was someone she cared about. "Have *you* set eyes on Fergus Bogle at all?"

A shake of his head. But was it rather too quick?

"Nae, lassie. Ne'er a whisper. Ne'er a breath.

Perhaps next time, wi' a death..."

***

30.

In which sorrows multiply…

Janet had been on guard for the third night in a row, with no sleep, frozen clothes, blue hands, broken nails and boots sealed to her numb feet. But at least her memory had returned. She'd tested it, going back year by year until her third birthday, walking hand in hand with Calum and her mother in the shipyards, alongside the *Pride of Argyll,* a black monster alive with sparks, destined to carry pig iron wherever pig iron was needed. Before that, nothing, except her mother's stories. How she'd neither crawled, nor drunk milk only water. Never cried when hurt and, how, unlike Calum, not given up on anything she'd started. Until that fateful March midnight…

*

At least she was breathing, unlike poor James Baird who reeked worse than the stanks at Ardnasaig House after the storms. Her buried pity rose up like a sudden tide to see him so dead, so bloated, but what if some passenger steamer should pass by? Or a fishing boat? Would she try and stop it to take him aboard? To let his father know? No. Because she'd be the first suspect and already had been accused of killing an old man she'd never even met.

She shifted position so she could better keep the gulls and other greedy beaks from what remained of the son of Ardnasaig House, while that star-filled night was now a purple haze, almost black over the hills and mountains either side of the loch, and dawn a cream smudge high on her left, reflected in the distant, open sea.

Opposite and below the towering slab of land shaped like an ape's head, lay that same settlement of green dwellings she'd seen during her swim. Baw Heid. Where else? Where she'd be wanted again.

To her right, more familiar views brought back other memories swept from her mind. As for her pursuers, they'd vanished, rowing away up the loch in silence. Perhaps lying in wait for her on the shore somewhere. Perhaps her thrown stones had done their work. She most fervently hoped so. Meanwhile, there were other, more persistent enemies.

"Leave 'im be!" She hissed as two fat crows hovered over that half-eaten face, whose unmatched eyes had already gone. "He used to harm ye once, but he cannae harm ye now."

But he *had* harmed her.

Yet as they flapped away inland, leaving behind an ominous silence, she plucked the maggots from his open mouth, spread more dead ferns over his face and let her fingers touch the two of his fingers that were left. Inky blue, puffed up like pea pods. Then she forgave him.

It was impossible to tell if he'd been wounded or not. She'd noticed no bullet holes or killing cuts. The greedy birds had done that. And with his rifle left by the Store before he'd run away, how could he have defended himself? As for searching his breeches' pockets and what was left of his coat, she couldn't.

"Did ye swim here like me, or take a bark from somewhere and let it go?" She asked him softly as if he could reply. Were ye lookin' for yer mother? For Rabbie? Or runnin' from Falcon Steer?"

The only answer were distant kirk bells beginning their six chimes and the faintest mew of gulls massing over the opposite shore. And then she saw why.

Boats. At least two, matching the sky's colour, pushing their way towards Blae Crannog.

As a farewell, she pulled a few matted strands of hair from his head and tucked them into her soggy skirt pocket. Then, having taken as deep a breath as her weary lungs would allow, clambered down through bladderwrack and the kind of dark, green seaweed she'd once used for her face, into the black water.

Christ Jesus...

Colder than last night, stinging her skin, her everything as she swam stiff-armed round to the far side and out of sight. What if one of those giant carp should nibble at her ankles? What if her heart gave out, and if she did have the start of a wean in her belly, would it shrivel and die?

"Stop it," she ordered herself out loud. Then, "swim... swim..."

*

The tidal, sea-going current bore her downstream towards the nearest shore where an invisible, pebbly shelf scraped against her body, forcing her to stand where nothing shielded her from the oncoming boats.

She soon found a rocky glen in which to draw breath and wring out her sopping skirt, while trying to judge the safest way towards the Kilforgan to Cranranich track.

Woodsmoke, just then, the sweetest smell in all the world. Two ponies tethered to a post. One brown, the other skewbald whose markings seemed familiar; sweat darkening its neck. An off-white sheet was strung out on a line slung between two pines.

There must be a dwelling, and someone must be at home...

She glanced behind her to see the two boats were gaining. Their oars frothing the loch. With her hair dripping down her neck and a length of seaweed lodged between her bubs, Janet ducked under the wet sheet to find a slate-topped bothy set in a plot bordered by a mossy wall. Both ponies whinnied a welcome and a dog yelped from inside an adjoining barn, but nothing swayed her from following the pathway to the front door.

"There she be!"

"The witch."

"Aye, a canny one, to be sure." The same woman's voice she'd heard on that boat near Baw Heid, made Janet spin round. "She strangled and drowned her brother's wean with nae a care. A murderer, tha's what she is. A *wean* murderer... And suppose I were to tell him what ye done, eh?"

Linnet Garvie's face with that wicked cast to her eyes, was almost unrecognisable. And all the while, Falcon Steer's rifle pointed at Janet's heart.

Jesus help me...

Constable Coyle toiled behind them with the minister panting and crossing himself with each step. One arm – which her stone had hit - lay strapped to his coat with a rope.

Fearn House. A miracle.

"Help!" she yelled. "Or they'll kill me!" Her numb, puckered fists hammered on its wooden door.

As if by another miracle, this door inched open and a elderly man whose grey hair stood up on end, pulled her inside. He slid the three bolts across while the roar of gunshot filled her ears. Of bullets striking stone, then orders being yelled. Linnet Garvie screeching out her name before she and her other pursuers retreated through the glen.

*

"Dauvit Hendry. Forestry worker for forty-two years." Her elderly rescuer held out a quivering hand of welcome, roughened by a life of outdoor work. "And I ken who ye are. Janet, the hoosekeeper's daughter from Ardnasaig. This is a terrible, terrible place."

Stiff-legged, still on alert, he pointed to the front window. "See," he added. "Cowards every bloody one. And I wonder who gave them the barks. Someone with nae conscience, that's for sure."

But Janet barely heard him, for the woman she'd known most of her short life was staring back at her from a distance, wagging a forefinger until she too, vanished beyond the curve of land.

"I'd heard about ye and yer mother from Master Baird." Dauvit Hendry looked straight at her. A man who'd spent his life among trees - growing them, cutting them for others to use, as well as for his own rowing boats. "Always spoken highly of ye both I'm sorry she passed on so sudden."

Both names came like cuts to Janet's heart. But it was too soon to reveal where the dead young man lay until she felt truly out of danger. If the former forester went running off to find him, she'd be alone. Surely God would forgive her selfishness?

"Thank ye, Mr Hendry," she said instead. The first words to come out, even though her mind was full of them. "And for savin' me life."

"I do unfortunately ken that roughneck Coyle and the minister," he said out of the blue. "But who were them other two?"

Janet told him, but shivering so much from nerves and cold, she had to repeat their hateful names twice. "Markin' me as a witch, they was. I've already been kept prisoner at Kilforgan and Baw Heid, where this dwarf gave me a special drink so I'd lose me memory."

"Baw Heid?" he repeated then tutted. "Is tha' where ye got yer bruise?"

"Kilforgan. In the Police House." Trying not to cry.

"We ken who's the *real* witch around here," he said, eyeing her up and down, from her bruised cheek and her loose teeth to her squelching boots. A look of concern and embarrassment on his face.

"We? And what witch do ye mean?"

"Where's ye coat?" Was his reply.

"Got rid. Too heavy in the water."

"Did ye swim straight across?"

She hesitated. James Baird would come later…

"Aye."

He seemed impressed.

"As there's nae other woman here, ye cannae be takin' off yer clothes to dry them. But I've a guid fire going. Come and sit yersel down. I'll fetch a rag for ye hair."

"Yer a kind man, Mr Hendry."

She followed him into a low-ceilinged room dominated by a gaping grate alive with flames. After McPhee's tricks, she wouldn't be going too close, but the offer of a solid oak chair was too good to resist. Set between two armchairs which, judging by their dented cushions, had been recently occupied, it was the second closest thing to Heaven. Smelling that woodsmoke had been the first.

While Dauvit Hendry placed more logs on the blaze, Janet unbuttoned her damp boots, placed them by the fire guard and stretched out her weary legs. She also pulled her wet, salty socks from between her toes and rubbed her skin to restore some warmth. Her rescuer wiped his hands on his old breeches and patted her shoulder. "I can fetch ye a dram and a bite if ye can manage it. Ye've endured what folks here ha' always feared. The power of bigots and the corrupt, like a festering sore in these parts, it is. And Colonel Ritchie's another one. I hope sleep brings him a quick death."

He moved again towards the window, then paused. "We're nae over yet, Miss Lennox. And I'm sorry we couldnae spare ye some of yer suffering, but…"

"We?"

His toothless smile caused deep creases in his weathered skin.

312

"I'll let me frein do the talkin.' Thinks a lot of ye, too, does Fergus..."

Fergus? Mr Bogle?

"That's impossible," she breathed, then turned to stare at the man, almost a stranger now, whose normally dour face had softened. She left her chair and threw her weak, damp arms around his neck. Saving her tears for later. For her mother, for Calum, even for James Baird, now food for the very birds he'd shoot for fun.

"I confess, Miss Lennox," came the handyman's familiar, gruff voice. "I cared for Miss McPhee more. Glaikit old eejit I were..." He eased himself from her embrace and paused until Dauvit Hendry left them to made his way to the kitchen. "Especially after seein' ye by the well almost three years back. Ye must ha' bin in agony, mind..."

"I will be. For ever."

"But we won't stand by and see a young woman hunted down. And all because o' pretty Catriona McPhee. 'Twere me who urged Mrs Fergusson to show Master Baird her brother's record of his second Footer's Cottage visit five years' ago. To warn him what the maid were really like. But Mrs Fergusson were too fearful to call at Ardnasaig, and got Dauvit to go instead. So," he scrutinised her whole appearance especially her damaged hands. "What 'appened? Why 'ave ye bin singled out? I must ken everything, Janet. I mean, everything, if ye want me 'elp."

Hadn't she done the same with Falcon Steer? But what choice did she have?

*

Afterwards, Mr Hendry duly delivered a piece of towelling and placed a dram of malt in her hands. The firelight reflected in the golden liquid made her long for sleep.

"A tad early, but drink up, lass," he encouraged. "Ye might still need it."

The powerful sweetness burned on her tongue. On her windpipe. In fact, all the way down.

"I'm sorry to bring danger here," she said to him, exhausted all over again from re-living James Baird's treachery and hearing the real reason why Fergus Bogle had left Ardnasaig for his own particular mission.

"Ne'er mind me, lass. It's ye who must tread carefully."

"He's right." Mr Bogle moved to the window, lifting a heavy grey pistol from behind a group of pine cones on a nearby shelf. "Our skite constable won't want to lose face now. I ken 'im from 'is Inverary days. Me guess is they'll hide up till we drop our guard." He turned to his friend. "The ponies should be locked away in the barn, or they'll take 'em. And me Bonnie like yourn, Dauvit, has been a trusty frein."

"I'll go," Janet said. 'Tis the least I can do."

"Nae lass." Mr Hendry laid down the oat loaf he was slicing, and unbolted the kitchen's back door. All at once, a brown shadow seemed to move between the nearby alders. Falcon Steer appeared, firing three shots at the bothy, sending squirrels higher into the birches, and birds into the sky.

*

314

Janet snatched the towel from her head and ran out to the stricken forester who, clutching his bloody side, staggered over to the two ponies already down, lying still. Of their killer, there was no sign.

"Mr Hendry! Stop!" She screamed after him. "I'll let the hound out while ye get yersel back indoors. He'll see 'em off..."

The huge, pale creature now free, leapt the boundary wall to give chase as she caught up with her saviour and, with Mr Bogle supporting him, pressed the towel against the oozing wound until they reached the bothy. With the moon's white carcass hanging overhead, Janet staunched the bleed and helped carry the stricken man back towards his hearth.

"Damn tha' De'il," murmured the forester, in agony. "Damn 'is soul..."

She'd never seen grown men cry before. Not even Calum when he'd said he loved her. But now, her tears came too. Raw, hot on her skin. And, as they laid Dauvit Hendry down on a makeshift bed and poured three drams down his throat for her to better prise the bullet from his body, she finally told a red-eyed Fergus Bogle about the architect's son, and where he could be found.

✱✱✱

31.

Where more necessary journeys are undertaken...

Just three days of the old year left, and good riddance.

At midnight, following a Day of Rest pacing the rooms and the grounds of Ardnasaig House, the architect had begged Catriona "to comfort" him again. And, as she'd been sleepless, imagining her father invading Ardnasaig's corridors, being everywhere he wasn't wanted, she'd thought at the time, this would be a welcome and useful distraction.

*

Before even the squirrels and cushat doves had moved from their rests in the rowan trees, or the sly capercailles from amongst the firs, Catriona left the impotent architect deep in sleep. Having thrown her cape over her nightdress and slipped her bare feet into those same luxurious boots belonging to his wife, she left the house, taking a short cut over the mossy grass where crocus buds and daffodil tips were already pushing their way into the light with far more vigour than he'd so far shown.

Why was she now risking a heavy cold or worse? She had no choice. Her father's knowing smile seemed to follow her all the way to that dank, sheltered graveyard where the first creeping light of day revealed the Dame of Nonach's stone.

She knelt down, letting her grazed hand stoke its solid, wet stump, the way she'd tried to pleasure the slumbering man. How her former friends in Cranranich had shown her. Twice, three times, to no avail, and her hand had grown tired.

"Once my son's found, then I'll show you what I'm capable of," he'd said on previous occasions, but she'd not been convinced. Her shiver of doubt added to those rumours that his rich, beautiful wife had strayed. Was this perhaps why?

Catriona lay down on the soaking, uncut grass, ensuring her stomach rested against the stone itself, and began the chant she'd been preparing ever since he'd apologised.

"Give me his seed and make it grow,

for nine full months with no blood show.

May our bairns thrive within this place

and Lennox perish without God's grace."

Yet any satisfaction she might have felt, was spoilt by the strongest feeling that the same presence she'd felt in the stable yesterday, was with her again. Touching her, pushing her. Keeping her deep amongst the neglect where a silent slug had crept on to her throat.

Having recovered her balance and sense of purpose, Catriona looked up to see Donald Baird's curtains still reassuringly drawn close. She brushed grass and other unwanted souvenirs from her clothes and, as if her supplication had revived her, set off along one of the marked paths that followed the track east towards Cranranich. The shore route would leave her too exposed. This way lay the cover she needed and the last but one obstacle to her dream.

*

The hall clock's six chimes accompanied her back up to the architect's bedroom where he lay on his back under the quilt and blankets, staring up at the ceiling.

"Sir?" whispered Catriona. "May I make a suggestion?" Another of Margaret Lennox's rules being broken.

"Indeed you may."

She came round to his side of the bed and he promptly sat up, clearly surprised to see her up and dressed. And then, too late, those creased-up eyes alighted on a muddy smear on the front of her cloak and the tips of his wife's fawn boots.

"So, where have you been so early?"

Her new lie was ready.

"I couldn't sleep, sir, for worrying about your son. I know my father's been out looking too, but I had to go searching myself. And it also occurred to me that while Miss Lennox draws breath, she may have lured him somewhere he might never be found. To punish him. And then you, sir."

He shook his balding head too quickly, as if the very thought was worthless.

"Miss Lennox is safely locked away until her hearing next Thursday. That I know. So, Miss McPhee, where *did* you go?"

"The loch, sir. I had the strongest feeling..." She placed a hand over her heart. Felt its quickening rhythm under her palm as he left the bed, naked save for his creased, fawn-coloured pantaloons, and stood by the window.

"But you told your father that James would head for the hills."

"I know, sir. I'm sorry."

318

"You argued against me when I'd said "down," remember? 'Up or down?' That's what he asked us."

Catriona sensed as if a crack was forming under her feet. She'd read about earthquakes with her mother. How in the blink of an eye, that crack can become a chasm, a void.

"So you think *this* is what we should do?" he said.

She nodded.

"I can make you some porridge sir. Warm you up for the day."

He began pulling on every item of clothing left out from yesterday. Vest, shirt, thick woollen waistcoat, jacket and brown cord breeches. Socks pulled up to his bony knees with a sigh.

"It may be best if I stay behind, sir," she tested him. "I'll only be a trouble to you."

"Excuse my impatience, Miss McPhee. My son's the trouble. From day one. But then your child is always your child."

"I can see that, sir." But the time still wasn't right to ask about how James Baird came into being and survived.

As she left the room to prepare breakfast, she smiled and waved at Isobel Baird's annoying portrait. Then stuck one of her very own boots in the air just to show her who was now boss.

*

Porridge lay trapped in one corner of his mouth. A haunted look in his eyes as they stood outside Ardnasaig House in that dull, drizzling day she'd experienced earlier. He gazed upwards at the elms' crowns high against the sky behind the house, where bird silhouettes flickered between their branches. This constant motion made her restless to be off. Made her also realise that if the Dame of Nonach couldn't help deliver her dreams, then someone else just might. After all, Catriona reasoned to herself, no-one would pay good money for a stallion that couldn't breed. Would they? And at that very moment, the one possible future claimant to Ardnasaig, might be lying inside Janet Lennox. If, after New Year's Day, she was still breathing and pregnant, then surely her new-found contacts would get rid of both, leaving the fertile James Baird a much more attractive prospect. Therefore, finding him alive could only be to her advantage and, given instincts inherited from her father, the loch would be a good place to start...

*

No refreshments, no encumbrances. Just the two of them with umbrellas, avoiding the pockets of snow still not melted in the rowan grove beyond which, the loch's water spread wide and dark, and the old black mooring posts bobbed and swayed drunkenly in the current.

"Our first port of call must be his godparents." Donald Baird said, picking his way over the bigger pebbles, stepping back when the tide's milky frill shimmied near his boots. "And you've already met Mrs. Masters..."

"Yes sir, but who are the others?"

"Just one. Did James never mention her?"

"*Her*? No sir."

"It's Mrs. Helen Fergusson. Bar-Beithe Cottage."

A small shiver, then a smile.

"Fine names, sir," she managed to say.

But if Donald Baird insisted upon her meeting this stranger, she'd have to be more than vigilant. With her own father too. Especially after his surprise Christmas present. Strange that James Baird had barely mentioned Fergusson, because she'd heard Roberta Masters' name many times. Why she herself had made a point of visiting the overweight boat owner on Christmas Eve to place herself in a good light.

"Helen's husband made clogs," volunteered her companion. "A fine craftsman."

Hideous things. Catriona recalled another big upset at Footer's Cottage when she'd refused to wear them. "Is he dead, sir?"

A nod.

She then had an idea. "None of Master Baird's friends called while you were away," she said. "Do any live around here?"

A rueful glance. "Another of our worries. He rarely mixed with anyone, even at school."

Our?

How she wished he'd stop using that word. It didn't help at all.

Now, as the smirr faded to a clinging dampness, they both took the same short cut she already knew well, and instead of that treacherous ice underfoot, lay water in all its forms. Where the main burnie's little footbridge swilled with a brackish flow from the land above, the architect took her hand, still reddened after the housemaid's madness. At other times, where black silt rose too near the top of his wife's boots, he let an arm slip around her waist for support, and in those brief moments, she felt protected from the dark forces she knew were gathering to unravel her future.

*

"Well, well, Donald," beamed Roberta Masters, the square-shaped widow, resplendent in a grey woollen nightgown with a double ruff under her fat chin. She looked from one to the other. Catriona immediately guessed her train of thought.

"What brings ye here at this time of a morning?" The woman then focussed on Catriona. "And ye, wee lassie, once again?"

The architect answered first.

"James hasn't been home since Christmas Day morning. Except for his keys, everything of his is still in the house. Even his rifle. Why I've brought Miss McPhee here, to lend her intuition."

The woman clearly didn't approve. "Intuition's a fine thing, Donald, but surely ye need the law? Have ye spoke with Constable Coyle yet?"

"Useless. He wasn't at Kilforgan on Saturday when we called. And Superintendent Lampard's off in the Alps somewhere."

"*We*, eh, Donald?" She repeated, dry as a stale bannock, glancing at Catriona.

He ignored her, while Catriona waited for that fleshy mouth to do its worst. Instead, Roberta Masters stepped down on to the path and pointed at the track that connected all the south lochside's villages.

"Up there were the constable with the Reverend McKinnon sitting alongside him, that very same day. Five, six o'clock in the

322

evening I'd say. Careering along. The brown cab were ne'er a police one, mind. Going like the Devil in all that wet..." She turned to the architect as if remembering something else. "Your James called here on Christmas Eve. Afternoon it was. To see if I'd a cart he could borrow. But the ground was too bad."

Catriona realised those hoof prints and the dung she'd seen earlier by the cottage, had been those of his cob.

"Please go on..."

"He seemed all in on hisself. I cannae describe it, and told him nae to bother wi' setting the traps. Perhaps if he'd stayed, we'd have had a cup of tea together and he might have told me things."

"Perhaps." And then his father repeated Lennox's cruel curse. Afterwards, the woman seemed too shocked to speak. Her hand stayed over her lips. "Tha's truly wicked. Where *is* this creature?"

"Where she should be. Now, Roberta, is there anything else you can tell us?"

But she seemed awkward. Her enthusiasm waning. Perhaps aware of her huge nipples showing through the wool. Her stomach and the bump of her sex below it. "I'd ask ye both in but as ye can see, I'm nae dressed to receive visitors properly."

"Please, Mrs Masters," Catriona spoke up. "Can't you see how much this mystery weighs on Mr Baird's mind?"

"Sometimes James'd come here wand'ring around looking' at me barks. Even the old ones up on the shore."

"That *is* odd," conceded the architect, casting his gaze to the pebble strand where, after every storm all manner of things turned up, from the pleasure steamers in particular.

"Didn't ye ken two of Dauvit's barks went missing just after yer dear Isobel?" The troublemaker speaking again. "A red one for setting bait. The other, white?"

"Roberta, you should have said. So should he."

"Well, there's been that much thieving round here, 'specially now with the Clearances, it didnae seem important at the time."

Catriona suppressed a third shiver, despite bright yellow ribbons of daylight forcing their way through the grey sky. "While you were absent, sir, Master James spoke of nothing else but security. He was very particular about keys." She shook the raindrops from the Fox umbrella and folded it. The best feature being its long, sharp spike at the end.

"And here's another thing," went on the Godmother. "We all ken yer wife's footprints ended by Dauvit's wall, but James was ne'er happy with that, was he? Always felt something was wrong about that story. How they so suddenly came to an end, nae like those of the dogs…"

Catriona watched every nuance in that porky face, aware of her own breath slowing up.

"Story?" The architect looked more than unhappy. "Mr McPhee's the best tracker for miles. Besides, we saw the prints for ourselves. Constable Wildman too."

Roberta Masters' eyes were on Catriona's feet. "So did I." She peered as close as her bulk would allow. "Like all well-bred women, Isobel wore boots just like these throughout the summer, and I'd swear to me God they was the same size."

"Because these *are* hers." Catriona, kept her turbulent thoughts to herself. Clenching her hand around Janet's coins in her cape pocket. "Mr Baird here, gave me permission to wear them."

Roberta Masters frowned just like the pug lapdog Catriona's grandmother once kept in Tarbet. Soft, with flabby folds of skin...

"Well, tha's an odd to-do. And dare I say, Donald, an' I hope ye'll forgive me, but it's nae wonder me poor godson's turned out the way he has..."

***

32.

In which snares are sprung and friends re-united...

Janet woke from a dreamless sleep to Dauvit Hendry's yelping hound and a room full of such violent sunlight that made her shut her eyes again and grope her way to the tiny window overlooking the wood behind. The huge, demented animal was running back and fore along the top of the boundary wall, ears on full alert.

Without bothering to splash her face with the stagnant water in the wash bowl, Janet scrambled into her still-damp clothes, glad she'd kept her boots on overnight, even though they reeked of the loch. She'd never feel safe again while she was here in this place of narrow tracks and overbearing trees. Not even with Mr Bogle by her side. And it was no good waiting for Calum. That note of hers had surely been lost. Besides, she'd already caused Mr Hendry serious injury and the deaths of two loyal ponies. She couldn't risk any more.

The former handyman stood at the bottom of the small flight of stairs, his trembling hand clasping the newel post. His bloodshot eyes glancing this away and that. He too must have slept in his clothes, and fresh soil lay on his boots and breeches. For the first time, looking down on him, she saw his bare head. How pale it was compared to his other skin. She'd never seen him without his usual tam o' shanter and not noticed it missing last night when he and a Doctor Johnston from Inverary had collected James Baird's body from Blae Crannog. Along with Dauvit Hendry, he'd been taken to hospital in Glasgow.

"How is Mr Hendry? Have ye heard? " Janet asked him, seeing a distracted shake of the head. "Like the doctor said, ye did well, lass, gettin' the lead out o' him. Ye saved his life, tha's for sure. Now yer own needs savin'."

But a certain question also needed an answer.

"And James? Had he been killed?"

"Nae, lass. Doctor Johnson believes it were cramps and exposure before the birds began feasting. He told me on the way out to his carriage. Having listened to me account of life at Ardnasaig, he's convinced the young man wanted to die. Nothing in 'is pockets neither. As if he'd seen hissel as a shroud already."

Janet shivered. Wondered out loud about his rifle that she'd last seen in the Store.

"Nae rifle."

"No keys? Or his purse?"

Another shake of that weary head.

Odd, she thought. Unless they'd been thieved…

"When will Mr Baird know?"

"Dr Johnson's calling in at Ardnasaig House early afternoon. He's assisting with an urgent appendix operation 'til then. And I'll re-visit that crannog soon as I can. In case something important's bin missed."

Mr Bogle's eyes began to water. He glanced at the window, clearly agitated. "Now that I've just buried the ponies, look over there! Those bloody cowards are back. Comin' up from the loch they are. All four o' them. Get down the cellar, quick. I can bring ye some porridge if ye need a bite…"

The prospect was tempting. She was hungry enough to devour two full bowls of the warm breakfast. But hunger wasn't for ever…

Janet hesitated, caught in a beam of yellow light that showed the real state of her clothes. Where on earth could she go, looking like this? And without a single coin to her name? "Thank ye, but…"

"Nae buts. Come along."

In that moment, like a burst of flame in a fire, she remembered something her mother had once said when they'd been ordered to leave Lismore before being paid.

"When I'm next in work, Janet, I'll be more canny. I'll tuck me money right safe away for our rainy days."

Rainy days… There'd surely been enough of those.

But where had she meant? In her room? Somewhere else? Or, had she spent all her wages on that trip to the Great Exhibition? Hardly, judging by the few items she'd brought back with her. A vase and those strange glass bottles. No time to wonder any further, for Mr Bogle was banging on the newel post.

"Do ye want to die, is that it, Janet? Ye saw Dauvit come close enough."

"Nae, but I have to go, Mr Bogle. I've bin too much trouble already. But I'm that thankful to ye both. I'll ne'er forget ye."

He suddenly gripped her shoulders. The last man to have done so in such desperation was Calum… "And *I* dinnae want to be pickin' ye up in in pieces like shot vermin. There's madmen out there, even though one calls hisself an officer o' the law and the other a minister who preaches brotherly love. Not to mention that De'il wi' the gun…"

And Linnet Garvie…

I ken all tha', but I must go, and come the New Year I…" she halted, unsure even then whether to trust him. "I might have Master Baird's wean to save."

"What?" Mr. Bogle's wrinkly eyes widened. Rested on her middle. "Did he ken?"

"Nae. But he did about me first. I told him. Just like I did to ye yesterday."

Mr Bogle pulled open the cellar door and turned to stare down into its gloom.

"Once I'd seen ye and the wean by the well that freezin' March night, I swore I'd ne'er breathe a word of it, as God's my witness. In these parts, a mother who takes her ane bairn's life is doomed. But if she's *due* one, can plead her belly." He looked again at Janet's middle, as if working things out. "I meant to tell ye that."

"So, if ye stay silent, and I'm caught and tried, I'll have eight months' reprieve?"

"Ye won't be caught if ye hide down the cellar here. And," he grew even more serious. "Some folk cud think ye have Master Baird's death on yer hands. Another cause to punish ye."

Janet sensed again that deep, deep water filling her up. A fat piece of kelp blocking her throat. "Don't think I'm ungrateful, Mr. Bogle, but me money's back at the house. And most likely me mother's. I cannae go anywhere with nothin' in me purse." She pecked his grizzled cheek. "Look after yersel. Dinnae worry about me."

"But... ye've nae coat..." he protested.

Too late. She elbowed her way past him and out of the front door whose three bolts were drawn back. Just then, as if sensing she might not get another chance, she turned round. "Before she died, my mother had a strange vision of Isobel Baird, and was able to repeat to me somethin' she'd said to her."

"I'm listenin'."

"Just tow me out on the loch and let my boat drift...."

*

Although the sun's position told Janet the time was eight o'clock or thereabouts, its strength felt more like midday. Full in her face as she crept around the bothy's far side and heaved herself over the moss-cushioned wall, into the woods beyond. Briar and bramble tugged at her skirt and in her panic to free herself, momentarily lost her bearings. Only when she remembered to bear left towards the plantation of birches, did she glance towards a track leading north towards Cranranich. And there, walking at a good rate, close as could be, were two figures. One tall, hatted, the other a bare-headed girl carrying a bag. Fair curls catching the sunlight.

The architect and Catriona McPhee.

Holy Mary.

Where were they off to in such a hurry? Just to see those curls bob-bobbing on her enemy's caped shoulders brought everything back, tainted by loathing. How she, Janet Lennox who'd once been the housekeeper's daughter, keeping the big house running from dawn to dusk, was now herself running for her life.

Suddenly, came the rustle of bare branches. Mr Hendry's hound with his tongue hanging from his jaws, was barking at her. A din she couldn't stop. She flattened herself against the wet, dead leaves; every bone in her body still aching from her frantic swim to that crannog. Every prayer she knew, spilling out under her breath.

"Wheeesht! Be off wi' ye!"

For a brief, alarming moment, her two betrayers seemed to stare in her direction before proceeding even quicker on their way, as if that pause had delayed them from some important plan. In different circumstances, she'd have caught up with them, told Donald Baird about his dead son. Challenged McPhee as to who she thought she was, stepping out with the Master of the house. Perhaps she'd forced herself upon him. Even threatened him. Neither seemed content, but they were giving her the perfect chance to retrieve her money from an empty house. Maybe find a change of clothes. A warm coat. A bite to eat…

To her relief, the hound bounded away in the direction of Fearn House leaving her in a sun-speckled silence, still full of danger, and those two hated figures growing smaller and smaller until the architect's top hat finally disappeared from view.

*

Calum might not be on his way to save her, but he'd certainly passed on his lock-picking skills learnt during training. She stood tucked inside Ardnasaig House's shaded front porch with a short length of bed spring from that cell in Kilforgan, a thin, torn strip from the Hanged Man tarot card and a large kilt pin she'd found at Mr Hendry's.

It was the Hanged Man's head which proved the most useful. Despite two soakings, the card was still stiff enough to slot into the keyhole without bending. With just three twists came what she'd been waiting for.

The click of victory.

Gritting her remaining teeth together, Janet checked no-one was passing by the gates at the end of the carriageway, before slipping into the hall and bolting the door behind her. The smell of wet clothes and a dense, biting chill immediately enveloped her. Why had McPhee let the place get so cold? Had she been too busy doing other things?

Under those stags' heads' watchful gaze, she tiptoed as best she could in her wet boots along to the kitchen where disorder reigned and, with a small, cooked tattie stuffed into each cheek, crept up the stairs, straining her ears for the faintest sound. When the grandfather clock chimed half past eight, she let out a yelp of surprise, scattering floury lumps from her mouth.

She scrambled past Isobel Baird's portrait tilting disrespectfully against the wall, caught in a dusty beam of sunlight. No time to set it aright and, in that too quiet house, as she reached the attic landing, her mother's story of her strange encounter with Isobel Baird's spirit came to mind again. She'd not heeded it much before, but was it because of her own nightmare in the loch water that she'd told Mr Bogle? Or, because she, Janet Margaret Lennox, would soon be on her way and the missing woman wasn't missing after all. But dead like her only son?

McPhee's door lay wide open. Her room bare. Even the pile of scripture books were nowhere to be seen. The bed stripped to its mattress. One look was enough…

Money…

In her own room now, like another phantom, haunting it; moving towards her unmade bed. The pillow still in place. Her blunted fingers searched for that stitched-up hole. The feel and weight of her coins. But someone else had got there first. Her hiding place lay torn open, with everything gone.

Thieving bitch…

Janet then pushed open her mother's door and immediately noticed her thick black Bible was also missing. Was this where her wages might have been hidden? Linnet Garvie had once shown her how to hollow out a book. But instinct told her to keep looking. The desk, like the wardrobe had been emptied of all its contents and, running her hand around inside its empty space brought a burning behind her eyes. Was there no end to the maid's sinning?

Just then, Janet's tired gaze travelled to a small inlaid cupboard in the room's far corner in which her mother had normally kept spare soap, a candle or two and a pair of white satin slippers she'd worn to her own confirmation as a girl. All miraculously still in place, giving off wax and lavender smells as she transferred them to the shelf above. That left the lowest, wobbly shelf which was easy to prise upwards, revealing a dusty space and a startled spider beneath.

At last…

Forgetting to breathe, Janet pocketed the neat bundle of at least thirty-one pound notes tied with a thin, black ribbon. Having returned the soap and candles to their usual place, she took the slippers for safe-keeping and shut the little door tight. She was just about to bid the room farewell, when there came a voice she recognised. A sound snaking around her like an evil spell, causing a sweet, sick fear to hit her heart.

***

33

Where blood has grown thicker than water...

Like Roberta Master's welcome, that early brightness hadn't lasted long, and as Catriona and the architect left Nonach Cottage, grey-bellied clouds over Baw Heid's mountain, drifted northwards to cover the sun.

Neither spoke as they followed these clouds towards Bar-Beithe Cottage, and with every step, Catriona's unease multiplied. What other lies might that fat dunt spread to him in private? And would Donald Baird defend his new love to the hilt? He'd not back then, when he'd had the chance, so how could she rely upon him any more?

She shivered again under her cape, while the architect lengthened his stride, looking straight ahead, fixed only on finding his son by the day's end. Driven no doubt by the knowledge that if he had somehow died, and Lennox's 'examination' resulted in the scrape-out that she, Catriona had pressed for, the likelihood of any heir to Ardnasaig was fading by the minute.

Having failed yet again last night to place his purply root inside her, Donald Baird had suggested a possible remedy. Seaweed cream applied by her fair hands. Lennox's mixture that she'd learnt to copy.

It had made no difference.

"When did this problem start, sir?" Catriona had enquired, with him sitting up in bed in despair. After a moment's pause, he'd gazed in the direction of the curtained window.

"When I realised I might be alone for the rest of my life."

That had left one more question, but just then, not the time to ask it.

"There he comes."

She started.

"Who?"

"Your father. He must have spotted us."

Catriona's heart missed more than one beat at the sight of Iain McPhee with his game bag on his back; his newly polished rifle under his arm, running down Footer's Hill like a new man. Where was the stoop she was used to? The drunken unsteadiness?

The Devil curse him…

*

"Me braw dochter!" His new, whiter smile seemed to darken everything as he kissed her cheek with his hot, wet mouth. "Tis guid to see ye again."

"Sir," he then held out his free hand to greet the architect. "I saw ye from the hill up there. Bin frettin' ye might have found trouble."

"No trouble my good man. I just want my boy home safe and sound."

Donald Baird removed his hat and, having wiped his brow with a clean handkerchief, returned it to his head. "Any news from yesterday?"

"Nae sir. Me and two others went as far as Ben Rochan. Terrible landslips up there, mind."

"Did you find anything?"

Her father shook his head. "We did our best, sir. We'll go agin once the ground dries up some."

The architect turned towards her. His cheeks mottled pink and white.

"We mustn't give up, Miss McPhee."

"I never do, sir."

Donald Baird then explained that they'd visited Roberta Masters with some small success, and were keen to speak to James's other godmother Helen Fergusson. He finished with a question that made Catriona start. "Have you seen anything of Miss Janet Lennox at all? Our late housekeeper's daughter?"

Why ask him that?

Catriona felt those flecked brown eyes on her.

"Describe her for him," urged Donald Baird. "Just in case…"

"I don't understand."

"Has Miss Lennox gone as well?" Iain McPhee frowned.

"She may have followed Mr Baird's son," Catriona volunteered. "Especially if she's expecting his wean."

Iain McPhee's newly-trimmed eyebrows raised. His surprise seemed genuine.

"Well there's disgrace for ye, sir. Why nae let her go?"

He's still keen on the handyman job, Catriona thought bleakly, but Donald Baird said nothing. And in the stillness of their surroundings, with the burnie's tinkling in the background, fresh turmoil filled her mind. Would he go so far as to save the witch and keep her child? For *her* to raise at Ardnasaig House? That prospect burrowed under her skin like a poisoned worm. The sooner she found a remedy for his impotence the better, or James Baird would soon be taking his place.

"I believe if we found Miss Lennox, we might discover him. So, Miss McPhee," those hooded eyes were on her once more. "How *would* you describe her?"

Catriona took a deep breath.

"Half my height again. A face like a cow's hip bone, with eyes black as winter peat…"

Her father's expression was the oddest she'd ever seen. Had she been too truthful? If so, it was his fault. She'd been brought up to call a spade a spade.

In reply, he cocked his polished rifle in the direction of the loch.

"Sir, tha's where we shud go," he said. "Back to where yer wife's footprints ended by Fearn House's boundary. If Miss Lennox *is* tracking yer son, he may not be far from there. Probably bent upon finding his mother, and that need's bin growing awhile."

The architect frowned.

"How do you know that?"

Iain McPhee tapped his forehead.

"When we was up the hills yesterday, with nae success, I had a vision…"

"A *vision*?" The architect's expression was now of bewilderment while Catriona for her part, willed his wife's terrible blue eyes not to appear. Seeing her chance, she took it.

338

"You've always believed in the power of the spirit world over this one, haven't you, father? No wonder Mother kept me away from things like that."

That smile again. Honey and steel.

"Ye ne'er turned yersel away as I recall. Always beggin' for more fairy tales o' this and that. A real bairn o' the Beltane, ye are, Catriona Mairi McPhee. Like a May kitten. And there's nae denying it. As for pressing me on that Dame of Nonach's ways, ye ne'er let up for a moment…"

Shutthatmouthshutthatmouth…

Donald Baird coughed. Adjusted his hat. Checked his fob watch.

"The day moves on apace, Mr McPhee," he said. "Tell me more about your vision."

"I were inside yer James's head, and all I cud see were his mother as she'd bin five years ago, calling to him to find her."

Silence.

"Well, then, you'd better lead on."

*

Catriona didn't catch her father's eye again. How could she? The man who'd driven his own wife to despair, was now doing the same to her. Didn't he want her to be happy? And when would be the next time he'd taunt her? Bring her to the edge of madness? She could have mentioned Mr Bogle's tartan cap hanging up by Footer's Cottage door; how she'd been face to face with him there on her first visit. The fact that unreliable handyman was still close by, would surely interest his former employer, soon to return to his faraway palaces.

She took a deep breath. Time to fight back and stop protecting the eejit who'd made her stay on too long in that dismal hole called Footer's Cottage.

"Sir, I've seen Mr Bogle," she said. "Close up, with my own eyes."

Her father slowed his pace. "Where? In these parts?"

"At yours, if you recall. Standing behind you that day I stopped by."

He stared at her. This was war.

"Ye mean the day poor auld Joseph Morrison met his end?"

The cone gatherer? Was that his name? Well, damn them both...

*

They were near the loch now. The water too still, too secretive. The slimy stones and pebbles sloping down from the overgrown world of bramble, too uncomfortable underfoot. Another tremor rippled under her clothes, while overhead, clouds almost black, merged together. Catriona wanted to stamp on her father's horrible feet. Pull out the last of his hair. Kick him until he went down... Down... begging for mercy.

"What's that supposed to mean?" She hissed.

Donald Baird, close to tears, took each of their arms. His hold so hard she flinched. "Enough, both of you! May I remind you, my son is the reason we're here. And if Mr Bogle is still in the area and paid Footer's Cottage a call, so what? He's certainly not been to see me, and I'm certainly not interested in rehiring him."

He suddenly let go.

So, his feckless son was more important than her hurt feelings? She'd have to speak to him about that. Meanwhile, as they followed the one who'd been partly responsible for bringing her into the world, and was now hell-bent on destroying her, Catriona noticed a small movement out on the loch. A lone figure rowing against the tide towards the sea.

Her father was too busy looking down, moving winter's heaps of wet leaves and other obstacles out of the way with his rifle barrel to notice. The architect meanwhile, seemed lost in his own world which, for the first time she couldn't reach.

*

"Bar-Beithe Cottage," announced Iain McPhee almost as if he owned it, setting off along the ragged pathway through the birch plantation until they reached a solid, pink house whose open barn alongside revealed not only the dead clog maker's workbenches and tools, but also too many unfinished and imperfect examples of his handiwork heaped up against the far wall. Catriona spotted a thin strand of smoke issuing from the one tall chimney. The same as she'd seen early that morning.

She hung back.

Her father of course, would plough on. Constable Wildman's testimony about that supposed curse, related to her not him.

"The doctor's carriage left Fearn House last night," he said. "In a hurry it were. Going towards Cranranich. Perhaps Mrs Fergusson ken something." He let Donald Baird lead the way to Bar-Beithe's partly-open back door. Its empty darkness suddenly ominous, while the raven perched above it, even more so. Although cooking smells eked from within, it didn't take long for Catriona to realise the widow wasn't at home. But why had that door been left open and a pot of cock-a-leekie burning black on the stove?

***

34.

Where water proves more deadly than blood...

Janet knew Linnet Garvie must have followed her from Fearn House, and now stood less than a foot away from her, looking twice her thirty-seven years, smelling faintly of incense. Her normally well-cared for black clothes were mud-stained and torn as if she'd spent the night out of doors. In close up, she seemed quite shrunken with half her straw-coloured hair gone, leaving an expanse of pink scalp instead of her usual parting. None of this had been noticeable from Mr Hendry's yesterday. Just the voice. Like now.

"Well, Janet," she sneered. "Some of us *have* done well for themselves."

"Yer trespassing."

"That I am, and ye'll have to excuse me appearance in such a grand house. Very nice too, and no expense spared..."

While Janet's left hand still gripped her mother's savings at the bottom of her skirt's deep pocket, her right hand felt for the loose mattress spring and the other wire she'd kept just in case. She was ready for a fight. Ready to win. She'd not survived for less.

"On yer own are ye?" she challenged her traitorous friend. "Or have yer three cowards come with ye?"

"Where's the difference? Ye'll be thrown to the hounds by nightfall. Even that's too good for them who kill their innocent weans."

"Ye said for me to do it. And I listened. I trusted ye..."

343

A strange laugh followed. "Where's any witness?"

"Me notebook that Constable Coyle took. I wrote all your advice, everythin' in it. And yer name."

A short, hollow laugh.

"Fairy stories. Ye said so yerself."

To McPhee…

"One piece of advice ye should have had was to stop at Baw Heid, but then ye always were a stubborn one. Still," she smiled bad gums and teeth that matched her hair colour. "I'm glad Calum ken what ye did."

Calum?

Janet froze inside. Her heart seemed to stop.

"So ye told him?"

"Me duty. Just like it was to inform the Bruce's what they were taking on. A simpleton and a witch with the power to decide who must suffer and who must die, including me wee kitten who passed on the day after ye visited. And didn't Lady Bruce's bad bowels almost kill her just after ye both arrived? Didn't her husband fall from their hay loft and break his leg so bad he won't walk again? Constable Coyle has their letter proving it."

"Yer a forger!" Janet steadied herself against the bed.

"We'll see about that."

"And yer letter to them betrayin' me?"

"Ha. Falcon made sure they burnt it. Falcon, whom I told to win yer trust."

Janet stared at her. Her own arguments evaporating in the presence of such a power which she'd believed with all her heart and mind. She wanted to ask how well the woman knew him, but just then, her brother dominated her mind. "Where's Calum now?"

"Guess."

An inch at a time, Janet pulled both her hands free of her pockets. Her right hand loosening its grip on her dead mother's money. The left, gripping that iron spring, and before Garvie could shake out the knife whose sharp tip had already appeared from the end of her sleeve, Janet punched her in the throat, using the coiled weapon to cause the most damage. Then she hit one cheek and the other, drawing bubbles of black, thick blood. The Sheffield knife stolen from the scullery drawer, clattered to the floor.

The woman from the better end of Fife Street, fell against the bed, babbling that Falcon Steer was on his way with a rifle. That if Janet spared her, she'd stop him blowing her head off.

"Just like he did to Dauvit Hendry?" Janet pulled a curtain from its hooks and tied her adversary's almost childlike fists tight together. Then, having torn the other curtain into two strips, bound those tiny, booted feet and finally, that dry, treacherous mouth. "Steer won't lissen to ye," she retorted. "He's a lunatic. And a rich one too, from what I heard. Too rich. Linin' yer pocket too, no doubt."

With the last of her strength, she dragged the enemy out along the narrow passageway until the linen room's two pitch-dark eyeholes beckoned her in. There was neither a key to lock its door afterwards, nor anything to block out the eerie cries which began the moment she walked away. Hanging in the air. A reminder of her sin.

Clothes...

Down to the next landing where Isobel Baird's room door stood slightly ajar.

It took her just minutes to shed her clinging, stale garments and replace them with those she'd only dreamt of. The double silk blouse was a wee bit tight, but the skirt in blood red brocade fitted exactly. One look in the mirror however, showed mutton dressed as a too-bright, new lamb. Next, shiny leather shoes the colour of hazelnuts, and a coat whose fur collar softly kissed her neck. Whose buttoned-up pockets proved even deeper than those of her old skirt.

She'd thought to hide her mother's small fortune in the sleeve of a black coat probably saved for funerals, almost hidden by the darkness at the back of the biggest wardrobe. But no. Especially as she'd ne'er be coming back to Ardnasaig House for as long as she lived. And as for that piece of James Baird's hair which she'd also reclaimed, that was for the future, too.

Before closing the door, Janet bade farewell to his mother, apologising for thieving her clothes, and hoping that wherever this exquisite woman might be, she couldn't see Catriona McPhee stepping out with her husband. That she was at peace.

*

Down the last dark flight of stairs where Margaret Lennox and those frantic bats had passed. Where the cunning maid had pushed her to her limits…

Left or right? Janet hesitated, feeling in every tingling nerve, that this warren of a house with its empty rooms and an air of death, was far too quiet. She turned right, as if her old domains of the Store, kitchen, scullery were calling her one last time. She noticed James Baird's rifle wasn't where he'd left it on Christmas Day morning. Nor any of his coats and capes…

Suddenly, something hard prodded the small of her back, pressing into her spine. The smell of oiled wood reminding her of James Baird's rifle. The whiff of carbine. A man's half-familiar voice.

"Well, well, Janet. You've smartened up. Nice clothes and shoes, too. So why not let them take you a wee bit further?"

From the corner of her frightened eye she glimpsed Falcon Steer, wearing one of James's brown coats fastened up to his chin. Then fear became anger. How dare he come here with that Garvie woman, as if Ardnasaig was theirs. She didn't care if she shouted.

"How did ye get in? Are those other criminals here too?"

"Scotland's my land, Janet, and I assure you, we're not criminals. As for keys, Master Baird kindly let me take his. And very helpful and peaceful he was too, up on Blae Crannog."

"And his three pound coins?"

"Of course."

"Yer more than sick."

Another prod that hurt.

"Have a care, Mr Steer. Tha' young man ye stole from and tried to bribe will come to haunt ye for the rest o' yer days. Ye've nae business in this house. Nor…" She stopped herself from saying that Greenock woman's name. "But what I cannae work out is where yer money's from, with ye lookin' like a beggar. And why pick on the likes o' me to suffer?"

His breath on her skin seemed to make the cold air colder. Her mind was fire, yet her heart was ice. She'd left Garvie's stolen knife behind. But what use would it be now with a loaded rifle pressing against her bones?

"You like stories, Janet. So here's mine," he began. "I made a fortune down in Greenock once the *Flora Macdonald* was finished. Heard of her, have you?"

"She carries steel to England. To make guns."

"Guns are useful."

"Nae to me. Anyway, ye said ye was from Dunblane."

A laugh echoed as if down to Hell.

"If I'd said Paris, you'd've believed me. Well, it may surprise you to learn I'd designed every part of that *Flora Macdonald* from her funnels to the last rivet. She was my own fine bairn until we had Morag. Just four years old she was when she fell ill, one month after meeting you. My wife and I paid for the best doctor in Glasgow to treat her, but he said the Devil had poisoned her blood. A second opinion said the same. After that, my sister-in-law told us who that Devil might be. Especially since her kitten died the very same day."

Linnet Garvie...

"Sister-in-law? She never said."

The mists of Janet's memory cleared to a fine May afternoon, just two months before she and her mother left Greenock for Lismore. Linnet had opened her back door into the garden where a beautiful little girl with huge brown eyes had been playing with a miniature porcelain tea set.

"Do you fancy a cup o' tea, Miss Lennox?" Morag had looked up to smile the sweetest smile when Janet had joined her. "I'm weel guid at making one, so auntie says."

"Auntie?"

Until then, Janet had never heard Garvie refer to any sister or brother-in-law with a bairn.

"Your best friend, o' course," Morag had explained before the straw-haired woman had interrupted them both with an odd look in her eyes. As if Janet and the bairn were getting on too well.

"Isn't this wee lassie just perfect? And taken to ye already, I can see." Garvie had then stroked her fine, young hair and blown her a kiss before moving away. Minutes later, after Janet had pretended to drink her tea, then handed Morag a daisy chain to go around her neck, her fashionably-dressed mother had called to collect her. There'd been whispers between the two older women, and for a moment before final farewells, Janet had felt uncomfortable. Excluded...

"We buried her on this very day," Steer interrupted the memory. "But we keep her wee heart in a special place, so she's always with us."

Another jab of the rifle against her ribs, and this time, Janet tried to wrestle the weapon away from him, but after her tussles with Garvie, he had the advantage. "There's too many of your kind in our land," he hissed. "Witches are a canker. A disease, and should I see Miss McPhee again, I'll apologise for likening her to you."

"Apologise to that snake?" Janet protested. "After what she's done? To the cocks? To me mother? And as for that stabbed man in the woods, she just happened to be on her way to Kilforgan at the time..."

"But she never touched our Morag."

349

"Neither did I. Only to make her a daisy chain."

"Move, witch! You've prattled long enough."

His rifle barrel pushed her along the passageway into the Store whose outer door lay wide open on to the wet, glowing courtyard lit by a sudden burst of sunlight.

*

She could still run. She knew the way through the elm grove to the drovers' track, away from where she and her mother should never, ever have come. But how, with Coyle and the Reverend standing by the well sharing a length of stout rope between their leather-gloved hands?

"Where's Miss Garvie?" Asked the constable whose normally stiff moustache drooped either side of his mouth. "We sent her upstairs to get a confession from ye."

When Janet finally spoke, her words felt like pebbles in her throat. "I ne'er saw her, and I've nowt to confess. *She's* the witch. Nae me." She turned to see how Falcon Steer's melting brown eyes had become hard as glass. She also registered a swift movement alongside her. The blur of the rifle butt lifted upwards.

Crack.

Her skull.

Crack.

Her ribs.

Voices, images fading as she fell.

"Yer wean's wee vertebra's in me pocket," called out Coyle triumphantly. "And yer fairy tale about Duns just another wicked lie…"

Plop.

"The gutting knife ye used for all your crimes."

Plop.

"Yer mother's eyes."

Plop.

"Your brother's confession to her. Your notebook," intoned the minister.

Plop.

They tore the shoes from her feet, the clothes from her limbs and the chilly morning air stung her bare, goose-pimpled body. Her mother's coins tinkled against the cobblestones.

"Hey, guid pickings 'ere, from inside 'er drawers," someone laughed. "Thirty-one pounds."

"I'll ha' that. I'm the next o' kin." Said a familiar voice while the rope ripped into her neck.

"Tighter… tighter…"

Blackness, whiteness.

Calum's voice again. She knew it was him. Tall as a tree, he looked down at her.

"She's 'eavy," he smiled. "I shud ken."

Plead yer belly…

Up, up, the sharp rub of the well's stone wall on her skin, then the suck of iced water in her closing throat. That dead March midnight all over again. The Dame of Nonach cackling her triumph…

"Go lie wi'our bairn and whate'er else is feeding off yer belly," Calum again. The one who'd loved her too much.

"Up she comes. Hold it…"

"Right. Down she goes. Getting' the hang o' this now. 'Tis time her blue vein was of use to us."

"Up!"

A small crown of bones in her hair. The longest, freed from her corset, sticking up like a mast.

"Down!"

Until her numb toes touched silt, then the top of her mother's Bible and what remained of that other wee soul gone before, gurning his own wee welcome.

All drowned by the Dame of Nonach's triumphant laughter.

Then, from above, came a gargled cry.

"Wait! We cannae do this! She's me ane flesh and blood. Bring 'er up! Bring 'er up afore it's too late!"

Calum's fear echoing through the years…

Next, came shouting. Gunshots. More shouting. The well's icy water spinning as all of a sudden, two strong hands grabbed her shoulders, gaining a grip beneath each numb arm, pulling, pulling until air and daylight met her face. The Dame of Nonach's gloating chuckles fading to nothing.

***

35

In which more traps are sprung...

To Catriona's relief, she, her father and Donald Baird hadn't stopped long at Bar Beithe, the other godmother's abandoned place. Instead, Iain McPhee had lifted the almost solid soup from the stove and closed the back door, wedging it shut with a lump of alder wood originally intended for clogs. All very impressive for a future handyman, she thought, aware of that same white-hot anger rising inside her which had led to too many risks. Not now, however. She must bide her time. Be the canny spectator of unfolding events.

"Helen may have heard something and gone to investigate," said the architect, squinting at a startling patch of sunlight deep among the birch trees. "But I'm afraid we can't wait for her. We must keep going. Let's hope Mr Hendry's at home. As I recall, he's never ventured far since his wife died."

"Fearn House is only half a mile away," said her father, still nimble. Still making an effort to impress. But not her. It was pathetic to watch.

Nearer the shore now, he chose a short cut over solid mud made passable by a mesh of broken alder twigs and winter's other helpful victims. Catriona was in no rush to meet Rustic Number Three and when Fearn House came into view, her jittering nerves made her laugh out loud. Her father turned towards her with a strange expression on his face.

Given that dwelling's name, she'd expected at least a solid villa - the kind her grandmother had owned in Tarbet. Not something probably knocked up in five minutes for forestry workers. She also noticed by the far boundary wall, two heaps of newly-dug earth each topped by a crude cross fashioned from broken branches.

Her father shouted out again. "Look at this, sir!" He bent down to pick up an engraved silver disc glinting in the long grass.

"A constable's badge, I don't doubt," said the architect. "And newly dropped."

Iain McPhee's hawkish eyes cast around again, until a large, honey-coloured hound powered its way towards them from a bank of bramble. Seeing the rifle pointing its way, its bark became a whine before it slunk away.

"Same bark as we heard earlier," observed architect, frowning. "Something serious has happened here, I'm sure of it." He then tried both front and back doors. "Locked."

"And the chimney's almost dead, sir."

"So it is. But why these new bullet holes in the wall?"

"Someone wi' a grudge?" suggested her father. "Ye never know."

And just as she was willing both men to beat a retreat, he removed his hat, scratched the grey hairs beneath it, and switched his gaze to the loch. "By all the Campbells' ghosts…" He crammed his hat back into place. Stood stock still. "D'ye see what I see? Someone's coming over the water." He cocked his own rifle then changed his mind. "I'd swear 'tis Fergus Bogle…"

So you do *know him…*

Catriona stood back while both her companions - just eight years apart in age, ran in a very different manner towards the stony beach and stood like two black scarecrows with arms raised above their heads, waving and calling at the solitary, bald-headed man in the rowing boat.

*

The former handyman had scarcely clambered from *Shona's Way* before the architect was hauling him up the pebbled shore. He must have recognised something in the older man's face. The red eyes, the air of grief as Bogle's adventure unfolded in fits and starts. How he'd first discovered James Baird lying dead on lonely Blae Crannog and begged the post van to fetch Doctor Johnson from Inverary.

"We cudnae find ye, sir. Tha's the truth, so yer son were taken to Glasgow, alnong wi' Dauvit Hendry…"

"Why him?"

"'Tis too long a story, sir. Enough to say there are certain enemies abroad…"

"Who? You're speaking in riddles," complained the architect.

"He has a right to know," Catriona stepped in and was rewarded with two black looks. Bogle's the worst. He hesitated as if about to hide something.

"Constable Coyle, the Reverend McKinnon, a black-haired thug wi' a rifle Steer an' some woman I ne'er seen before. They killed me an' Dauvit's ponies, an' hurt 'im bad, but it were me they was really after. I'm lucky to be alive."

Catriona recalled seeing those two earthen mounds and their hurriedly-made crosses. Something wasn't adding up.

"And this 'thug' shot at Fearn Hoose?" Her father butted in before her lover could react to the fact that a Constable and vicar together with someone who could have been Falcon Steer and a woman had found Bogle so important.

"'E did. An' when they'd gone, I rowed back to Blae Crannog a second time."

"Why?" demanded Donald Baird, continuing to disappoint. What little flesh there was on his face, crumpled in despair.

"In case I'd missed anything. And sir, let me say how calm yer son looked in death."

Catriona stared at his stupid mouth, spelling out the end of her dream. Her last chance of producing the heir to Ardnasaig House.

Damn his filthy, rotten soul…

To add insult to injury, she might well have been invisible. The once paternal handyman from Ardnasaig House was treating her like a total stranger, but why, she couldn't begin to guess. That dirty old tartan cap lined by flakes from his scalp was still safe in her pocket. More proof he'd been keeping company with her father.

"And?" The architect pecked at him for more answers like a ravenous gull. "Was he harmed at all? You must tell me."

"Nae by a human hand, sir."

"Birds?" ventured her father, looking up to cast another odd glance her way.

"Aye, a few, but nae like some I've seen."

Silence, save for the lapping water against the shore, with gulls' cries diminishing out to sea.

"Yer James 'ad the makin' of a fine man, sir," Bogle said as if to divert him from thinking of greedy beaks and scratching claws. "A fine, braw man. A credit to ye and yer wife... I'm so damned sorry."

"So am I, sir," Catriona added, wanting to take Donald Baird's hand to show him she cared. Because she did. Very much. Also to show their closeness. How she'd managed to crawl from her dismal but and ben and into his bed.

At this, both her father and Bogle glanced her way while the architect lowered his bare head. His thin shoulders lifted up and down as he stifled his sobs until a large, red handkerchief took the first of his tears.

"Was there any trace of Miss Lennox having been near my son?" He finally managed to ask.

"None, sir," said Bogle quickly.

"And this Doctor Johnson can't say for sure how he... how James died?

"The Post-Mortem shud tell us. Meanwhile, 'e has 'is opinions. The main one bein' Master Baird did it hissel, if ye get me meanin,' sir. All we ken is there were nae rifle and 'is pockets was empty..."

"Empty?"

"Yes, sir."

Keys, thought Catriona, because nobody else had. She took a deep, cold breath. "If he *had* ended his own life, it was down to

Miss Lennox. The foul things she'd said to him. I heard her more than once curse his soul."

This brought another silence and more stares sharp enough to kill, from Bogle and her father. Would she never learn? And why hadn't Donald Baird agreed with her?

"Nay. 'Twere a broken heart," opined Bogle. "I shud ken."

Catriona started.

"What do you mean by that?"

"Ye'll find out soon enough."

Bogle took the architect's arm. "And now, sir, ye must away to Glasgow." He turned to her father. "Mr McPhee can call on Mrs Masters for transport. She's sure to oblige again. James *were* her godson after all. "I'll arrange with the post due any minute, for the Inverary police to be told. Those four criminals have probably scattered far and wide by now. A proper hunt's what's needed."

The architect still in a daze, seemed content to let others do the organising. He'd obviously forgotten that fat boat owner's unhelpful remarks. Then came a panic Catriona hadn't seen in him before.

"Mr Bogle, you should have used *any* means to find me." He wiped both eyes with that wet handkerchief. "Any means at all. The three of us have been tramping from here to there for several hours…"

"I 'ad to be sure, sir."

"And we have to see him. Never mind Mrs Masters, there's the cob and trap."

"We?" An odd look in his eyes.

"Yes, myself and Miss McPhee. As before."

"Sir, with the greatest respect, more will be achieved if yer maid returns to the house at once. She can make it secure again."

Yer maid?

How she hated the ignorant peasant. Meanwhile, the architect was looking at her. Doubt in those grief-filled eyes. "What if pilferers or worse are there at this very moment?"

"I'm sure sir," said her father giving her a knowing stare, "she'll soon see 'em off."

*

She should have had a spring in her step but didn't. Her father's look stayed with her too long. His easy companionship with the handyman another worry. Why Ardnasaig House couldn't come quickly enough. Her domain, where Donald Baird would, by the end of the day, be by her side, too stricken to think up awkward questions or press for her father to work there. She could always hire casual labour for wood cutting and repairs. And who was to say, that once grief for his son had passed, the architect mightn't be able to stiffen enough to father a child?

After all, he must have, once upon a time.

Rather than take the longer but clearer way back, she chose the shelter of birch trees and bramble, and soon felt sweat tickle her skin. That ever-present headache now so intense, it made her feel sick and dizzy enough to stumble and fall.

She reached out to steady herself only to feel something soft, barely warm beneath her bare hand. The hand of another human being, not young, not old. Fingers and thumb knotted together.

By the Devil's heart...

She felt sick, pulling back the wet, brown ferns to see Helen Fergusson's upside-down face and her lips moving like two slugs feasting on Iain McPhee's sprouting cabbage. No blood. Not yet. Not until she'd pulled away her carefully laid obstructions and checked that the man-trap's steel jaws were still clamped around that sturdy waist.

"Help me…" The nosy bitch murmured. "Help…"

"I don't think so. Your brother, the constable, could have ruined everything for me." Then, having apologised for feeling ill herself, Catriona willed that same creeping sick to find its way upwards. To surge into her mouth behind her teeth, and land on target.

A handy stick with a snapped-off end was perfect to finish the godmother off with a stab to her pulsing heart. Afterwards, with the slimy ferns back into place, and the tell-tale, bloodied object flung into the nearest burnie, Catriona continued on her way, watchful for that same quartet Bogle had mentioned, lurking nearby.

*

Ardnasaig's front door was closed and locked. Likewise the Store's rear door. The cob whinnied from inside its stable; an urgent, frightened noise, and when she glanced up, noticed four crows perched on the lean-to's tin roof, watching her. She felt a sudden shrinking of her skin. Instantly old. Barren and old. The future had arrived like those clouds above, rolling too rapidly northwards to hide the sun, and she'd be shackled for ever to that bottomless silence that slowed her running heart.

She reached over to slide back the stable's bolts and fling open its half door. Isobel Baird had harried her there, so perhaps letting in daylight might do the trick, combined with a curse she'd dreamt up while walking back.

"Away foul Demon, leave this place,

go set your eyes on another's face…"

The cob's flank brushed her cape as he lunged from his prison and cantered once around the well. His big hooves made sparks against the cobblestones before he went, tail up, head up, into the elm grove with more spirit than she'd ever seen before.

Then something small and red trapped between the cobbles, caught her eye. A brocade-covered button that seemed to burn in her palm. She tossed it into the well and ran back to the front of the house.

*

One by one, she explored each cold room in turn, finding nothing disturbed except a blackthorn bush missing, another lopsided in its bucket, and two fallen baubles on the floor. Whoever had taken James Baird's keys, hadn't been here to steal objects of huge value that would one day be all hers. However, she kept her senses on alert for the slightest sound, the merest unfamiliar smell as she climbed upstairs in the dead woman's boots; her usual energy returning. Her father and sly Mr Bogle far from her thoughts.

The architect's room with its shared bed was locked as he'd left it. But his wife's…

Good God…

Even without sunlight, the disorder of clothes and shawls, indeed her whole wardrobe strewn everywhere, was unmistakeable. Then, hearing a faint noise outside, Catriona stopped and negotiated her way over the garments to the window where an unfamiliar rough-haired pony stood saddled up and tethered to the wall below.

Who on earth did that belong to?

*

"Still wearing 'er boots, I see. Just like them grey moleskin ones ye was wearin.' Take 'em off this minute."

Catriona jerked round to see a red-faced Fergus Bogle complete with wading boots and holding up that same portrait whose blue eyes seemed more invasive than ever. He set it down against a chair, but there was no time to wonder why he should have brought it into the room, because he was pulling a stout, grey pistol from his shabby coat, aiming it at her heart. With what felt like too many fingers, she duly undid the first heeled boot, then the second, placing them together on the carpet.

"Where's 'er comb?" He clicked the trigger. "The ivory one."

"Hers as well?"

"Aye."

The room suddenly sombre. Those snow clouds were settling too close over the house, and Donald Baird was well on his way to Glasgow. Catriona plucked her pretty keepsake from inside her skirt pocket, unable to stop her hand from trembling.

"What was it to you, old peasant?" She let the comb drop by his feet. He bent to retrieve it, wheezing, then twining that trapped blonde hair around one of his coarse fingers. He sniffed it, laying it in a rag of a handkerchief as if some holy relic. "Ye stole this from me bothy. Yer father saw ye goin' in, hangin' around."

So he'd *been the mysterious figure stumbling away...*

"Don't believe a word he says. His last breath'll be a lie."

"Like yersel, then. And where's me piece of newspaper, wi' news of Mrs Baird's disappearance?"

"I never saw it."

"Tha's a ham-a-haddie if e'er there were."

Then came other noises. She turned to listen. Were they footsteps on the stairs? Hard to tell as the old eejit with the pistol wasn't finished. "'Tis time for some truth, Miss McPhee. When ye thieved this comb, did ye ken it belonged to Mrs Isobel Baird? A fine woman and mother gone in her prime?"

She swallowed hard. Still tasted sick at the back o her throat. Willed those haunting eyes to stay away for ever.

"I had no idea. How could I?"

"Yer a lyin' little twister. What wud ye ken aboot love?" He gestured towards the painting, "I loved her with all me heart, from the moment I first set eyes on her. This comb were a wee memento I cudnae bear to lose."

Catriona couldn't disguise her grimace at the thought of him lusting after such a woman who seemed to have acquired a sainthood. Saw where this was leading. That she herself was now the one in his sights.

Here it comes...

"When yer father told me last Tuesday what ye'd made him do that August night after Cranranich Fair, I were torn between either shootin' or befriendin' him. Ye can surely understand that? After

363

five years bottlin' it up, and nae being a kirk man, he had to tell someone afore another Hogmanany came round. So I took pity. Called round to say I'd do anythin' I cud to find 'er remains. Wherever they was."

'... what ye'd made him do...'

Catriona faced him, enjoying his struggle to continue.

"Fact is," he said eventually, "'e'd first met her nineteen years before, at the Feeing Fair near Eagle Bridge, and 'ere's another truth. Are ye ready? James Baird who came into the world eight months later, is... is yer ane step-brother. And yer poor father still dinnae ken."

One brown eye, one blue...

Any enjoyment soon ended. She felt sick again, worse than before. In her stomach, in her head. Everywhere. Disgust too, that such a drunken reprobate had helped make the heir to Ardnasaig. And who cared about *her* feelings? If Lennox *was* after all with wean, there'd be a step-sister or brother. A first grandchild for him, treading the earth. And then came the big question she'd also saved for that half-man architect...

"No-one goes full term near this loch. How did she manage that?"

Bogle frowned, whether trawling his memory or cooking up more lies, she couldn't tell. "Bein' a believer in the Dame of Nonach's powers, she went back to 'er 'ome town. Nae a soul ken her condition 'til she returned wi' the wean. Nae even Mr Baird or me or ye father. And, if ye please," he snarled, fingering his pistol. "*I'll* be the one tellin' him."

How she loathed her enemy's wet lips. His rat-like eyes. She couldn't let him win. Couldn't let Lennox win, wherever she was.

"But Mr Baird must have been able to father a child at the time," she argued, "or he'd not have accepted James as his own. Perhaps he then caught a disease…"

Bogle eyed her in a way she didn't like. "Ye've a brain under them pretty curls, Catriona McPhee. 'I grant ye that. Pity ye've nae used it for guid. 'Tis a very strange thing to say."

"Typhoid's been killing hundreds in the Crimea," she persevered. "Perhaps he caught it too or took up with the wrong women and caught the clap. Or…"

More footsteps on the landing beyond the open door, cutting short her theories which the roughneck hadn't denied. Next, a cough, followed by heavy breathing.

The adulterous betrayer himself…

*

He arrived complete with wading boots like Bogle's and his rifle under his arm till he set it and his game bag down on the nearest chair. Despite the chaos of his dead lover's clothes. his gaze stayed fixed on her. Fists ready. Nothing had changed and Catriona still knew the signs. Iain McPhee was after all, her father.

The two men didn't greet each other. In fact, stood apart. Her jury. She, the accused with right on her side.

"I was only thinking of my poor, hard-working mother," she addressed him first. "How *she'd* feel, tossed aside for someone younger, more beautiful. I planned to give the Tail a fright, that was all. Till you took over."

The veins in his neck were pumping too much blood. Good.

"Yer a cunning little vixen."

"And you never said she was Isobel Baird. *The* Isobel Baird. So what kind of father are you? Only when I saw her portrait here, did I realise. And how was I supposed to manage after that? You could have ruined everything for me."

She would never mention *The Scotsman's* photo she'd found while searching Bogle's bothy. That was her business.

"Ye can throw words around 'til they make the story ye want, young Madam, but it will nae be the truth, because ye cannae face it. E'en to yersel."

"Why was *she* so special?" Catriona put an end to the poetry. "My mother wasn't some old hag."

Her father wasn't listening. Just staring out at the water.

"I wasnae the only one who'd thought Isobel Baird had been born with a silver spoon in her mouth," he began. "Then marrying into yet more money. But truth was, she'd begun life in a bad part of Helensburgh, and went into service at Ardnasiag House when fifteen, with nothin.' Nae religion, nae family to turn to. But she treated people with respect. Even me."

"And never said James was yours?"

A silence as deep and dangerous as the loch at spring tide filled the room, while that face she'd known for sixteen years, belonged to a stranger.

"It were for *me* to tell him when the time were right. *Me.*"

"And when would that have been?" she challenged, with little to lose. "Never?" A little smile reached her lips. "After all, be honest, you both wanted to be inside her."

Lightning had struck.

"Ye cursed little yellowhammer!" Bogle, whose cheeks had purpled like plums, raised his pistol again, but her father wrenched it away. Put himself next to her.

"If Mairi McPhee had borne a son," he growled, "I'd have given him that very name." She saw those fox-eyes skimmed by tears never shed during her mother's last moments, and thought how easy it would be to twist his scarf around his bobbing throat.

"'Tis a proud name, to be sure," nodded the other old barnacle, still purple. Still shocked by what she'd said. "And 'ed have done ye proud."

"The Tail only went with you because Donald Baird can't perform. Did she mention that?" she dared.

Mistake. Move on…

But two startled faces were turned on her.

"Who says?" Her father first.

"He did."

She wasn't the only one with a forked tongue.

"Yer just a maid," said Bogle. "He'd ne'er speak o' such things to ye."

Say it.…

"I take his sausage don't I? Or at least, I try."

Another violent silence followed.

"He pretended all along that James was his. He had to."

"I cannae believe ye," her father murmured. "But aye," he added, "I can."

*

Catriona was suddenly back in that late summer's heat and its hordes of clegs and midges, waiting for the familiar target and her two soft-coated setters to step from the birch wood into moonlight. And there she was, the architect's wife, smoothing down her dark blue dress. Her painted mouth half-open in expectation. Her surprise at hearing a twig snap behind her. Her cry as the rope had met her throat. Now, five summers on, Iain McPhee was still hiding the truth while Bogle's cracked lips were busy again.

"Yer father blackened his soul at yer behest. To cover up for ye, a twelve year-old. Ye played on his loyalty. His love. Nae wonder he didnae want ye at Ardnasaig."

"If he expects me to be grateful," she snapped. "I'm not."

"I ne'er wanted gratitude," said Iain McPhee. Just yer happiness. Why I've protected ye ever since. Fool that I am. And now... now me son's dead." He wiped his nose along his coat sleeve. "I can ne'er work at that cursed house. Not e'er..."

He resembled that cowardly black setter who'd run away from trouble. She was glad when he began searching in his game bag. But not for long.

No...

"Recognise these, dochter? Ye shud do, after the thoughtful Chritmas present I brought ye."

From a torn piece of brown paper, he dangled three familiar slivers of peach-pink material edged in beige lace. Part of a petticoat she'd hidden. Then came that sapphire-studded wedding ring, still shining.

Her tongue went numb. Bogle let out a gasp. Reached out for them, but her father was too quick.

"No?" she replied calmly. "I don't. Should I?"

"Aye. After ye'd strangled her, I saw with me ane eyes how ye removed her undergarments and this wedding ring. Then when ye thought I weren't looking, buried them up Footer's Hill. And by the by, I've kept all yer other hidden oddments. Just in case." He jabbed a black-nailed forefinger into her arm. "Weren't it enough to kill her and Tam, the other dog without degrading her so?"

A nervous laugh exploded from her mouth.

"Your witnesses?"

That finger pointed to himself.

"And who'll believe a droothy layabout over me, Donald Baird's mistress?"

At this, Bogle let out a grunt.

"Ye made sure o' that quick enough," sneered her father.

"How kind."

"Me all over." He handed the pistol back to Bogle, who gripped it tighter than ever.

"The law will say you tired of her," she retorted. "How you fancied someone new and she was in the way. Everyone knows your reputation. I can also admit overhearing you arrange to meet her in the birchwood, because you'd said they were the trees of love. How I saw *you* strangle her and that black dog near Fearn House, then drag them down to the loch like two pieces of meat. How *you* put both in the bark you were towing and rowed to the neck of the loch where you let go of it, hoping the tide would carry it out to sea. Then *you* buried her things on Footer's Hill. Not me."

Iain McPhee stood mute as a ghost, while Bogle moved his pistol from side to side. If he thought that might frighten her into saying sorry and confessing, he was mistaken.

His horrible lips were moving again. "Ye left a young man to grow up with nae mother," he said to her, "and yer father ne'er to ken his ane son. But tha's nae the end o' yer cruelty, Miss McPhee. The poor man ye stabbed to death in Draighnish that Tuesday, were - are ye lissenin - me auld uncle Joseph. Ye've left an ill wife and three bairns who've only fresh air to their names. But why trouble yersel over that? 'Cept 'e did describe ye clearly to me frein who found 'im before 'e died, and I've nae wish to blaspheme in Isobel's bedroom."

Don't admit anything...

Too late.

"He had an axe. He'd have cut my head off."

"Pity 'e didn't. Then Miss Lennox might be 'ere now."

That name again, staining the day. Would it keep cropping up to spoil the rest of her life? Would it?

"Where is she?"

"What's it to ye? I ne'er saw her agin after she'd stopped at Fearn Hoose. Said she were comin' back 'ere to find 'er money. I wonder if she ever found it."

Catriona felt her cheeks redden, yet her feet were more than cold without those nice boots.

Damn everyone.

"*You'd* called her a witch. Remember?" she protested. "Nice, kind Mr Bogle. And I overheard you tell her that she and her mother had brought a curse to Ardnasaig."

His suddenly trembling mouth was about to reply, but thought better of it.

"Empty yer pockets, lass," he said instead. "Afore we're away for another wee walk."

"In my *stockings?*"

But nobody answered.

✱✱✱

36.

Where moorings are loosened but danger still smiles.

No sun in the Elm Grove behind Ardnasaig House, with snowflakes shivering in the air beneath the huge, bare trees.

"Stay here, out of sight," she heard Calum say, having wrapped her bare body in a rug he'd found in the stable. Its coarse fibres harbouring too many fleas making her itch. Its pungent smell a mix of horse and dung. "Make nae sound, and I'll soon be back wi' warm clothes."

Yet something in his voice suggested he had other things on his mind.

"Was it ye who took our mother's money?" She finally ventured. Yes, he'd saved her life, nevertheless she'd had to ask ever since he'd brought her to this hiding place.

"Constable Coyle demanded it, or else 'e'd ruin me career. What wud ye 'ave done?" He challenged her. "Besides, ye took away me wean and…"

"I loved him," she interrupted. "Ye must believe me. He were ours, and God ken I will always be sorry."

How could she mention Linnet Garvie, probably dead? What lies she'd spun.

"God ken nothin,' an' does nothin. But *I* did."

Janet could only stare at him.

"What's tha' supposed to mean?"

"With everyone gone from the courtyard, I scooped out all the wee bones I cud find from the well." He patted his coat's bulging, damp pocket. "Me ane wean too, remember?"

"Dinnae leave me here, Calum. Wait, I beg ye!"

But before Janet could even begin to raise herself, he'd mounted bareback on James Baird's chestnut cob and turned him away. It was only then she noticed a rifle strapped to the other side of his saddle. Judging by its condition, it must have been James Baird's, taken from the Store. Although every one of her nerves was chilled, her head seemed full of hot coals as the cantering hoof beats diminished. Until all fell silent in the softly falling snow.

*

She couldn't sleep any more. How could she, clinging to the memory of those same wee bones in the well water brushing against her body, when all she had left was that corset bone still trapped in her dripping hair?

Having pulled it free, she gripped it tight in her puckered palm as her other hand scraped a hole in the earth beside her. She had to pretend the thing was real.

Part of that little body come from hers. With her prayer to Jesus finished, she wept out loud for what that treacherous thief Constable Coyle had bragged was 'yer wean's wee vertebra,' so she could bury that too.

Having made the sign of the Cross, she murmured, "and please, me wee one, where'er ye are, forgive yer wicked mother. And yer father."

She should have given him a name. Been able to imagine him safe in the Lord's arms, but like all the unbaptised, he was probably spinning around in a wild, cold place their Greenock vicar had called 'Limbus.'

No more crying. Someone or something on the prowl might hear her. Instead, Janet wrapped herself even more tightly in the smelly rug, telling herself Calum would soon be back. But deep in her heart, knowing he wouldn't.

With daylight on the wane and no helpful sun to tell her what the time might be, Janet realised Calum had gone for good. And who could blame him? From now on, she had to look after herself and whatever might be hiding inside her. But where to start? Because of those murderous thieves, she had neither money nor any of those lovely clothes with which to cover her modesty. Besides, she was shivering so much that whenever she tried to stand, she stumbled.

"God help me, she breathed into the thickening snowflakes, which on another occasion might have seemed Heaven-sent, not another obstacle. For a few moments she sat on the nearest fallen elm to get her bearings, and through those massive trees that had survived preceding winter storms, could still see Ardnasaig House's dead chimneys. Heard the silence surrounding it, and wondered where those inside it had gone.

However, when her infected eyes moved towards the loch, she was certain she heard voices. McPhee's in particular, along with those of at least two other men. One she also recognised as belonging to Fergus Bogle.

What was going on? Janet wondered, and then, sensing that if they chose to turn her way, she might well be seen. Having gathered the harsh rug more tightly around her, she followed the cob's clear hoof prints through the elm grove, hoping they'd lead to the road to Kilforgan to the west and Cranranich to the east. With every hurting step, she also hoped Linnet Garvie was already beginning to rot. Her sole aim now was to leave this godforsaken place and ne'er even dream about it.

*

With the snow beginning to settle and cause her feet to feel more like solid blocks of ice than flesh and bone, Janet reached the road where earlier travellers had cast any settled snow away. It was impossible to tell from amongst the mingled prints of hooves and carriage wheels, which way Calum had gone, but what mattered just then, was that someone she could trust might turn up.

She eventually found a convenient stone on which to sit and, with both numb feet clear of the ground, waited for her mother's roving soul to somehow help. But with each passing second, death's breath seemed to be intensifying on her skin.

"Janet Lennox? Is this really you?"

She almost fell from the stone, then saw the familiar figure of Elspeth Farquhar sitting up in a trap behind a white pony. Her mother's friend belonged to the kirk in Kilforgan. A devout woman still trying to lay Margaret Lennox to rest.

Her kindly face registered shock then pity.

"Who's been hurting you, then?" the widow clambered down from her seat, leaving the pony to graze by the roadside. "What on earth...?"

"Me dead feet!" Janet cried out, struggling to stand. "I cannae afford to lose even one."

"You won't. Not if you come with me. I've extra blankets to wrap them in, and while we go home, you can tell me why you look like a ghost. A half-drowned one at that. And your teeth. Your poor teeth..."

*

But Janet's story didn't start until the blazing log fire in Glenholm Villa had warmed her through and through, and the clean, plain clothes on her back together with hot porridge and tea, made her feel human again. That there would be a tomorrow after all, even though her 'wee frein' was overdue and Linnet Garvie still inhabited that linen room.

"Your mother worried about you from the day you both went there," admitted Elspeth, clearing away the crockery once Janet's incomplete tale had ended. "Too soft, she'd said. Too sensitive and," she peered at her, "she was right. Bullies need standing up to. Especially jealous bullies. Heathen bullies. That greedy Constable Coyle is a disgrace to his profession, and as for our vicar..." She paused, as if choosing her next words. "I'll be reporting him to the highest authority. Make no mistake. As if his treatment of your dear, late mother wasn't bad enough, he thieves her savings."

Janet felt sleep begin once more to slow her pulse, lessen her headache and make her cosy surroundings recede to such an extent that she pictured herself in quite a different place, far away from that gloomy loch and the Dame of Nonach. She was in another warm room, this time with the sweet, yeasty smell of new bread rising in its ovens.

Since she was a bairn, she'd loved baking, but at Lismore and Ardnasaig, the ready-made bread had come in by cart. In her vivid dream - wherever that was - her hands were coated in flour as she pulled and pushed the waiting balls of dough into shapes to please the eye. Shapes she knew James would have liked. His wean, too?

His wean…?

*

She woke with a start. On her own, with the log fire more settled, but not her mind, for in her deepest heart, she knew that come next autumn, there'd be new life in her arms. A wee lassie, she was sure of it, who already had a name.

"Janet? Are you alright?" Interrupted her saviour from the nearby well-stocked kitchen. "Do you fancy a wee dram of something?"

"I've decided what to do wi' me life. I want to make bread," Janet said instead of replying. "I'm nae mad am I?"

Elspeth laughed. For too long an unfamiliar sound. "My dear girl, there are only three things that matter here on earth. Our dear Lord, a smile and a warm, crusty loaf." She bustled in and poked the fire back to its earlier glory. "And where exactly will you do this baking?"

"I saw a map of England once," said Janet. "And father used to speak well o' Cumberland. He had a cousin in Carlisle. I cud try there…"

"And I can help you get started, and have your teeth mended," Elspeth settled herself opposite in a matching armchair. "My beloved Kenneth left me a considerable sum when he died. We ne'er had bairns, and my last living relative is in hospital, unlikely to last the winter, so," she leaned forwards, a sparkle in her frank, blue-grey eyes. "Why ever not?"

*

While her generous benefactor - sworn to secrecy about this future plan - busied herself with tasks in the kitchen, Janet set to with a pencil and paper, making a list for next morning, beginning with a train south from Glasgow. Merely to write the words representing her future, was excitement enough, but it wasn't long before they grew blurred. Overlaid by images she'd hoped never to see again. Her enemies, faint at first, becoming frighteningly real. Linnet Garvie, whose decaying lips formed an angry grimace. Falcon Steer, staring as if into her very soul, and Catriona McPhee, no longer young and pretty but aged in earth, alive with maggots. Except for her eyes - but not *her* eyes - startlingly blue, flickering, it seemed, a warning of danger.

Janet let out a gasp. Slapped down her pencil and turned her list over, wishing she was already on her way, convincing herself that once this cursed area wasn't even a memory, all would be well.

Mother...

Amidst all the torments she'd forgotten her, and resolved that once settled elsewhere, she'd ask Elspeth to find her grave by Kilforgan kirk. Send her money for flowers or a small tree to be planted on it in her memory. One day, perhaps, she might even return with her bairn. Even Calum.

One day...

***

37.

Soft specks of snow like those scalp flakes inside Fergus Bogle's tartan cap, began to settle as Catriona struggled down to the loch and eastwards along its bumpy shore. Both men who'd lusted after Isobel Baird hemmed her in on either side, and with each jarring step, she sensed worse to come. Handing over Bogle's unsavoury cap, the cheese knife, dried hen's claw and Lennox's savings had been humiliating enough. Now this latest indignity, with neither bully saying a word.

Nonach Cottage was merely a grey blur between the trees when the threesome suddenly followed the sloping shore into the loch itself, over the frilly wavelets whereupon the pebble shelf dipped sharply away.

"I can't go on!" she cried out, unable to feel her feet. "It's too freezing!"

Her father only pushed her in deeper; his grip hard around her arm until they reached what had once been a working jetty before the architect had refused any moorings off his land. The rusted iron rings for the steamers still lay in place, while beyond this stone-built convenience, swayed those skinny, black posts used to secure lighter craft.

"What are we doing here, anyway?" She cried out again, feeling her calf muscles seize up. Her throbbing headache return.

Bogle let out a spiteful chuckle, while he held his pistol clear of the water and kept her close. Too close. His smell worse than the cob's stable.

"'Tis for ye to find out."

Catriona remembered his tale of the lucky caul which had covered him at birth. His talisman against drowning, so he'd boasted. However, her father who'd let go of her to steady himself, was another matter. He'd only used his legs on the land, so she could easily tip him forwards into the water, hold him under and claim his rifle. Afterwards, there'd be nothing left of either troublemaker save a few bubbles breaking the surface. And her long-held secret of August 14th 1846 would be safe for ever.

But would it?

As for Lennox with her prominent blue vein across her nose, she hoped it would soon bring the drowning she deserved.

"I cud fetch Helen Fergusson," suggested Bogle. "She doesnae miss a trick as far as Loch Nonach's concerned."

Catriona blinked in surprise at hearing the name of the busybody who was missing more than a few tricks now.

"That mad wifie?" Her teeth juddered together.

"Ye shud ken all aboot madness," Iain McPhee insulted her before Bogle continued airing his knowledge without once looking round. "Helen's a decent sort. Not long after the shock of Mrs Baird goin' missing and Constable Wildman's death on the railways, her memory returned. She'd spotted one o' Dauvit's red barks driftin' up the loch and, judgin' by its direction, guessed it could be trapped in any one of the jetties along its length. Tha's what she told Dauvit, anyway. Too feared to tell anyone else. Until a dream sayin' 'er days was numbered."

Think. Quick...

"It was my friends in Cranranich who said she was gone in the head. Not me," said Catriona, wary of where this was leading.

"Was?"

The sky grew dark enough for thunder, with snowflakes bigger now, landing on her nose. She prayed for the contents of that man-trap not so far away in the woods to remain unseen. Rot quickly.

Be careful...

"How do you know all this about her?" she asked, hardly recognising where they were. Over the years, rough weather had re-shaped the exposed shoreline. Brought fallen trees and other driftwood ashore. More stones, flotsam and jetsam from all kinds of boats,

"Shall I say?" said her father.

"Aye."

"Mr Bogle found two letters tucked between rocks on Blae Crannog," began the man who'd always kept her in her place. "One from Janet Lennox that she were expecting James's wean..." His voice raised in excitement. "Me grandchild. Think of it..."

Catriona did.

"James must have ta'en it wi' him when he'd left Ardnasaig House, and it fell from his purse..."

"Very interestin' it is too," purred the other betrayer dipping into the top pocket of his rough coat, and opening up a crumpled piece of lined paper. "The ink's run a bit, but bear with me. This cud be me ane chance to read it out to ye, afore it goes to Glasgow for examination wi' the other one. 'Tis his farewell."

*

Afterwards, those mean eyes met hers. "So James Baird killed hissel from guilt at nae protectin' 'er. Of sendin' 'er and his wean to the waitin' wolves as 'e called 'em."

Catriona's empty stomach seemed to burn with bile.

"That can't be true."

"I suggest ye lissen to this, then, Miss McPhee."

With his pistol tucked in a lower pocket, Bogle then withdrew a mess of blue paper and in a trembling voice, read out Helen Fergusson's warning message to her godson.

Iain McPhee kept both eyes tight shut throughout. Mercifully there were no more tears, but instead, another accusing stare, making her heart beat too fast. Faster than the repeated rattle of loch water shifting pebbles.

*

When Bogle had finished reading, he placed this damning find next to the other, deep inside his top pocket. Then he jerked his pistol to his right where a stack of kelp-covered rocks sloped downwards into the deceptively gentle tide. They formed a protective basin which, from most angles, might appear empty.

Not so.

For in the middle of this watery berth lay something that made Catriona slump forwards as if all her leg muscles had suddenly succumbed to cramp. A skeletal wreck of what had once

383

been a red, wooden bark lay filled with the solid remains of whatever time, tide and winds had deposited there.

"At last, the yellowhammer's cradle…" muttered Bogle under his breath, before the wintry breeze bore his truth away towards the sea. "I'm nae poet, but tha's the ane way to describe it."

*

"Had a guid few barks in them days, did Dauvit," said her father, wading forwards, taking Catriona with him. His hold on her arm tightening with every step. "Rented to Glasgow folks for fishing. Made such a fuss about losing two after that August night, I lived in constant fear. And all for ye. A cunning, wee twelve year-old wi' the strength of someone twice her age." His grip was cutting off her blood supply. She felt dizzy and faint. The bitterly cold, salty water had reached her knees, burning her bones. "But how could I say aught? We'd both have bin strung up. Or deported."

Catriona turned away, but then felt a different, icy hand on her back, pushing her onwards so strongly, her father put out an arm to restrain her.

"Let her go," said Bogle, landing a kick on her ankle for good measure. "To show us wha's really in this bark."

"Dig," came the insistent, female voice occupying her head. "Hurry…"

"Dig, ye Dei'l! And be quick aboot it!" Repeated the copycat, letting go of her arm. And she did, until her filthy, scraped hands releasing the fetid stench of death, could dig no more, until the delicate remains of a dog came into view. Its skull buried in silt beneath another bigger one whose two moss-lined eye sockets weren't empty by any means.

She heard Bogle cry out. Her father too, as she leant in closer to see how each watery hollow harboured a dazzlingly bright blue eye.

***

38.

Where the noose is tightening...

With one local search party under way for Constable Coyle and his three associates, and another for Janet Lennox and Helen Fergusson, two constables from Inverary waited in Ardnasaig House's cold drawing room for the doctor and Donald Baird's return from Glasgow.

Having reached the end of their official questioning, they stood grim-faced and silent, giving nothing away after recording one untruth after another from her father and Bogle now keeping themselves busy with the fire, making little difference to the chill. Catriona, on the other hand, who'd answered each question fully and honestly, positioned herself behind them as they added more snapped-off blackthorn branches to the flames.

"It may be useful to remind ourselves again of the background to this mystery," the taller Constable Watson again produced his thick record book to read out the tiresome tale of how Isobel Baird had first met the former herdsman at Cranranich's Feeing Fair in the March of 1830. "If ye recall anything to add to what ye've already said, best do it now."

A dead silence followed, broken only by the sound of crackling branches and the constable clearing his throat and reading.

"Iain Hamish McPhee, an already married man had been looking for work from local estate owners," he began. "Until Lord Melhuish offered to take him on. After several secret assignations

386

with Isobel Baird on the other side of Cranranich, well away from Ardnasaig House, she'd seemed to cool..."

Her father looked up from the fire. Its flames lighting up his eyes.

"I ne'er did ken why she'd stopped away for so long. When I enquired, folks said she'd bin caring for an ailing friend. Why shud I have believed any different? Or ken aboot the wean she'd had? And once we three McPhees were in Footer's Cottage, I were out working noon and night, too weary to wonder."

He glanced round at Catriona. Spit on his lower lip just like that hot night after the Cranranich Fair when he'd hit her everywhere. Hate in his eyes, all over again. "Then ye began growing up. And when I dared meet with her agin - at *her* request, mind - ye had to punish us both in the most terrible way."

Too easy. Too easy...

"That's an extremely serious allegation, Mr. McPhee. Does this cancel your earlier answer?"

"It does."

Rather than rise to this crude bait, Catriona concentrated on the Persian carpet she'd cleaned by hand only last week, spoilt by fresh dark mud stains brought in from outside. She should have ordered her father and the throwback to take off their wading boots immediately they'd re-entered the house. That they'd no right to take her blackthorn to burn in the fire. But with no Donald Baird to defend her, she was like a hog on a spit, turned inch by inch for a thorough burning.

"E'en the master believed her story," added Bogle, just when she thought he'd buttoned up for good. The pistol still jutting from his coat pocket. "Hurried back from London to see 'is new bairn. But *I've* ne'er bin so ready to believe other men's tongues. 'Cept this wee lass here fair took me in till I saw 'er runnin' from the cocks'coop wi' blood on her hands. And what were Margaret Lennox's eyes taken out with, if it wasnae a neat little cheese knife? Me *ane* knife?"

*

Her father tried to raise himself, a rickety old man again, gripping the marble mantelpiece. He searched her face as if she was a stranger, but couldn't speak.

She knew why.

"Suspicion's ne'er enough," said the shorter, older constable. "'Tis solid proof we need." He stared at Catriona with nothing in his eyes. "Like the gutting knife we found under yer wardrobe, still bearing human blood - Joseph Morrison's blood as it happens - on its handle. As for Mr. Bogle's cheese knife, like the smooth-soled boot he found and passed on to us, it had been well cleaned. But nae quite clean enough."

Bogle's smile showed not one good tooth in his mouth.

"That left boot were hidden in a pile of swedes in the Store," he said, enjoying the attention. "I cannae think for the life o' me who might have left it there, but it matches what Miss McPhee wore that very day. *And* the footprints I spied by the coop and me bothy where she'd helped hersel..."

"You're the thief, not me!" Catriona snapped. Her head heating up too quickly, unlike her toes.

"Yer in nae position to call any kettle black," he countered. "Janet Lennox also looked at the tracks after the killin's, and came to the same conclusions as mesel. That boot sole o' yourn leaves a rare impression for these parts. Plain, with a separate small heel. And there was enough of them going right up to the coop until ye re-appeared to rub 'em out."

"You liar."

"I also spotted a patch o' pink snow close by the coop, where some clever cleanin' 'ad gone on."

"A thief, a liar *and* a trespasser..." Catriona added, with nothing to lose.

"Ne'er a thief, lassie. Ardnasaig's always bin like a second 'ome to me. Why I kept me Store key safe." He looked up at both constables. The taller one still writing. "Tha's nae agin the law is it? You see, I never really left. Kept mesel occupied. Kept a look out, once I realised this wee yellowhammer had the De'il's blood in her veins."

Catriona flinched.

"Spying on me, you mean?"

His big backside invited a push so hard, he'd tumble into the fire, just like clumsy, ugly Janet Lennox.

"I shud've spoken out, and p'rhaps poor Mrs Lennox would still have 'er eyes. But stalkin's a long process as ye ken. The target must have nae suspicions. See nae movin' shadows... Hear nae sound..."

Now the same constable was staring at her. Swayed by this rubbish, she could tell.

"We'll be exhuming Mrs Lennox tomorrow to compare the damage to her eye sockets with this cheese knife's blade." He said. "But it might save a lot of effort, Miss McPhee, if ye could explain why ye took it from Mr Bogle's bothy in the first place, and what exactly ye did with it."

"Before I answer anything, Constable, I still have two question for him." She turned to the bald-headed eejit, who seemed suddenly taken aback, making it easier for her to stick a different kind of knife in. "Referring to Margaret and Janet Lennox, what did you mean by 'them's twisted sisters, make no mistake. And on me deathbed, I'll tell ye things ye shudnae' ken?'

Her cowardly target jerked his head away. Held on to her father for support. But she wasn't finished. "As if it was yesterday, I remember you adding, 'If I fall to Death's messenger, get yersel to me side.' So, could you kindly explain what that means, or will you be taking your dirty secrets to the grave?"

Only the sounds of the blackthorn spitting and cracking in the grate, broke the quietude. Before she returned to Constable Watson's question and began her story. Whether or not both constables believed her desperate compulsion to rid the dead housekeeper of Isobel Baird's accusing eyes, was hard to tell, as neither had spoken. Nor those two consummate liars, her father and Fergus Bogle. But he was certainly full of surprises, looking first at her then her father before snatching a big Bible from a nearby bookcase and smacking his right hand hard over the gilt cross on its black cover.

"I swear to almighty God tha' what I'm aboot to say is the whole truth and nothin' but the truth. So help me, God. I have to say it."

She and her father watched his crabby mouth re-open to report everything his trusting 'friend' had confessed to him about that August night by the loch more than five years ago, with no detail spared, ending with Iain McPhee helping his daughter fill one of the two rowing boats she'd stolen from Dauvit Hendry.

"And when Isobel's bark 'as bin examined," the traitor's voice shuddered with emotion, "I'll burn it to ashes and free 'er spirit for ever. Tha's me promise."

*

Fergus Bogle slumped into the nearest chair with his head in his hands. The Bible splayed open at his feet as the shorter constable moved towards the window, anxiously waiting for the overdue architect to arrive. To Catriona, her father seemed invisible.

Now.

She mustered all her cunning and in a deliberately brighter tone, addressed Constable Watson who was still busy writing down Bogle's account.

"May I please change out of these wet clothes?" she asked. "I've been in them far too long. If not, I'll catch my death of cold..."

"Two minutes." He didn't look up, and before he could change his mind, she hurried towards the door, deliberately ignoring the motionless, silent Iain McPhee.

Of course he looked numb. The constables' black-curtained carriage and its two horses was already outside, waiting to carry them both to Inverary Gaol.

*

The air, instead of warming towards the next landing, seemed almost frosty, bearing a strange, rotting smell intensifying as she climbed upwards past her dead step-brother's locked sanctuary and the architect's room with its useless double bed. She stopped by the door to his wife's disordered haven, where she snatched up the portrait and carried it up to what had been her own attic room.

She felt a stranger there all over again, her sodden, stockinged feet still leaving their damp imprint on the wooden floor behind her. Her pulse oddly steady.

That noticeable stink ekeing from the linen room had grown stronger, but she had other, more important things on her mind than to investigate. Having laid the portrait glass side up on the floor, she jumped on it once, twice, until the glass split and splintered, tearing through her stockings, into her skin and her veins, bringing vivid red sprays of blood that obliterated that vengeful Tail's face.

*

She was thirteen again, back in Footer's Cottage, trapped by more than bad weather as that crow's body had hit the window. The thud of flesh and feathers against glass. The way it had fallen…

At least it was free.

"Ye destroyer."

Her father.

He'd followed her upstairs to torment her again while red ribbons of her blood colonised the floor.

"You mean Bogle?"

Silence, except for his laboured breath.

"Did ye ken that last September, me son had been left everything? 'Tis down in black and white wi' Donald Baird's executor in Inverary."

Nothing was worth turning round for any more.

"How does that make ye feel, having driven him to freeze to death?"

"Go away."

"When Falcon Steer's payment arrives for ye, I'll see it builds James the best braw grave in Argyll. Ye've had too much already. And shud Janet Lennox e'er be on yer mind, I heard a whisper she survived a slow drown yesterday, and has me son's wean in her belly... Think on that..."

His words didn't matter any more. Only hers.

"You mean the son you called 'the young Jock who's ne'er done a day's turn in his life?'"

He sucked in that same raspy breath. A stranger she had no wish to know.

"Rot in Hell, dochter, ye waste o' skin. See if I care..."

She'd stopped listening, and despite her feet sticking to her own blood, she heaved up the small sash window letting the snow hit her face, her neck, her arms, before squeezing her upper body and the rest of her out beyond the eaves.

Fly...

So she did, trailing skeins of redness behind her, glimpsing again those dark, mossy hollows alive with that Tail's eyes, watching her from between the lime trees' branches. Then her white jaw bone of perfect teeth opening in a beckoning smile, while far below, a pony and trap rattled up the drive to join the black-curtained carriage still waiting. It bore two men. Another stranger and the widower - whose pale, uncomprehending face was, for a fleeting moment, lost in shadow.

✳✳✳

Epilogue

Dead chestnut leaves the same colour as the young woman's hair, flutter on to her bonnet, even settle beneath the collar of her new, tweed coat as she crosses Glasgow's wet and busy Priory Street. Having carefully avoided an extremely deep puddle, she then finds Cowper's Lane leading up towards the cathedral. Here, to her left, the Birtle & Bowker, Commissioners for Oaths' prominent sign swings back and fore from its iron bar.

What is it about water that makes her blood turn cold? Even as a young child, she'd screamed whenever her mother had bathed her, and as for that huge Loch Nonach she'd seen five years ago when visiting the abandoned Ardnasaig House for the first time, she knew she could never live anywhere near it. She'd be lying awake night after night, in one of the vast bedrooms wondering what if those sly, silky waves were to creep towards its granite walls, up the stairs and drown her in her bed? Drag her down to the earth's core to join the other forgotten dead?

Oh yes, those walls were thick, but to her mind, having listened to that very old man in a ragged tam o' shanter who'd stood by the house gates, repeating her name as if a curse, they'd never be thick enough. He'd told how the badly decomposed body of a woman had recently been found in the linen room. All very mysterious and, according to *The Scotsman*, possibly another suicide. How a wean's pitiful cry can still be heard nearby, and the spectre of murderer Catriona McPhee, is sometimes seen floating downwards from an attic window. Her stockinged feet red with blood.

"Which still stains yer namesake's braw portrait," he'd added. "And to think that Iain McPhee, hanged in May 1852 at Inverary Gaol, ne'er uttered a word to 'is ane son."

Her mother had rarely mentioned either of the McPhees, so she'd asked this unsettling stranger if they'd been buried in a grave. He'd shaken his toothless head. "Nae, lass. 'Tis for the best. I saw to tha.' I also watched him swing. Three times it took, if ye please, which to me, were only fair."

*

Those dark histories still envelop her as she plucks the last stray leaf from her bonnet before stepping into a gloomy hallway lined with broth-coloured portraits of bearded lawyers grown fat on the misfortunes of others. Hers is no different, but at least after the forthcoming sale of Ardnasaig House, she'll be someone of means, free to make her own choices. She pauses by a mirror set between several damp, black overcoats and a full umbrella stand, where even the poor light cannot disguise her two blemishes - the noticeable blue vein across the bridge of her nose, and her odd-coloured eyes - now twenty-one years old. Long enough. Part of the sale proceeds will pay for the best surgeons in the land, to remove that vein and try making her two eyes match one another. Brown not blue.

"Miss Isobel Margaret Baird?" comes a man's voice from above.

The name always unsettles her.

"Yes. That's me."

"I'm Charles Bowker. Do come on up. Everything is ready for you."

His new client feels her heartbeat quicken, not least because the man's face bears a smile in a world of too many deaths. Her uncle Calum's, in 1854, from wounds during the Battle of Balaclava had been the first. He'd saved his only sister from drowning, but not from water on the lung which had plagued her days as a baker in Carlisle and the cause of her death last June. Six years after Donald Baird, the unseen man she'd first assumed to be her grandfather. He'd died in his sleep from a recurrence of the typhus first suffered in Sebastopol in 1832. Someone her mother had falsely, but understandably claimed, passed his drawing skills on to her.

"I should wish you a happy twenty-first birthday," observes the young lawyer, indicating a chair the other side of his mahogany desk, then handing her the late architect's Will and property Deeds for signing. "However, the expression 'curate's egg' does come to mind."

She doesn't quite understand, but he continues nevertheless, avoiding eye contact.

"Unlucky for some, there, that's for sure. And as for your mother's cowardly assailants, save one, rumours persist they fled to Ireland. But from there, who knows?" His gaze then meets hers. "Did she ever speak of a Glaswegian, Linnet Garvie?"

"Not that I recall. Was she a friend?"

His reply is to nudge a pen, blotting paper and a full inkwell towards her, then check his fob watch. She takes the hint and studies the finely-scripted detail of what seems a straightforward enough Will dated 24th September 1851 signed by Donald Baird and countersigned by an Andrew Stephenson, his then lawyer and executor in Inverary.

"As you already know, Mr Baird, fearing his wife was after all, dead, changed his existing Will from her to James, and subsequently in the untimely event of *his* death, to the first of his issue upon reaching the age of twenty-one. Which of course, is you."

"But he'd surely realised later how James was fathered by Iain McPhee?"

"Indeed."

"And that James in turn, impregnated my mother?"

The slightest blink of surprise at her no-nonsense verb. A small cough.

"Guilt is a powerful motivator, Miss Baird, and, having said that," the lawyer slips his hand into that same large envelope," he also left you this."

He places a substantial red brocade-covered button on the desk and she notices how on its reverse side, the small silver ring is badly rusted. "One of the more - how shall I say - ordinary items. Also a smoothing iron and ruined Bible found in the well when it was finally dredged before he passed away. He'd confirmed this button had belonged to his dead wife whose name of course, you share."

She suddenly feels as if winter has invaded that office. Both her hands grip her body to suppress a shiver, sensing this Charles Bowker is still keeping too many secrets.

"What are the less ordinary items?"

He coughs again. "Did your late mother confide in you about her earlier years in Glasgow? The fact that she'd kept a private notebook?"

Her daughter frowns. "No. Why?"

"Please sign and date the Will and Deeds where shown, Miss Baird, and I'll explain how it fell into the wrong hands..."

"Wrong hands?"

"Yes. There may be those still living who could cause trouble for you and attempt to discredit her memory. One of whom is a certain retired Constable, still with connections in high places."

"Who?"

Pause.

"Coyle. Seumus Coyle."

She repeats the name under her breath.

"I don't understand. She was a wonderful mother. The best I could have had." Yet her daughter's writing is less controlled than usual, and an unsightly blob of ink lands after each signature. "What exactly do you mean by 'discredit her memory?"

He passes over a piece of clean blotting paper and a wrinkled, black leather-bound notebook signed with her mother's name on its frontispiece.

"Keep this as safe as your soul."

A strange thing to say. But that's not all, for a ragged portion of thick, black hair has also been inserted, harbouring an unusual smell. "Your father's, I believe," says the lawyer.

Isobel doesn't speak, instead touches it gently, thinking of their neat graves lying side by side in the Presbyterian churchyard just around the corner. Also of her other grandmother, Margaret Lennox, whose remains, like those of the McPhees, have yet to be found.

She turns the water-stained pages where dates written above the entries are almost unreadable. Except for one. Uncle Calum's confession.

Upon reaching the end, she uses the young lawyer's unused handkerchief to dry her eyes, then, having retrieved her gloves, pushes away that 'more ordinary' souvenir so hard it rolls from the desk, clatters to the floor and perhaps luckily for her, vanishes from sight.

END

Glossary

auld - old
bairn – child
bark – boat
braw – beautiful
besom - slattern
burnie - stream
but and ben – small cottage
cocks – hens/chickens
dochter – daughter
droothy - drunken
frein – friend
gowk – awkward or foolish person
glaikit – thoughtless or lacking intelligence
Ham-a-haddie – an unlikely story
heavy – whisky
'necessaries' – lavatories.
Ne'erday – New Year's Day
smirr – mist
stank - lavatory
stoater - excellent
Tail – prostitute
tumsties - turnips
wean - baby
whaur - where

Published by DEATH WATCH BOOKS

Made in the USA
Charleston, SC
25 August 2016